The
Fenland Spell

A Father Eadred
Tale

Lindsay Jacob

Matador
Unit E2 Airfield Business Park,
Harrison Road, Market Harborough,
Leicestershire. LE16 7UL
Tel: 0116 2792299
Email: books@troubador.co.uk
Web: www.troubador.co.uk/matador
Twitter: @matadorbooks

ISBN 978 1803136 660

British Library Cataloguing in Publication Data.
A catalogue record for this book is available from the British Library.

Printed and bound in Great Britain by 4edge Limited
Typeset in 11pt Adobe Garamond Pro by Troubador Publishing Ltd, Leicester, UK

Matador is an imprint of Troubador Publishing Ltd

Acknowledgements

My thanks to historian and award-winning historical novelist, Annie Whitehead, for sharing her considerable knowledge and experience of writing historical fiction and the intricacies of publication. Annie has always given me wise and honest counsel, encouragement, and conveyed with a gentle humour. Jenny Quinlan provided developmental and copyedits for my manuscript. Jenny immersed herself in the body and personality of the story, enhancing it at all levels. She guided and questioned with acute technical skill, consummate professionalism, empathy and with an accessible and cooperative spirit. I had a few ideas for the cover design and a sense of the mood I wanted to convey. Mike Bastin employed his skill, judgement and collaborative approach, and created something that exceeded my expectations.

The Spell

Two small pots, the comb, stick, knife, and the platter with its collection of leaves, were placed on the woollen cloth. The hooded, kneeling figure took a few attentive moments to arrange them. He blew at a taper until it birthed a flame and lit five candles around the area where he sat. The shadowed osier, alder and ash trunks to either side of him and their bald branches overhead seemed to form a natural channel through the surrounding tangle of wood to the mere's edge a few feet from him. The candles were his only light, which pleased him, for this was necessary to achieve the greatest potency of the spell. The air was still and fragrant with the scent of the earth and chilled by the nearby water.

He brushed his fingers against the trunk to his left. This was the one: an ash. Three days earlier, he had cut the marks of magic into its bark. He felt their contours, and with his blade he sliced them away, catching the shavings and sprinkling them onto the platter. His chant into the darkness began; some words in Latin and others in a tongue that would defy most people's comprehension. All the words were sung slowly, at times diffidently, almost as a child would haul them from their memory. Pouring the contents of the pots over the platter, he continued.

"Here, the milk of a pure white cow, and here, my own seed. I stir them thus with a stick given power by Matthew, Mark, Luke and John, their names inscribed upon it. On this comb belonging to the fair Sister Edith is a single hair from her head." The man then tipped the platter so the concoction spilt over the comb, and he sang more strange words, concluding in Latin. All with the same deliberation.

"I entreat Abraham and Solomon and the angels in heaven to bless this comb. That when it is used again by our sister, her affections turn to me, and she comes to hate the very name of Eadred the priest, who has abused her kindness and drawn her into sin." He then wrapped the comb in a linen cloth and placed it under his cloak.

A smile replaced the stern concentration the spell had needed. The man reflected that he had done everything correctly, in the right order, in the language required for each stage. He anticipated success, for the comb and its single strand had fallen, seemingly fortuitously, into his hands. It spoke of spiritual forces working in his favour and against the vile priest. This knowledge gave him confidence that the comb would find a way to return without suspicion into Edith's hands.

He retrieved a box from behind his back, opened the lid and drew two of the candles closer. Their gentle light fell upon his face, the flint expression returning. He cupped his hands around his nose and mouth and groaned. For a minute or so, the enormity of his proposed action weighed upon him, and he knelt, immobile, staring ahead. When determination returned, he looked at the box and removed the left hand of a recently executed thief, a man who had put himself beyond the protection of the Lord God. The power of the spell rested in the left hand; the right hand was useless. Despite retching when he picked up the cold flesh, he was resolved. The instruments of the first spell were put aside and a further set were positioned carefully on the cloth. A pot, a platter, the head of a raven and a knife with a handle inscribed with runes.

The hooded man began to speak in a tongue not used by men other than to entreat the powers of darkness to assist in some act of evil. Once more, each word was pronounced slowly and with care, as taught by his master. Not one mistake was permitted. The man stopped twice, trying to recall the correct words, then moved on. The bird's head and the hand were placed on the platter and the substance from the pot poured over them. He took the knife and sliced the blade into his own forearm, dripping his blood over the platter. Next, he raised his arms.

The roar began in the distance, in the trees on the distant side of the mere, then the gusts smashed through the clearing in which the man knelt, sending the candles flying. He cried out in terror, but he could not stop.

"I adjure you, creature of hell, to do my bidding. I bring down a curse upon the head of Eadred the priest. Deliver him into our hands—that his name is destroyed and his life ends in humiliation and torment, not by an honourable death, but when he is hanged as a common criminal."

Strangely, the clouds parted, and by moonlight the man, exhausted and trembling, threw every object he had used in his wicked venture into the mere, apart from the comb. As he hurried on his way, he pondered that he was used to being obeyed, and this secretive method of gaining another's heart and disposing of an enemy was not to his liking. It made him feel weak, but soon he would be stronger than ever before. His life, though successful according to most men, had not touched the potential he imagined for himself. There was much more to achieve, and to share his domain with Sister Edith was worth anything. The price demanded by the demon he had called upon was not harsh, but would involve some risk. Yet, even if the Christian God did prevail over darkness and the man's soul was plunged into the fires and abominations of hell, memories of Edith's pliant, arching form and inflaming caresses would surely sustain him.

Everything now depended upon the comb and returning it without suspicion to the woman he loved. For the spell to work, it had to be washed with holy water just before the sun rose on the third day following the ritual and then used by her sometime in the week to follow. The more times the comb embraced Sister Edith's hair, the stronger the magic would become, and he would harvest his reward, made even sweeter by the tortured end of the upstart priest.

ONE

A Disturbing Order

Eadred knocked gently on the door and pushed it open. "Ah, my boy, come in, and be sure to close it." Bishop Aethelbert sat in his small reception room at Snailwell Minster, double-cloaked but still shivering in winter's bite. He beckoned Eadred to the stool in front of the table.

A wave of sadness washed over Eadred, seeing the old bishop growing more infirm by the day. He glimpsed the jar of dried, dusty herbs on the table that seemed to reflect Aethelbert's withered form and fragile hold on life. Yet, even if his body quivered, the bishop's smile was still possessed of warmth, though Eadred thought he saw a hint of grieving in the old man's face.

"Now, how long has it been since you returned to us?"

"It has been almost a twelvemonth since my time at Elmstow Minster, Reverend Father." Eadred realised from the bishop's faint smile that, although it was a truthful response, he had fallen into a trap.

1

"Is it that long? And look at how you have recovered! You had barely a muscle when you returned and now have the frame of a warrior."

"It was my good friend, Brother Tatwine, who encouraged me to strengthen my body in case I again needed to protect my life. I almost lost it at Elmstow."

"Indeed, I remember, but that is in the past now, dead and buried," the bishop replied. "We must look to the future, for we are promised eternal life. You have had a whole year secluded within these walls; at my bidding, to be sure. It has given you time to draw closer to the Lord God and to restore your body and your mind, but now it is time to venture out. Eadred, I have a mission for you."

Eadred failed to suppress a groan. The last time Aethelbert had said such words, Eadred had been sent into a viper's nest at Elmstow Minster and met people with blacker hearts than he had thought possible. He opened his mouth to object, but the bishop continued without pause.

"You have doubtless heard of the fenland feud?"

With reluctance, Eadred replied, "Who has not? Brother Oswald's family lives on one of Lord Forthred's estates and talks often of the misery of the common folk. The feud has spilt blood and sown fear. I am told it is as bad now as in ages past."

"I fear that is true, and worse," the bishop replied. "I have no idea how it all started, but the enmity between Lords Forthred and Cerdic is consuming the blood and wealth of rich and poor alike. Forthred is a greedy, wolfish man, too ready to make claims for contested land, livestock and rights, even when there is no foundation. His reach across the kingdom expands year by year. Cerdic, thank the

Lord, has a more moderate disposition but is as defensive of his property and rights. Both are rich, and as the rich do, they want ever more. Forthred has already had two wives, both died young, and he inherited land from both. He is now almost as rich as the ealdorman and doubtless seeks as much power. But, despite the greatness of his wealth, it is widely said that Forthred has always been jealous of Lord Cerdic's estates, especially an area of abundance in the deep fens. It has the richest pastures and meres in the kingdom."

Eadred wondered why the bishop was telling him this. He soon found out.

"I am afraid the feud has grown even worse over past months, and the ealdorman has had to involve himself. It is damaging the kingdom. Only recently, ale got the better of some of the youngbloods from both families, and men died. Cattle are being senselessly slaughtered and left to the wolves. Ealdorman Aelfric has urged both lords to find a way for the next generation to break the bloodshed. He has proposed a union between Forthred's only child, Edmund, and one of Cerdic's daughters, and it is said by some that King Athelstan himself has offered financial benefits to both kindreds for it to take place. Edmund has been raised as a warrior and has the strongest sword arm of any man in those parts by far. It is Edmund's strength that secures his father's commands. These are not men to cross. Thank the Lord God, I hear that the marriage has now been agreed, and this is where you are to help, my boy.

"The wedding is to take place in a week or so, and you are to conduct the ceremony at Deerstow, where Lord Forthred has his great hall."

Eadred felt the colour leave his face, and he began to

3

shake. "But, Reverend Father, surely I am of too low a rank, in the kingdom and the Church, to undertake this important task? There is now Abbot Cuthred to help you. He was assuredly elevated to—"

"Hear me out, boy!" the bishop snapped, then breathed deeply and stared at the wall behind Eadred for a few moments before continuing. "What I tell you now is for your ears only. Do you understand?"

Eadred's guts twisted, but he nodded.

"I do not care for the new abbot for many reasons. I did not choose him, as the laws of the Church require. The decision was made by the king, and he was not well advised, but I am not that foolish to object. Abbot Cuthred is a worldly man with vast ambition rather than a caring soul. If he becomes bishop when I am feeding the worms, I fear he would treat the Church as his own estate, to be managed for profit and his own enrichment.

"You and I know—most of our brothers and sisters in Christ know—that the Abbess of Elmstow would be a far more pious and humble leader of our Church than Cuthred. What she has done to clear the vermin from Elmstow and to rebuild its foundations of faith is beyond understanding. Yet she will need to bow before Cuthred. If she were a man, I have no doubt that she would become the next leader of our Church."

The bishop groaned loudly. "Near enough, he does as he will. He rarely seeks my permission. I have little knowledge of what he does, but I have had one great victory." The bishop's voice fell to a whisper. "Last summer, when he was still Abbot of Wexning, Cuthred consecrated Lord Forthred's new church at Deerstow. He would be delighted to go himself now to unite the families in marriage and to raise his own stature, but I have kept knowledge of the wedding from him and from others. It will only be a modest affair, so calm yourself. I am sorry, dear boy, to put you through this, but you must also attend the wedding feast as my representative. I know you are not comfortable, or indeed talented, representing Holy Church at such gatherings."

Eadred blushed. The memory of his humiliation at Elmstow Minster summoned itself. He had sought to leave a debauched feast only to be hauled back in tears at the former ealdorman's orders. He doubted the remembrance of the laughter at his expense would ever leave him or do anything other than bring him to tears and trembling.

"This will not be such a gathering as at Elmstow." The old bishop patted the back of Eadred's hand. "The old ealdorman was a bitter man, his power had corrupted his nature, but he is now dead and gone. And if the rumours are true that he called on demons, he is now enjoying the torments of hell.

"Unless I am much mistaken, this will be a short feast. You will attend and have only one task. You, dear boy, must keep a careful eye that it remains peaceful. We cannot have a continuation of this feud. It has cost Christian blood, unsettled the people, and if it continues, it will weaken Lord Aelfric's position—perhaps see an end to it. That is not what we want. He is showing himself to be a friend to the Church. As you know, he made a generous endowment to Elmstow to set the minster on firm foundations, and he has promised to endow churches in areas of the kingdom that need to have a stronger touch on their lives from the Shepherd. He also has a high opinion of you for what you did for him at Elmstow. It is a powerful benefit, Eadred, to be esteemed by so great a man as the kingdom's ealdorman. We must do all in our power to support him."

Eadred could not disguise the desperation in his voice. "If this union is so vital, he will surely attend the wedding? There can be no more important task for Lord Aelfric."

The bishop sighed. "If it is possible, I am sure he will be there." He sat speechless for a few moments, then spoke quietly. "The word is that dark forces within the kingdom have sensed that Ealdorman Aelfric is not yet sure or strong, and lawlessness is springing forth throughout our land. King Athelstan has despatched him to quell the violence. I have no knowledge of his whereabouts. I am afraid that you should not rely on his presence at the wedding. But ask Lord Forthred if he has heard from the ealdorman more recently. I am sure he will have better tidings for you. Now, this is not the end of it, my boy. There is a final part to your mission."

Eadred's stomach knotted. For the past year, under the bishop's protective hand, he had all but forgotten that he was a priest and not a contemplative monk.

"After your duties in Deerstow, I want you to take the path deeper into the eastern fens to a place called the Cauldron by the local folk."

"Holy Father, I do not know the path to Deerstow, let alone this Cauldron! Who is to come with me?"

"No one! I can trust no one else. In the days ahead, you will understand why. As for directions, go and ask Brother Anselm; he came with me and will remember far better than I. He is known for his exceptional memory. Now, do not interrupt again. Just listen.

"A number of years ago, not long after being made

bishop, I ventured into the eastern fens with the king's warriors and with fire in my heart. I baptised many of the Cauldron Folk over several days, I have to say with the warriors' help. For most, it was skin only. Many pagan hearts beat still in that watery place. If you need to, you can always identify a secretive non-believer by whom they call upon for help. Never the Lord God, Christ, the Holy Spirit, the angels or saints, but upon their own ancestors. Now, there will be a church there; I had it started during my visit, and on the return journey to Snailwell, I began the building of one at Deerstow. I also installed a priest, Father Ingeld. He lived with the Cauldron Folk, and he completed and consecrated both churches. I think you must have met him on some of his visits back here. He is of an impressive height."

"I do remember him, Holy Father: tall and thin."

Aethelbert nodded. "Ingeld used to return here twice a year for a week or more, generally when the days were growing longer and then once the harvest was in. He would stop at Deerstow on the way to care for the people's spiritual needs. Sometimes, Ingeld drove a cart to carry what remained of the people's tithes after he had taken what he needed to live, or if the road was well nigh impassable, he came on horseback. As the days were beginning to lengthen close to a year past, a farmer visited here: one of the Cauldron Folk. He was on his way to the higher ground to collect his cattle, where they had been at their winter pasturing, and to return them to the low mere country for the warmer months, as is the way with farmers from the Cauldron. Well, the farmer came on Ingeld's cart and with the usual share of the tithes, which Ingeld wanted him to deliver. He passed on a message from Ingeld, saying that he had fallen ill with the fen ague and had neither the strength nor the endurance to leave the Cauldron to make his journey but was recovering and would see Snailwell again after the harvest. We gave the farmer lodging and food for the night, and on the following day he took one of the horses, with our thanks and blessing, and continued his journey. Well, Father Ingeld has not since returned!

"I suppose my mind moved on to other concerns, and my health has fallen away, but it is no excuse. I forgot about Ingeld and have become dilatory about other duties. There are matters I must put right, Eadred, while I still can." Aethelbert began sobbing, as he did often these days. "What it is to grow old, to look back at the many days you have had and to see terrible mistakes you have made because you sought your own comfort.

"Eadred, you must be my eyes, ears and hands. Tell the lords at Deerstow that you will officiate at the wedding in my name. Seek out Lord Forthred or his son, Lord Edmund, as soon as you arrive; they will expect someone from here. Listen carefully to what they say. Tell anyone else who wishes to know of your journey that you are going there to care for the souls in those parts, and do not speak of the wedding to anyone other than Forthred, Edmund, Cerdic and the ealdorman, not even your closest companions, or it will go badly for both of us. If Lord Aelfric does not come to Deerstow, I am depending on you to ensure that this wedding takes place. Is that understood?" Eadred nodded. The bishop stared into his eyes, as if he were seeking to sear the instruction into Eadred's mind, then he beckoned for the young priest to embrace him. "And see what help Ingeld needs. You need to grow in wisdom about the ways of the world, and it will not happen if you hide in the cloister. The Lord God be with you, my boy. You will come to understand the necessity for concealment and haste. You leave tomorrow." Then he wiped the tears from his eyes.

Eadred left his audience with the bishop, bewildered and dismayed. He knew the day had to come when he would need to venture once more beyond the safe and predictable walls of his beloved Snailwell Minster, but he had trusted that the bishop would allow him to take gentle and secure steps. Instead, Aethelbert seemed to have thrown him without warning into a raging torrent. The bishop had seemed agitated, and he had rarely given Eadred such specific commands about what he could and could not say—and to whom. Eadred's mind raced with what he needed to do and what he had to pack for the journey. But how to get to his intended destinations? Despite the chill of the air, Eadred felt the sweat roll down his spine as he ran to the dormitory to find Brother Anselm.

"It has been close to a dozen years ago, when I had just past my thirtieth year, that I travelled with the bishop into the deep fen. I confess I was scared witless." Anselm chuckled and tapped his skull with his knuckles several times. "I put the path in my memory, for I imagined that I would need to return one day, but it was not to be. The Cauldron is a fascinating place. There is only one rise in the land of any consequence, and from there a man may look out upon a mere that is shaped like a cauldron, and he is at its base with a finger of land to his left and his right, like sticks of a fire. I heard that for this reason, the people who lived there called themselves the Cauldron Folk. There were half a dozen vills and other scattered farms and houses. It was a good living for the folk who lived there, as I remember."

Anselm had never learnt how to read or write, a weakness he tried to keep hidden, but the longer-serving monks knew, and the bishop had let it slip to Eadred. So, as with the great scops who memorised the songs of their people, when Anselm conveyed directions to Eadred, he did it by way of a song he had made those many years ago and never forgotten, and he was patient in trying to teach an agitated Eadred the words.

"Come, Eadred, let us sing the song once more after the midnight service and again tomorrow morning before you leave. Your mind will be more settled then. Deerstow is a straightforward road, but the Cauldron is a little more complicated. But the song is quite simple once you have mastered the rhythm. Yet why could the bishop not have given you more time to prepare for your mission? It seems to be a needless haste." Eadred agreed but said that the bishop was determined that it was time to resume the calling of an ordained man and for Eadred to care for the souls of others, and not just his own.

*

Eadred had the bishop's dispensation to absent himself from the three o'clock night service, but he lay awake, staring into the blackness. A whirlpool of fears and memories filled his head. It had been Aethelbert who had sent him to Elmstow Minster a year or so earlier to check on the rumours of declining standards. Such evil and depravity had made a nest in God's house that Eadred, even now, shivered at the memory. It had consumed good souls and perverted creatures alike. In the midst of the swill, a neighbouring kingdom had attacked, eager to take advantage of the disorder.

The minster had been finally cleansed of its black brood of murderers, but at such a sacrifice of blood that the kingdom even now remained weak. Eadred's name had been raised throughout the kingdom as the one who had used the gift of his mind to discover those who sought to hide their guilt by guile. But rather than rejoice in his newfound fame, Eadred had since hidden away, back in the cloisters of Snailwell Minster.

It was his nature to avoid the company of those he did not know and not to venture into circumstances where the road ahead was unknown. He had prayed for the day when Bishop Aethelbert would say that he could live a monk's secluded life of contemplation, but it was not to be. And he also understood in his heart that it was not the Lord God's chosen path for him. Eadred's duty was to be a priest. To bring men and women to the Lord, to teach them the Scriptures and how they should use their time in this earthly life to protect their eternal souls. To baptise, marry and bury the faithful. To stop them from fornicating, from thieving, from murder, from calling on demons. To hear their confessions, give absolution and prescribe penance. To delve into the darker corners of men's hearts and minds.

These were places that distressed and appalled him, but here he also served his Maker. For at Elmstow, Eadred seemed to have demonstrated a special gift: one that some others and he himself had since doubted. At that dark time, and in that place of evil, he had looked at the bodies of those who had lost their lives through secret violence; he had searched the places where they had died or where their bodies had lain; and he had asked questions of those who had been nearby. He had talked and looked and drank wine until his mind had been addled—and without seeing anything. He had also prayed for insight, and when he had least expected it, it had come. On contemplating the landscape of evil afresh, a pattern had emerged so clearly, as though a confusion of letters had suddenly taken the form not only of words, but of a poem.

His dear friend, the hermit monk Tatwine, had told Eadred at the time that he had a God-given gift, and it was an affront to the Lord God not to use it. Eadred recalled being uplifted because he had entrapped those who had taken the lives of God's people. Yet there had been another emotion. Up until then, he had been an unremarkable priest, but Elmstow changed this. When muscled warriors had called him by name and sought his blessing, and the smiles and words of lissom nuns had teased and provoked, he had felt a worldly pride, but surely he deserved it? Or did he? He had also saved a woman from the gallows. But in the days after the defeat of evil, Eadred the priest had fornicated with her—but once only. What anguish it still caused him.

With tears streaming down his cheeks and contemplating his departure from Snailwell in the morning, Eadred prayed that sleep would release him. He remembered that only a few nights earlier he had given profound thanks to the Lord God for his secure and peaceful life, but in a few hours, when light returned, he would be plunged into an entirely different world.

TWO

Trials of Priesthood

The smell gave Eadred hope, lifting some of the gloom that sat upon his shoulders. He breathed in the smoke, yearning that it signalled he was approaching at least a farm, but hopefully a vill. His first night spent in the open air for almost a year had been unsettling and virtually sleepless. Half a day's light had now passed on the second day of his journey. Eadred turned a bend in the path, and there, scurrying towards him, was a woman.

"Welcome, Father. One of the villagers told me he saw you nearby on the road. Do you wish to stay the night? I am Eadgifu."

"Is this the vill of Deerstow?"

"It is, Father."

"Then I have reached my destination," Eadred said with a smile of victory, and he crossed himself. "Thank you, I am Father Eadred of Snailwell, sent by the bishop to spend

13

some days here delivering the sacraments." Eadred realised belatedly that his stare was causing Eadgifu discomfort, and she was awkwardly trying to be polite while turning her disfigured face from him. Eadgifu's dress hung over a skeletal body. Her right hand seemed unable to clench or to open fully, and her face had been pulled from its natural shape by swirling eddies of tight, glossy, reddened skin. She also wore a blackened eye. But Eadred sensed a welcoming warmth radiating from her.

"That is good news, Father. We have not seen a priest for a while, and the Lord God help us, we are in need of you. There is a house where you can stay. I will take you there now, if you wish, and then get some food and ale. You will be tired if you came by foot?"

"I am weary, to be sure, Eadgifu. I left the minster yesterday and spent the night in the open air. A fire and hot food would cheer me. I cannot seem to warm myself. My feet ache with the effort of these past few days, and I can barely move, so you lead the way and I will follow."

On the way, Eadgifu stopped by a house and emerged with a handful of flaming dried sedge grass. When they arrived at Eadred's shelter, she used it to light the small pile of tinder, then, with barely another word spoken, she hurried away.

Eadred fed the fire, rejoicing in its budding warmth. The air in his lodging was damp and stale, but a few hours of the fire's heat should remedy that. It was bare, just a crude bed, two stools and a small table, upon which rested a cup and two candles. A crucifix hung on the wall, and Eadred wondered if this simple dwelling had been set aside for Father Ingeld when he visited. Eadred heard his name being called, and he bade Eadgifu to enter. The door creaked open, but it was not her. He sprang to his feet.

"I am Eadburga, Eadgifu's sister. She asked that I bring you this." The contrast left Eadred speechless. Her face had a striking beauty that her surly expression failed to disguise. Long blond hair flowed over her shoulders, and when her cloak opened, Eadred stole a glance at a strong, willowy body and a slender neck. Surprisingly for a peasant woman, a chain of gold adorned her neck and chest. Eadburga's scowl informed him that his attention was displeasing. She hammered the platter of stew and bread and the cup of ale onto the table.

"Thank you, Eadburga, this is kind of your sister and you."

"You are here to preach?"

"Yes, and to deliver the sacraments."

"To impose penances on the wicked?" Eadburga continued.

"It is part of my duties," Eadred replied. "Christians must confess their sins, receive penances and seek God's help in fighting against their sinful ways." He was tired, but there was food on the table, a roof over his head and someone who seemed eager to confess something. She was also beautiful. "Would you like to stay awhile and talk further?" Eadred moved one of the stools to the other side of the fire.

Eadburga pondered for a few moments, then sat down, motioning for Eadred to eat. He took a couple of mouthfuls. "There is something troubling you. If you name it, I can pray with you." There was a further silence, then she spoke.

"I speak for my sister. You have seen her condition. Her husband, Brihtwold, is a pig. Her life has been made hard enough, but he makes it worse."

"Did he cause her deformity?" Eadred asked in alarm.

"No, but he does not help. It was an accident the winter before last. There was a knowledge before then that whoever gained my sister as his wife would be a fortunate man. Her face used to be as mine, but her heart has always been the better, even now. She slipped and fell into the fire, and it melted her face and arm. Men were sorry for her, but none wanted her then."

"But what of her husband?"

"No woman wanted him either. Ask others and they will tell you why. Make certain that Brihtwold confesses to you, and make him treat my sister better. She used to say that God had blessed her. Even now, she prays and praises despite the pain she endures, but each day gets worse. Eadgifu is a good woman and does not deserve the life she leads. You are a man of God; you have power that is seen and unseen. Give my sister something to reward her faith!"

Eadred had forgotten the trials of priesthood, and Eadburga had reminded him with a blunt axe. "I will do all within my power for your sister. This I promise." As soon as he had said the words, Eadred regretted the expectation they seemed to create. Eadburga nodded, said that the platter and cup would be collected later and left.

Eadred spent a few moments musing on Eadgifu's plight and her sister's clear affection for her. But he thought as much about his own difficulties. He had entered Deerstow with some lightness of heart, having followed Brother Anselm's instructions quite easily, only to be reminded of the struggles of most common folk beyond the minster's walls and how he had to explain to them how God walked with them. Remembering the bishop's instruction, he also had to seek out Lord Forthred or his son. So Eadred bolted down his food and ale and walked out into the mid-afternoon sunlight.

Deerstow was the home of the infamous Lord Forthred and many of his kindred, as well as the freemen who had built their wealth serving their lord. It was correspondingly large and with many well-built houses. In the distance, further along the road that sloped downhill and on to other settlements, Eadred could also see the crammed shacks of the poorer peasants and slaves. He had already noticed the great hall and the church while he had walked with Eadgifu, so Eadred returned along the road for a while, then took the gently rising land past the great hall to see a cluster of solid dwellings at the highest point in the vill. Several warriors stood around these houses. He walked towards the closest guard.

"I am Eadred, priest of Snailwell Minster, here as representative of the Bishop of the East Angles. He has instructed me to seek an audience with either Lord Forthred or Lord Edmund and that I am expected by these lords."

Without a word of response, one of the guards entered a house. A short while later, he returned and was similarly terse. "Wait!"

Eadred anticipated the door would open in a few moments and he would be beckoned inside. The time passed. The glare of the setting sun, almost blood red through the smoke of many fires swelling into the sky, caused him to turn and face away from the guard. He wrapped his cloak closely around himself and sat down.

He was shivering when he heard a voice boom from within the house and saw the guard disappear once more through the door. Eadred had practised the words he wanted to say many times and quickly started mouthing them to himself once more. The door opened, and Eadred clambered to his feet. The guard reappeared.

"Go to the great hall. Lord Edmund will see you there. You will find food."

Eadred suppressed a moan and nodded. With darkness trespassing, he hurried back down the slope and entered the welcoming warmth of the hall. The only occupant was a woman, who was stirring a cauldron of stew. Eadred introduced himself, telling her who he was waiting for. She let out a cry, finished her work quickly and left.

The gentle, meditative and recuperative months at Snailwell were over, and Eadred knew he had been plunged once more into the truculent realm of warrior kindreds. But he felt, or at least he hoped, that he was not the callow boy who had faced humiliation at the hands of the muscled brutes at Elmstow. Eadred understood that a warrior's purpose was to protect his lord, and to succeed at this he needed to build his combative spirit as much as he built his frame. A warrior earned honour and glory by his bravery and his loyalty to lord and companions. Eadred had known firsthand the virtue of such a spirit, but he had also seen how easily it could decay into meaningless violence, self-indulgence and depravity.

So much, Eadred mused, depended on the nature of a man's leader. The former ealdorman had become corrupted by power. He had lost the disciplines of leadership somewhere in the years of bloody conflict and let his men misuse the common people rather than protect them. He had let the fenland feud fester. His son, Lord Aelfric, elevated by the king to become the new ealdorman and, in name, the second-most powerful man in the kingdom, was as different from his father as a man could be. As far as Eadred could discern, he had the seeds of a great leader, but he had to live long enough for the sapling to flourish. The door opened.

"You are the priest?"

Eadred bowed his head. "Lord Edmund, I am Father Eadred of Snailwell."

The young noble snorted. "The bishop is too old to travel, but what of the abbot? He should have come. We know him—from a noble, if minor, family—but I have not heard of you." As he was speaking, Edmund soaked a wedge of bread into the stew and began eating.

"My lord, the bishop instructed me to tell you that I am as adequate to the task as our new abbot. Bishop Aethelbert has other duties for me to undertake for his flock here and in the deeper fens and considered that only one of us should undertake the journey. The bishop has need of Abbot Cuthred's help at Snailwell."

"Does he?" the nobleman replied. "It is of little importance. What have you been told?"

"I am to officiate at the wedding of yourself and Lord Cerdic's daughter. That I am to tell no one of this purpose until I speak to you or your father and receive direction."

"Well then, priest, these are my directions. It is to take place in three days' time. You talk to no one about it but me. No one! There will be carts carrying provisions for the wedding feast appearing from tomorrow. People will talk, rumours will spread, but you will say nothing. My father has ordered all who live on his estates to come to you for confession, so you have your tasks to occupy yourself. I

19

will see you when the wedding has to take place." Edmund turned and walked to the door.

"My lord, if you will." Eadred hoped that his voice would not begin to shake. "It is the Church's practice for the officiating priest to spend some time with the couple before they marry, to speak to them of God's purpose in the sacrament of marriage and—"

"Priest, it is clear you know little of our families and how we despise each other," the young thegn spoke over Eadred. "Just do as I said and your time here will be well spent. But breathe one word of this wedding and you will wish that you had never ventured beyond your minster's walls. It is a long and dangerous journey back to Snailwell." Edmund opened the door.

"Lord, the bishop did ask whether Lord Aelfric would attend your wedding."

Eadred sensed Edmund's irritation at being questioned once more. "The ealdorman was, of course, invited, but I have no idea whether he will come. He is searching out the criminal bands that have been tormenting us. He could be anywhere." And with that, the young thegn left.

Eadred closed the door and took a stool close to the fire. A deep misery weighed upon him. He warmed his hands and groaned. A marriage between two great families that had feuded since before memory. Surely, the ealdorman needed to be there, and also the abbot, but Bishop Aethelbert had sent him—a simple priest—to ensure that the union took place! And the groom was treating his marriage as little more than a transaction. This was beyond Eadred. He loved Bishop Aethelbert as a father, but he felt his anger rise. The senile old man had let his annoyance at Abbot Cuthred cloud his judgment and, as he had at Elmstow a year past, he had sent Eadred into the wolf's lair.

Why this secrecy about the wedding? Even if it were not a voluntary union of companion souls, but a peace treaty, surely it needed to be proclaimed, not hidden from view? There was also a menace about Edmund that alarmed Eadred. He found it impossible to imagine that the aggression simmering under the thegn's skin would end through union to an age-old enemy. This world that Eadred had been thrown into was not one that he understood. He needed to stand on firm rock, but found himself looking into a dangerous quicksand.

Eadred found himself muttering the words he would use in the marriage ceremony. Even in his solitude, Eadred's voice quivered as he imagined himself standing before a throng of hostile faces and speaking words that meant nothing to them. He knelt and prayed, but all that came to him was a sense that there was evil in Deerstow and that the so-called wedding was part of it. Eadred could see only one small flicker of light, and that was if Ealdorman Aelfric would come, and this was what he prayed for.

THREE

Abbot Cuthred

Abbot Cuthred stood on the small, bare hill in the village of Thornham, smiling, his arms outstretched to welcome the man striding towards him.

"Cousin, this is a special day." Cuthred almost laughed the words, finding it impossible to contain his joy at that moment. He embraced his cousin, Leofric the thegn.

"This is indeed a wonderful day." Leofric sighed with contentment and gazed skywards, then admired the building rising before him.

"I am pleased to see your delight," Cuthred replied.

"This has been a desire of my heart for some while," Leofric clasped his hands together, "and to see it now is a miracle. It is beyond joy to have imagined a perfect child, to have watched it grow from birth, for it now to stand fully grown before my eyes and for it to be even more glorious than the dream!

"This is the only building of stone this side of the Gronte River between the eastern meres and Snailwell Minster, and it is mine. My own church! Not even Lord Forthred's church at Deerstow is of stone. How the mason has shaped the blocks with such care, and see the arch around the door! It is crafted with such skill! And bricks from the time of the legions. There are more than I imagined. How did he get those?"

"He has a precious store of them, collected from the ruined houses and monuments of the Romans," Cuthred replied.

Leofric's smile faded. "Cousin, I was once told that by chanting words of dark power within a building made from the stones of the Romans, evil men could call up the gods of the legions. I pray that this could not happen within my church?"

Cuthred groaned and shook his head. "Sadly, there are still many in the fenlands who have not turned to Christ, or they deem our Saviour to be one of many gods. In ignorance, or wilfully, they conjure demons. I will correct this in time, now I am made Abbot of Snailwell. Be at peace, cousin, all stones and bricks from the days of the legions which have been used in this church have been cleansed with prayer and holy water. It would need a frightful spell to defile this church."

"That is reassuring. I am forever grateful for all of this, cousin. This church is wondrous—and raised with such speed. How is all of this possible?"

Cuthred smiled. "I have my connections in King Athelstan's court, and through them I was able to advise the king of the growing weakness of the bishop's health and mind and its injurious impact on the Church's own health. I offered my own services to lift the burden from the bishop. It has taken a while, but the king and queen came to understand that Bishop Aethelbert could no longer perform his onerous duties, and they undertook to ensure my elevation from Abbot of Wexning to Abbot of Snailwell Minster. I knew that I had secured the position some months before it was announced, and in that time I planned and had a start made on building this church, as well as other projects. Once I knew that I had the authority given by the king and Holy Church, it was only right that I assisted the pious hunger of my kin.

"You also have the cemetery you asked for beside the church. Be certain to encourage the families of the dying on your estates to have them buried here. I want an end to the old burial places. Their time is over. In the heat of last summer, when I was still Abbot of Wexning and called upon to consecrate the new church and cemetery at Deerstow for Lord Forthred, I said the same to him. It is time the dead were buried with their Christian family, not with their blood ancestors, where the baptised and heathens lie side by side. This change must be led by our leading families so others will follow. And be sure to bring your son here for baptism. He has a great lineage and is heir to much wealth. He must have God's protection and blessing."

"I will not fail," Leofric replied, "and I promise that my tenants will know of my expectation. And, cousin, I shall meet your other wish and redouble my efforts to purify the minds of those of my tenants who still call upon the old gods and spirits. And, in addition to the lands and the mill I have bestowed upon Snailwell, I shall see that you personally obtain your just reward for creating this building and for the other gifts. I give my word. Our family will be raised up, as it deserves."

Abbot Cuthred gave a slight bow. The two men turned towards the doleful sound of chanting rising from the wood in the middle distance, now distinct from the songs and cries of an abundance of birds taking to the air. From the pathway, the first monks appeared. Behind them came all of the men, women and children, free and enslaved, from the vills and farms belonging to the thegn. The procession laboured towards and then up the slight hill on which the church stood, led by six monks shouldering a coffin draped with linen cloth. Around the heads of the throng hovered their chilled breath.

"You have, I pray, kept your word and not yet entered the holy building."

"Cousin, I swear I have not," Leofric replied.

"Then prepare to witness the greatest gifts." Abbot Cuthred raised his hand, and the column halted. With mutual acknowledgment, Cuthred and Leofric parted. The abbot hastened down to the head of the procession and led it towards the church. As instructed by Cuthred, the thegn stood at its door with head bowed to welcome the gift from God.

Two monks opened the western door. Leofric entered, gaped and issued a gasp of wonder. The walls hummed with vibrant images in red, yellow, green, brown and even rich scarlet hues. Adam and Eve, Noah, Moses, King David, Jonah and many more. But the greatest vision for the Christian flock was upon the eastern wall. The Lord God sat enthroned and before him, his son, crucified, defiant, upon the rood, and between them flew God's spirit, as a dove. Below the sacred figures, two angels sounded their trumpets, calling the dead from their graves. The saved climbed a ladder to heaven; the damned were pulled into hell by demons.

"It is the Last Judgment," cried some of the cloistered men. Disaster loomed as villagers, hearing exclamations of joy and disbelief, pushed towards the narrow opening, buffeting the monks who carried the coffin. The cloistered men strained with the weight they carried, shouting for a path to be cleared to the bench that awaited them. Leofric barked an order, and several of his warriors cleared a way, but nothing short of a cudgelling could stop the explosion of awe. Cuthred had a more effective approach.

"On your knees before the glory of God, the saviour of the blessed, and judge of the fallen. See how his angels call the saved from their graves into heaven and the sinners are pulled down by Satan and his demons into the fires and torments of hell!" Monks and villagers alike wept. The thegn had a troubled eye.

"As wondrous as are these sacred images, painted upon these walls as though they were a calfskin Bible, this is not all of the Lord God's gifts today. Sing!" the abbot boomed. Once more, the monks began to chant. A reproving eye from Cuthred sent the thegn to his knees. The service began.

The abbot chanted in Latin, and holy brothers responded, also in Latin. He gestured to one of their number, who nodded to others, and they moved to the bench and lifted the linen cover. Cuthred's thundering voice quelled the whispers and caused those who were edging forward to withdraw.

"Behold the casket of Wulfmaer, first abbot of Snailwell and brother to King Athelstan's great-grandfather. His saintly body has rested within this simple wood since his death many years past, protected by a stone sarcophagus, buried within the minster church.

"Listen, for I must tell you of something that is both marvellous and dreadful. In a dream, Saint Wulfmaer came to me. He spoke of the condition of Holy Church in the Kingdom of the East Angles, the land he loves still, even though he now abides in heaven with Christ the King.

"Not all is well. Our sister minster at Elmstow was cleansed of the corruption that had delivered it into the devil's hands. It had nurtured debauchery, drunkenness and all manner of perversion. The safety of our own dear kingdom hung in the balance. We all know that we were delivered, but at what cost? The blood of so many good souls ran like a river when the Lord God and his army of angels came in fury to smite down the sinners who had made Elmstow their home. Their lives were made sacrifice to free us.

"Yet do we think the sin that almost broke our dear land, leaving it open to the ravages of our enemies, found only one home in the kingdom? Are we that foolish?" Cuthred stopped. The only sound was breathing—from him and from the souls who stared at him, eager for his next words. His lungs heaved.

"The pestilence that lay waste to Elmstow was born at Snailwell. Our Saviour, Jesus Christ, made the Church to be his bride. Yet in our land, the Church has become as Jezebel," he roared, "welcoming the gold of sinful, corrupt, ungodly men, desperate for the fleeting joys of the flesh." Even seasoned cloistered men gasped at the image summoned by Cuthred's words. "It grieves me to say such things, but it is my duty as your new abbot.

"Bishop Aethelbert has been a blessed Father to us, but he is now infirm. He is struggling to bear the yoke of leadership. It is beyond sadness to tell you, good people, that his failing health and distraction has turned to neglect.

"I do not say that he has evil in his heart, for that is not our Father. But he was called to nurture, to lead and to be wise in his decisions, as were the apostles before him. With his strength failing, his duty was to choose others who possessed experience, of sound teaching and standing within our Church. Instead, he has relied upon one green priest who may possess a peculiar gift, but who certainly lacks all the high virtues of faith and leadership.

"I tell you this openly, for I know there has been fear and confusion. The Church family has acted and elevated me to the position of Abbot of Snailwell. I tread humbly in the footsteps of our own great Saint Wulfmaer. Following his sacred instruction, I will be diligent in teaching you God's word and leading you in his ways to protect your eternal souls.

"The blessed saint also gave me this command. He has rested in Snailwell for many years and yearns still to help his people. In this, the youngest church in the whole of the kingdom, he wishes to settle. To be a beacon for the renewal of the faith of his countrymen. His spirit is already in heaven, but here, in Thornham, he wishes his mortal remains to lie. His bones are blessed, and his presence will bless this church and this community.

"So let us continue to kneel and in our hearts pray that Saint Wulfmaer will speak to God on our behalf." With a nod of his head, the abbot signalled to the nervous monk who had been watching carefully for the sign, who then disappeared through the open door.

To the deep, ethereal waves of chanting voices, six more holy brothers appeared, bearing upon their shoulders a pristine casket of oak. On each side, six figures were incised, and on each end, angels; four on one and three on the other. On the lid, a single name, 'Wulfmaer'. The casket was placed alongside its venerable ancestor.

"Here today, in the sight of his people, let us give Wulfmaer's saintly bones a new shield of wood." Cuthred gestured to the monks to take up their chisels and knives and to begin to prise away the lid. It had been a solid home, and the effort took some work. With the task completed, he again began to chant in Latin, then spoke in the native tongue so all would understand.

"I sense the spirit of our glorious saint here in his church. Whenever we come into this beautiful building with prayers for our needs, however simple, Saint Wulfmaer will take them into the throne room of the Lord God." He gestured for the lid to be removed.

Cuthred cried out in horror. Some monks gasped, some shouted, one fainted. The assembled villagers clambered to their feet and rushed to see what had caused such turmoil. They too struggled with what they witnessed, and the church erupted with frenzied voices. Abbot Cuthred, who had rightful pride in his imperious control over common and finer minds alike, stared speechless into the open box. He saw bones—plenty of them—jumbled unceremoniously at one end of the casket, but most of the space was taken up by someone else.

"Who is it?"

The villagers and monks shouted in response to Cuthred that they had no idea. "He is not from these parts, lord, and see the burn of a rope around his neck, and his hand is missing."

"Defilement! Some fiend seeks to desecrate the church." Cuthred's voice shook, his face blanched, and he fell to his knees. He grasped hold of the bench to stop himself falling further. "Remove that body and return the saint's bones to Snailwell. Lock the church until it can be purified. Lord God have mercy on us."

FOUR

Penance

E adred slumped upon a stool in the church and rested his
back against the wall. Light from three candles kept the
encroaching darkness at bay, and he gave thanks that his day
was nearly over. He could soon rest in the house provided
for him.

Eadred was approaching his third night at Deerstow.
On his first night, he had maintained the monastic routine
of participating in three periods of prayer and praise in the
church, albeit as a private devotional. Last night, he had
managed only the midnight service, and could otherwise
only whisper a few pleas from his house for the Lord God's
protection and forgiveness. He missed the familiar bell that
chimed to draw the minster's inmates to their church, and
he missed the collective encouragement of his brothers. His
mind and gut were also churning from the tension of the
wedding he had to perform the following day. Eadred felt
exhausted, lonely and indeed melancholic.

On the first full day, he had preached and then started to meet the folk from this vill and from the settlements and farms nearby and listened to their confessions. Bishop Aethelbert had instructed him to hear confessions privately rather than a single ritual of public penance. In this way, the penitent would hopefully be more forthcoming, and Eadred could also talk of the Scriptures and of faith as to a friend. The bishop had proven correct, but such a bottomless pit of sin and misery had emerged that Eadred had wept himself to sleep the previous night.

Almost half of those who had been obliged to confess did so in a careless, disinterested fashion, almost as if they were reciting from the same book, before receiving the same scant penance and absolution. They left as quickly as possible. But it was the others who troubled Eadred the most. In the quiet and intimate scope of the church, he found that many men and women came to speak deeply about an oppressive and wanton spirit in the community. They told of a rapacious lord who responded to the mindless slaughter of their herds by taking more and more of their dwindling number of beasts to keep his table full. They told of a lord who was heedless of the rule of law, so courts were not called to hear grievances, and feuds were allowed to burgeon in bloody attempts to gain justice. Despite the rich bounty of the region, poverty was spreading; unidentified babies were found dead in shallow graves, buried by parents who could not—or desired not—to care for them; and attractive girls were preyed upon by Forthred's kin. Unconfessed sins had abounded for want of a priest to hear them: theft, fornication, rape and other abuse of women, married and unmarried, and ill use of the old. Such things,

Eadred prayed, surely could not be the experience of the common people throughout the kingdom, but came from Forthred's sinful nature. A few folk had admitted to calling sometimes on false gods and spirits, and Eadred struggled to explain to them that they were calling on demons, which threatened their eternal souls.

Eadred had done what he could to bring hope, but it seemed an almost futile effort. He may be unable to set things right in Deerstow, but he was determined to do his best for one of the villagers. He had seen the genuine love of the Lord God in Eadgifu's eyes when she had welcomed him to the vill several days back, and her husband should soon arrive for his confession. Eadred had also made a rash promise to Eadgifu's sister, Eadburga, but he was not sure what he could do. A more seasoned priest would have chosen his words more cautiously and not let expectations swell, but the image of that forceful and lithe woman was in his mind when the door opened.

"Brihtwold, you are welcome." The heavy form moved slowly from the shadows with a sense of weariness about it. The middle-aged farmer looked strong of frame, but it was his face that required Eadred to stifle a gasp. It was full of warts, eruptions and cankers.

"Brihtwold, kneel here, if you will." The man dropped onto his knees with a loud sigh. "This is your opportunity to confess your sins and to seek forgiveness from the Lord God. It will remove the impediments to God's grace and allow you to partake of the sacraments." Eadred waited, and after a few heavy breaths, the farmer commenced to lay bare his sins. There were many of the venial offences Eadred had heard already dozens of times—bearing false witness, use of immoderate language, occasional drunkenness—but nothing relating to the gross behaviour that many of the villagers had connected to Brihtwold. Then the farmer continued.

"I confess that I have made lewd requests of some women and touched them on their private parts. And I have, once or twice, hit my wife for little reason." Brihtwold sighed but said no more.

"This must end! Look at me!" Eadred demanded the farmer's attention. "Other men have spoken to me of your behaviour. Surely, after you have been beaten twice, or is it thrice now, by the husbands and kin of women you have hounded and worse, you must know that there is retribution in the world of men for those who seek to take what is not theirs?"

"Father, I give you my word that I try, but I struggle against temptation."

Most of mankind does, Eadred mused, *but we are called to imitate Christ, however hard that might be, not to stew in our sinfulness.* He looked at the weary farmer and wondered whether he would ever be saved. From what he had heard, Brihtwold was not a man whose word was worth much. Yet, despite his own artless, youthful face, sometimes cloaked in pious reflection, Eadred also held an awkward assessment of himself. He might, unfortunately, have similarities to the man kneeling before him. Eadred could also find an excuse for most of his sins. There had to be something that made him a better man than the one who faced him other than the words of judgment he had learnt and the purity of his skin.

"You are married now, and to a good woman. You have been blessed. Eadgifu is younger than you and could still bear you children, if it is God's will. A man who marries late in life should feel himself fortunate to have such a companion. And her sister has also come to live in your home to help with the many burdens of the house. And tell me, how could you take your cattle to the upland for winter if you had no women to do the farm work while you were gone? You would be poorer without the coin your oxen earn ploughing those fields."

"Father, I have not taken my cattle to the upland this winter. The journey is not safe anymore. It has cost me good money."

Eadred nodded, for the bands of outlaws killing men and cattle had struck fear into all the fen-dwellers, but the point was still good, and he would make it understood. "That is sadly true, but I hear that last winter those who were fortunate to own oxen joined together to move their beasts and earned good coin. I was told that you were one of them, and that the season was the best for many a year."

The blotchy farmer sighed and could not evade the truth. "Yes, I was away until almost Easter last year. It was a good season."

"See, there are blessings from marriage, so why behave improperly with other women? It is a sin and also so foolish. Penance is not a punishment that can just be taken and forgotten, but an opportunity for you to repent. To truly repent is to strive to turn from sin to God's ways."

Brihtwold looked up at Eadred, who was at least ten years his junior. "When I was younger, my life was consumed by caring for my father, who lost his sight, and my mother, whose mind became feeble after my sister died. They returned to God only two winters past, and my life was then returned to me."

35

"I know of your burdens, Brihtwold. They have been hard to take."

"I was a good son; it is widely known. But the fleeting years of my youth had passed or been stolen. Father, when crops fail and there is famine, we hope to survive on bark, acorns and roots, and our stomachs ache for good bread and meat. But when seasons of plenty return, do we not all feast and gorge ourselves?"

"There is no excuse for fornication! We are more than just base flesh. Your penance this time must be far harsher."

"But, Father, the devil is shrewd and may tempt all men, whatever their rank." The farmer hesitated but continued. "It is said by some that even you have been enticed by a woman's charms to journey further than is proper, and is it not worse for an ordained man to taste—"

"I have confessed and am paying my penance!" Eadred thundered and flushed red. "For continuing to interfere with married women, you will fast for two days each week for six months. Brihtwold, go to your wife and behave as a husband should. Eadgifu deserves to be treated better than this. Now, let us pray fervently to the Lord God that he will strengthen you against your improper yearnings and actions, for your resolution alone is clearly inadequate." The prayer was one-sided. Brihtwold kicked the church door on his departure.

Eadred sat alone, his chest heaving. He had made one mistake, and even a pockmarked womaniser could ridicule him for it. He had shared carnal love with Sister Edith—a serious sin for a priest—but he had confessed his error with a contrite heart, accepted the penance and received absolution, as had Edith. He was not the first, and assuredly would not be the last, man of the Church to allow affection to proceed further than chaste spiritual communion, but his enemies had pounced, especially Abbot Cuthred. Cuthred had already openly questioned the fame Eadred had gained from his efforts in uncloaking evil at Elmstow Minster, and the abbot had no intention of seeing a priest from a poor family raised above his station.

The attacks had also been aimed at Bishop Aethelbert. Eadred would never forget or forgive himself for the terrible dilemma he had caused the bishop. Those ready to condemn Aethelbert for his lack of discipline had been too ready to give him advice. The bishop had spoken to Eadred about a visit from Cuthred he had endured, when the abbot had left him in no doubt that the recommended penance for fornication with a nun, laid out in the minster's penitential, was a fasting period of three days a week for seven years, but that there had been occasions when priests had been divested of holy orders for the same sin. This latter penalty, the abbot had proposed, should be seriously considered. But the bishop had stood his ground and had not assigned the full penance, and Eadred remained a priest. He knew that Cuthred would try again to have him removed from the priesthood.

As he walked back to his shelter, Eadred remembered something he had almost forgotten in the day's misery. Several folk had told him that their last confession had been to Father Ingeld in the previous spring, close to a twelvemonth earlier. But the bishop had told Eadred of the message from Ingeld, carried by the farmer who had visited Snailwell at that time, saying that Ingeld was too ill to travel from the Cauldron to Snailwell. Had Ingeld subsequently recovered sufficiently that he had journeyed as far as

Deerstow, but no further? What made these recollections from Deerstow's parishioners even stranger was that Ingeld seemed to be in robust health and his visit had been shorter than usual. Only one person could untangle this confusion, and that would be Ingeld himself, when Eadred came to meet him at the Cauldron.

*

Eadburga scampered back into the house. "Your husband returns," she whispered to her sister. "He has a dark look." Eadgifu rubbed away her tears.

"Come, my love, the priest would have filled him with fear far better than we can. I can see it in his eyes. This will get better now." The hope in Eadburga's voice was desperate. She remembered her sister from better years: seldom frivolous, but not often oppressed by the thought of each coming day's toil and troubles. There had been a sense of promise in her that her future would improve. Eadgifu had more than a hardworking nature, she had a kind heart, and it shone through her guileless blue eyes and gentle smile. The accident had changed it all, and her marriage to Brihtwold had added to her burdens.

Eadburga was Eadgifu's younger sister and only sibling. Brihtwold had suggested to Eadburga that she should come to live with them to help Eadgifu with the work and the necessities of life. She had not objected, inspired by her affection for her sister. Under the same roof, Eadburga had hoped that she could protect Eadgifu, but she had a beauty in her features, her long blond hair and lithe body that caused unwanted attention.

"More fasting!" Brihtwold slammed the door shut and spat the words with a string of invective. "Six months this time, two days a week! It has only ever been a day a week for three months."

"Is that all? Nothing more?" Eadburga's impulsive sharpness earned her a punch to the cheek, which sent her crashing to the ground. Her hope that the priest's visit might have brought sterner punishment for Brihtwold and a miracle for her sister had been dashed, as before.

The wart-faced farmer bent over Eadburga, eyeing her amber earrings, fingering the chain around her neck. It was not the first time he had looked at her array of jewellery, given to her by eager men, even, it was suspected, by Lord Forthred's son, Edmund. "Whore, I know how you gained these trinkets. And God's blood, is that not enough penance for me! What is the difference between that priest and I? We both sin, but he is the one to give me penance. I hate them all. How much can a man take? Without food in my gut, how can I provide for us?"

"Here, eat now. This is not a fasting day." Eadgifu served her husband a platter with thick stew and bread and a cup of ale.

"And I can do more," Eadburga spoke, smiling gently at her sister. But she knew that it was time to escape.

It was not the life she had wanted or expected for Eadgifu. The physical pain alone rarely eased. She could hear her sister at night, whimpering with the torment to her body as she turned in bed. Eadgifu would pray fervently for some flicker of light to shine in the darkness. Only one small candle against the gloom. Eadburga also stifled her pain. Behind the woollen curtain around her bed,

Brihtwold would commence his regular nightly practice, when not drunk or unconscious from ale. The thrusts and the grunts would continue until his excitement exploded in unconcealed gasps. The first time he had grabbed her chest, Eadburga had twisted his manhood and received a punch in return when he had recovered. Brihtwold had made it clear then that she could either give him release or he would continue to make her sister's life a misery.

FIVE

Aelfric, the Ealdorman

"Horses passed recently, lord; perhaps seven or eight. Here, they took another track." The crouching warrior pointed to an obscure pathway into the thicket.

"Can we catch them today?" the ealdorman replied.

"If they are heavily laden or carry wounds, it is possible."

Aelfric, Ealdorman of the East Angles, looked up. The sun issued a pale light through the treetops and in this late winter season left the heavens quickly. His troop of close to twenty warriors watched him in silence.

"They are not our prize. Leave them."

"But, lord, they have murdered and raided. We have them. They are running from us. We can finish them and be on the road to Deerstow when the sun rises."

Aelfric looked at Hygelac, the greatest warrior in the kingdom, and thought about what he had said. "We follow then, and with low voices. One rider goes ahead."

In single file, the horses left the main path through the forest, their riders suppressing their voices. Some were seasoned warriors and not overwhelmed by the risks of battle, but many had less experience to see them through. They were exhausted, their stomachs depleted, and some bore wounds from several clashes with bands of thieves and murderers. But Aelfric knew the main concern they all shared. It was not hunger, fatigue or the unknown, but him.

It was close to a twelvemonth since he had been elevated to the lofty position of ealdorman. Aelfric's father had been ealdorman for many years, respected or feared by all as a tough, incisive, brutal leader.

Aelfric was of a different mould and suffering from bitter blows that would test any man. Though only in his twenty-third year, the few souls he had loved were all now dead. He had heard the whispers that his mind had not recovered and that he had not risen in prowess since the king had bestowed the title upon him, though none questioned his courage or loyalty. This campaign had been dispiriting. For four weeks, he and his men had been hunting criminals. They had inflicted some damage, killing three or so handfuls and hanging half as many again, but losing too many of their own. Despite Hygelac's persuasive torture, none of the captives had owned to slaughtering livestock. Injuries and doubts gnawed at those who now rode with Aelfric along an unfamiliar path. In normal times, common criminals would not warrant his direct attention, but lawlessness had taken the opportunity of disarray and weak leadership and now plagued the kingdom.

Aelfric had ridden the length and breadth of the

kingdom with his father when he was ealdorman, and now in his own right. He thanked the Lord God that peace in the land of the East Angles was a desire for most men. God's grace and their own toil fed most families well. The realm was flat or with low, gentle hills. The upland areas sustained good crops and livestock, but it was the low-lying fens that yielded the greatest bounty. The earth here was rich and black, with meres and strong rivers that teemed with fish and eels, and all manner of birds filled the skies. Too damp for many crops but rich in pasture for cattle, sheep and pigs. But the fens could show a different temper and do so with daunting speed.

Aelfric had kept an eye to the heavens these past few days and smelt the air. He was certain that rain was heralded, but how much? When the rains hit hard and long or when the great northern sea smashed into the coast, sending waves over the land, the fenland was all but buried in water. During this current campaign, he had again been astounded at how the restless rivers and meres had shifted in their shape and size over the years he had crossed the land. What had once been solid earth under his feet had now become more water than land. He had known thick mists to obscure everything for weeks and fevers and demons to rise with the vapours. The fens were treacherous to the body and the soul.

Most men gave thanks to the Lord God and handed over their tithes to the Church with gratitude, but some took the opposite path. They saw the blessings bestowed on others through the eyes of greed and envy, and rather than accepting God's gifts, they took what was not theirs.

Aelfric's faith told him that a state of peace and order in the kingdom could only be achieved when God was honoured. Those who committed unlawful acts could redeem themselves by accepting their guilt and the king's punishment and by confessing their wrongs and doing penance, as prescribed by Holy Church. But there were now too many folk who scorned this and who departed from peace and from God's commands, and they made a sanctuary in the deepest and most secret parts of the fens.

Aelfric remembered what his father had told him, that the gods of these outcasts despised the Lord God, for he had turned the people against them. Most of these deities would have accepted him as a brother god, as had been their practice for countless generations, even as a greater god, but the Church, in his name, threw them from the heart of the kingdom to the darker, more forbidding places and called them demons. Some were and may have deserved their fate, but others were good-hearted. These were the spirits of the meres, rivers, trees and hills. Of limited domain, they had no desire for power, but to see the seasons pass in union with their folk. But Aelfric's father was no lover of the Saviour of man and called upon all manner of spirits to aid him in life's battles. He was not disposed to consider as evil those spirits the Church called demons.

It was towards one of the forbidding places that the group of East Angles was being drawn. The path became more confining. The thorns, at first a mild nuisance, had become increasingly vexing and now cut and ripped at tunics, breeches and flesh. Men drew their cloaks around their heads and swore. The horses groaned and bucked, their hooves sinking in the stinking slime. Then they splashed in flowing water, and for the past few minutes all could feel the gloom of the retreating sun. Aelfric knew his men well enough to share their unnerving sense of growing danger, but unable to stop from plunging deeper.

"Ahead, not far, there is open grassland. A small area but enough to camp."

"And beyond it?" Aelfric responded to the returning rider.

"Thick branch-work and reeds, then a mere."

The band of warriors approached the clearing with weapons ready. "And what of the thieves and murderers, where did they go?"

"To the mere, lord. The water was their only way out of here. There is no other but the path we came along."

The ealdorman nodded without lifting his head. To do otherwise would have shown his dejection. "Then we camp here."

"I will have the shoreline checked while we have light. They would have left some sign of their withdrawal."

"Yes, do that, Hygelac. It is wise. Their horses must be here somewhere. They surely could not be taken by boat."

The clearing was waterlogged but did possess two areas of slightly higher land. Upon these, the East Angles made their camp. As the flames of the fires began to quiver, a shout of victory rang out from one of the returning warriors.

"Lord, the thieves may have escaped, but they left their horses along the mere's edge, all dead. I counted eight, still warm, their throats cut, ready for our fires!" The joyful cry was universal. Knives were drawn and kept busy with butchering the dead beasts. Soon, the rich, encouraging smell of horsemeat began to flavour the damp air.

"This is a prize we did not expect, lord," Hygelac gloated. "Your resolve forced those base men to take a path that led to the killing of all their horses. Whatever they stole could not repay this loss. Not only their value in gold, but this also depletes their ability to plunder. And we eat well!"

Aelfric's eyes lit briefly as he looked at his warriors around the fires. He sat with Hygelac, his closest hearth companion, away from the others. "It is good to hear their laughter, Hygelac. I wish for all the world that they could hear mine."

"Take some cheer from us, lord. You have responsibilities that would crush the toughest warrior. These days are harsh, full of evil, but each one provides a lesson if we can see it. The day will come soon when your heart and your mind will be as strong as your arm."

"Without my hearth companions, where would I be?" The ealdorman shook Hygelac by the shoulder and stared past him into the darkness. He spoke slowly, assessing the purpose and impact of each word. "I know that I have disappointed many. The king's choice to make me ealdorman is questioned widely, and also by me. Perhaps my nature has never been that of a warrior. It is hard to rise each day without joy and to face my burdens. Each night, I see the faces of the many warriors whom I have led to their deaths by my mistakes. They deserved better than to die without purpose. I find cheerfulness to be rarer than a hoard of elvish treasure."

"Lord, a warrior's duty is to follow and protect his lord, wherever that may lead, often unto death. It is not their purpose to question him. There is not a man here who would not follow you to the ends of the earth. And there is not one great leader who has not made errors that cost lives—many lives—but by learning what makes a poor path, a leader learns how to choose wisely. But that journey takes time."

"You would make a better ealdorman than I. Warfare is natural to you."

"You are gracious, lord, but it is not so. I can fight, and I can lead men into battle, some say. But there is much that I cannot do, tasks that irk my head. I am not made to build alliances or to talk with our enemies to exchange hostages or to think about how to feed an army. God gave me a simple warrior's head and heart."

"More than that, my friend. You are the only man I can talk to about the cares I carry. You are the only man who knows that I faltered in resolve at the first clash of the battle at Elmstow."

"It was a momentary hesitation, lord, and none question your courage. Nor should you."

Aelfric sighed. "I can, without fear, face the man who comes at me with his blade, for all that would happen is his death or mine, and neither concerns me. But to choose which path to take for my companions and the king's army in the face of unseen dangers troubles my heart. And this past year has seen the witless decisions I can make and the numbness of indecision. Criminals and the corrupt have taken heart from my mistakes. I am more than glad that our king has now released you from his court so you can be by my side and help me thresh and winnow the good paths from the bad.

"But there is something else happening. I can sense it but not understand its nature. The lawlessness and unrest in our kingdom these past months is like nothing that I have known. Surely, it is not only from my failings?"

"I feel it too, lord," Hygelac replied. "There have always been those who would defy the king's law to enrich themselves. There is more darkness in what is now happening. This senseless slaughter of cattle and other beasts, leaving them to be torn apart by wolves, has sown a deep disquiet amongst the lawful."

"It must be stopped," Aelfric spoke, "or famine will waste the people in coming seasons. It will waste us all if the land is not worked. I pray to God that the marriage between Forthred's son and Cerdic's daughter will stop the fenland feud. I harbour a deep fear, my friend, that much of the unrest across our land is caused by these warring families, but I cannot be certain. My father, in his great wisdom, over his years as ealdorman, found men in all parts of the kingdom—and some in other lands—who would alert him to dangers. He told me once that they were to be found in our most populous settlements, in the two great minsters of our land and in the households of our great lords. He told me, when he was full of ale one night, of one sign that they all had in common: they, like he, did not follow the Lord God, though they had to profess to the king's faith. For that, and for other reasons, he kept their names to himself and never talked of them again. I wish to God I had those eyes and ears now. They saw everything for him and kept his life safe for many years.

"I need to be at Deerstow to make certain the wedding does happen. I have devoted too much time to bringing the families together, but I fear for its completion. But come, Hygelac, the fires are ebbing and the air is damp. That is enough misery for one day. We all need some rest. Tomorrow, let us return to the main path before rain falls and journey to Deerstow. There is still time before the day of the wedding. I am weary from the past weeks' labours, and our wounded need to find somewhere to heal, or fever will take more of them."

*

The sharp clash of metal made for an unwelcome and urgent waking. Hygelac was the first to react. "Shield wall!" he screamed out the order into the darkness. The arrows made an unnerving sigh in the air. Before the wall was formed, one of the points hit a man; he groaned. They came from the direction of the track from the clearing back to the main path. There was not a candle of light in the air. Hygelac barked another order, this time for his men to return fire.

"One has hit leather and wood—a shield!"

"They bar our way back to the Deerstow road," Aelfric moaned.

The minutes passed, and the drizzle strengthened. Once in a while, a few arrows crossed to no great effect other than to keep each force from advancing.

"One or both of us must charge when we have but one spark of light," Hygelac said.

"I would sooner know at what. Their numbers? Their condition?" Aelfric replied.

"We must force ourselves past them, lord, whatever their strength, or perish. We would do best to surprise them."

A deluge now fell from the sky, and the earth between the contending groups turned treacherous for whoever attacked. The eyes of the East Angles strove to follow the emerging grey contours of the force facing them. Some appeared strongly armed, some only with knives and scythes. Some were horsed, most on foot. Their number hard to determine but equal to the ealdorman's force.

Aelfric pulled Hygelac closer, and the two men spoke. Hygelac then left to talk to some of the warriors. He soon returned.

"Are you ready?"

"We are, lord," Hygelac replied.

"Then give the order."

Hygelac held his hand high, then dropped it. A dozen of Aelfric's men had picked their targets: five men and their horses. Their arrows flew, and four of the enemy toppled from their mounts. With sudden pain searing through their flesh, the animals bucked. They trampled, slid, collided and fell.

Aelfric and his men locked shields, and without a word, they advanced steadily across the waterlogged clearing. Some men slipped, but none fell. They were almost within striking distance of their unsettled adversaries before any enemy arrows found their way with purpose. One hit an East Angle in his thigh and another in the foot. Then the foe charged, and from behind those who could be seen came others on either side. They pounced on Aelfric's flanks.

The sudden response by the enemy unnerved Aelfric, but it was not long-lived. From the corner of his left eye, he saw Hygelac attack like a clawed bear. Whether to his front or side, the great warrior hacked and roared with no apparent concern for his own life, like the great beasts of the forest. The fury of his attack spurred others, including Aelfric. It soon became obvious to him that most of their adversaries were not warriors, but criminals and outcasts, who fell easily to blows and thrusts and soon turned to flee. But to Aelfric's dismay, there were some men made of rock, and despite the efforts of the East Angles, these men withdrew without showing their backs. They filled the narrow path back to the main track and roared defiance.

Hygelac attacked. His sword lacked the room to smash shields, so he thrust, but each time his blade was thwarted, as were those of his countrymen who sought to follow his example. The morning wore on, and wounds and death were hard to inflict, but once in a while metal did have the advantage over flesh for both contending sides. Slowly, far too slowly, Aelfric sensed he was gaining ground, and with resilience his men would prevail.

The deluge had redoubled when Aelfric's force finally broke into the main path and his men could engage with their enemy without constraint. Nightfall came early, and the few remaining of Aelfric's foe turned and ran. The East Angles fell to their knees in gratitude and exhaustion.

"We have won, my lord. Most of them lie dead."

Aelfric managed a weak smile to his countryman. "We fought well but at a cost."

"Four only of our side are heaven-bound, my lord, and most of those with wounds should heal with rest and care."

"But we have paid in time. When light returns tomorrow, we must ride to Deerstow, and I pray to the Lord God that all goes well with the union of the fenland kindreds, whether I am there or not."

The night was wretched. No one had seen rain fall as fiercely or for so long. And when light finally returned, Aelfric and his battered band of warriors started towards Deerstow. The horses slipped and slid. One, then two, broke their legs.

"Lord, we cannot continue. Let us rest awhile and wait for this storm to ease. There is not enough rain in the heavens for it to last much longer. Our horses cannot move in safety."

Aelfric nodded. *God help me,* he thought, *we should not have pursued that band of thieves. It has cost me a day, at least. I pray that I have not erred yet again.*

SIX

The Wedding

E adred had conducted fewer than a handful of weddings in his short life as a priest. This was enough, he thought, for him to feel comfortable with his role. He was a serious-minded young man, though partial to red wine, often to excess, who had desired to walk closer with his God since his fifteenth year. His parents, poor but free, had eventually agreed, and he had left his younger brother and elder sister and entered Snailwell Minster with the intention of becoming a monk. Around eighteen months later, he had been ordained as a priest.

Despite the depth of his conviction to join the Church and to bring souls to Christ, Eadred could find little joy at the weddings he conducted. He would counsel the couple in the months before their union, and without fail he came to like them. Several of the folk he had known for years. They were mostly of his age and from families of hardworking men and women. As Eadred did not have the necessary seniority or rank in the kingdom or the Church to officiate at the weddings of noble families, these were the folk up to now whom he had been called upon to marry.

But as he spoke of God's blessing to the couple at the ceremony, there was always a moment when he discerned the seductive turn in the bride's smile to her beloved, and the groom's chest rose and fell with anticipation of the night ahead. Eadred's face would marble and perhaps he would stutter, and he would feel tormented. Eadred had struggled with his own chastity since Elmstow. It had been a single occasion of fornication, but not a day had gone by since then when he had not relived it in his mind's eye. It was a sin and it had borne evil fruit, for he had tasted carnal love, and his contentment with priestly life had suffered a wound. How he prayed for that memory to fade, but it became stronger and more unsettling. At least, Eadred hoped, with the couple standing in front of him, there would be no desire-laden glances.

"Marriage is a sacrament. It was established by God so that the desires of the flesh may be contained, for the begetting of children and for them to be raised in love and in God's ways. A man and woman accordingly should not be compelled into marriage against their will. It is their mutual affection and respect that God builds upon."

Eadred stood with an awkward smile before the church on the road into Deerstow and looked at those facing him. The groom, Edmund, and the bride, Censwith, surrounded by their kindreds, could have been statues. The looming black shroud of storm clouds approaching with flashes of lightning and booming thunder added to his disquiet.

"As we know," he continued with a strain in his voice,

"women are natural peacemakers, and if a woman of her own volition seeks a marriage to bring together families to end a bloody feud, then the marriage is doubly blessed."

Eadred could afford no mistakes, so when the wind suddenly rose and the threatening storm spat its first drops, and the rich men and women in their fine clothes eyed the church door, Eadred led them inside.

The interior issued the same damp odour as it had the day before when Eadred had heard confessions, and it was as void of joy as then. If he had witnessed the same scarcely suppressed hostility between the families in a marriage of folk of a lower rank, he would have refused his role and counselled the pair to think deeply about their intentions. But under strict instructions from the bishop not to interfere, he proceeded with the ceremony. At least his wish was granted and there was not the slightest hint of warmth between the new husband and wife.

The wedding feast was destined to be similarly uncomfortable. There had been talk that although Lord Aelfric had missed the wedding, he was riding hard towards Deerstow so as to attend the celebration. Eadred's eyes searched in all directions before he entered the great hall. There was no sign of the ealdorman.

The guests had assembled. Forthred's close kin and guests sat at three tables and Cerdic's at three others, with the great fire separating the families. Husband and wife sat at their own table facing the assembled witnesses to a new day in the relationship between the two families—hopefully. The door opened, and women entered carrying jugs of ale and wine. It had been a while since Eadred had tasted the ruby liquid, and his eyes pursued the vessels.

Cerdic's wife, Hilda, rose from the bench and took one of the jugs. Known far and wide as a peacemaker, she went firstly to the bride and groom and served them wine. She performed the same service for Forthred and finally for her husband. Her poise, charm and the disabling warmth of her smile, meeting all of the flint faces she encountered, filled Eadred with admiration.

Forthred nodded, and Eadred rose. He said grace and the feast began. To his disappointment, the wine was reserved to a few guests, and he lamented his cup of sour ale. He returned it to the table after a few sips.

There were not many benefits to remaining sober at a wedding feast, but Eadred accepted that there was an advantage in his case. As the alcohol swilled around the room, inevitably tongues began to loosen. At first, the banter was constrained to each kindred group, as if they were feasting alone. But as the sound of laughter grew, so did Eadred's anxiety. It was more than tongues that began to enjoy the freedom found in the emptying of a cup.

One of Forthred's kin—a heavy, ungainly boar of a man—rose and limped slowly closer to the fire to warm his hands. Eadred, who was further from the hearth than the man's table and without the effect of wine, still enjoyed more than a pleasant warmth, so there was no necessity in the man's actions. Eadred's gaze followed his every arduous movement.

Some four dozen folk filled the room, more than half of whom were men. Years of hostility provided the nourishment for a far stronger blaze than crackled at the hall's centre, and addled heads fanned the flames. Eadred prayed silently that there would be no spark, for if there were, the bishop expected him to smother it.

"A fight at a feast starts between two men," the bishop had told him before his departure. "One inflicts some damage on the other's honour. He says some immoderate words or there is some hurtful action, and the other responds by instinct. Ties of kinship draw in others in a blink of an eye, and the violence spreads as it will without constraint." Eadred could not forget the bishop's warning. "You, my boy, have two chances to stop the fire spreading. Block the spark. If you see discord brewing between two men, go to them and let them know their names will be cursed if they harm those who attend a wedding feast. Tell them to return to their seats and spend the night in harmony. If a fight has started, shout loudly that all who join will bring down a curse upon themselves, for marriage is a sacrament. Besides, neither side will want to lose the king's gold, so all should be well."

The man-boar stopped to take in deep breaths, stooped and lifted a log. He withdrew a few paces, then tossed it into the burning centre. Embers exploded over the bride's family. Eadred let out a cry. The oaf stood back and raised his innocent hands, but the foolish smile could not be easily smothered. Men and women tore at their hair to rip out the throbbing embers.

Cerdic and his two sons rose. Eadred had met them earlier. All men had left their swords and axes at the door, but most still carried their knives.

"Hold! In the name of the Lord God, I say hold!" Eadred's voice was lost in an eruption of angry voices. Food and drink spilt over the floor as a table was overturned and others pushed aside. One of Cerdic's sons and the heavy member of Forthred's kin traded blows. Blades flashed and bit into each other. In a heartbeat, all the men had engaged each other.

"All who break the peace of this wedding feast are cursed in the sight of God." Eadred stood to the side of the brawl and bellowed the words several times. But blood was up, and no one heard his words. "The king's protection lies over this feast. Those who fight break his law and will pay the penalty." He looked on in horror as a blade slashed a man's face.

A scream, high-pitched and insistent, cut through the grunts. The flames lifted into the air. Lord Cerdic's wife, Hilda, stumbled from the hearth, the bottom of her dress alight. Her husband ran to her with his cloak.

"Get water." Speaking words of reassurance but with a voice flushed with panic, Cerdic threw his cloak over his wife, who had fallen to the floor, writhing, crying. "Quick, in the name of God!" One of Cerdic's sons, fired by desperation, threw a jug of ale over his wailing mother. It was a timely action, and two more were similarly used.

Eadred looked carefully at Lord Forthred's expression while the Lady Hilda was being cared for. The lord seemed uncertain. Eadred wondered whether he was troubled that the violence had broken out or because it had been stifled. Eadred moved quickly and went to speak to him. "I pray that a tragedy that would have blighted the marriage has been averted, my lord. The king's gold is still on the table if peace is restored." Forthred did not reply.

With the cloak covering Hilda's body, another of her daughters examined her mother's legs. The water arrived and was poured over the limbs.

"How is the pain, mother?"

"My left calf and ankle burn but are bearable. Otherwise, I think I have been fortunate." Hilda raised her head. "For all that is sacred, put down your weapons. This alliance is blessed by God, and any man who harms its birth must answer to the Almighty."

Cerdic shouted to his kin to sheath their weapons, and Forthred did likewise. Both men had to repeat their order. Cerdic looked once more to his wife.

"All is well, my love." He sighed with relief. "God has preserved you. Come, we will take you to our house and care for you." Hilda's sons helped raise her to her feet.

"Our lady was pushed. I saw a hand." The accusation was met with cries of anger, and blades were raised once more.

"I cannot say I felt a push. I think I stumbled in the confusion," Hilda shouted to be heard above the voices. "Let us have peace!"

"If anyone tried to harm my wife, he must be uncloaked and suffer the consequences. There can be no peace between us until there is justice," Cerdic thundered.

Forthred muttered, then nodded. "If one of my men has violated my hall and stained my name, I swear I will find him and see that he is punished, and you will be compensated."

Cerdic breathed deeply, watching his wife being helped from the hall. He nodded in return.

The hall emptied. Among the last to leave was the married couple. "God's blessing on you both. Hilda is in good hands and will recover." Eadred turned to Edmund. "Your father will discover and punish the culprit. The virtuous behaviour of both fathers augurs well for the future."

"There will be brighter days," Censwith sighed.

Edmund's face was as colourless as that of his wife. He looked at Eadred but did not repay the smile.

As Eadred was about to leave, a serving woman, whom Eadred had met when she came to confess her sins, approached and whispered, "Father, is it not a wonder that the two lords remain at peace despite the violence of this evening? Is it the promise of gold or the power of a peace-weaving woman? I pray to God that this gentleness between the lords continues, but it will take a miracle."

Outside, the skies had opened and nature roared. Eadred threw his cloak over his head and ran to his shelter. He had a journey to start in the morning and prayed that the day would be fine.

SEVEN

Journey

Eadred stretched out his hand and looked skyward. A few drops. It was as good a time as any to start his journey after the rampant storm of the night before. His feet slipped and slid, and he moaned at the prospect of mud gathering around them and dampness creeping up his body. After four cheerless nights at Deerstow, he was eager to leave the village. Hunger vented its displeasure in his stomach after his meagre mouthfuls at the dismal feast. His other meals had been provided by each of the poorer households. For the most part, it had been a grudging contribution. Eadred understood well enough that parting with hard-won food in the grim poverty of winter was unpopular.

A great lord could obtain his food renders by right; so also, the Church. The uncompliant faced penalties, which could be harsh. But for a young priest, alone, near the outer measure of the bishop's reach, Eadred received hostility, close to defiance at times. He took sparingly and assured the donors that he would record their contributions carefully and have them taken into account when they next paid their tithes.

A few souls had seemed to welcome his visit, like Eadgifu and her sister, but after Eadred had given Brihtwold his penance, Eadburga simply scowled at him. He had preached and given Holy Communion to the community. He had looked carefully into all of their eyes, and some had the spirit of the Lord animating them. Most could just as easily have been looking at a dung pile.

Eadred sensed well enough that his relief at leaving the settlement was an emotion returned by most of the villagers. He had felt himself to be an intruder rather than a welcome visitor. Eadred did not doubt the dogs that strained against their tethers, baring their teeth and snarling as he broke into an escaping run, reflected their owners' opinions of him.

The disaster at the wedding feast troubled him. The heads of the two families had talked of a just settlement if Hilda's fall had indeed resulted from a deliberate attack, but the bishop had spoken of generations of bloody animosity that would need a miracle to bring to an end.

Eadred had a deep belief in his faith and strove to see Christ in all he met and to see the best in a fellow man until his behaviour showed that the devil had his soul. Even then, if a man did evil, Eadred believed he could still be redeemed, as was Paul the Saint. Thus, he had to accept for now the word of Forthred and Cerdic. The laws of man also needed to be obeyed, and if a wrongful deed had been committed, then the unknown assailant had to be discovered and face justice.

If circumstances had been slightly different, Hilda might have become disfigured and disabled, even worse. Eadred mused over the actions of the limping oaf who had started the brawl and wondered if he were simply ale-addled and a solitary fool, or if others were involved, who were part of a deeper plot to ruin the union of the families. Whatever the truth, it had been made clear to Eadred that it was time he left Deerstow.

He was disturbed from his thoughts by a figure moving off the path ahead of him. Eadred broke into a run to catch her. "Eadgifu, wait." She seemed in two minds but did stop. "Let me carry those." Again, Eadgifu seemed uncertain, but Eadred took the bundle of firewood from her arms. He let Eadgifu lead, which she did in silence, apart from a few quiet words of thanks. Although Brihtwold's house seemed to take him away from the road out of Deerstow, Eadred considered that there had to be something more he should do for the poor woman, although he had no idea what it might be. He tried to think quickly. It was to a flimsy house in a grim, waterlogged part of the settlement where she led him. She opened the door and let Eadred enter.

"What is he doing here?" Eadburga seethed.

"Good morning, Eadburga," Eadred replied. He unburdened himself of the pile of firewood. "I saw your sister and hoped to speak to her husband. He does not appear to be here. Is he close by?"

"Who knows? He comes and goes as he will. He left before it was light."

"I see a bruise upon your face."

Eadburga touched her cheek lightly. "It is the price of defending my sister."

Eadred turned to Eadgifu. "I gave Brihtwold the strongest penance that the bishop would allow for his sins. I know it vexed him greatly, for others have told me how he complained. I still hope and pray that the thought of another such penance if he continues with his behaviour will restrain him."

"It may curb his lust for other women, but it will fuel his violence towards his wife! Who will stop that?"

Eadred gulped back his feeling of impotence. "I am sorry that there is little more I can do. But what of Lord Forthred? Can you not raise Brihtwold's behaviour with him?" Eadburga's laughter served as an answer. "Then I swear to you both that when I see the ealdorman, whom I have rendered services to in the past, I will plead your condition with him."

"I am grateful for your concern, Father," Eadgifu replied. Her sister sighed and kicked the ground. "Have you food for your journey?" Eadgifu continued.

"If you have any to spare, it would be welcome. I have a long journey ahead of me." Eadgifu cut a heavy loaf of bread and gave half to Eadred. "Thank you, it is most welcome. Now, I must be on my way. There is rain in the air, so I will hurry." He said a quick blessing and turned to go. It was a great surprise to Eadred to see the flames of the fire gleaming off some silver pennies that had spilt from a bag half-hidden behind a pot in the corner of the house. By the look of the size of the bag, there was a tidy sum within it. Brihtwold's land might be waterlogged, and he cried poor, Eadred pondered, but his cattle were bringing him wealth.

His track followed a river heading eastwards. Eadred had queried the villagers he met over the past few days at

Deerstow about his path, and those that replied seemed none too helpful, almost, he thought, attempting to dissuade him with suggestions that he would be better off returning to Snailwell. So he put aside the sullen counsel of Deerstow's inhabitants and prayed that Anselm's memory contained as accurate a reflection of the route ahead as the monk imagined, including that it was no more than a day's good walk further on from Deerstow, so long as the path he chose were true.

Now, into his sixth day after leaving Snailwell, Eadred was the furthest, by far, that he had ever been from his beloved minster. Yet his face wore a faint smile that once in a while creased into a boyish grin. It was in Eadred's nature to wonder why his spirit should feel so lively as he made his way across pastures and sedge fields, through woods, and beside meres and unfamiliar river courses, for the routines of the religious life that he loved so much were nowhere to be seen. He spoke to the few people he met on the way, whether they walked the path or drifted gently down the river in shallow boats.

Eadred pondered that happiness had three reasons for its visit. Firstly, it was beyond joy to have Deerstow and its inhabitants behind him. It had been an oppressive, dismal and challenging time for him. Secondly, as he ventured further into the unknown, he found that Brother Anselm's memory appeared to be remarkably accurate. At each distinct landmark Eadred recognised from the monk's description, he found himself not only singing Anselm's words, but also a song of victory.

Anselm had warned that some sections of the country Eadred would traverse were open to constant change, as flooded rivers challenged their current course and land melted away or emerged around a stand of trees. Yet even when Eadred was confused by what faced him, through prayer, keen wits and some effort, he found the true path once more, even if he had to explore several alternatives.

But it was the third reason that really delighted and amazed him. From his time at Snailwell Minster, Eadred had formed the belief and the habit that only within the regular confines of his cell or the minster church could he come nearest to contemplating his Maker. It was only in isolation, in God's house, with no burden on his senses, where he had the greatest opportunity to turn his mind from the constant weight of life's impositions to the great mystery of God. But here, in the unfamiliar expanse of creation, with constant possibilities of distraction and worry—which should have troubled his ordered mind—Eadred was aware of God's presence more strongly than at any time since he had last been with his friend Tatwine. That wonderful hermit monk was closer to God's spirit than anyone he had ever encountered. He had heavenly visions and spoke prophetic words. Eadred remembered what his friend had whispered to him once.

"There are no more demons in the fens than in the gentlest hamlet, though this is not what we are supposed to tell the people. You will never hear what I say now from a bishop. We warn Christ's sheep not to venture to certain meres or caves, groves or hilltops because they are home to demons. Yet I have seldom found that to be the truth. Demons may seek to attack us even in God's house. We tell folk this lie because those parts of our country remind people of their former gods and spirits. It was in such places that pagans worshipped. We must claim all such rocks and cracks in the earth and rejoice in them, not fear them, for

God has dominion over all creation. Let us then see our Maker in all of his creation, and not let the pagans claim nature, as they did before they knew of the Lord God and still seek to do."

That memory was of Tatwine at his best, when neither night nor clouds could shroud the light. But God did not entirely possess the monk; there was a side to his nature that Eadred feared. Tatwine had joined the cloister to save his troubled soul, but the devil could still stir his heart. "Do not fear demons, Eadred, fear men. Satan may light the spark, but it is men who decide whether it dies or burns and consumes."

Near to day's end, with light leaving the world, pushed on its way by a return of forbidding black clouds, Eadred came upon a ruined farm building, probably once used to shelter precious cattle. It crowned the only higher land that he could see. One end had collapsed and taken the thatched roof with it. He took his knife and moved quickly to cut handfuls of sedge and threw them over the dilapidated, slanting roof, then stood fallen branches to hold his repairs in place. The rain he had expected began to fall, with Eadred hurrying to gather twigs and underwood for a fire.

Suddenly, the sky opened and he flung himself under the pathetic cover that he prayed would protect him from the freezing deluge. From his woollen bag, he pulled some dry moss and two precious flints, which his numb hands could barely hold. Fumbling as a baby would play with pebbles, he grew ever more anxious that the fire his body ached for would remain beyond his power. His dead hands fell beside him.

Eadred crouched low, pulling his cloak tightly around him. Nearby trees blurred into a shadowy mass. The air seemed liquid and roared with sound. The earth streamed past him but, thankfully thus far, not through his timid shelter. He groaned and prayed—there was nothing else he could do—and darkness descended.

A night without sleep and without comfort was no stranger to the young priest, and he huddled low in prayer as the hours passed. He imagined that if he could see into the black fen or hear beyond the thunder of the deluge, he would look upon a land in motion from the power falling from the heavens, surging into life.

*

When a touch of light struggled through the gloom, Eadred gave thanks that he and his dwelling had survived the night. His cloak was wet but not soaked, and the earth beneath him was damp but not dissolving. If he had slept, it was in momentary bursts.

With no enthusiasm, he rose with groans of pain in his back and joints and emerged crouch-backed. He looked at a terrifying world. The oppressive clouds covered the earth like a black skin, and still the rain fell, undiminished, assailing his eyes when he arched his back. The path Eadred had to follow had become a shallow, fast-flowing river littered with broken underwood.

So overwhelmed was Eadred at seeing what confronted him, and pained by the misery of his cold, wet condition, that the sound from the north seemed a distant concern—until he turned his eyes.

A sound like a waterfall. Crashing through the trees, the fury of a river having burst through its channel. A swirling, curling deluge of black water and mud, dragging torn and splintered branches, reeds and sedge burst into the meadow. Eadred let out a scream and stared. The monster came on towards him. There was only one way to safety. Eadred fled, struggling along the path, knee-deep in water.

A few moments later, the torrent broke over the rise where the cattle shelter had stood. What was left of the structure bent, broke and was swept away. Eadred feared turning to look, for the river, freed from the confines of its banks, sped on, unchained, smashing across the path along which he had just fled.

The hope of the previous day was gone. Eadred continued wading along the path Brother Anselm had sung to him, tiring against the current. The tree cover began to thin and gave way to vast meadows of sedge—a sea of grass to the horizon. In places, it reached up to his waist, swaying with the currents flooding through it. Eadred stood silently, overwhelmed. The path would resume in the far trees, but he had no idea where.

In his mind's eye, he had once seen the gentle rise that Brother Anselm had described, with fleecy clouds reflected in the cauldron-shaped mere, hemmed by sedge grass, stands of reeds and osiers and with the call of ducks, teal and snipes echoing to the heavens. It was there ahead somewhere, no more than half a day's walk in fine conditions, but not as in Eadred's earlier musings. The mere would have swollen, broken through any impediment and flooded in all directions.

He was soaked and frozen to the bone, grey-faced, shivering, more dead than alive. Eadred began to sing—or perhaps, more accurately, moan—a psalm, and he set off through the featureless mats of grass.

EIGHT

The Cauldron Folk

The cry was repeated several times. Eadred imagined it was a fen bird, distraught for some reason, squawking over and over. "He wakes!" It was from a child. The door opened and banged closed. The smells were different, the bed he lay upon, the cloak covering him, and the breeches and tunic he wore! None were familiar. The hissing of the rain brought a memory, but this was not the church at Deerstow. Eadred tensed his muscles.

"Holy Father, come on. Open your eyes. Speak to us. You are safe here." Eadred's eyes flickered. "That is better." The heavily bearded man smiled and turned to others in the room. There was a murmur of joy. All Eadred could see was the man's smile returning to face him.

"I am Alfred, headman of our village."

Eadred's mind still struggled, and his eyes betrayed his fear.

"I found you propped against a tree trunk when we were bringing our sheep to safer ground. You must have come from Holm or Deerstow or one of the other vills from that direction?"

"I came from Deerstow. It must have been yesterday."

"Not yesterday, Father. This is the third day you have lain here. We were fearful you would not survive. You were as cold and still as the grave, and we have no more dry wood for a fire. So we dressed you in fresh clothes and have watched over you. Praise God, you are alive."

It was only then that Eadred realised how close he had come to death, and he gave a heartfelt thanks to Alfred. "I am Father Eadred from Snailwell Minster. Do I give thanks for my survival to the Cauldron Folk?"

"Welcome, Father Eadred. You are indeed with the Cauldron Folk. It is the name we call ourselves, and we are pleased to hear others call us this. It rings better in our ears than being named 'Webbed-Feet People'." Eadred heard more chuckling. "The great mere around which we live, and over which we have rights, has sustained us for many generations, though it threatens us now. It is getting ever larger from this onslaught. Some families have already left their homes to find drier land, though nowhere is safe now.

"You are from Snailwell, where our bishop lives?" Eadred nodded. "Then you have been sent to replace Father Ingeld?"

Eadred lay silently for a few seconds. "When did you last see the father?"

It was Alfred's turn to look bewildered. "We have not seen Father Ingeld for close to a year. He left us to return to Snailwell as last winter was passing, as was his way. We

71

expected his return a few weeks following that, but he never came. I thought the bishop must have decided against his return. Most here miss him deeply, for he was always a good friend to us and brought us God's blessing. Some were fearful for his safety, though he has made the same journey many times. He always carried what was left of our tithes with him, and there are many thieves these days waiting to take what is not theirs, but he said the Lord God is greater than all of the thieves in the kingdom, and he never showed any concern. I pray to God that he is safe."

"He never came to Snailwell, then or since," Eadred replied. "The bishop believed he was too ill to come and still rested here and sent me to see after his welfare. I have since discovered that he did arrive at Deerstow last spring, but then no one knows what happened when he left. It is a terrible thought that he might have been attacked by thieves on the journey, and neither the bishop nor you knew of it."

It was when Eadred was speaking these words that he recalled what the bishop had said. Eadred continued. "That is indeed strange and vexing. Bishop Aethelbert told me that a farmer from these parts, who described himself as one of the Cauldron Folk, had visited him at that time on his way to collect his cattle, with a message from Father Ingeld that he was ill from ague and too weak to leave here!"

"I can make no sense of that, Father," Alfred replied. "His health seemed strong as far as I can remember, although I cannot be certain. He could have been harbouring an illness that worsened at Deerstow, but as far as I know, no one from here was sent to the bishop with such a message." Alfred turned to the faces behind him, which were similarly confused. "You have been ill for a while. Perhaps your memory needs time to recover?"

Eadred was reliving his talk with the bishop as Alfred spoke. "You are probably right. In a few days, I will be able to remember what the bishop said. I find that my mind is as weak as my body, but both will recover, God willing."

"Rest now. You are in Father Ingeld's house. We have kept it repaired and ready for his return. It has fought well against this rain thus far. We have missed Father Ingeld and are grateful the bishop has sent you. Tomorrow, if you are ready, I will talk to you about our needs here. Without the Shepherd's hand to guide and protect our souls, some of the flock have wandered, and some have been taken by the wolves. Now, we will leave you to your recovery. Have some food, you look as if you need it."

Eadred's body ached, and he sensed the weakness in his limbs. The rain was a constant whisper. On a stool next to his bed, he found some thick slices of smoked meat, a jug of ale and a cup. It was good to eat and drink. There was nothing in him to encourage his rising, and he closed his eyes. Later, he heard the door creak open and then close a few seconds following.

It was sometime in the night when Eadred woke again. Blackness and silence surrounded him. The rain must have eased or stopped. It was time for prayer and to be grateful, for he was alive. After a few attempts, Eadred realised that he could not free his mind to give thanks. There was a voice that had grown stronger within him over the past year or so, and it was intruding on him now. One that was no friend on the path to quiet contemplation of his Maker. It asked questions and engaged the priest in speculation—not of the divine, but of the crimes of men and how they might be understood and the perpetrators brought to justice. It spoke to him now about the disappearance of Father Ingeld.

Bishop Aethelbert was weak in his body, and his memory suffered, but he had not lost his wits. He may not have remembered much of the detail, but he would not have mistaken the message from the visiting farmer that Father Ingeld had wanted the bishop to know of his illness and that it prevented his return to Snailwell early that year. Then Eadred remembered that Brother Anselm and other cloistered men at Snailwell had also told him of the farmer's message of Ingeld's illness and how it prevented him from leaving the Cauldron.

As Eadred lay still, pondering what may have happened to Ingeld, a faint and brief smile broke across his face. He recalled the way his mind had moved away from its well-worn paths of thought and behaviour when he had tracked the dark intentions of the murderers at Elmstow Minster a year before. He sensed the strength of that gift rise within him once more. He imagined that he was seated beside a warming fire and his dear friend Tatwine, the hermit monk, was facing him. A jug of wine rested beside them, and they were both enjoying a cup. The one-eyed monk was listening attentively as Eadred explained his thoughts.

Alfred of the Cauldron Folk says that Father Ingeld left for his usual journey to Snailwell when winter was passing almost a year back and seemed in good health, but he did not arrive, although he was seen at Deerstow, which is on the road to Snailwell. The unknown farmer who gave the message of Ingeld's illness said he was from the Cauldron Folk, but how are we to explain his visit and message to the bishop? Either the message was true, and Alfred and his countrymen are lying, or it was false. If it were true, then how are we to explain Ingeld's arrival at Deerstow? And if it is false, who wished to tell the lie and for what purpose? Then, with self-recrimination, Eadred continued, *When in Deerstow, I should have asked if men remembered whether there was anything strange about Father Ingeld or his visit!*

As his mind pondered the possibility that Alfred might be lying, Eadred's heart began to race. The stories he had been told about the Cauldron Folk spoke of a people who lived in the treacherous swampland not only at the edge of the mere, and not only between the lawful and the criminal, but also between the true Christian faith and the worship of demons and dark forces. Eadred groaned that his weakened body was now in their hands. The food he had eaten and the ale he had drunk could be poisoned.

*

His eyes opened to beams of pale light piercing the gaps around the door, and his ears awoke to the sounds of voices— adults and children. The rain had stopped. Eadred listened for a while to the frenzied sounds of activity, the chirping cries of the young, the occasional bleat of an animal and, in the background, the rampant rush of water. He was, to his surprise, alive, and it was time to venture beyond his walls.

Eadred's home for the past few days was one of around a dozen houses spread along what was now a low-lying ridge—narrow, but with a length that disappeared amongst the trees ahead and behind him. Two other dwellings lay in ruins further down the slope with the torrent gushing through them. Eadred managed to smile at the man coming towards him.

"Father Eadred, it is good to see you out of bed, and the rain has stopped! You have brought God's blessing to us. Have you eaten what we left for you?"

"Good morning, Alfred. Yes, all of it."

Alfred's thick, greying beard accentuated his smile. He seemed to Eadred to be approaching his middle years, slightly stooped but otherwise agile and energetic. The priest had seen enough savage, unforgiving faces over the past week or so, and Alfred's appearance seemed very different to these; it seemed familiar. He could easily be at home in a cloister, but Eadred had been wrong before. It was prudent to remain cautious, he thought, but the dark fears of the night before seemed to have ebbed.

"That is a good sign. You will recover quickly. The Lord God brought you to us, and we must care for you properly," Alfred continued. "The wrecked building you see over there was our church. It had stood safely since it was built by Bishop Aethelbert and Father Ingeld but fell to the flood a few days back. We will build another when the water melts away, this time on higher land. As you came from Deerstow, I think that you may have been there at the marriage of the daughter of our Lord Cerdic to Lord Forthred's son?"

"Indeed, I was, Alfred. I conducted the ceremony myself. It was a day that I shall never forget."

Alfred smiled. "There has been much enmity between their families, but we here all pray that the marriage will bring peace. Lord Cerdic is a good man, and his wife is a blessing to us. Ah, here comes my own wife.

"Elfwyn, look here, Father Eadred is out of bed. He has eaten everything you gave him and is restored!"

Eadred flushed with embarrassment, looking left and right, but finally his eyes were forced to confront the overjoyed face of Alfred's wife, who was rushing towards him with arms outstretched, despite the risk of slipping in the mud. Elfwyn could have been Eadred's sister, Gertie, in her unbounded happiness and earnest warmth upon seeing him. Elfwyn's appearance also reminded him of Gertie, with Elfwyn probably just a few years older. Blue eyes that seemed to take up half of her face and a slim, almost slight body. Above all, a smile that seemed birthed from years of deep friendship and understanding. She managed to contain her elation at the last instant.

"Father Eadred, your journey has been hard, and you are among strange faces, far from Snailwell, but be assured that you are among friends. My dear husband found you and brought you here, so put from your mind any thoughts that we mean you harm. For if that were the case, it would have been inflicted by now." Elfwyn knelt on one knee and kissed the back of Eadred's hand.

Eadred flinched, as much from the ease with which Elfwyn must have read the disquiet in his expression as from the unexpected honour she bestowed. "I am a simple priest, Elfwyn, unused to such kindness. Please rise. I am indeed grateful for the care you and your husband have shown to me, and I intend to repay it. I will raise the cross here again, and once the waters that threaten your community are dispersed and the path to Snailwell safe, I will ask the bishop to build and consecrate a new church. And I will preach, hear confessions and bestow the holy sacraments while I am with you. I am no farmer or woodworker, but my body feels stronger, and there must be useful tasks for me to repay your kindness?"

Alfred and Elfwyn looked to each other with a smile. "Father, if it is no trouble," Alfred said, "while those who live here clean the muck from the settlement, lay reeds and sedge over this mud and care for our beasts, you could try to find wood for a fire? The ground is soaked, but there are dead trees that might provide a harvest of branch and twig we could dry and, God willing, have our first fire in a while. Be careful, though, for there are many deceitful paths; the torrent has added to their danger, and there are trees ready to fall."

"Husband, the father does not know our land. We will send a young lad with him," Elfwyn scolded Alfred. He looked suitably chastised.

Eadred intervened. "I will be caution itself, I promise. I should enjoy walking and praying alone and giving thanks for my recovery. If you give me some directions, I will get about my work." It took Elfwyn a few seconds to agree, which she did with an unconvincing smile.

Alfred spoke again. "Then that is settled. Take the wide path behind you. It links the five settlements and many isolated homes around the Cauldron. You will find tracks leading from it, but never venture far from the main path. There are any number of other pathways linking our people to the mere edge and off to other parts of the fen. Some are well used, but others fade into thick underwood or disappear into the swirls of mere and river. Do not be tempted to take one of those. And here, take this shepherd's crook and knife. They will help in gathering dry wood from the trees."

Eadred took a hefty wedge of smoked meat that Elfwyn offered him and set off on his mission. He followed Alfred's instructions and walked eastwards along a wide trackway and then took one of the narrow paths to the right, which led away from the mere. Eadred came to an abrupt halt on turning a corner to see the black water from a burst stream surging across his path. He smiled, seeing a small osier on his side of the flowing water that had once been pollarded for use in basket-making but then forgotten. He took the shepherd's crook and the knife, and, pulling the dead stems towards him, he was able to cut away a few lengths of wood.

Eadred continued with this labour for a good while, exploring the paths that led from the main trackway, looking for dead wood of a small enough size that might dry quickly. He gathered his harvest into a pile, then began to search along the paths on the other side of the track. These led to the swollen mere, where Eadred found that the ferocious currents had toppled a few dead trees, and the wood was thus drenched and unusable.

Close to an hour passed, and the pile of wood grew into a substantial treasure. Eadred gazed upon it and sensed that his mood had lightened from the murky fears of the night before. He had taken to Alfred and Elfwyn and had performed a useful service. He had little skill in woodwork, metalwork, healing, husbandry or artistry of any kind, and he was uplifted whenever he could undertake a task with his hands that benefitted others.

With the work now accomplished, apart from the effort of carrying the pile back to the settlement, Eadred mused that he could allow himself a brief time to witness the power of the torrent without the fear of having to negotiate a path through its flow. His fear of the surge had dissipated, now it was no longer being fed from the sky. The black pelt that had hung with menace over the fens for days had given way to the fleece of shaggy white clouds that Eadred had seen in his daydreams.

He decided to explore another pathway towards the mere and a while later found a seat on a fallen tree trunk and soon had become entranced by the rush of black water that surged through the mired osiers and alders a few feet from him. In the distance, outlining the original perimeter of the mere, the water now covered stands of reeds up to half of their height. It was a scene of power and beauty, made doubly imposing by its proximity to Eadred. He had never felt the terrifying grandeur of God's creation as much as he had these last few days. He had heard stories of the glory of the pounding waves at the eastern edge of the kingdom and hoped one day to go to the coast and witness the Northern Sea, but he could not contemplate it being more imposing than the scene upon which his eyes now stared. Islands of fallen trees and reeds, ripped from their moorings, and broken branches sped past his eyes.

Eadred had a vague sense of his duty to return to Alfred with the firewood, but it was failing to surmount his desire to continue his solitary exploration of this strange world. The matted branches and underwood appeared to create an armoured wall either side of where the priest was seated, but Eadred found a low, narrow gap not far behind him on his left, and, with childlike joy, on his hands and knees he shuffled into the space. The thick branch-work continued for further than the priest had imagined, and he began to doubt that it did anything other than end in an impenetrable, knotted barrier. So when it did give way to an open area, Eadred chuckled.

He rose from his knees and stood in a small meadow, and over him spread a gnarled alder tree. Already inspired by the sights, sounds and smells of the Cauldron, Eadred gazed at the confusion of bald branches, imagining them to be a creature that could lower its tentacles and sweep him into the sky.

Early in his time at Snailwell, Eadred had heard a song that spoke of a dream giving voice to the rood upon which Christ was crucified. The precious tree spoke of the brave man who went to his death as a warrior facing his inevitable end. Eadred had only heard the words a single time, for the bishop was uncharacteristically vehement when he spoke of his opposition to it being sung at the minster.

"Holy Church faces a daily battle to turn the minds of so many of our people away from their old religion. Despite this being a Christian kingdom for many generations, many still believe that spirits abide in rivers and meres, on the summits of hills, in the depths of caves and in trees! We must remove this perversity. Though this song tells of the crucifixion of our dear Lord, we cannot allow a tree—a thing without spirit or soul—to have a voice. The song will confuse weak minds and remind people of their former ways, and I will not tolerate it!"

At the time, Eadred had seen the sense in Aethelbert's command. Though it was a man's dream that gave a voice to a tree, Eadred had no doubt that it could inspire men to return to the spirits and gods of their past. For he, like many in the Church, believed that demons would take advantage of the door that might be opened. Yet standing here, beneath the limbs of this noble living wood, he could not help but think of the words of his dear friend Tatwine, who had no spiritual fear of any created thing.

"All creation belongs to God. If a man dreams or believes that there is a spirit in a rock or a river or a tree, tell him it is God's spirit that dwells there, as it dwells everywhere. If you see the markings of a follower of some demonic being carved into a rock or a tree, then destroy them and cleanse the tree with prayers to return it to God."

Eadred knelt at the base of the trunk. His eyes had been drawn to several small wicker figures hanging above him. He searched and saw others on more distant branches. He had seen these idols before. Scores of decaying wickermen had lined the road not far from Elmstow; some the size of a man, others as small as a child's thumb. They had been placed there by generations of men who had helped build or had used the road, to entreat the help of the spirits that lived in the region in keeping travellers safe.

When Elmstow was established as a Christian minster, such reminders of deities that the Church saw as contenders for men's souls were not welcome, and they were replaced by crucifixes. Yet their presence was never completely destroyed, and once the minster's slaves had returned from repairing the road and other concerns consumed the bishop's attention, the wickermen returned. Not in as great a number, but enough to tell the bishop that even at the gates of a minster there were souls who had not abandoned the spirits of old and who were willing to face the king's laws against idolatry should they be caught.

There was a set of marks cut into the bark of the tree. Some formed shapes and others, Eadred supposed, words.

He peered closely, but they formed no words that he knew, and certainly there were no signs with which he was familiar. This was not the work of Christian hands. His eyes scanned the ground around him. He counted the remains of three small hearths. In one, the burnt wood remained intact, thus recently made. He rubbed his hand along one of the charred logs—it was sticky. He put it to his nose—it was vile, of burnt flesh and other unpleasant smells.

Eadred felt his heart pumping hard, and though the air was cold and damp, he sensed sweat trickling down his spine. With his back against the trunk, he breathed deeply and prayed for protection. His eyes darted around the clearing, not knowing what to expect other than it would be evil, whether in physical form or in spirit. What he did know and feel was that something vile and sinful had been undertaken there, and recently.

It came to Eadred that while not walled and roofed by shaped wood, stone or reeds, he was within a temple—a pagan temple. His mind then understood the truth of Tatwine's words. It was not the hidden meadow or the spreading alder tree that unnerved him, but the activity of the pagan priests, their demonic signs and words and their iniquitous offerings to black spirits. He understood what he needed to do.

Eadred, priest of the Lord God, knelt and clasped his hands together. "Father in heaven, maker of all that is seen and unseen, hear these, the words of your servant, Eadred. All of creation is your temple. There is no place forbidden to your spirit. Here, under this spreading tree, wicked men have made a temple to demonic spirits.

"Here, in this place of beauty, these men have called upon the creatures of darkness to cause harm. Lord—"

He stared skywards. A pall of darkness descended, and colour drained to grey. There was a roar, and Eadred was pushed back against the tree by the wind. He cried aloud. Branches twisted and moaned. Dozens of eyes opened and looked to the priest through the weave of twigs and underwood. One pair burned unlike the others, red and piercing. The beast pushed through the wall of wood.

"Lord God, preserve me." Eadred struggled with the fear mounting within him. Shaped as a giant black dog, almost the size of a bull, the beast prowled before him.

It had been at Eadred's wine-soaked evenings with Tatwine where he had sat, open-eyed, and had learned more about the ploys of demons than he ever could within the safe walls of Snailwell. "They will seek to terrify you, my dear Eadred, until your heart bursts with fear, or they will tempt with wanton sights of womanly nakedness or marvellous riches or exalted rank. They will sense your weakness, if it takes them years, and if your faith or resolve fails, they will grasp for your soul. But always remember, though the flesh may be doubted and you see only your certain death, God will repay your faith. So be resolute!"

Eadred closed his eyes and began to pray. The beast's stench of decay and the rancid reek of its greasy pelt filled the air. He could sense it moving closer, the foul stink of its breath drawn from the lost souls in hell.

His voice shook. He paused, then tried once more. "In the name of the Lord God and all of the armies of heaven, I command that you return to the dark and wretched place from whence you came. Demon, you have no power where Christ the King has dominion. I stand on his word that all creation bows before his name, and I say go now!" Eadred heard the howl, and in his mind he heard the whispered taunt. *There will be an hour, my friend, when you are weak, and I will return and take you.*

Eadred dared not open his eyes for a few minutes. The pale blue sky was a thing of joy. The earth issued the scent of life. He wept. No hint of the demon remained, and Eadred mused whether the beast had lived only in his fretful imagination, but he did not intend to remain a second longer. He remembered one final task. Taking his knife, he shaved away the demonic marks from the trunk and threw the slivers to the wind. Then he bolted through the low gap, back onto the pathway, and fled.

It was only after he had been running for a while that Eadred understood his predicament. He had failed to take to mind his route thus far and was lost. The hour had arrived when the day's light in late winter turned melancholy and a timid heart turned anxious. The pathways were indistinguishable, and though he yearned to turn a corner and see his pile of firewood, it did not appear. The path bent around a stand of trees, and Eadred saw the way ahead rise before him, as it did on the way back to the settlement. His mood quickened, and he ran. The wooded ridge was soon achieved. Eadred screamed.

Below a branch to the side of the road, the beak-scavenged body of a man hung by the neck. His arms dangled loosely, both hands cut away. Eadred possessed no curiosity to look further and turned and ran back down the slope.

He continued without slowing, extending the distance between he and the corpse as quickly as possible.

"Father Eadred, this way!" Alfred stood at the top

of another ridge, carrying the pile of wood. "What has happened?"

Eadred's addled mind exploded with fear. Was he running towards a murderer or to his protector?

NINE

An Intriguing Evening

Alfred blew gently at the twigs and moss in his hands. The wood crackled for a few seconds, then the doubtful flame turned to smoke. A brief, nervous smile at Eadred and he blew again, softly but sustained. A flame, small and sickly, but it carried hope. Alfred's breath nurtured it gently, and it took hold. He nestled it at the centre of the hearth and fed it with a cautious hand, stick by stick, stooping low to continue to breathe life, singeing his beard. A happier smile. "Now, Father, we can welcome you to the Cauldron properly."

An hour later, just over two dozen men and women sat on stools around the hearth in the great hall with almost half as many children seated on the floor. Their contented faces glowed deep with colour; their eyes captured by the pulse of the flames. Stomachs filling with stew and bread and with cups of ale to hand. Piles of drying wood hissed and smouldered. It was a scene of happiness, but Eadred needed to know more about a subject that unsettled him. "It is a sad sight to see a boy's body hanging not far from where we feast."

Alfred shook his head. "His name was Coenwulf, executed on the ealdorman's order," he replied. "He was one of our younger folk from further east around the Cauldron, never contented with his life. He had taken small belongings from other people when younger—cups, a knife, a coin or two. His parents were dead. He had an uncle, but the man never cared much for him or put himself out to correct his ways. The uncle was not much of a man, and his own son, Boisil, even less. Poor Coenwulf was readily swayed by dreams of easy wealth, and most here think that Boisil led him into even darker places. Boisil was a vicious and unpleasant creature, and wily. He was a thief—we all knew it—but never caught. Anyway, the uncle refused to pay any compensation for Coenwulf's thefts. The boy had been warned at our assembly. I think all that did was to make him more secretive; it certainly did not change his ways. He was troublesome, but there was never any violence back then.

"When the days were warm, after Father Ingeld had left, Coenwulf was seen untethering another's man's ewe in the early light. Foolish boy, he drew his knife and slashed at the owner, drawing blood from his arm. Then he ran. The hue and cry went after him, but it is easy to hide in the lonely places hereabouts, and he would never have been caught. After that, two ewes and two cows were killed, some by arrow fire, some by blade, and just left where they fell. We had never feared for our animals before then, but we became ready to protect our beasts and kept a watch at night. Even then, we lost some horses and cows, again left to the wolves. What madness is that? We thought Coenwulf was involved, that he had fallen in with other criminals.

"One morning, not long back, when the days had drawn in and the bitterness of winter gnawed at us, the boy took his knife to another man's sheep but was caught. In the struggle, he wounded the man in the thigh. It was deep and will weaken his strength for the rest of his days.

"It happened that no less a man than the ealdorman was in these parts a week or so later with a troop of warriors. We had sent a plea to him, for the losses had been hard to bear, and it was causing harm to our peace as well as to our living. We heard from one of the warriors that lawlessness had arisen over many areas of the kingdom, and the king was seized with the need to restore God's peace to the land.

"A few men had been caught, we were told, and had been executed. That was the fate of Coenwulf. Elfwyn and I were saddened by his end. He was not a bad lad when he was a young boy, but he never had a father or other kin willing to straighten him out. I suppose I should have done more, but my dear wife and I have had our share of troubles." Alfred paused and stared at the flames.

Elfwyn rested a gentle hand on her husband's forearm and spoke. "My first husband died from wounds suffered in the Mercian wars. He survived for a few months but never looked as if he would recover. Life became very hard. Trouble has also visited Alfred." She looked lovingly at her husband and waited for him to speak.

"My wife also died, taken by a sickness. We had a son, who was born weak, and he became dearer to me than my own life. One day, he started coughing, and it only ended three days later when the Lord took him. The air here in winter can kill worse than a blade."

"What losses for both of you to bear. I can see the love in your hearts for each other, and I pray that might heal your wounds." Eadred looked at the youngsters playing and laughing. "Are any—"

"None. God has not blessed us in that way. And when I saw Coenwulf, who was younger than you, bellowing with pain and fear before they took the stool away, I was beyond sadness. Still, Elf and I have found happiness with each other, and we are blessed more than most. When you have rested well, I will take you to visit the rest of our people. I have prayed every day that a devout man of faith would return. There is much need for you."

It was clear to Eadred, unfortunately, that Alfred hoped he was to be the replacement for Father Ingeld. Worse, if that were possible to think upon, the bishop might indeed decide to install Eadred as the local priest for the Cauldron Folk! Aethelbert had, of late, expressed his opinion that Eadred's growth as a priest required that he move outside of the minster's walls and take on pastoral duties amongst the community.

There was within Eadred a desperate desire to return to Snailwell before his fear was fulfilled. But he could not bring himself to explain to the eager soul sitting next to him that the mission Bishop Aethelbert had initiated was already accomplished. There was no Father Ingeld to care for, and Eadred could rightly consider his task as completed, and his duty was to return to Snailwell with the unfortunate news. Eadred would try to persuade Alfred and the bishop that there was a better choice for pastoral care than this young and callow priest.

"Alfred, is there not a monastery close to here from where a priest might travel to visit your folk and bestow the sacraments?"

"The closest is almost a day's ride, at Wexning, to the east and north of the Cauldron. It is a small house, and, if things have not changed since I was last there a few years back, there is but one priest.

"Father Ingeld was a wonder. In the years he was with us, he grew to become one of us. I can say with my hand on my heart that of the hundred or so grown men and women around the mere, we all near enough came to love him.

"Many who had been baptised by the bishop had no idea what glory had been bestowed upon them. But the father patiently taught them, so they knew what the life and execution of Jesus meant for their souls and how they had been freed from sin and could be restored to the Lord God. He heard our confessions so we could partake of the body and blood of our Lord. He taught us the stories from the Holy Book and baptised, married and buried those who had need.

"And even more. He stayed and prayed with the sick. He never moved from the side of the dying until their soul had been safely released from its house of bone. He even cooked and brought them food." Then Alfred's smile at the memory of a thousand good deeds by the priest left him.

"He did what he could for poor Coenwulf when he came to see that the boy could not see good from evil. He became like a blood father. I believe if Father Ingeld had not left us, he would have changed him. At his trial, Coenwulf swore to the ealdorman that he had slaughtered no animals. No one believed him. The boy had harmed too many people, but I do not think anyone wanted him dead. That was not how the ealdorman thought. A warrior told me that he had heard the king had chastened Ealdorman Aelfric for failing to uphold peace in the kingdom and ordered him not to rest until he had scoured the land for criminals and brought them to justice.

"Poor Coenwulf, there was no priest to pray for his soul. Lord Aelfric demanded to know the names of his fellow thieves and he would get a quick death and his body interred, but he said he knew nothing of the stolen animals. There was a vicious sort of man who was the ealdorman's chief warrior. He gave the order, and they cut off one of the boy's hands. Coenwulf still said nothing other than his screaming. So he lost the other and died with his secrets.

"Just before Father Ingeld left here the last time to return to Snailwell, he drew me aside. He asked that I keep a weather eye on Coenwulf. He knew the boy was troubled, but there was something else that worried the father. He thought the boy may have fallen into bad company. Father Ingeld had a look about him that he was harbouring some distressing knowledge that Coenwulf had told him, but he said nothing of it to me. Father Ingeld said that when he met the bishop, he would see if Coenwulf might be accepted into Snailwell Minster as a postulant. He knew of no other way of repairing his behaviour. It was never to be."

"That is beyond sadness, Alfred," Eadred replied. "It is hard to see someone so young executed. To see a boy turn bad would have weighed on Father Ingeld and all of you. But why have you left his body to rot and to be ravaged in plain sight? At least let us bury what is left."

Alfred groaned, and his eyes moistened. "Coenwulf's body had not stopped twitching when the ealdorman's chief warrior commanded me to leave the body on the tree for all to witness, saying that it was the king's wish to show all who passed by what would happen to criminals. I will not defy our blessed King Athelstan."

The gloom was slowly pushed aside as the fire grew and more jugs of ale were found. Eadred had not drunk this much since his return to Snailwell from Elmstow close to a year earlier, and the impact was pleasant. The contrast between his happy companions here, around a welcoming hearth, and the discord and animosity he experienced at Deerstow could not have been more compelling. He sat back and listened to the conversations and stories swirling around him. His mind was becoming quite addled and sanguine, something he could not have imagined or risked earlier in his mission.

And it seemed that the Cauldron Folk, thus far, were taking to him, as he was to them. They seemed to delight in having a priest amongst them, and Eadred, despite his misgivings when sober, was feeling that this was not a bad place to be. Not permanently, but for a few months, when he could really live out his calling as a priest and serve his God. And he had a mission that he had to take upon himself, and the thought of it was giving Eadred that same feeling of exhilaration as he had felt when he had to piece together the secret steps of evil at Elmstow.

His mind returned to the disappearance of Father Ingeld. Sadly, it was most likely that the priest had been murdered. Eadred had dismissed his earlier concern that Alfred had lied about Ingeld's departure. Although Alfred talked of the people's love of Ingeld, it was possible that one of them had borne a secret grievance and set upon the priest after he had left Deerstow, but why not sooner, once the priest had left the Cauldron? In the days to come, Eadred would talk more to the Cauldron folk and see if he could unearth whether Ingeld had enemies here, but his mind was turning more to the notion that Ingeld's disappearance had more to do with Deerstow. He was certain that the farmer who had visited Snailwell had lied. Who was he, and why had he spun this deception? Surely, it was not simply theft, for most of the tithes Ingeld collected would have been consumed by him at the Cauldron, and he took little with him to Snailwell on his visits. Coenwulf's behaviour also troubled Eadred. It seemed that the boy had been wayward but no great trouble until after Ingeld had left, then his thieving had become far more grievous and violent.

Ingeld had been told something by Coenwulf, or he had otherwise discovered it, which bore some connection to the boy's growing lawlessness. Could it be about the boy's accomplices? Whatever Ingeld had unearthed could well have led to his death. Eadred surfaced from his musing when Elfwyn offered him another platter of stew and bread and refilled his cup. Her smile and attentiveness seemed to out-glow the fiery hearth.

"The flames take us to other places and times, do they not, Father?"

"They do, Elfwyn."

"Where do they take you?" she asked with a disarming intimacy.

"I was imagining myself to be Father Ingeld, then the poor soul Coenwulf, to see if my mind could understand what they were doing and thinking that led to their deaths. They were not joyful thoughts, but they have their use. It is right that I try to discover what happened to my brother priest, that whoever cut his life short is brought to earthly justice. No man should feel that he can take another's life or possessions without just consequences, or our kingdom will suffer great harm. A priest is covered by the king's protection. It must be upheld."

"We all feel the same, Father. Coenwulf's execution has unsettled our community, and now we know that Father Ingeld, whom we loved dearly, has probably been killed. What has happened here? We have never known such trouble."

"Elfwyn, I know the ealdorman myself and did him a service once. I must try to talk to Lord Aelfric about Father Ingeld's disappearance and the slaughter of your beasts. You said that he only left here not many days past. Did he say where he was to ride next?"

"No, Father. They were closed-mouthed about such things."

Eadred sighed and would have happily continued to speak to Elfwyn, but Alfred had returned after taking a piss, and Eadred needed to unburden himself of his thoughts. He spoke to husband and wife.

"When I was collecting wood for the fire, I came upon a clearing. It was well hidden, and I had to crawl under the branches to enter. There was a great tree that was like a roof, and I felt joyful at first to be there. But then I noticed strange signs cut in the bark, and there were the remains of fires and burnt sacrifices. I tell you honestly, as I sat there, the pall of evil overcame me. I smelt it. I heard it. I saw it. The devil's brood has been conjured there, and only my earnest prayers saw the return of light. I cannot believe there are men here who would call on demons!"

Alfred groaned. "Since Father Ingeld left, problems have come our way. There are places around the mere edge where evil has come to live. These are not the spirits of our folk and our land, but are demons."

"All spirits are evil, Alfred. Call on the Holy Trinity, the angels and saints, but not on the false gods and spirits you believed in before your people knew of Christ."

Alfred looked perplexed. "That is not what Father Ingeld taught us."

"Where are these so-called spirits?"

"They are everywhere. In the great mere, in special trees, in our rivers, in the graves of our ancestors. These are not bad spirits, Father."

Eadred had returned his platter and cup to the ground. He rubbed his face with his hands. "I cannot believe that a priest of God would say other than these spirits of your past, which you should have denounced, are demons. What did Ingeld say?"

"He told us that most of them had accepted the Lord God as their master."

"Did he not say that it is idolatry to believe that rivers and sticks have spirits within them?"

"No, he told us that all of creation has the spirit of the Lord God within it."

"And what of your ancestors?"

"The father said we should honour our elders, alive or dead. They have great wisdom and can talk to the Lord God on our behalf."

Eadred's instinct was to condemn Ingeld for having confused these minds, and worse, for endangering their souls, but he decided not to give voice to his concerns, at least not now. "In the days to come, Alfred, I will teach you what is written in the Holy Bible. I am sure Father Ingeld had his reasons for saying what he did, for he was a good Christian, but perhaps he had forgotten some of what Christ the King taught us. Tell me, though, you said some men have gone too far with these spirits. How am I to understand this?"

"Bad spirits come from the devil," Alfred replied, "as it is written in the Holy Book. Father Ingeld told us that someone must have called on these black beings. He had sensed the presence of evil, but his prayers kept it leashed. I fear you must have found one of their lairs. We will try to find it and destroy it. But Father Ingeld was certain that it was not Coenwulf who had called forth demons, but someone far more sinful and who was skilled in raising these beings."

"Why would anyone in this land of plenty want to call on evil?"

"I do not know," Alfred lamented. "Someone who wishes to harm others in secret and who drips with sin."

It was not the end of the day that Eadred had wanted. He hurried back to his house in the bitter cold. There was so much that was good in the Cauldron, but he had witnessed the presence of evil. It was gaining strength, and he, more than anyone else there, had to stop it. After his prayers, Eadred drew his cloak closely around him and covered himself with another he had been given. Sleep did not come easily to his troubled mind.

TEN

Return

"Two riders on the road from Deerstow, not far away. One seems a warrior." The villager gasped the message to Alfred, Eadred and the other men, who were sitting around a fire a few hours after first light, nursing their heads. Within a few moments, Alfred and half a dozen villagers stood with weapons at the ready, barring the road to the Cauldron. Eadred stood with them. The riders each raised a hand in a sign of peace and stopped at a safe distance.

"We come with peaceful intentions. I am Offa. I serve Ealdorman Aelfric, and at his bidding we seek the priest Father Eadred. Not for any crime, but because our lord has high regard for him and has need of his skill. Our lord is now in Deerstow. We hear that the father could be here and need him to return with us as quickly as possible."

Eadred stepped forward. "I am Father Eadred. If you are who you say you are, then I would gladly serve your lord, but evil men who pretend good intentions abound these days. How do we know this is not a trap?"

"The headman of this vill should know my face. We were here not long past with Lord Aelfric and hanged a thief," Offa said. "And to you, Father, my lord says you did him a great service at Elmstow, which he will never forget."

Alfred focussed on the man's bearded face. "I do remember you, and you are welcome. Come then, have some food and ale. You have the look of men who have slept under their cloaks on a cold night. And we will see that your horses are cared for."

The offer was gratefully accepted, and soon the two newcomers were seated around the fire with Eadred and Alfred. Eadred anticipated that Offa would explain the reason for the urgent action, but none was forthcoming, so he spoke. "I am happy to return to Deerstow with you but would like to know the purpose."

Offa finished his stew quickly, belched loudly and shook his head. "Father, you must trust me, as you would trust my master. I cannot say more, but you understand that Lord Aelfric would not have us search for you without the cause being great." Eadred tried once more to extract some explanation for his extraordinary summons, but Offa apologised and remained silent.

Not an hour later, Eadred was ready for his journey. Husband and wife raised their arms to bid him farewell. "We barely know you, but we know you are a good man. God and his angels be with you and keep you safe."

"Be diligent in laying waste to the demons' lairs," Eadred replied. "I will pray for your protection and will return."

At midday, they set off. There had been a reluctance to talk in front of the villagers about Eadred's recall to Deerstow, but now, as the prudent hooves tracked through the flowing fen waters, Offa was more forthcoming.

"I fought at Elmstow, so I know of your skill and courage. You had a good teacher." His eyes scanned Eadred's form. "Your muscles have developed well since then; I would scarcely know you by sight. It is good to see a man care for his body."

Eadred smiled, happy that his efforts to build his strength by working in Snailwell's fields had been noticed. It was the first time that anyone outside of his community had remarked on the change. It had been Tatwine who had urged him to guard his life in the flesh, as well as in the spirit, by physical work, after warning that Eadred's skill in uncovering murderers would put him in danger.

Offa continued. "As you have been told, our purpose is to quell the rise in lawlessness in the kingdom. It has been a difficult time. Some days past, we followed a band of thieves and villains, hoping to finish them off, but fate was against us. We found ourselves cut off and confronted by a larger group. We fought our way out, and then the heavens opened, and our progress slowed to a crawl. It took three days to reach Deerstow. Our lord's great concern on the journey, which sapped his spirit, was his desperation to attend the wedding between the children of Lords Forthred and Cerdic to ensure that all went well. So much depends on their union."

"But it has taken place, as you would know if you have come from Deerstow, and I did perform the ceremony myself."

"You did, Father, but there is more to tell. On the day we arrived at Deerstow, we saw the ravages of the torrent. The flood had broken through the earthen wall that protects the communities, especially one called Holm, not far from Deerstow."

"I know of it. I met folk who live there."

"Who *lived* there, Father. The vill is no more, washed away by the flood."

"And the souls who lived there?"

"All but a few are now dead. Drowned and smashed by the water's fury."

Eadred moaned and crossed himself. "I will see to their funerals."

"There is more to tell." Offa's voice was grim. "When the bank broke, the flood surged through the graveyard and even washed some of the dead from their rest. Yet when the bodies had been gathered, they found some who should not have been there!"

"What do you mean by such words?"

Offa appeared to think very carefully upon what he said next. "There were bodies of those who no one thought dead! Some who carried the marks of violence upon them and who had breathed only a few days earlier. Their presence had been overlooked in the disaster of the flood, so no one had missed them, but their bodies had been concealed in the cemetery."

"God forbid!"

"When Lord Aelfric was told that it was you who had performed the marriage of Lord Edmund and Lady Censwith and had only recently left for the Cauldron, he ordered that we fetch you."

Eadred turned to the local man. "Were all the dead from Deerstow and thereabouts?"

"Most were, Father." The man exhibited a great reluctance to talk.

"Lord Aelfric will speak to you further about the bodies, Father," Offa intervened. It was obvious to Eadred that Offa and the guide knew more but had said too much. He continued to throw questions but was met by silence. It galled him that there was some vital and disturbing knowledge that remained just beyond his reach.

The journey proceeded slowly. Black water foamed and raced across every path. Time and again, they stopped to confirm the direction they should take. As light faded, they made camp for the night.

"You will be happy to see the ealdorman again?"

Eadred had not been expecting Offa's question but was certain of his answer. "I will. There is a light deep within him, in his spirit, which is seldom seen by others. He will, I am sure, be a great leader of men. He has suffered much, and his father's shadow veils him. I pray constantly that his torments will fade."

"As do we, his hearth companions. We see touches of what the man can become and will defend him to the grave, but many see him as he is now, and his enemies grow in strength. Be wary, Father."

Eadred saw the disquiet in Offa's face. "You will need all the wits that Lord Aelfric praises in you. Tread carefully in the days ahead."

*

102

They rose early and were close to Deerstow within a few hours. "There is an earthen wall at Holm," the local guide spoke. "When the flood surged through that protection, it destroyed it all, killing those poor souls who were there. The water came through here but was weaker by then, and Deerstow lies on higher ground. Some of the houses were taken, but the others will stand with some repair." The guide pointed ahead to a throng of activity—clearing away the debris and mud and repairing dislodged and broken timbers. "You remember our lord's great hall and the church; they did not fare too badly. They are being repaired. Lynden is another nearby settlement and had hard damage. I am from Lynden, which is also on Lord Forthred's estate. It will be repaired . . . sometime."

The guide looked at Eadred but remained silent. Eadred understood well enough that he was speaking of his lord as he might a rapacious merchant. Eadred was taken to the great hall, where he was told that the ealdorman was to be found.

"Lord Aelfric, it is good to see you again. God's blessings on you."

"Father Eadred, a year has passed since I last saw you. When I was told that you were the closest priest to here, it pleased me." The ealdorman rose and approached Eadred, who bowed. "You look more like a warrior now." Aelfric clasped Eadred's upper arms. The familiarity surprised Eadred, and he saw the same reaction from those in the room.

"This priest did me a great service, and he is in my trust. I wish everyone to know that if he were a warrior, he would be my hearth companion." The impact of Aelfric's words could not be contained, and Eadred uttered a quick cry of joy. A figure moved from the shadows, and Eadred addressed him.

"You have weathered a hard year."

"I have," Hygelac replied. "A few gashes in my thick hide, but nothing worse. Whoever takes me on in battle will leave a woman to mourn him."

Eadred smiled at the warrior as he would at a fierce dog that growled and strained at the leash but was unable to sink its fangs into the passing man. Hygelac's fighting skills were unparalleled, but Eadred had become wary as he had learned more since Elmstow of the man's savagery. He had no doubt that it was Hygelac who had removed Coenwulf's hands before his execution. Eadred rubbed his nervous fingers together in the sure knowledge that if Aelfric needed secret information that Eadred held, Hygelac would, without misgiving, cut it from his hands. And Eadred harboured a doubt whether Hygelac's ferocity was solely for his lord's benefit, for any man who was feared throughout the kingdom must surely have his own ambitions.

"Now, Father, we have need of you to perform the tasks of your calling. Offa has spoken to you?"

"He has, Lord Aelfric, but said that you will tell me more."

"The battered bodies of the dead, killed by the torrent or pulled from their graves, have been gathered and placed under a roof away from the vill, waiting for Christian burial. It will happen tomorrow. Now, come."

Aelfric led Eadred to a storage hut at the edge of the village. It was locked and guarded. When the door was opened, the stench of open, rent bodies, barely disguised by herbs, overwhelmed him. He fell back against the wall and retched.

Offa entered, carrying a lighted candle, Aelfric and Hygelac following. Other candles within the hut were lit. Eadred's body was shaking, but there was no alternative, and he took hold of the door and struggled into the reeking darkness.

"I had forgotten this smell."

"Look upon these two bodies, then we may leave," Aelfric replied.

Offa gave Eadred a candle. The glow fell upon two bodies lying side by side on a table. He moved his quivering hand so the light flickered over the first face. "I know this man," he gasped.

"It is Edmund, son of Lord Forthred. He was killed by knife thrusts to his back," the ealdorman spoke.

Eadred shook his head. Whatever misery he felt at seeing the marble face of the dead man was forgotten when he moved his light to the other body.

"Oh no, how is such misery possible? Tell me I am wrong!"

"No, Father," Offa groaned. "It is Censwith, Edmund's wife, also killed by a blade to her back. When they were not seen, it was thought that they wished to have time to themselves after their wedding, and the flood was consuming everyone's concern, but they were already dead and buried. We would not have known their fate but for the flood that washed their bodies from the earth."

"Can you be certain they were buried in the cemetery and dislodged from it?" Eadred asked.

Offa continued. "They were found with some old bodies

leached from the cemetery and thrust together by the power of the torrent, and with all manner of wreckage from the fen, all matted together in such a confusion that it would be impossible for them to be there by any other means."

"But their bodies do not seem battered or gashed as would be the case if they were dragged through the fen by the power of a flood."

"Here is another mystery," Aelfric said. "Edmund and Censwith had been wrapped from head to toe in shrouds of good linen, as with a proper Christian burial. The winding sheets gave their bodies some protection, and the distance they were borne was not great."

Eadred's voice was heavy. "I married them. What soul could be so black as to inflict such agony?"

"Father, we will bury them tomorrow with the others. Do you need to see any more?"

Eadred raised his hand to Offa and bolted for the door. Once he had spat out the last of the bile, he returned, almost as white as the corpses.

"Were there any other marks upon their bodies other than the blade thrusts?"

Offa spoke. "One of Censwith's kin, an aunt, unwrapped and washed her body and said there were cut marks on her arms and chest. Some were deep. And see the scratches upon her face and hands." Eadred pushed the covering away with a gentle finger and saw the deep furrow of a blade running down from Censwith's throat. It would have travelled onto her breast. "The aunt told me that the shroud was barely flawed, so these injuries were inflicted by the killer, not the torrent.

"Edmund was cleansed by one of his kin, who spoke of

no other marks upon him, just two deep thrusts to his back." Eadred used his finger as before, and, as Offa had said, there appeared to be no signs of damage inflicted by a blade upon Edmund's chest or arms. He nodded and was soon out of the hut, leaning on a tree for support and breathing deeply.

"There is no suspicion on the other deaths?"

"None, the others lying here all died naturally. Some had already received Christian burial in the past, and these were pulled by the torrent from the cemetery. Then there are those who died in the flood. There is no suspicion on any of these."

"Were there signs that husband and wife had been bound?"

"No, not on wrists nor feet," Offa replied. "It seems that death surprised them."

"Is it not strange," Eadred pondered aloud, "that the bodies of the married couple were not crudely disposed of by simple burial in the nearby wood? They were likely taken from the settlement a good distance to the traditional burial ground of these vills to be buried with their kin and, somehow, without anyone noticing?"

"Father, the skill you used at Elmstow to unearth the killers, I need you to employ it once more. I see that you are still eager to search for the truth."

The young priest smiled at the ealdorman. He had slipped, without thought, into that way of thinking that had enlivened him and brought him success in the pit at Elmstow.

"These are not the murders of simple folk, but from great families. There will be retribution, and it may spread far beyond this region. The kingdom has enough problems, and I am needed everywhere," Aelfric sighed. "Your service will not go unrewarded."

It was a beguiling request. Everything in Eadred wished to assent, but it was not within his power to do so. "Lord Aelfric, I am a simple priest and owe obedience to Holy Church. I have no authority to accept, despite my own wishes. I must seek the bishop's agreement."

Aelfric tapped his fingers on his thigh. Hygelac strode forward until he brushed with menace against Eadred.

"Lord Aelfric, you are a Christian man. You understand that a kingdom flourishes if it fears the authority of Almighty God. My own desires are irrelevant. My obedience is to God."

"That I understand. The Lord God is also my protector," Aelfric said. "But tell me this, how is it that I was kept away from here when I had pledged my presence? I missed attending the wedding, but worse, I was not here the days after, when these murders were done. If I were here, would the fiends have dared to take these lives? God have mercy on me." Aelfric looked skyward. He stared at Eadred with anguish in his eyes. "Then I will talk to the bishop." With that, the ealdorman, Hygelac and Offa left.

Eadred walked back to the same house that had sheltered him on his first visit. He was disconsolate. For a few minutes, he had experienced the excitement of his mind that he had first felt at Elmstow, when his thoughts alone had taken to combat against a hidden enemy and sought to outwit murderers and bring them to justice. He wanted to enter that fray once again, for his mind to sift through the myriad details of a crime and to see how they became a pattern that led to the perpetrators.

He had no doubt that if the ealdorman spoke to the bishop, Aethelbert would agree to the request, for when the powerful spoke, the Church listened, and the ealdorman was a strong supporter of Christ's Church. And Eadred had also witnessed the unease that was gripping Aelfric. It was hard to see this budding leader so burdened. Yet what deeply troubled Eadred was something more immediate. It was the inevitable reality that solving murders involved dealing with the motivations and actions of viciously sinful people. If only it could be an act of quiet contemplation, an exercise of thought on his part rather than entering dark places to see decomposing bodies, throttled or killed by cold-blooded knives or burning poison. To look a murderer in the face. One who has sought to hide the filth of his thoughts and behaviour from the world. One who would risk his immortal soul.

Eadred moaned aloud at his confused existence. There were men fortunate and happy enough to live quietly within the cloister and within their own ruminations, and there were those who relished the brutal realities of the world— men such as Hygelac. Eadred knew that, although alluring, a life of seclusion would eventually stifle his mind, but to immerse himself in the worst of the world was sickening.

*

He felt awkward but accepted the ealdorman's offer in the knowledge that a rider had been despatched to obtain the bishop's agreement. By the time of the evening gathering at Forthred's great hall, Eadred's hesitancy had turned to contentment. He ate with relish, and when a few jugs of wine appeared alongside the ever present ale, he drained two cups in quick succession.

Eadred's mood differed from those around him. It was a strange experience to be more buoyant than the men of power and muscle. He looked across to Forthred, who sat alongside the ealdorman. The two men spoke occasionally.

Offa came and sat beside Eadred. "He covets my lord's position."

"Ah, I thought I noticed difficulty between them."

"The lands Forthred has gathered to himself probably make him near as large a landowner as the ealdorman, and he has that skill to turn land into power."

"He may have wealth, but he is not a leader of men. There is a darkness in him," Eadred replied.

"Help my lord where you can. He needs us all at this time, whatever our calling." With his wish made clear, Offa left.

Forthred had lost his only son through murder, and with Edmund dead, the branch that would have continued to build the dynasty had been cut away. Forthred had married twice already, and Eadred imagined a third union might be anticipated. He pitied the woman. Eadred's gaze fell upon Hygelac. He watched him for a while. The brutal warrior's eyes were stalking the limping oaf who had caused the fire to erupt at the wedding. The man stared back. This was another sign of the anxiety of the ealdorman and his companions. Eadred looked closely around the hall, and each of the ealdorman's men looked tense and fearful, for Aelfric was in the lion's den, and Forthred was Darius. Eadred returned his full cup to the bench. He had enjoyed his moment of pleasure, but it was over. He rose and approached Forthred.

"It is a bitter blow for a man to mourn his son and the promise of a new generation. Thank you for the food and wine. I will retire for the night to pray and prepare myself for tomorrow." He bowed to Lord Forthred. The nobleman failed to reply.

"Father Eadred unearthed the murderers at Elmstow Minster. I have asked the bishop that he be given the same task here. He will find the killers."

"He will indeed," Forthred replied to Aelfric. He turned to Eadred. "I have my own eyes and ears, and they tell me what you did. Do the same here, and you will be well rewarded."

Eadred bowed once more and took his departure.

"Priest!" Forthred shouted to Eadred as he opened the door. "Do not fail."

ELEVEN

Burials

Eadred rose early and met Offa, who crouched beside a fire in the centre of the vill, warming his hands. They took the track to the storage hut at the edge of the vill in the company of several other warriors, a handful of Forthred's slaves and two wagons.

"We will take the common bodies to the ancestral graveyard of the community. Those of Edmund and Censwith have already be borne from here and will be buried beside the church. It is the wish of both fathers."

Eadred blanched. "How many?"

"Ten were killed by the torrent, all from Holm. They were found broken and rent by the force. Four others were leeched from the ancestral cemetery."

Eadred was more prepared when the door opened, but he still groaned. Candles were lit, and the sombre interior glowed darkly. Those recently killed by the flood lay together, identified by their names crudely scratched on their winding sheets with charcoal. The putrid remains that had been resurrected prematurely by the torrent that had cut through the cemetery, dragging them without dignity from their graves, lay in a heap. The slaves began their task and loaded the dead upon the wagons for their short journey to the ancestral graveyard. Eadred walked behind with head bowed.

A short while later, the sombre procession arrived at the cemetery. It was the first time Eadred had seen the ground that had been used by the community since before memory to hold their dead. It was closer to Holm than Deerstow, and a good distance from the path between the vills. The wound from the deep channel that had been gouged by the torrent was clearly visible, but already the slaves had exhausted themselves in repairing the damage. They had done the same to the earthen bank.

Eadred looked at the living souls who had gathered there, four men and two children, and he despaired at the sight. These were the only survivors from Holm. The rest had been hurled to their eternal sleep when the earthen bank was ruptured and the torrent swept through the vill. The graves had been dug. Eadred began the service. He looked at the misery, the precious candles of life swept away and those left above ground, more dead than alive in their spirits. It had to be a short service, for he needed to return to the church for the burials of Edmund and Censwith, but he owed these poor souls more than a few passing words.

"This land is full of plenty and feeds its people well. But those souls who made their home in this place also know of its dangers. The gifts and the perils are as either side of the same coin. The Lord God made us. He knew each of us while we were in our mother's womb, and he knows the time of our passing. Today, this community buries many of its loved ones. Each was baptised as a Christian and now rests waiting for judgment, as we all will do."

Then he went to each burial hole, named those who rested in its earth and prayed for each in turn. As he heard the sobbing of those who loved the still and torn bodies lying beneath their feet, Eadred cried inside for God's spirit to help them, and he began to cry outwardly. He had dissolved into misery by the last name.

"I pray for each of those gathered here, mourning their loved ones. Lord God, give them the strength and the grace to continue with their lives, and bless them as they suffer. We are made of flesh and spirit. Our flesh will wither into the earth, but our spirits will soar and live with you forever." He spoke to those around the graves for as long as he could, but knowing that he was now perilously late, he took to a horse and rode to Deerstow.

*

Offa, who had ridden on before, stood with a few folk beside the church. Forthred, Cerdic, Hilda and their kindreds were nowhere to be seen. Neither was the ealdorman. Eadred's heart sank.

"Have they left? And the bodies?" Offa had a dark look. To have left some of the most powerful in the land waiting, and waiting to bury their children, could see Eadred removed from the priesthood—if not worse. He imagined himself being taken to the border with Mercia and pushed from the kingdom into exile without support, to become a slave. "I must beg for their forgiveness!"

"Come here!" Offa beckoned to him. The warrior turned to look with others at one of the burial holes. Eadred dismounted and joined them.

"What is that?"

"A body. The slaves came upon it when digging the graves." The group looked at the upper torso of a blackened winding shroud, three parts submerged in a pool of darkened water in a shallow grave. The head and lower body were still hidden beneath the earth.

"Surely, it is not so surprising to strike an earlier burial in a cemetery around a church? There is enough ground here to dig a fresh hole."

Offa did not share Eadred's indifference. "Do you know nothing? This is Forthred's church. He has just told the ealdorman that he has never sanctioned a burial here. The dead for time beyond memory have always been interred in the ancestral ground from where we have just come. This was to be a place solely for Forthred's family's dead. He is up there in his hall, in fury. We have questioned the community, and no one knows who it might be. Why would they? There should not be a body here! Why is it that this place has bodies where they should not be?"

Two slaves were sent quickly back to the hole to continue the effort of uncovering the corpse.

"Nothing was found while digging the other hole?"

Offa shook his head.

"We must find out if anyone has disappeared in strange circumstances over the past few years," Eadred added.

One of the slaves murmured a small victory. He had

prised the head of the body free of the encasing earth. Together, the two slaves then manoeuvred the corpse from the hole and laid it upon the ground.

"Whoever it was, they were uncommonly tall," Offa said as he took his knife and began to cut away the cloth from the head. "Let us see what remains." He peeled the shroud from the head. Even Offa appeared disturbed. Confronting them was a blackened but largely uncorrupted face, twisted horribly in death.

"Oh, I fear it is poor Father Ingeld." Eadred looked up at Aelfric, Forthred, Cerdic and some of their kinsmen coming towards him.

Absorbed in his task, Offa pulled a ball of cloth from Ingeld's mouth, then exposed more of the tunic and shoulders. "Help me turn him over." The men slipped the body onto its front. "His hands have been roped together, and see, there are marks of violence upon his neck and shoulders, like strong blows."

The young priest's eyes moistened. "Who would do this to a man of God?"

Forthred held his vexed head in his hands. "We can do nothing for him now, but what about the funerals? They must go ahead. It is unseemly that our children decay in sight of everyone. Priest, you are ready to do your duty?"

Unfortunately for Eadred, there was an impediment he was obliged to raise. "It is beyond sadness that Father Ingeld's murdered and defiled body has been secretly buried within the boundaries of this consecrated earth without the proper rites. Whoever committed this atrocity may have done more. Lord Forthred, I seek your permission for your slaves to dig further across this cemetery to ensure there have been no other wrongful burials, and to have any bodies removed and reburied with Christian rites. Once we are assured that this ground has not been polluted, then we can proceed with the burials of your children."

Forthred issued a cry of annoyance. Eadred responded quickly.

"It is to protect the souls of Christian dead. You have rightly had this ground consecrated for your family to rest within when it is their time. If it has been desecrated, then it is no longer a fit place."

Forthred simply stared. Eadred understood that the mysteries of ritual space would probably not be familiar to the landowner's ways of thinking, but this was about protecting eternal souls, and Eadred had to speak the truth.

"I think the priest may be right," Cerdic spoke. "You had this ground consecrated to make it an acceptable place for your family, and now my daughter, to protect their souls. It has clearly been used for unlawful purposes. Who is to tell if there are not other murdered bodies within this ground? Is there not a way we can bury our beloved dead today? I see that there is a small section of the cemetery on the other side of the church. Is it possible if you bring more of your slaves that they can dig there to see if the land is pure, and in the days ahead they can do the same here?" Cerdic looked to Eadred, who hoped that what he would say next would be acceptable to those present.

"Lord, if that small section of the cemetery is shown to be pure, then the burials can be achieved today."

"Very well, so be it. Get more slaves and dig on the other side. Tell me if all is well—and quickly." Forthred then glanced at Cerdic, and the two men wandered back to the hall.

"They have both lost a child, but it may have brought peace between them," the ealdorman said to Eadred and Offa. "It has banded them and given them common purpose."

"And hopefully made your task the easier," Offa replied.

A short while later, with the slaves having completed their work without discovery of further bodies, the families gathered around the graves.

Eadred felt tense. He had not expected such an onerous duty, and the sight of his brother priest bound and murdered frightened him. Words came to him with difficulty. He prayed that his halting, gasping speech would ease and he might proclaim the promise of Christ for the faithful dead, but calmness evaded him.

At the end of the burial rite, with the earth returned to cover the bodies, he wished he had said more, and with conviction rather than in fear of his own incompetence. Eadred's eyes flitted nervously across the faces of the mourners and saw their deep sadness. The enmity and aggression of the wedding seemed to have been buried with the married couple. The group began to disperse and return to the great hall, where they would feast and honour the dead. Eadred stood alone, hoping he could avoid the event and creep back to his shelter. But it was not to be.

"Priest!" Eadred looked up to see Hygelac motioning to him with the slightest move of his hand. What a monster that man was. He was a wild beast. Eadred felt no certainty whether the warrior was loyal to Aelfric or waiting for the moment to pounce upon his master.

What did Eadred have to offer? When he was content with his life, he felt God had blessed him with a special gift, but his mind did often return to his apparent success at Elmstow. In truth, he had blundered in the mud for most of the time, missing obvious lies and failing to see where twigs led to branches and to the core of the truth. If he had found anything useful, it had been because he had looked longer and harder than others. In his mind, there was no gift behind what he had done. He felt the weight of his body and the dullness of his mind as he meandered towards the hall.

Over that short distance, Eadred made up his mind to talk to the ealdorman and to beg to be freed from his task and to return to the Cauldron Folk, where he might do some good and serve God in the way expected of a priest.

TWELVE

A Welcome Change

Sleep was thoughtless with Eadred that night. He had slumped onto his bed, his misery diluted with ale. The ealdorman had not granted him leave to speak, but had spent his time, late into the night, deep in talk with Forthred, Cerdic and Hygelac.

Eadred had sat alone, staring into his cup, apart from a brief time with the gracious Hilda. She had thanked him for his service at the burials of her daughter, her daughter's husband and the drowned villagers and said he would be paid shortly. Eadred felt like forgoing the customary payment but knew it was not his decision—the fee belonged to the minster.

In the dead of night, he awoke, his mind filled with unpleasant thoughts. He recalled the few times he had noticed Father Ingeld at Snailwell. He had been, now Eadred thought more on it, a sincere priest, dedicated to caring for God's people. The poor had been especially in his heart. Eadred managed a brief smile at the memory of Ingeld talking to the slaves and blessing them, which he had often done. There had been no special dispensations for the rich or the Church's patrons. He had on a few occasions given wise advice to the younger priest, most of which had passed Eadred by. Several times when Eadred had been engaged in comforting the recently widowed or those who had lost infants, he would look up to see Ingeld walking past, nodding with a gentle smile to encourage Eadred on his journey.

Yet when Ingeld had taken to his bed ill or collapsed exhausted against the wall after days of serving the poor, Eadred had been so consumed with his own activities and burdens that he had never reached out a helping hand. Now, it was too late. Father Ingeld had lived Christ's message but had been brutally murdered. Eadred sobbed himself to sleep after hours of misery and remorse.

"Father Eadred," the ill-tempered voice boomed yet again. He had imagined that his fraught mind had been dreaming, but the increasingly angry demands proved to be real. He opened his door. Offa glared at him. "Lord Aelfric awaits your presence." Offa led the way with the dishevelled Eadred trotting to catch up. Their destination was the storage hut where the bodies of the dead had lain. Aelfric leaned against a tree away from the door, talking to Hygelac.

"Lord, forgive me. I have kept you waiting."

Hygelac spoke for the ealdorman. "The ealdorman's father would have had you whipped for this, but we remember your past service." Eadred was pleased that he was not meeting Hygelac alone. Aelfric did not reply, but rose and went to the door, which the guard opened. Eadred followed with Hygelac close behind.

The sickly odour of the mixture of death and herbs had not dissipated; indeed, it seemed even stronger. The glow of half a dozen candles fell across the body of Father Ingeld lying on a table. Eadred crossed himself.

"It is God's sign that Father Ingeld was precious to him. His body is miraculously intact."

"Perhaps," Hygelac replied. "I have seen bodies found in the fen waters looking like this. Some years back, when a channel was being dug to bring water to a new mill, two bodies were found, their skin intact and coloured by the peat. They had the tunics and swords of the legions and had lain there for generations."

"I had his body checked," the ealdorman said. "He was bound hand and foot, and there are marks of a struggle on the back of his head and his shoulders, but no sign of a killing thrust. He was likely subdued by a blow from behind, but his end was worse than a blade."

"This look upon his face." Hygelac pointed to Ingeld's twisted expression. "It is not from the stretching of decaying flesh, but from the manner of the man's death. These are the marks of fear and dread. He was buried alive."

"Oh no, no!" Eadred cried out, clasping his head. "He was a gentle, caring man. Surely not. And who would risk their eternal soul by doing this to a man of God?"

Hygelac continued. "See here, how the muscles around the mouth are shaped. His scream was stifled by cloth pressed into his mouth, and by the shroud before the earth was piled upon him. And his eyes strain wide in panic."

"It cannot be. You are mistaken."

Hygelac shook his head. "I have seen it before with men buried alive."

"No man deserves such a fate," Eadred spoke, in tears.

"You are wrong. I have buried enemies alive myself and then dug up their bodies and hung them on a tree so their companions knew what awaited them if they failed to answer my questions."

Eadred stared without words.

"But never to a true man of God," Hygelac added after Aelfric raised his eyebrows.

The ealdorman spoke. "I had you brought here to show you the nature of the men we are dealing with. The son and daughter of great families murdered in the days after their wedding. I had a rider sent to inform King Athelstan of the crime, and he returned saying that the king was shaken to his marrow. An honourable man of the Church not only murdered, but tormented. I will tell you more. There is lawlessness and murder across our kingdom as no one has seen before. Some say it was my father that kept order across the land with his sword arm, and that I must learn to do the same. Evil men waited for my great father to die to unleash their sinful actions. So I bear much responsibility, and it weighs heavily upon me. I do not find excuses for my actions, or lack of them, but I sense there is something more. I have crossed the kingdom several times these past months, and there is a spirit of evil that seems to be at work.

"I have questioned those we caught. Each claimed they stole or murdered alone. But that could not have been. There are those who commit small crimes against their neighbours, and when caught, they pay compensation and come to lead honourable lives. Yet what I have seen often now are crimes even against the greatest in the land, and with much thought to making them happen. I had thought the slaughter of cattle and horses to be senseless, but it is so vast in number that it must have a purpose." Turning to Hygelac, Aelfric continued. "My noble friend here can be very persuasive, but even he has failed to break through the cloak of lies. There is a greater power at work here than we can see, and I confess I am troubled."

Eadred looked at the Ealdorman of the East Angles, the second-most powerful man in the kingdom, and before Aelfric managed to wipe the fear from his face, Eadred saw a man buckling under the weight of the unknown that confronted him.

"My hearth companions and I will hunt as warriors do, and if you use again the vision you shone upon the crimes at Elmstow, together we may discover what is happening and destroy it."

*

Eadred wandered back towards his house. He knew the ealdorman to be a good man, one of the few of rank not to be driven solely by self-interest and the fever of power. Men like Forthred waited for Aelfric to fail so they might advance their claims to replace him. Others, like Hygelac, counselled the ealdorman to become like his father: brutal and merciless. What Eadred had seen in the former ealdorman was a man turned by power and endless struggle into a vindictive monster, capable of anything in protection of his king. There had been nothing in his being that cared for the ordinary man or woman. Eadred wanted so much to support Aelfric with whatever small gifts he had, but he felt undeserving of the faith placed in him. He ached for an earthly kingdom led by God-fearing men, but they were heavily outnumbered, and in the battle in which they were engaged, they were losing ground.

"Eadred!" From the side of the house appeared a figure like a giant and strange beast from some foreign land, a muddied and bedraggled being. "My dear, dear friend." His grey hair was irregularly tonsured, and he was garbed in a great pelt cloak. His single eye burst out from above a thicket of greying facial hair that had not seen a blade or comb for many months. He ran towards Eadred with arms outstretched, laughing without constraint.

The thoughts that had burdened Eadred disappeared in the blink of an eye. His legs, which had left Aelfric's company tired and leaden, could now outrun a hare. "Tatwine," Eadred shouted the name three or four times until the two men collided. They embraced, laughed, shook each other and refused to part in case it were a dream. But it was real.

"I heard that you had recovered well, and look, you thrive," Eadred giggled. "And the pain?"

"It is a miracle. For half a year, my head throbbed, and behind my former eye, a stabbing pain that made me cry out and fall to the ground when it hit. But it slowly calmed, and now the pain seldom visits. I have forgotten what it was like to have two eyes. I do not miss it. And you! I feel muscles on your arms. You could wield an axe all day."

Eadred blushed. "But, my dear friend, why are you here, so far from your cave at Elmstow?"

"Sit, and I will amaze you." Tatwine sat upon a log next

to Eadred with his arm around him and continued. "Several nights ago, perhaps a week, I was fortifying myself in prayer, ready to renew my battle with the demons who still try to remove me from the cavern which I took from them. At the hour when they are accustomed to appear, their stench began to fill my nostrils, and I saw their lumbering movement in the shadows. 'Come, foul spirits,' I shouted, 'let us do battle.' They prodded me with their talons. They stared me in the eye and mocked me for the loss of its brother, saying it would soon happen that I will lose the other. I laughed at them and shouted the names of the angels of heaven and the saints of our people. And then they surprised me.

"I heard the screams of a man, tormented by wounds upon his body and in his mind. Then I saw his figure in the dark air, with his hands bound behind him, and evil men were wrapping linen bands around his body until he was sealed, apart from his head. The monsters turned him to face me, and they taunted me to leave my lair and help him. Then they continued their foul work until his screams were muffled by the encircling cloth. The demons laughed as he groaned in ever greater desperation. There was a pit in the earth, and they threw him into the gaping hole, and I heard the howls and bellowing of hell, and they began to cover him with earth."

"Father Ingeld!" Eadred gasped. "You saw the murder of Father Ingeld of Snailwell Minster, for his body has been found. He was shrouded and buried alive, as in your vision."

"Sadly, I know of it. The ealdorman's warrior, Offa, told me of the murders. I met the father several times. He was a gentle and kind man. What evil heart could have done this to such a man of God?" Then Tatwine spoke in a sombre whisper. "My dear friend, I must tell you the truth, I saw you! It was your face. I saw men and demons conspiring against you."

Eadred stared into the distance and gulped.

"There is more, my friend. Once the demons left, I spent the night in prayer. The following morning, I heard the sound of horses. There are always horses on the Elmstow Road, but I seldom hear them. These were close by. Then men shouted out my name. They were riders from Lord Aelfric, who came to persuade me to journey here to give help, in whatever way I can, in your efforts to unearth the murderers of those poor souls you had just married. I needed no persuasion.

"And, Eadred, be calmed. The vision I had does not mean these things will come to pass. Do not be fearful, but be wary. It is a warning. In my prayers, I discerned that it is likely that some evil man or men are summoning dark forces against you. I will continue to pray, as you must, and never forget the prophecy I had about you at Elmstow: as long as you are engaged in God's work and have faith, the Lord God will send his angels to surround and protect you, as he has already."

The one-eyed monk continued. "I cannot understand how God works, nor should I try, for my small mind makes him smaller. But I feel his hand working, for when my vision told of the danger you will face, was I not then summoned the following day to walk with you? Is that not miraculous? You are here for a great purpose, Eadred, and I am here to help you."

Talk of his great mission and the perils he would face did not inspire Eadred. The expectation raised by Tatwine's words fell heavily upon him, and it showed.

"Come, Eadred, is it not a wondrous thing to know that you go about God's work, and that he is arming you to battle evil and to win? What greater purpose is there for a priest?"

Eadred shook his head. "I am not the man that the ealdorman or you think I am. This responsibility is too great. As for purpose, I have no idea what I am meant to be. All I want in life is to be a simple priest. At Elmstow, the murderers were uncovered, and the ealdorman believes I am capable of such an exploit here. Yet, dear friend, there is nothing in my mind. Nothing!"

Tatwine smiled. "Then let us sit and talk as we used to and see what light can be shed." The two friends entered Eadred's house, and the smells and sights caused him to laugh.

"How did you get these?" He looked upon a giant joint of boiled lamb and two loaves of heavy bread. Beside them were three jugs of wine.

"We are serving the ealdorman, and he was happy enough to help secure these. So come, let us eat, drink, talk as we did at Elmstow. The Lord God will guide us in our thoughts and actions, and this liquid will give us encouragement when we need it."

THIRTEEN

Questions

Eadred watched as the flames took hold of another log and the fire's heart pulsed, and he smiled. "I have a happiness in my heart from seeing you again, good Tatwine, and sharing a cup or two. Although I am bewildered how I seemed to unearth anything at Elmstow, I will tell you what I know of these present killings, and let us see if it leads anywhere.

"There have been years of feuding between the families of Censwith and Edmund, and both were murdered once wed. If one were killed, then the other family might well be suspected. Is there someone else who does not want to see peace between the families?"

"From another kindred?"

"Yes, or from one of the families themselves. Someone who believes there is more to gain from the feud than from peace. Yet, as far as I can determine, the deaths seem to have drawn the two fathers closer. The murders appear to have done more to bring about peace than the marriage."

"I cannot make sense of it."

"Nor I," Eadred responded. Both men stared at the fire in prolonged silence and refilled their cups. The brooding silence continued until Eadred sobbed. "Poor Ingeld! Who would have inflicted such a defilement upon him? He was a dear man, and Christ assuredly dwelt within him. It is the work of demons, surely. They have captured some evil souls and aroused them to the most wretched of crimes. If I fail in everything else, so be it, but I will find his killer and see him hanged slowly."

Tatwine cloaked his arms around his friend and held him tightly as Eadred's body shook with weeping. "We will find the culprit, and he will perish, and his soul will face the endless torments of hell. I swear to you, my dear friend, I will do all in my power to help you."

"I know you will. You are the bravest soul I know, and the closest to God's heart, and I am beyond fortunate to have you with me in this task." Eadred looked at the hermit and saw the passion burning in him. He saw the swirling furrows of flesh where his eye had once lived and remembered how this brave monk had lost it. Alone, he had ventured into enemy land to save a group of nuns from defilement, and in the fight he had lost an eye. Though he struggled back to safety, the fever almost took him. His courage knew no bounds.

"Let us then make a pact, here and now," the hermit spoke, "and promise to the Lord God to work as one to unearth the murderers and bring them to justice. If we do not devote ourselves to this purpose, then the fiends will escape, for they are shrewd, and evil will win."

For Eadred, the task seemed like a mountain stretching up before him, but after a moment or two his faced creased in a boyish smile. He rejoiced in the company and infectious optimism of his friend. He knelt, and the hermit followed. Tatwine was quick to start praying. Eadred would have continued quietly with his passion contained—not so the hermit monk. Very soon, Tatwine's voice was building into a thunderous chant. Eadred felt awkward, but, as if a building storm suddenly unleashed its torrent, the words the hermit sang formed such images in his mind it was as though the murderers stood veiled just beyond sight.

The wicked men mocked him to follow their footprints and the trails of blood if he were capable of so doing. They kicked dust across the paths they had followed and goaded him to challenge them and bring them before the courts. They laughed, drew swords to threaten and threw silver coins to show their capacity to corrupt. But Eadred knelt in resolution. The more they ridiculed his poverty and low rank, the more determined he became. Tatwine ended his adjuration for God's blessing upon their task, but Eadred was not yet ready.

"Listen, whoever you are," Eadred shouted. "There is no evil so great that we, the servants of the Lord God, cannot overpower. We are coming. We will find your steps and see through your false words, and you will face justice in this world and in the heavenly realm. Be assured of this promise. You will not prevail!"

The two friends clasped each other's forearms, their eyes shining. They filled their cups and drank deeply.

"Now come, my friend, use that gift of yours and tell me what it shows you about Father Ingeld."

Eadred closed his eyes and spoke with care. "Ingeld left the Cauldron Folk late last winter to journey to Snailwell to see the bishop. He was murdered in Deerstow or close by, for otherwise why take the risk of torturing and burying him here, where there are many eyes that might see? His body has been in the ground for many months, discoloured, but free from decay. I have spoken to some folk who remember that he arrived here but that his stay was far shorter than usual. The manner of his death was also grim. It was not just to silence the poor man, but to punish him or attempt to discover some knowledge he had, which in the end, he took to his grave. There are those here in Deerstow or in the vills nearby who know more of this."

"You have the authority of the ealdorman, Forthred and Cerdic to question and to search. You must use it while there is still zeal for your task."

"Tomorrow, my friend, I will start the work of questioning everyone who dwells here," Eadred replied. "Forthred had the cemetery surrounding his church consecrated for the burials of his family. If he had been involved in Father Ingeld's murder, surely he would be concerned that the burials of Edmund and his wife might unearth the body? He showed no such fear. From what I hear, Forthred is the most violent and ill-disposed man in this region. I admit to you, I thought he was the most likely to harm other men, although I have no reason why he would wish Father Ingeld dead.

"And there is a darker thought in my head. Poor Ingeld was buried alive in the only consecrated land here, beside the church. The ancestral cemetery, where I buried the dead from the flood, is older than memory. It has not been formally sanctified by Holy Church, and Christian and pagan rest side by side. I have a fear that this could have been a deliberate perversion by some foul hearts to mock him and to desecrate the cemetery."

"By pagans?"

"I fear so, Tatwine. Who else would bury a priest alive in consecrated ground? It is a defilement of the man, his faith and of the purity of the soil. The ealdorman spoke to me of his fears that there was some unseen hand directing a surge of evil in the kingdom. The powers of darkness may be at work. We must pray together daily to protect the kingdom and ourselves. And let us not speak of our fears to anyone."

FOURTEEN

An Unexpected Opportunity

Eadred's plans were changed early the following day. He was summoned by the ealdorman to the great hall. It was well guarded, and he had to wait before the warriors let him pass. As he entered, his heart began to race. The hall was filled with men who had been hurriedly assembled from the nearby communities, and at the furthest end sat Aelfric, Ealdorman of the East Angles. He rose.

"The trial of Cuthbert and Dudda of this vill has been lawfully called. Lord Forthred, thegn and lord of this region, is their accuser." Aelfric nodded to Forthred, who rose. He stood silently for a while, his chest rising and falling. Eadred, and undoubtedly others, could see a man who seemed to have lost his purpose. Eadred heard someone whisper, "Our lord is a crushed soul." Then Forthred spoke.

"At the wedding feast of my son, Edmund, and his wife,

Censwith, an attempt was made to harm the Lady Hilda, mother of Censwith. The feast was in my hall and under my protection. The attack fouled my honour. I wish to proclaim to Lord Cerdic, to whom I am now related through grief, and in front of this assembly, that I have been exacting in seeking out the culprits. I have searched the hearts of my kindred who attended the feast. Each one came before me to swear on their honour.

"This man, Dudda, who is son to my cousin, has admitted that he deliberately created mischief to spoil the wedding feast and to allow this man, his brother, Cuthbert, also to cause harm." Dudda was the weighty, cumbersome man who had thrown the log onto the fire, scattering embers to create disorder. His brother looked underfed and a weakling in comparison. "They have shamed me and deserve their punishment."

Eadred looked at both men: they were bound and had been beaten hard. A dozen thoughts tumbled through his mind. *Lord God in heaven, give me the chance to question them.*

"Dudda of Deerstow, do you accept the accusation?" Aelfric spoke.

"Lord, I do." The man broke into sobbing and fell to his knees. "Lord, I did throw a log because I was addled with ale and had malice in my heart, but upon my honour, though my brother and I had agreed to blight the wedding feast, I did not know that he would seek to harm the Lady Hilda. I am slow-witted, as men will tell you, but—"

"That is a lie," Cuthbert screamed. "We agreed that we would try to ruin the feast, but I never said that I would cause harm to the lady, and I swear I did her no harm. I did not push her!"

Dudda lowered his head from the gaze of his brother and the court and burst into tears. Aelfric turned to Cuthbert. "Do you accept the accusation?"

"Lord, it is true that my brother and I talked of causing discord at the feast, but upon my honour, I did nothing."

Eadred moved towards the ealdorman. A guard stopped him, but Aelfric motioned for him to come. Eadred whispered in Aelfric's ear. Shortly after, the ealdorman rose.

"There are disagreements between the accused. It is important for the two kindreds before me and to the kingdom that there be lasting peace between these houses. The truth must be found and justice met. I have asked Father Eadred to question both men. He has served the kingdom well in this purpose before and is in my confidence."

Eadred turned towards the sea of faces. It had been around a twelvemonth since he had first questioned accused folk in court. His involvement had not been particularly welcomed then, not only because of his lowly rank, but because this was not the customary practice at trials. However, Eadred had been tolerated.

Communities of free men and women took collective responsibility to maintain peace. In the case of most crimes, the victim had to accuse the likely culprit and bring them to trial. In a society where men valued their honour, and in vills and settlements where most folk were known to each other, crimes were generally admitted and the culprit or his kindred paid customary compensation to the victim. The sin was also confessed to a priest, and the culprit repented and atoned with a prescribed penance. That could well be the end of it, and life continued.

What troubled folk was when a crime was denied, as this

involved the dilemma of gathering proof. Much depended on the character and standing of a person, whether accuser or accused. An accused man or woman would need to provide a certain number of 'oath-helpers', men who would swear that the accused's word—their denial—was true. If those charged were of good character, such oath-helpers were most likely furnished. The accused was then freed, and the accuser risked the likelihood of being found guilty of bringing false accusations.

The standard of proof rose if the accused were of poor reputation, having been found guilty of earlier crimes, especially if they had denied their guilt. Higher numbers of oath-helpers were required, or this path was denied altogether, as their word was useless. Then the accused had to undertake a trial by carrying a bar of hot iron or plunging their hand into hot water. God then showed their innocence or guilt through the healing or otherwise of the hand. The difficulty was that Holy Church had to interpret God's message, and this was a fraught task with many shades of grey, as inevitably the hand bore wounds.

The worst type of crime was secretive, where there was no easy way of identifying the culprit. In these cases, the community, not only the victim, was affected, as suspicion then fell upon neighbours. If a thief were caught in the act, they could legally be killed on the spot. Customary law and order struggled with hard-bitten, shadowy criminals—the skulking, shrewd, invisible murderer or thief. It was in this crevice that Eadred had a skill. One that might be called upon, even by those ruled by custom and who disliked his lowly birth, when the consequences of unsolved murder were too grave.

Eadred had been keen to question the two accused, but his zeal had run ahead of his preparedness. He felt his limbs shake, and his first attempt at words was lost in a coughing stutter. His mind blanked, and the questions he had formulated a few minutes earlier disappeared. He had to take his eyes from looking at the faces staring at him, and he tried once more.

"Dudda, why did you create mischief at the wedding?"

The man looked to Aelfric. "I have said why."

"Just answer," came the curt reply.

"Because it is not in my nature to look kindly upon Lord Cerdic's kin. For generations, they have been our enemy. That is the way it is. I looked at faces I have always hated, feasting happily in my lord's hall. Drink had the better of me, and I did what has been natural to me for my whole life."

"Did you decide before the wedding feast to create the disturbance with the fire?"

"We decided to see what chance arose, and that is what I chose," Dudda replied.

"To create problems between families who had just been joined by a holy sacrament?" Dudda lowered his head and remained silent. Eadred repeated his question, and the unfortunate Dudda mumbled his agreement.

"But your lord had agreed to the marriage. It is not for you to question his decisions, is it?"

The accused man looked manifestly uncomfortable. He groaned, then broke into tears. "No, I am not worthy of my lord. I am sorry. I have failed him and all my kin and accept my punishment." Dudda shook his head and burst into intense weeping.

"Are we to believe that you and your brother alone decided to abuse your lord's trust?" Eadred's eyes shifted to Cuthbert, who began to shake. "No one would believe this. Who told you to wreck the alliance between the kindreds?"

The wretched man shook his head.

"You almost succeeded. Blades were drawn, and injury, death and the ruin of the alliance were a heartbeat away if not for the courage of the Lady Hilda. How else could the alliance be torn apart if not at the feast?"

Dudda raised his head. Tears streamed down his cheeks.

Eadred suddenly shouted, "What do you know of the murder of Edmund and Censwith?"

"Oh, God help me." Dudda shook his head, moaned, but said nothing more.

"You tried to destroy the alliance at the feast. It failed, so you were ordered to murder Lord Cerdic's daughter."

Cerdic jumped to his feet, wailing like a wounded dog. Dudda covered his head in his hands.

"But why did your lord's son also have to die?"

"Do not answer!" Cuthbert yelled. A guard punched him in the side of his head.

"Answer me," Eadred bellowed. Dudda whimpered, shaking his head.

The assembly, up until now, had been silently absorbing the unprecedented scene playing out before them, with two of Lord Forthred's kin being questioned by a lowborn cleric while the second-most powerful man in the kingdom governed the proceedings. But that now changed with the accusation of murder of the newlywed couple.

"What have you done? Speak! Animals!" Abuse was hurled at the two men, who cowered and wept.

"Silence!" Aelfric slammed his sword on the bench. His warriors, by instinct, lifted their weapons and stepped forward. Calm was restored. All eyes were on the young priest.

"Did you bind their bodies and bury them, so they would never be found or identified, and you could escape penalty with the silver paid to you?"

"It was not meant to be like this. Forgive me," Dudda wailed.

Eadred continued quickly. "But the Lord God would not let your crime be hidden. His flood has unearthed your murders."

"I swear on the blood of my ancestors, I wanted none of this."

"Be quiet!" Cuthbert yelled. He was punched again, this time in the stomach.

"Who paid you to murder?" Eadred continued to question but with no response.

"Face me," the ealdorman spoke to the accused men. "I give you one last chance to tell me who paid you, or other methods will be used." The brothers could not speak through their blubbering but shook their heads. Aelfric dissolved the proceedings.

Eadred was familiar with Hygelac's violent approach. Unfortunately, if men did the most evil of acts, caring nothing for their honour or their neighbours, and sought to hide their crimes, then brutality was sometimes necessary to free the truth. What disturbed Eadred was the smile he saw in Hygelac's expression when a poor unfortunate man or woman was screaming in pain. It seemed to encourage him the more when the blood spurted from hammered or sliced flesh, when fingers fell to the floor or eyes were torn from their sockets. And certainly, his methods were not always the most effective way of winnowing truth from lies. Eadred had seen tortured men say almost anything to stop the pain.

Eadred approached the truth in a different way. He had been gladdened before, when he found that his questioning of an accused man let clues surprisingly escape from the culprit's mouth. A seemingly innocent comment would yield part of a dark story, and the sudden realisation by the villain that he had exposed his actions would dismay him into further mistakes. Or arrogance or false pride when questioned by a lowly priest, while a community watched on, would lead to the offender disclosing some small part of his offence, which Eadred would store in his mind.

Sometimes, Eadred would leap upon the man's mistake, and, as if it were beyond his control, the wrongdoer would then stumble from one fault to another and condemn himself. But more often Eadred would sit alone, or with Tatwine, and ponder the words he had heard and the things he had seen, and after many mistakes and false paths on his own part, he might glimpse a pattern emerging. The time would come when all he had gathered and sifted would come together to suit his purposes, and Eadred found some part of the truth, great or small, which would lead to trapping the sinner.

Today, Eadred had taken a warrior's risk, and to his delight it had drawn blood. The feeble-minded Dudda was tormented that he had broken the sacred tie between a man and his lord. Forthred was known to instil fear and loyalty, so what would make two of his own kin attempt to destroy an alliance that would have brought their lord greater wealth and the promise of the continuation of his house? Some other malignant and powerful force had to be involved.

Someone did not want the alliance to proceed. This person had somehow persuaded the brothers to attempt to reignite the feud at the wedding feast by an affront to Lord Cerdic's honour. It did not work. So were the murders of the newly married couple another attempt? It was worth a question. With Dudda distraught at what he had done, Eadred had pounced by asking him what he knew of the murders. The man's mind had unravelled, but not to the point of disclosing who had ordered the murders. It was now Hygelac's turn to see if he could extract what they knew.

*

A few hours before sunset, in a hut beyond earshot of the good folk of Deerstow, Hygelac's questioning commenced. Eadred had contemplated for a few seconds whether Forthred himself had kindled the unrest at the feast but dismissed the thought. If Forthred had instigated the mischief, he would have made sure that Cuthbert and Dudda could not have been questioned.

Eadred entered the hut. It was lit by solemn candlelight, and it stank. Sweat was the least of it. Blood, bile, piss and shit. He could never harden himself to the stench from a man enduring the worst pain imaginable, and he spat out the muck that had risen from his throat. Forthred, Hygelac and several warriors rested against the wall. Cuthbert and Dudda were tied by the wrists above their heads to a rafter, and their feet were manacled to the ground. They were naked. Once Eadred's eyes had adjusted to the dim light, he gasped at their battered, bloody faces.

He approached Hygelac and whispered, "Were there any wounds or signs of struggle on them before your men started?" The warrior shrugged his shoulders.

"Priest, one last opportunity for you to question these lordless animals, then my men will continue." Hygelac gestured for the two warriors in front of the prisoners to stand back.

"Cuthbert, Dudda, for the love of God, confess what you know. I beg you to answer, for you know what awaits you if you do not," Eadred wept. "You both have wives, and Cuthbert, you have a son. Please!" Neither answered, just sobbed. The impatient response from Hygelac was brutal.

A warrior punched Dudda in the stomach, then in the face. Teeth flew from his mouth.

"You were my kin, but you murdered my son." Dudda could only groan in reply to Lord Forthred.

"Do what you have to," Forthred said to Hygelac.

The chief of Aelfric's warriors stood so close to Dudda that the prisoner must have felt Hygelac's breath spurting into his face. "Who ordered you to kill them?" Hygelac hurled such abuse that Eadred clasped his hands to his ears. But the unfortunate Dudda was to be treated far worse.

"Cut off his ears!"

Dudda shook his head and cried for mercy. None came. A warrior pulled one ear free of the protection of Dudda's upstretched arm, took his knife and sliced away the ear. The poor wretch wailed. His second ear was treated similarly. Eadred knew there was only one outcome from this manner of questioning.

"Dudda, please. Your wife will be cared for if you tell us who ordered the murders." Though blood poured down his body, Dudda remained silent. Before Eadred sensed what had happened, Cuthbert's deafening scream pierced the gloom of the hut. Hygelac rested the axe on the ground after it had separated half of Cuthbert's left foot. The man continued to scream until a warrior shoved a ball of cloth into his mouth. Cuthbert's head toppled forward; he had fainted.

"How can I question him now?"

Hygelac ignored Eadred and flew in a rage at Cuthbert's accomplice. "Tell us who ordered the deaths?" With no intelligible response, Hygelac kicked the poor unfortunate between the legs.

"Dudda," Eadred spoke as softly as he could to still be heard against the surging waves of misery and pain. "I know the killing of Edmund and his wife was more than could be accomplished by you and your brother alone. Another man was there. Who helped you?" Still, Dudda remained silent, apart from the gasps of pain. "Then tell me this, why did Edmund and Censwith both have to die? It could not be to stop the families from uniting, for their deaths have done more than the marriage to bring the lords together. Come, tell me."

The broken man raised his bloody head. Such a groan of misery came from his torn mouth. "Tell my lord that we never intended harm upon his son. Edmund died fighting to defend his wife."

"Who ordered her death?"

Dudda groaned. "My brother."

Eadred looked across to Cuthbert's ashen face, misshapen by blows, and the blood pumping from his wound. Eadred did not expect Cuthbert to speak again.

"I will pray for you both."

"No! No prayers. We do not need them."

*

They were murderers, but surely a Christian man should show some mercy. Eadred and any villager who passed through Deerstow on his way to the great hall or church from that night on would see them and know the cost of crossing their lords.

Cuthbert and Dudda, or what remained of them, hung by their necks on a tree at the edge of the village clearing. Eadred shuddered. After he had left the hut, Hygelac had ordered further, and the most despicable, mutilations. Their hands and manhoods had been cut away.

Eadred sat close to his small fire on a bitter evening. Tatwine had offered him companionship, but Eadred asked for his friend's forgiveness, for he had no spirit to be with anyone. He had hurt his friend with that response but knew he would be poor company. There was only one thing that might dull what he had seen, heard and smelt that day. He filled his cup again with ale.

Had the miseries of hell that he had witnessed added to his understanding of the murders? Over and over, he tried to work through what scraps of knowledge he had gathered at such a cost in blood and horror, but each attempt was torn apart by the brutality of the day. He drank more, and finally sleep released him, but not for long.

In the small hours, violent images woke him in sweat and gasps. "Oh, Lord God, help me see some shred of the truth," he prayed. Again, he tried to understand what he had heard. He repeated the Lord's Prayer over and over, and finally he managed to settle his mind and gather his thoughts.

It is beyond doubt that Cuthbert and Dudda did try to ruin the union of the two warring families at the feast. It was poorly conceived and failed. A day or two after the wedding, they did murder Censwith for the same purpose, but Edmund also died in the struggle. Someone else ordered so great a crime, and he may have been the third murderer. Surely, it would have been too great a risk for the two physically deficient brothers, with one of them weak in the head, to overpower the greatest warrior in the region and his wife silently. And why risk taking the bodies the distance to the ancestral burial ground and not simply bury them in the wood? The deaths achieved the opposite of the murderers' intentions, although they left Forthred with no heir. Dudda named his brother as the instigator of the murders, but by that point Cuthbert was beyond hearing and speaking.

Eadred was exhausted and prayed that some tranquillity of mind would come his way. He resolved to question Forthred and Cerdic as soon as possible when day came. His head pounded, and his guts ached. Eadred fell back upon his bed. If Dudda spoke the truth, then they never intended to kill Edmund. There was a dark mind behind these murders that even souls under extreme torture would not name. This attempt to ruin the alliance had failed, but whoever it was would act again, and more blood would be spilt.

FIFTEEN

Troubling Thoughts

"You do not look well, my friend." Tatwine rested his hand on Eadred's sunken shoulder. Eadred breathed deeply and slowly, eyes closed. The hermit gave him time to consider the words he would use. They eventually came.

"I know that some men deserve to be maimed and to forfeit their lives for their crimes and to be tortured if they deny knowledge that will help in tracking down their fellows. That is justice. But it is still hard to witness, and the more so if the act of retribution exalts violence and denies the uncloaking of some key part of the crime.

"Yesterday, at the torture of Cuthbert and Dudda, I felt that some details of the truth were being forced from their mouths, but I could not make sense of what they meant. My mind needed to think upon them awhile and then to try again to prise more information from them, but from a different path. But I could not stand against Hygelac, and before I had opportunity to question Cuthbert on some matter that his brother had said, the warrior had all but killed Cuthbert, and the chance was lost."

Eadred continued with his wretched self-reproach. "My dear friend, I do in faith have to believe that the Lord God has given me a gift to bring evil men to face justice, but so often my courage fails. It is not God who falters, but I. If a warrior has muscled arms and skill with sword and axe but runs from a man coming to attack him, he is nothing and may as well be a weakling. That is how I see myself."

"Come, I do not doubt your courage for an instant, brave priest," Tatwine replied. "Most warriors live by instinct, or they die. There is seldom time for them to think through their actions. They are creatures who take great risks and whose ferocity erupts in an instant. As they are unpredictable, so they create disquiet in an enemy. It is a necessary part of a warrior's nature on the battlefield, but it has its weaknesses elsewhere.

"You are a warrior who uses a different weapon, and it needs time to defeat an enemy. You are a contemplative man by nature, and I have seen you brood over a problem until it becomes clear to you. That is your strength. Do not imagine that other men think like you, that they have the will or the mind to delve into the unknown day after day until what was shadowed becomes clear. Yet you also have the capacity to strike suddenly and with a clear eye, so that what is just a possibility becomes certain. I saw it when you struck a blow against Dudda.

"I have watched Hygelac and seen a brave man, but he is one who is ruled by instinct. He does not value your gift but knows that Lord Aelfric does. I think Hygelac sees you as his rival. Do not rue the opportunity that was lost yesterday, but let us see together how we may find another way to the truth. Now, tell me what you are thinking about the murders."

The two men walked to the great hall, where Eadred had been granted an audience with Lord Forthred. Tatwine was allowed to join him, which greatly pleased Eadred. Unfortunately, Cerdic and Hilda were already on the way back to their vill, in the direction of the Cauldron, so there would be no audience with them yet. Forthred sat beside the fire sharpening his sword. He spoke without enthusiasm. "Well, they are dead and received the treatment they deserved."

Eadred looked at a man whose best years were over. He had spent his life amassing wealth by any means to give himself the excesses of luxury and to nurture his dynasty. But with the shoot of his tree dead and buried, he was only a flabby body, devoid of spirit.

Forthred sighed and addressed Eadred. "Did their final words tell you anything?"

"I will continue to pray for the souls of Edmund and Censwith and that our Lord will give you peace as the days pass. Dudda did say that his brother ordered Censwith's murder and that your son died defending her. It was a courageous and honourable death.

"Yet I cannot believe that Cuthbert devised the plot, and Dudda certainly did not. Lord, was there anything about the two men that could have led them to this? And while I am no fighting man, I cannot believe that Dudda and Cuthbert alone could have overcome Edmund and his wife. I would value your thoughts. Is there someone else, a great enemy, who could have turned to murder to stop the union of your families?"

The thegn aimlessly prodded the embers with his sword point. "Could they have killed Edmund and his bride without the aid of another man?" Forthred shook his head. "My son was the greatest warrior in this region, strong, nimble, always alert. He had eyes in the back of his head. You saw those oafs. Dudda was a slow-moving, slow-witted pig, and Cuthbert weak of muscle. Neither were warriors. They would not dare risk a confrontation with my son without at least one other man with them.

"I have done my utmost to raise my family above others. Many from these parts objected to my methods. I have been a ruthless man, as you would have heard. I do not think the Lord God will care much for me. Perhaps the death of my only child is his vengeance. I do not know. But those who owe me fealty know not to cross me.

"The brothers were not much liked within the kindred. Weak-willed, stupid malcontents. My men, other than those two, are hard but with honour between them and towards me. Ask any if they would take gold to dishonour their names, and they would answer that they would rather die. But ask them who might be the most likely, God forbid, and they would give the names of Dudda and Cuthbert. I had their houses searched last night. I should have done so earlier. Each had a bag of silver coins buried in the dirt. They were paid to ruin the union of the two families. Who would destroy his kindred for money?" Forthred threw his cup into the fire and stared past Eadred at the wall.

"Lord, whoever wished to stop the alliance would not

have waited until the wedding feast. Did anyone try to stop the marriage?"

"Not many knew of it. It was not going to be popular for either Cerdic or myself, or Edmund and Cerdic's daughter, so we kept knowledge to our closest kin and, of course, the bishop. Aethelbert was sworn to secrecy. Dudda and Cuthbert were not told. Some were dismayed, but once they knew my mind, none objected. I cannot remember any other impediment. But I will tell you of some strange attacks against me. They started in the warmer months. It took a while to realise this was different from petty thieving. I lost some sheep, then a few cows. I increased the guard. I had a herd of twenty-odd cows and oxen moving to new pasture. There was an ambush. Eight cows and two oxen were not stolen, they were killed by arrow fire! Three of my men were slain by arrow points and several wounded. Who would needlessly slaughter cattle?

"All was then quiet, though I kept my beasts well guarded. I thought the shits had gone. Then, when we moved the herds back to the upland for winter, they struck again. I had good warriors protecting them this time, but points flew from tree cover, and I lost a dozen or more cattle, including oxen, and four good men with their horses. A day later, on the other side of my estate, there were more attacks, and I lost three bulls, half a dozen horses and some fifteen cows. Every attacker escaped. All we found, apart from the arrows, were a belt and buckle of Mercian design. Since then, there have been more attacks. I was bleeding!

"I could not lose so many cattle, and my honour was stained. I thought at first that it was Cerdic's work, but he was suffering almost as much. I do not care for the man, and he feels the same about me, but we had to do something. His kindred is not the force it used to be, but it was better we tried to ally ourselves.

"There is no one in these parts strong or bold enough to challenge both Cerdic and I if we work together. Who paid the brothers? Whoever is behind the cattle raids, that is who. I have no name and no idea. Cuthbert knew him, and now he is dead. I would have had Hygelac flogged, but he is close to Aelfric, and not a word of blame has come from the ealdorman's mouth."

Eadred could have added to the criticism of Hygelac but decided it would do him no good. "Lord Forthred, when was the last attack on your livestock?"

"It was a day or two following Edmund's wedding. I lost close to twenty cows and two dozen sheep. My son would have been overseeing the protection of our herds, but he had gone to check the condition of the earthen bank, for the storms were upon us. We have never caught or seen any of the attackers. They fire their arrows, then disappear. I understand the desire to steal, to want what is not yours, but to kill the animals we depend upon! If I wanted easy wealth, I would steal. If I wanted to harm someone, to lessen their power and weaken their authority, then I would destroy their wealth—their cattle. That is the only reason I can see in it. Someone wants to destroy me, and I have no idea who it is!"

*

"These poor souls," Tatwine spoke to his friend. "The worst flood for many a year and some dark mind behind the destruction of their cattle and other beasts. The thegn

Forthred is as close to a criminal as you can be without being found guilty, but I feel some pity even for him."

Eadred looked vaguely towards Tatwine. "Forgive me, I did not hear all you said. I fear I was distracted."

It was the smile of an understanding companion that greeted Eadred's shallow smile. "Come, dear Eadred, tell me what are you thinking. You look exceedingly troubled."

"I was thinking of something Lord Aelfric said to me. Lawlessness has been rising across the kingdom these past months. He has blamed himself for not being the man his father was. I thank God that he is different, but Aelfric takes too much of the burden upon himself. He told me that he sensed some malignant hand or spirit stirring evil across this kingdom. I think, my friend, we are seeing it at work here. Lord Forthred is probably almost as wealthy as the ealdorman, and until the death of his son, he had a fierce ambition. It could be he who is nurturing dissent and crime to weaken Lord Aelfric and take the position for himself. Dudda told us that Forthred's son, Edmund, was not the intended victim, yet Forthred has suffered worse ravages upon his herds than Cerdic. The path ahead is far from clear.

"Is it not a danger to all who live in these fens that the beasts on which their lives depend are being slaughtered and left to the wolves? Not only cattle, but I hear horses, sheep, pigs and goats are dying, all from arrow fire. Where will folk find milk? How will they plough the earth? I overheard one of the villagers speaking—Forthred is now taking more than his customary share of their pigs to replenish his table and strengthen his warriors. Give thanks to God that ordinary fen folk can fish and catch birds aplenty, but not all the ordinary folk in our land are as fortunate to have such bounty. If these attacks are being made across the kingdom, then our whole land is in danger."

Eadred grabbed at the hermit's cloak and turned to face him. "I wish that this thought was not growing within me. The kingdom may be under attack, as much as if our borders were being invaded."

"The Mercians?"

"Forthred said that a belt and buckle of Mercian craftsmanship were found after one of the attacks. It is the only kingdom that would attack us; we have been enemies for generations. This time, it is by endless raids and without showing themselves. If they crossed our borders in force, then we would know we were under attack, but these secretive, creeping encounters are harming us just as much, if not more, for we cannot see our enemy and believe it is one of our own countrymen. My mind returns to their defeat at Elmstow Minster last year. I fear they may be coming for revenge.

"Is it possible that what we thought was the hand of criminals is an attack devised across the border by our ancestral enemy, and their gold and silver are buying traitors? Tatwine, this is a greater menace than I first believed."

"The ealdorman would know much more," Tatwine replied. "He has crossed this land many times these past months."

Eadred failed to hide his doubt. "I hope it is so, but he is a tormented and distracted man. I pray he knows more than he tells and that this concern we have is no surprise to him. Even if the minds behind this villainy rest in Mercia, I think they may have recruited many of our own countrymen— men who would take foreign wealth to harm their own neighbours. They skulk in the woods. We have to capture and question one. Then we will know more.

"When I was with the Cauldron Folk, they told me of a local lad, not a bad soul at first but easily led and his behaviour became worse. He took to stealing and butchering livestock. Aelfric had him hanged. A man would not risk his life for no purpose. He may well have taken Mercian coin from someone he knew or met. As with Cuthbert and Dudda, he was unsatisfied with his life, easy prey for someone who could offer him riches in return for mischief.

"I think I will return to the Cauldron, for now I would ask questions of those folk with greater purpose. Often, if you sit peacefully with a man and ask him a question, he will search his mind and things that had been forgotten are remembered, and some may be important. I would welcome your company."

"Gladly, my friend," the hermit monk replied. "Let us leave early tomorrow, and we should arrive by nightfall."

Eadred again became distracted. A young woman moved quickly between huts to avoid the two men.

"Eadgifu, wait!"

She stopped and spoke without turning. "Father, I am busy now."

"A few moments only, please. Could you turn around?"

It was not what she wanted to do, that was clear, but the young woman turned slowly, still without looking at the priest.

"Eadgifu, what has happened to your eye?" Eadred reached for her chin and eased her head to face him.

"I slipped, Father, and caught it on a pile of wood. It is nothing. I must go." She smiled briefly and hurried off.

"The poor woman has been struck."

"Yes," Eadred replied. "Her husband, a foul being called Brihtwold, mistreats her. At his last confession, I gave him more than the prescribed penance, but it seems almost useless. He has been beaten by other village men for disturbing their wives, but I think his behaviour has not improved. I even spoke to the ealdorman to see if Brihtwold could be brought before a court, but Aelfric said, with reason, that he has more important things on his mind. Eadgifu is a good Christian woman. There is a kindness in her, and a gentle heart, but neither the justice of God nor of man seem able to help her. I fear for her safety."

"Well, my friend, let me tell you what we must do." Tatwine smiled. "I will get my axe, and we will go to this Brihtwold's house. Tell him to come outside. You will say that you have a friend, a man with a single eye, whose wits have been damaged by his wound and who thinks he is a saint sent to protect those who have been deformed in some way. I will tell him that if I hear of any further mistreatment of his wife, I will bind him and cut away his privies. And I will do it, Eadred. I pray it will not come to this, but it is not just idle talk. There are men who ignore the laws of God and of man, thinking they have a dispensation, and sadly, often they go unpunished."

Eadred looked steadily into his friend's eye, hoping a further smile would emerge. It did not, and he gulped hard. Then the hermit's great beard split, and he laughed aloud.

"If I saw this loathsome man face-to-face, I might well be led to make such a threat, but I would not turn it into the deed. You know my past, my good friend. I have let fits of turbulent violence overcome me and killed men who should have lived. I ended the life of a good friend and even now have no memory of the cause. The needless fury was so great within me. I have cruelly executed harmless captives, God help me. I pray daily that I might be rid of such evil, but I fear it may still be unleashed. I am sorry, my dear Eadred, that you have witnessed how savagery can overcome me. The Lord God, who is my only hope, spoke to me, saying that I must live a solitary life, away from the burdens that living with others can press onto a man, until I am safe in the company of disagreeable souls."

"Father Eadred," the voice repeated. It was one of Lord Forthred's men, running towards them. "Two riders have arrived from Snailwell Minster. You are to return with them."

"On whose instructions?"

"The abbot. Tomorrow, at first light."

"No, I cannot!"

"The ealdorman has agreed. Do not cross them."

"Then I will talk to the ealdorman," Eadred insisted.

"You will not gain an audience. Lord Aelfric leaves as we speak to hunt down more criminals."

Tatwine pulled Eadred around to face him. "Go with them, my friend, you owe the abbot obedience. I will come with you."

"No," Forthred's messenger bellowed, "the order is clear. Father Eadred journeys alone."

The priest kicked the dirt and groaned. "I am conspired against! Now my head begins to work on these crimes, I am constrained to return to Snailwell. While I am gone, will you go to the Cauldron and see what you can discover?"

"Of course," Tatwine replied. "Until we find the nest of

these murderers and criminals, and destroy it, there will be no peace."

"Search as best you can. Speak to Alfred, the headman. He is a good soul. Take care, my dear friend."

SIXTEEN

Unease at Snailwell Minster

His journey back to Snailwell was dismal in the extreme. The two warriors sent to fetch Eadred remained tight-lipped, talking briefly to each other but never voluntarily to him. He had asked at the outset the purpose of his summons. They had replied that they did not know, for they were from the estate of the abbot's cousin, Lord Leofric, and all they knew was that Eadred's recall was at the order of the abbot. Some way into the journey, he was intrigued by a few words exchanged between his reluctant companions.

"That was the strangest of happenings. Has anyone named the body that was found in the saint's coffin?"

"No one. All I hear is that he was a thief or murderer; there were the marks of a rope around his neck, and his left hand had been removed."

"It greatly troubled Abbot Cuthred. Lord Leofric's new

church has still not been blessed and stands unused, and the saint's bones have been returned to Snailwell. There is talk of devilry."

Eadred could not stay silent. "I have not heard of this! Do you talk of the consecration of the church at Thornham? I knew it was to happen while I was away with the fen folk. The blessed body of Saint Wulfmaer has been defiled?"

"It is not for us to say more." The warrior added that it was pointless Eadred ask them anything further. Given their annoyance, he reluctantly agreed.

The remainder of his journey was consumed by frustration. What else had happened in his absence? And with Cuthbert's premature death, the path ahead to understanding who ordered the murders of the newlywed couple remained deeply shadowed. Eadred dared hope that someone amongst the Cauldron Folk would have some sliver of a recollection about the poor, unfortunate boy who had been hanged for killing livestock, which could provide some sign to the truth. If such a shred existed, then it was now Tatwine's task to discover. The hermit was a truly wonderful man, to be sure, but Eadred harboured a worry that he might miss the smallest of clues that could have led to a great discovery.

Eadred also felt anxiety gnawing at his guts. Cuthred had made it clear since his recent appointment as Abbot of Snailwell that he saw Eadred as a simple, lowborn priest with limited talents who had been lauded with some inappropriate renown because he had stumbled upon the perpetrators of a crime. Unfortunately, Eadred was often burdened with the same view of himself. It was also certain that the abbot was covetous of Bishop Aethelbert's position and barely disguised this ambition beneath regular claims that the bishop was too senile to continue. Again, unhappily, there was much truth in this. But there was not a bone of warmth or compassion for his brothers from the abbot. He was a hard steward with no heart.

A few hours of light remained on the second day of the journey back from Deerstow when Eadred entered Snailwell's gates. Eager to see his companions and share stories of what had happened over the past few weeks, he headed for the chapter room. He did not arrive. A monk whom Eadred did not recognise took his arm as he walked across the courtyard, gave a meagre smile and encouraged him in another direction.

"Father Eadred, welcome back. I am Brother Diuma from the monastery at Wexning. The abbot asked me recently to join this house, and I have not long been here. He is keen for you to tell him of your time away. Come."

"Thank you, Brother Diuma, and welcome." The monk kept a brisk pace and reserved bearing across the courtyard. Eadred was looking at quite a burly man of thirty years thereabouts with a distinctive harelip. Eadred spoke again, more through unease at the silence than any desire for knowledge. "I have much to tell the abbot about my journey to the fen country. Have you been to that part of the kingdom?"

Diuma seemed to be preoccupied. "I went to Deerstow once, last summer, accompanying our abbot at the consecration of the church there. Our route from Wexning took us through the fenland."

"It is wonderful that the abbot chose you to enter the minster from his previous monastery. He must have a great purpose for you."

"I will visit some of the nearby settlements to hear confessions and officiate at Mass, and I am called upon to deliver other services for the abbot."

Eadred nodded. Some of Diuma's words were difficult to understand with his deformity. He imagined this made the monk reticent to speak. "While I wait, I will quickly see if our bishop can see me."

"That will not be possible. The bishop became seriously ill and is bedridden. His earthly journey is nearing its end."

"No," Eadred groaned. "I had hoped his body might hold out awhile. I must see him one last time."

"Talk to the abbot. He is now head of the minster. And we have seen other troubles these past few days. They are consuming my attention. Come."

It was disconcerting for Eadred to be taken to the room that Bishop Aethelbert had used to welcome visitors and to wait there until Abbot Cuthred was ready to see him. He looked around and grew more melancholy. The four stone walls enclosed a space empty of life. A small table, two stools and a candle, without books, without the sprigs of herbs that the bishop loved so much, without even dust. No heart or spirit. Time dragged, and Eadred's misery turned to anger.

"The abbot is ready." Brother Diuma brought Eadred to the bishop's main reception room. The abbot sat in the bishop's chair. He was tall and richly attired, more excessively than Eadred had ever seen with the bishop. Eadred's distaste for the man was heightened when he saw that alongside the crucifix around his neck the abbot wore a worldly medallion of gold with a rearing horse carved upon it. He gestured for Eadred to sit. The abbot's minimal movement reminded Eadred of Hygelac's arrogant motion of his finger to give effect to his instructions. It added to Eadred's apprehension of the man.

"Father Eadred, I do not have much time. You may have been told already that the Abbess of Elmstow was murdered not far from here two days past?"

Eadred sat in wide-eyed shock and silence.

"Then you have not heard?"

"The abbess was murdered!" Eadred gasped. "Such infamy is not possible. Lord God help our land if such a thing can happen. The abbess was fierce in defence of Holy Church."

"Perhaps too fierce," Cuthred replied. "She had gathered many powerful enemies. We all, of course, mourn her death, but I have much to do. Her funeral is to take place in a few days, which I am conducting. Now, to the purpose of your recall." The abbot continued speaking, but Eadred heard nothing. He saw Cuthred's lips move, but his mind had been frozen by the enormity of what he had just been told.

"How did she die?"

Cuthred stared at him. "I do not care to be interrupted. She was found hanged in the woods not far from our walls. The abbess had journeyed here at the bishop's request to report on the condition of her minster. She had taken an early morning ride to enable solitary prayer, as was her daily custom, and never returned. Some of our slaves found her body close to midday.

"Now, be silent and listen. Bishop Aethelbert sent you into the deep fens to see to the welfare of Father Ingeld. I have heard from a rider from Ealdorman Aelfric that our brother in Christ was killed. While sad, I am not surprised. Criminals across this land see an opportunity to test the resolve of our new ealdorman. God be praised that Ingeld was destined for heaven. The people of those parts have, unfortunately, now been without pastoral care and direction for some time without our knowledge, and that must be remedied soon. Having discovered Father Ingeld's fate, it seems that you forgot your duty and decided, without authority, to remain in Deerstow to inquire about his death. That is not your concern. I needed to remind you and order your return. In due course, I will find a suitable replacement for a priest to serve the people of the deep fens, but, again, that is not your concern."

"He was buried alive, Reverend Abbot, and in consecrated earth. We must not—"

"You must not do anything! I will say this once and once only. Your duty is to me, it is not to meet the ealdorman's requests. Because you had some small and chance part in uncovering the murders at Elmstow last year, you are forgetting your calling. I will not tolerate you stepping beyond your duties again. Thus, you will make no inquiries about the abbess's death. If I hear of one further offence, I will see you removed from the priesthood. You do not serve two masters. You would benefit from reading the *Rule of the Master*. It lays out, better than any other instruction, how cloistered men are meant to behave and what happens to them if they fall into error. I have placed my copy in our library for you and other inmates to consult. I sent a message to the ealdorman to remind him that you are under my authority and I expect obedience from you. He understands this, which is why he agreed fully with your recall to Snailwell. I can assure you that it does not serve you well to imagine that the ealdorman is your patron and protector. Now, is that clear?"

Eadred gave a dispirited acknowledgment.

"To my next concern." The abbot glared at Eadred. "Our ailing bishop made a very serious error in sending one who is of lowly stature and authority to perform the ceremony to join two great families through marriage. He should have consulted me, and I would have gone myself. I know the families well and consecrated the church at Deerstow last summer. Yet I knew nothing of the betrothal! The bishop purposefully kept that knowledge from me. I imagine that you were told by the bishop not to let me know of your mission? Such behaviour is intolerable, and it ends now." The abbot's chest heaved from anger, and he looked away from Eadred while he composed himself. Then he continued.

"Now, tell me of the spiritual condition of the people in that part of the kingdom. How have they suffered without a priest, and what were you able to remedy? Has there been any lapsing into demon worship? How many did you baptise?"

By the end of the abbot's inquisition, Eadred felt exhausted and dizzy. Abbot Cuthred continued without pause.

"A final issue. I have assumed leadership of this minster, given the bishop's rapid decline. The king has been informed, and the need for a quick decision on a new bishop has been stressed. I have already told the community, and now I tell you. Bishop Aethelbert has been relieved of the burdens of his position and will see out what days he has left in his chamber. There are prayers daily that his soul will be freed soon from his failing body to make its heavenly journey.

"Because of your attachment to him, you may feel a

desire to visit the bishop before he leaves this life. While I understand this, the bishop sleeps most of the day and cannot talk, only make sounds that carry no meaning, like a newborn. I have decided that each day, members of our community can visit to pray in vigil by the bishop's bedside and to see to any small ways to care for his comfort. So that each inmate may have the opportunity to see but not distress the bishop, the visits will be in pairs, one in the morning and one in the afternoon. Because of the bishop's condition, it is not possible to be precise about this arrangement, but you will be told when it is likely to be your turn.

"I trust that you understand fully that life here in Snailwell will be different from now on. Discipline will be tighter to remedy the weaknesses allowed by the bishop. I have told every inmate that those who cannot improve their obedience will be turned out of holy orders. Most of our brothers in Christ welcome the change. We will see how you fare. I will be watching you closely."

Eadred was dismissed, this time by the abbot's silence and casual glance at the door.

*

Eadred resumed his participation in the cycle of prayer and praise with the midnight service. It was, unfortunately, a disconcerting experience. His heart had felt lighter with the thought of seeing his brothers in Christ once more and sharing worship after the misery of his time with the abbot. He smiled openly at the first few faces he knew so well. Some smiled briefly and hurried past; others stared blankly at or ignored him. His hopes had been high for the reunion.

What had happened in his absence so that his companions would seem to disown him?

Finally, a faint, disguised smile and a whisper. "Let us seek to talk tomorrow. Not all is well here." Brother Anselm's expression turned harsh abruptly, and he moved on.

Eadred lay in bed staring up into the blackness. Snailwell was his home, and now it felt like a strange place, where he knew no one and where unknown dangers threatened. The bishop had started on his path from this earthly life, and Abbot Cuthred had not allowed Tatwine to accompany Eadred to Snailwell. Tears trickled down his cheeks. The Lord God seemed as distant as Tatwine and as bleak as Snailwell. Prayer was impossible.

Once again, Eadred's thoughts drifted into the darkness of a crime. It was a consolation. Even if Snailwell felt lonely, his mind was free to dig into the perplexing circumstances of his days at Deerstow. What was he missing? There was a plot to stop the alliance between the families of Lord Forthred and Lord Cerdic, and this had led to murder. Someone was also destroying the main source of wealth for both families and for those who lived on their estates: cattle. Surely, these two deeds were related, like attacks on a battlefield from two directions.

According to Forthred, the marriage alliance was contrived secretly, thus the opportunity to halt it before its birth was limited. Those who opposed the marriage had to break it. Was it another noble family, who feared the arrogant power of Forthred, or was it the Mercians, who wanted the feud to consume the East Angles? Or could it have been instigated by some of Cerdic's kin but went terribly amiss when Cerdic's daughter was killed? Dudda and Cuthbert were the only trespassers who had been caught, and they were now beyond questioning. As he sifted through these thoughts, his mind turned even darker. Almost the last words Dudda had spoken before Eadred left the torture hut were for the priest to tell Lord Forthred that the two brothers intended no harm on Forthred's son and he had died stoutly defending his wife. Now, with the benefit of his silent contemplation, Dudda's words did not ring true. Eadred recalled seeing the bodies.

It was the groom who had been murdered suddenly and by surprise, not the bride. Edmund had died by two swift knife thrusts in the back, and with no other signs of struggle. Censwith had the marks of the brutal encounter on her arms and chest—while another killer had sunk his knife into her back. She had fought back, not her husband. Dudda had been remorseful for his role in murdering Edmund and lied to mask the appalling truth that the death of Forthred's only child was intended, and Censwith also had to die, perhaps so no witnesses to the crime would survive. There surely had to be at least one other man involved in the murders. Forthred had spoken of the warrior strength of his son. Besides, Eadred conjectured, having failed to end the marriage alliance at the feast, the two brothers would have taken no chances with their next attempt. They clearly feared the man who had paid them the silver and could not fail to deliver their part of the transaction. Was the third man at the killing also the mind behind the wave of crimes?

Eadred did not like where his thoughts were taking him. They made no sense, for a death to both families would not cause the feud to explode, but could unite them in grief, as indeed it seemed to have done. Did someone want revenge on both houses? There were many things that Eadred did not know or understand. But he did know that Lord Cerdic and his wife had left for their estates around the Cauldron very soon after the tortures and executions, and they and their family may still face danger. He thought of Tatwine. "Lord God, I pray for your protection over my friend for his journey to and from the lands of the Cauldron Folk. May his wits stay sharp and keep him safe from danger."

SEVENTEEN

Escape and Capture

Faint light smeared the eastern sky. Tatwine pulled his cloak closely around his shoulders and stamped his feet on the frosted earth. The pall of mist had rolled through the bald branches to his left and now shrouded the path through Deerstow. He fingered the droplets on his beard, contemplating the dangers of the journey. The Cauldron was ahead of him, up to a day's unknown walk, which now seemed even more testing. Yet he had faith in the villagers from the night before. To a man, they had told him that the mist would rise before he had to navigate the most difficult parts of his journey, so he decided to set off.

Less than ten paces later, he stopped. He opened his cloak and drew his knife. "I see you. Stop, now!"

"We are unarmed. Please do not raise the alarm." The forms of two entwined figures stumbled into view from the right of the path. "It is Eadgifu, whom you met yesterday, and my sister, Eadburga," she whispered in a trembling voice.

"You are alone?" Eadgifu confirmed that they were. Tatwine took a few steps backwards, watching the women carefully as they walked from the side of a storage hut. He remained suspicious.

"You are on the road early, Brother Tatwine, and not in the direction of Elmstow," Eadburga spoke with a hushed voice.

"I travel into the deep fen. Father Eadred was to journey there, to the country of the Cauldron Folk, but had to return to Snailwell Minster. So I go to bear witness to the Lord God. And I see that your sister has a cut lip. Perhaps she has slipped again? I see also that you have brought some food for a journey, and without your husband?" Tatwine's inquisitive eye went from woman to woman and to their bags.

Eadgifu broke into gentle sobbing. Her sister wrapped her protective arms around her, and she stared angrily at him. "You have no right to question us. Yes, you see a woman who is abused daily by her drunken lecher of a husband. Her shrunken, bruised body gives her more pain than most of your sex will ever face. And who brings the pig to face his crimes? Not the lord of this vill nor the ealdorman, not the Church. For all the foul words that Brihtwold hurls at the backs of priests for their penances, the only real penalty he faces is from the men whose honour is affronted when Brihtwold grabs their wives' tits and tries to lift their tunics. You wonder why we want to escape!"

Tatwine raised his hands as if to fend off Eadburga's anger. "When men have no fear of the Lord, all manner of evil is possible."

"I have known many men whom you call heathens and decry, yet they had more honour than most of the churchmen I have met," Eadburga replied.

"Sadly, there is some truth in what you say. I am sorry, Eadgifu, you deserve better. Where do you go?"

Eadburga answered, "We know what we are leaving—that is enough."

"It is unlawful, as you know, to leave your lord's estate without his permission," he replied.

"We know, but if we stay, my sister's life will be short and full of misery. We will find some joy together before we are found."

Tatwine found himself in an unexpected and unwelcome position. He knew his responsibilities to the Church and to the law, but a memory from before the time he had entered the cloister, of how he had failed a young woman in need, spoke louder.

"The Church and man have failed you, but as long as you have not harmed Brihtwold, then I will stand in court and defend you against his foul behaviour, and I will swear to your good word."

"He remains safe," Eadburga scowled. "We are not that foolish as to harm him."

As he looked at the two women—one battered, burnt and thin, and the other fierce and protective, walking into the fog—Tatwine fell into disbelief at their courage. "The land is lawless and unsafe. If you have a mind to journey with me to the land of the Cauldron Folk, we will be safer. Father Eadred has told me that they are good people, and the meres there are full of food."

Eadgifu turned to talk to Tatwine. Her sister took

her hand and pulled her away, but Eadgifu resisted. She whispered to Eadburga. Some strong words were exchanged, but finally Eadburga relented. They kissed each other's cheek and exchanged a brief smile.

Tatwine voiced his thoughts. "The Church of the East Angles is not free from sin, far from it. There are many cloistered men and priests who do not follow the rule of chastity, and that is the least of their faults. I failed once to protect a helpless woman. She was misused by men and then murdered, so she could not speak of what she knew. I will never be free of the guilt I feel, but I swear on the Holy Book that I will not harm either of you in any way, if that is your concern, and in memory of that young woman, I will fight to keep you safe."

"We are grateful to you, Brother Tatwine, and would be happy to journey with you." Eadgifu smiled, and her sister nodded.

"Come then, let me carry your bags. They look heavy, and we will move the quicker if you are not laden."

"No," Eadburga responded with a ferocity Tatwine did not expect. "Take my sister's if you will, but I am not weak." Eadgifu passed her bag to him. The departure had been delayed, but now the trio moved quickly before their absence was noticed.

Tatwine had always admired his own ability to consume apace the distance he needed to walk to reach a destination. He was accordingly cheered to find that his companions had a similar capacity. The Lord God help the sisters if they were caught now, and this surely kept them moving. He was also relieved to find that the sisters were familiar with the path towards the deep meres. The track they confidently took at each junction seemed to agree with the instructions he had received from Eadred, so although the lack of visibility proved to be a stubborn difficulty, he followed their directions without much concern and without comment.

After an hour or so of good and silent progress, the sisters slowed their pace. Even with stretched, featureless skin masking her expression, Eadgifu's disquiet was clear. "In this fog, we are uncertain whether we have taken the right path. Our memory went no further than where the way last branched. We could have made a mistake."

Tatwine looked to Eadburga, who stared stone-faced into the distance, so he spoke. "Father Eadred gave me careful directions, which I have been following as far as I am able. Living alone in a cave, I have developed my own way of remembering a journey. Often, in the black of night, I move from my home to special trees, where I meet the demons to do battle; sometimes to three or four trees in a single night, spread over the hillsides. After the struggle with the beasts of hell, my mind is tired but exhilarated, so I have disciplined myself to find my way back to warmth. I give a number to each time I need to decide which branch of a path I must take. So at number four, I take the left pathway. At number five, I cross a stream and follow the path to the right. I have trained my mind to remember well.

"I sat and talked with Father Eadred while he remembered his journey to the Cauldron and back. He learned the way there by way of a song he was taught, but I use my own song. There are fourteen times when a choice must be made on the journey from Deerstow to the Cauldron. I have them all in my mind's eye. The last branch was the fifth, and I would have taken the same path as you. As you do not have a memory of travelling any further, I will happily now take the lead."

"We are thankful to you, Brother Tatwine." Eadgifu's eyes sparkled. Once more, her sister looked elsewhere and said nothing. Tatwine, in return, ignored Eadburga. He had now to remember each part of the trip without any other support. The fog, which the villagers had been certain would rise, also chose to be defiant.

The pace of their progress slowed. The ninth point where a judgment needed to be made could not be far away. Tatwine recalled what Eadred had said and peered ahead for a narrowing of their path, almost to the point where a nervous mind might feel that the way did not exist. Yet if they shouldered past this, the path again should appear, but there would still be uncertainty, as the mere may have swallowed it for a distance. And indeed the bare, enclosing branches began to press against Tatwine and his companions, forcing them to strain against the wood to labour forward.

Tatwine knew that his God had granted him a special gift of prophecy. Eadred had himself been a recipient and had come to understand that Tatwine moved within the spirit realm almost as easily as he walked in the world of men. It was this gift that guided him now in an instant that separated life from death.

"Lie down, now!" Tatwine turned and threw himself at the two women, sending them flying backwards. Screams, shouts, abuse followed. Eadburga drew her knife against him as he lay on top of her. Tatwine grabbed at her wrist, but she was strong and spat in his face.

Something whistled through the air above them and was

gone, almost as if it had never been. Then others. "Arrows!" Eadgifu cried.

Tatwine stared into Eadburga's eyes and took his hands from her wrists. It came to him to suddenly cry out in misery, as if he had sustained a wound. Then he rose and ran forward into the mist, drawing his knife. He collided with a man who, from his expression, must have considered that the arrows had done their work. The man dropped his bow and grasped his knife, but Tatwine thrust his own blade into his opponent's throat and onwards into the head. The monk could hear several voices ahead. He had a warrior's heart and instincts and sensed the importance of his next move. He picked up the bow and some arrows, knelt, waited a few moments until figures emerged from the mist, then he fired three times. The meaty sounds told of some success, as did the screams of unexpected pain. Tatwine leapt forward and slashed at the face of the first man he encountered. His opponent had sustained arrow wounds to his thigh and shoulder. Tawine pushed him into the underwood as a second man loomed quickly before him. This assailant appeared unharmed by arrow fire. The attacker grabbed Tatwine's raised knife hand and went to unsheathe his own blade. Tatwine managed to hold on to him, and the two men fought. Some damage was sustained from their blades, but Tatwine was proud of his strength and agility and soon felt he had mastery of his opponent. His mood was lightened further when it seemed there were no further attackers. There were cries of a man and woman from behind Tatwine, and he managed to turn his attacker so he could see Eadburga plunging a knife, over and over, into the body of the man he had earlier thrust into the thicket. Her eyes then fixed on Tatwine's, and she came towards his attacker's exposed back with blade raised.

"Do not kill him!" he yelled. The man turned his head to see Eadburga. He fell with a kick to the stomach and a punch to the head from Tatwine.

Tatwine slumped onto his knees, breathing heavily, but he smiled. He tore strips of cloth from his opponent's tunic, rolled him over and bound his wrists. "We needed to capture one of these unknown animals. He has secrets we might prise from him if we can get safely to the Cauldron. And I see that you have had your own fight!" He looked at the blood dripping from a knife wound to Eadburga's forearm.

"It was an easy win," she replied while zealously gathering silver pennies that had spilt from her bag.

Tatwine's head was full of more immediate concerns than the woman's apparent riches. "When our captive has recovered, we must move quickly. If I remember Father Eadred's instructions, there should be a safer place to rest not far ahead. If we tear cloth from the tunics of the dead, we can use it later to bind what wounds we have." Eadgifu had also enjoyed her own victory, and she held high a length of rope that one of the dead had been carrying.

Within the half hour, they came to the mere's edge, then waded and searched, taking false tracks while the light of the sun took its end-of-day journey. Tatwine exclaimed his victory when he came upon the path forward and finally a sufficient expanse to rest and see to wounds. The sisters had bruises and Eadburga a shallow cut, but they were otherwise safe. Once the sisters had tended to each other, Eadburga came to bind a gash on Tatwine's left forearm.

The captive had small gashes to his right arm and shoulder, but Tatwine's wish had come to pass—at least thus far—and the man's wounds were far from fatal. But Tatwine and the sisters still had to find the safety of the Cauldron. The prisoner's mouth had been bound in case more of his companions were nearby. He sat, resting his back against a tree, his wrists and ankles bound with rope. He stared out to the mere, occasionally flinching, forlorn. Tatwine's hope was that this man was one of the furtive cattle killers.

"How did you know that arrows were coming towards us? I could see nothing ahead." He smiled at Eadgifu's question. "It was not of my doing. I have been granted a gift of foresight by the Lord God. I saw the points leaving the bows as clearly as I see you now, but not with my earthly eyes."

"Praise God that such things happen! That there are miracles still in this world." Tears began to fall down the woman's face.

"Eadgifu, I know of the torments in your life, and not just the scars upon your body. I will pray that your future is blessed." She smiled and moved away to wipe her tears.

"You mean well, and you are doing more than just saying words to help us, but do not give my sister false hope." Eadburga spoke slightly less aggressively than usual. "For that would make her hardships even worse. Churchmen have put their hands together for her before. Though her husband hurled the foulest abuse behind the backs of priests for the penances they gave, they were useless and did not change him. Then the men of the Church forgot her. Do not treat her as badly." Eadburga finished tying the cloth around his arm.

178

"I have felt what power lies in the world of the spirit. I call upon God many times daily, but he is beyond my understanding. I cannot be silent about his blessings to me, and the hope he can give to others." The hermit's face broke into a grin. "You are a fierce warrior. I should not like to meet you in battle! You protect your sister and your silver well."

Eadburga's face turned crimson. "It is a small share of Brihtwold's coin. He owes my sister that, at least. It will help us, wherever fate chooses to take us. For all his wailing about penances, he was never fined or forced to pay her compensation. If he risked the loss of his precious silver, he would have thought twice before beating her!" Eadburga snatched up her bandages, and the two women went to bind the captive's wounds. They were not gentle.

The hours of darkness were not kind to Tatwine. He was somewhere between Deerstow and the Cauldron. He was certain that there were more than the group of men who had attacked them waiting somewhere amongst the trees and reeds, ready to silence them before one of their kind gave up his secrets. In the early hours, in prayer, he heard their whispers and heartbeats.

EIGHTEEN

Brother Anselm

Snailwell Minster sat on a gentle, chalky hill with the village settlement resting at the base of its southeastern slope. It was in Eadred's nature to feel content and well rooted when he walked the path from the cloister down into the valley and the vill, crossing the bridge and taking any of the tracks that led along the riverbank or off into the woods.

It was Bishop Aethelbert's custom on important feast days to lead processions around the village and then into the minster church, and this had given the pathways a wonderful otherworldly dimension for Eadred. He might start a solitary walk burdened with earthly cares, and as he progressed he imagined that this skin of worries slowly peeled away, allowing his soul to hear God's gentle voice. But not today.

Halfway down the slope and off to the right of the track

stood four great oak trees with an abundance of undergrowth. On hot summer days, inmates of the minster would rest there for a while on their journey from the minster's fields or returning from pastoral duties. It was here, not long after the mid-morning service, where Eadred waited.

"Greetings, Brother Anselm."

The monk looked carefully behind him, then came and sat beside Eadred. "God bless you, Eadred. I am pleased that you have returned safely, although this is not the homecoming I would have wished for you."

"This is my home, but my brothers in Christ look at me as if I am a criminal! What has happened?"

Anselm sighed with the weight of what he had to say. "Many things. Some I understand, but many I do not. I have thought carefully about what I want to tell you, so if you would indulge me, let me say it all before you ask anything in case we need to bring our little prayer time to a quick end." Eadred nodded his agreement.

"It is no secret that the abbot has a very different view of you than does the bishop. Abbot Cuthred is rising, and our dear bishop is declining. I prayed by Aethelbert's bed a few days back. It will not be long before his soul leaves the house of flesh. He recognised me but could not speak. I have seen many men facing their last days, and there is no doubt that the bishop is on his final journey.

"The abbot has spoken to us recently about the declining health of the bishop and said that he would now take on the duties and authority of leading the minster. A new bishop will then be chosen. He spoke about some new arrangements he would initiate to remedy areas of loose behaviour, as he put it, that the bishop had allowed to creep into our daily activities. He told us they had weakened our discipline and the sanctity of our purpose.

"As an example of our parting from our sacred duties, the abbot mentioned you. In fact, he spoke at length about you! I might say that most of us were surprised. He talked of the murders at Elmstow Minster a twelvemonth past and how you had been allowed to speak before the court and to question the accused. Cuthred said that allowing this was a grave error on the bishop's part. He had not observed the time-honoured procedures for how a court should work, and if there was a need for an inquisition, then a senior man should have undertaken the task."

Anselm shook his head. "The abbot ignored, deliberately, what we all know—what even the king knows—that you found the killers. I am sure, Eadred, that he harbours jealousy. It infuriates him that you have been honoured above him, a member of a great family, and that the king and the ealdorman hold you in high regard.

"But there is something more than jealousy." The monk breathed deeply and chose his words slowly and carefully. "I think the abbot fears you. He fears that gift of yours, my dear boy. There is something about him that is secretive. I see it in his eyes. There is something he wishes to keep hidden. I think he would have you banished from the priesthood if he could.

"The reason your companions here are nervous now to embrace you is because the abbot spoke of your sin, your fornication. It was another of the bishop's failings, he says, that your penance was too light, and you have been treated better than your brothers. He as much said that we brothers befriend you at our peril. Watch your back carefully. He is turning the community against you."

Eadred hunched forward. "One mistake!"

"No, one excuse. He has set his face against you. It has been good to see you, Eadred, but take care! Now, I should leave before I am noticed."

Anselm rose, but Eadred held his wrist. "Please, before you go, the abbot told me that the Abbess of Elmstow was murdered here a few days past—found hanging like a common criminal! She was the hope of many of us to renew Holy Church once the bishop takes his heavenly journey. What is happening?"

Anselm returned to kneel beside Eadred. "There is evil lurking in our kingdom. Many feel it, but it lies hidden in the darkness. It was not killed off at Elmstow. You are right, the abbess was a great force for good. You know the condition of Elmstow when she became its head. She stood against its sinfulness and powerful patrons and weeded out the debauched. The bishop would have gone to the queen to seek justice, for her royal heart understands the dangers for a woman of lofty position, and she was always a support to the abbess. Aethelbert would have instilled in the king and the ealdorman the importance of finding the killers. He would have done all within his power. But Cuthred is burying the abbess with immoderate haste, and unless he is taking action in the shadows, I have not seen or heard of any resolute steps on his part to find her murderers."

Eadred sighed. "I hear that an executed criminal was found within Saint Wulfmaer's coffin and almost installed within the new church at Thornham. It speaks of dark magic."

"Oh, Eadred, demonic forces have been called from hell! They touched Elmstow a year past and now Thornham.

I fear Snailwell is next. I have said too much. I have been away from the minster long enough and confess that I grow fearful that my absence will be noticed."

Eadred spoke quickly. "One final question, Brother Anselm, before you go. Tell me, have there been attacks, senseless slaughter of cattle, horses and sheep, especially by arrow fire, while I was away?"

The monk reflected for a few seconds. "I have heard that the thegn Leofric has set extra guards on the beasts within his estates. Perhaps he has heard of attacks elsewhere."

"And what of our cattle and sheep here on minster lands?" Eadred continued. "We have one of the biggest herds in the area."

Anselm shook his head. "I have not heard of any attacks, and the abbot, as far as I know, has taken no steps to increase our defences." The monk clasped Eadred's shoulder, then he looked along the pathway and left.

Eadred watched his tears fall to the earth. There were many vicious, lying, corrupt and arrogant people—men and women—in the kingdom, and Eadred had met his share. They ruined the lives of their victims, and it gave them pleasure. What had he done to deserve the abbot's attacks? He had been given a gift by God, one that served a good purpose and did the Lord's work, but it also brought Eadred suffering. This was his cross, or was it an attack by the evil one? Eadred could understand that those who committed the foulest crimes might want to stop him—he had faced a slayer's knife before—but to be the object of another churchman's venom, and one with great authority! He felt sick, helpless and alone.

Yet, even when he felt such misery, Eadred's mind could

still rake over the details of the crimes around him. It helped him cope with his own condition. Why had the abbess been killed, and by whom? She was known for her reforming zeal, and there would be enough rich families across the kingdom smarting at her expulsion of their pampered, ungodly daughters.

He also pondered Brother Anselm's reply about the absence of unlawful cattle slaughter on the estates owned by Snailwell Minster. Eadred understood that the lands owned by Elmstow Minster had also been free of such attacks, and both were closer to the border with Mercia than were the deep fens. He took some comfort from this. It was less likely that the Mercians were behind the wave of killings, for if they were planning an attack, then the border regions would be the first to suffer.

Such thoughts consumed Eadred on his walk back to the minster, but as he entered its gates, a few dark faces reminded him that it was no longer the refuge it used to be.

NINETEEN

Life's Slender Thread

Tatwine had not felt as anxious for many months. The attack of yesterday, and the nearness of death, had reminded him of how he needed to guard his soul, for life's end could steal upon him at any hour. He was grateful to his Saviour for reminding him of the frailty of man and for saving him on this occasion, when his spirit had sensed the killing arrow points hurtling through the vapour.

The journey continued, in silence, from first light. Wisdom suggested that the prisoner should take the lead, bound, gagged and with a rope around his neck, as some minor protection for his captors. However, Tatwine had no doubt that there were more of these sinister men concealed along the pathway, and one of their arrows might serve to silence the captive from telling his secrets. So, with every sense heightened, he instead took the lead, with Eadburga gripping the rope around the captive's neck.

The eleventh time when a decision had to be taken arrived, some twenty paces ahead, a bend to the right, around the trunk of a great tree. If Eadred's instuctions and Tatwine's memory were accurate, a fork in the path should follow. Then there was a rustle.

Armed men—four, perhaps five—appeared from around the crook in the path. Tatwine groaned. A clash of metal caused him to turn. The path behind him was similarly blocked.

"I am sorry," Tatwine said in a soft, anguished voice. "There is no escape this time."

The captive tugged at the rope and tried to shout. Eadburga held it firm in both hands.

Tatwine already had his knife in hand and held it to the man's throat. "I will kill him!"

One of the murderous band laughed. They raised their bows. Then a thud.

One of the attackers behind them fell forward, the shaft of a spear extending from his back. Then more screams, ahead and behind of Tatwine. The attackers were under attack. They panicked to replace bows with blades, but the surprise was deadly. A rush of blows and thrusts and all lay dead.

Shouts of victory filled the air. An axe blade took the head from one of the bodies, and it was raised high with exuberant cries.

"I am Alfred of the Cauldron Folk and headman of our vill. Whom do I speak to?"

Tatwine shouted out the words Eadred had bid he use when he approached the Cauldron and its inhabitants. "I am Brother Tatwine of Elmstow Minster and companion of Father Eadred, who visited your people recently. He is not with me but sends greetings and blessings, especially to you, Alfred, and to your wife, Elfwyn." Then he added, "These women are from Deerstow, and we travel together for safety. This man was one of a band who attacked us."

"Praise be to God! You are very welcome, Brother Tatwine." Tatwine's fingers edged towards his knife as the bands of men before and behind him approached. Alfred raised his hands and smiled. "You have faced many dangers, but you are amongst friends now. Believe me." In a fearless stride, Alfred came up to Tatwine and clasped his shoulders, his eyes gleaming. Tatwine responded, and any reticence evaporated, but Eadred had asked him to convey sad tidings to Alfred, and Tatwine was keen to remove the burden from his mind.

"Father Eadred asked me to bring you word of a terrible discovery. Father Ingeld's body has been unearthed at Deerstow."

"It was murder?" Alfred's voice trembled.

Tatwine nodded. "Prepare yourself. He was buried alive."

Alfred clasped his head in his hands, looked to the heavens and screamed as one who had sustained a vicious wound. His misery was echoed by his companions. "What animal could have committed such evil? A rider from our Lord Cerdic has these past days told us of the deaths of Lady Censwith and her husband, and that some traitorous kin of Forthred and perhaps others did kill them. And now we hear of Father Ingeld's murder! I will avenge him. I pledge to God that I will." Then Alfred saw the captive.

"I know your face." Alfred rushed towards the bound man, who tried to pull away. Eadburga held him fast.

Alfred took his knife and sliced away the cloth around the prisoner's mouth.

"Boisil!" Alfred had not even finished saying the name when he punched the man hard in the stomach. Boisil bent double, gasping, and fell to his knees.

"His miserable father is over here." Another of Alfred's band pointed to one of the dead attackers.

"Are any others known?"

Hands pulled the bodies from each other, and their faces were checked. "None," came the answer.

"Pig! Slaughtering your own people's beasts." Alfred dragged the captive to his feet. "And the Lord God himself will not be able to help you if you had anything to do with Lady Censwith's or Father Ingeld's deaths. I will tear you limb from limb!" Alfred stared into Boisil's impassive eyes. "I will skin you alive. Where are these men from?" Alfred spat into his face.

Boisil turned away from Alfred. The headman stepped behind him and wrenched his head back, piercing one side of his throat with his blade. "Tell me!" No answer came. "And Lady Censwith and Father Ingeld?" Again, no answer. Alfred swore and put his boot into the man's back, sending him crashing forward. Two of Alfred's men took the headman by the shoulders and begged him to calm his rage, saying there would be time to question Boisil later and that Alfred's own men had wounds that needed attention.

Tatwine also spoke. "He will not tell. I have seen this in Deerstow. Two men, accused of the vile murders of Lady Censwith and her husband, would not confess the truth of who ordered the crime despite torture. We must use other methods."

Alfred seemed unimpressed. "This excuse for a man deserves the worst of deaths. I will make him talk." Alfred turned to his companions. "Take their heads. Someone might recognise them." The dead bodies were decapitated, and the group set off for the remainder of their journey.

"Brother Tatwine, you know Father Eadred well?"

Tatwine smiled at the memory of his friendship. "I do, Alfred, but it may seem otherwise. We met first only a twelvemonth past and since then have barely been by each other's side. But we have been connected by God and by our natures. We have fought the Mercians side by side, ate and drank together and shared our deepest thoughts.

"Father Eadred spoke highly of you and your wife and of the too short a time he spent here with you. He would want to be here now but was recalled by his abbot, so he asked that I come in his stead. I am from Elmstow, not Snailwell, and my abbess has sanctioned my journeys as a wandering hermit, so I am able to embark on missions such as this. The father asked that I provide what spiritual care I can, although I am not ordained. I know you have been without a priest for close to a year, and that has weighed on Father Eadred. Now he is back at Snailwell, I am sure he will speak to the bishop about your needs."

"Your friend is missed," Alfred replied. "Elfwyn and I drew close to him quickly. And what of the two women?"

Tatwine repeated the words he had devised since the sisters had agreed to journey with him. Eadburga had bristled at them but accepted that there was no believable alternative. Tatwine hoped she would continue to lie.

"As you see, the one called Eadgifu has been deformed by fire. Her sister, Eadburga, cares for her. They come from a poor family but have hearts for God and were journeying to Elmstow alone, hoping to be accepted as postulants. Yet the way was more dangerous than they thought. I met them on the road, and they were happy to journey here with me. When I return to Elmstow, they will accompany me. It will be safer for them, and I think they were encouraged when I told them I would speak to the abbess on their behalf. Our journey here proved more perilous than I had contemplated, but, thank God, you saved us from certain death. Father Eadred was right to praise you and your people."

Alfred was clearly happy to hear Tatwine speak of Eadred's love of the Cauldron Folk. His chest and his tangled beard rose and fell with contentment. He continued with another subject that pleased him. "We had been hunting that band of arseholes for three days. Their arrow fire killed four cows, but our folk have become more watchful, and they have become careless. They moved quickly but made mistakes, leaving prints in the earth. It was a bigger band than in the past, but I had organised our men to be ready, and we were in quick pursuit."

Another sign of pride brought a grin. "While they were watching you, they were unaware that we were shadowing them. You helped us catch and kill them!"

"I sensed we were being watched," Tatwine laughed, and then turned more pensive. "I have heard and seen with my own eyes the scourge of these lawless bands. Here, in Lord Cerdic's lands and in Lord Forthred's. For all I know, they are happening elsewhere." He lowered his voice. "This man, Boisil, is the only one of them we have in our power. His tongue could tell us much. Yet, as you witnessed earlier, there is some immense fear or power that stops them speaking of their crimes, even when tortured and facing death. I cannot understand it, but we must keep him alive, at least until he gives up his secrets."

*

"Elf, this is Brother Tatwine, a friend of Father Eadred, sent by him to ensure that God is with us."

Alfred's wife beamed an excited smile. "You are very welcome, Brother Tatwine. You have already brought us God's blessing."

"It is a joy to be here, Elfwyn. Father Eadred could not praise you, your husband and your folk highly enough. This is Eadgifu and Eadburga, sisters who wish to join the cloister. Alfred saved our lives, so we also feel blessed."

"Then it is a feast tonight, and look at this bounty!" Elf clapped her hands, watching the severed heads of her people's enemies being exhibited on ash poles and the children throwing stones at them. "Boisil! God's blood, if you are part of this pile of shit!" He gave a provoking smile in return to Elfwyn.

"Come, dearest," Alfred smiled, "leave him for now. There are a few wounds to see to, and there is sad news. Brother Tatwine has told me that Father Ingeld's body has been found. He was murdered. His killer remains unknown." Elfwyn shook her head in disbelief and bellowed her grief. Alfred drew her tightly to him. "It is certain that he is with God now, and we will find his killer. But we are all returned safely with the heads of our enemies, and with Brother Tatwine and his companions. So let us build up the fire and see what the store huts hold. Let joy prevail, at least for tonight."

Tatwine knew well enough that the homecoming feast after a battle or an unsettling hue and cry always flowed with mixed waters—dark with loss of loved ones and the damage of severe injury, but also clear with relief for those who remained alive and who had escaped disfigurement or the certainty of a slow, agonising death. There were certainly tearful memories of Father Ingeld for those who stared awhile into the flames or watched the shadows move across the walls. But a great victory had been won, one of the bastard criminals had been captured, and the folk of the Cauldron were welcoming a man of God.

"We cannot spare a sheep or pig, but we trust that this fare is acceptable?" Tatwine raised his cup of ale in response to Alfred. "I am blessed to be safe, and to share in the riches of your land and your waters." He had two thick slabs of bread; one covered with roasted chicken and the meat of fen birds, and the other piled with roasted eel and smoked cheese.

"Brother Tatwine, the past six or seven months have been the worst for us Cauldron Folk for as long as men can remember. The attacks on our livestock have done much damage. We need their milk, their muscle and their meat. A man can be as rich as he needs one day, but the next his cattle and sheep lie dead, and he has no way to feed his family or to secure his old age. The recent flood has damaged us, though not as much as for many. And we lost dear Father Ingeld. His murder saddens and disgusts me. But Boisil is bound and well guarded. We will see to him tomorrow, and I swear if he had a hand in the father's death, I will have him regret the hour he was born."

TWENTY

Escape

A tepid smile or two, a few nods and a couple of mumbled 'Eadreds'. This was all of the positive recognition he had received during the two days he had been at Snailwell. Mostly, it was the same avoidance or reticent stares and glances, but at least there was not open hostility. Then, at the end of mid-morning prayers, a few whispered words. They were from Brother Anselm.

"I saw the bishop for a few moments yesterday afternoon. It was not my allotted time, but I crept into his cell quickly. I had to tell our beloved Aethelbert that you had returned. He cannot speak in a way that we understand, and he can barely move, but he struggled hard to say your name. There was distress in the noises he made, and his eyes stared into mine. He yearns to see you, my boy."

"But how? I have not been given a time, and when I do, it is unlikely to be soon," Eadred replied.

"Take mine, just before the lighting of the lamps today."

Eadred grabbed the back of Anselm's hand, squeezing it, and mouthed his thanks.

"And, Eadred," Anselm continued, "watch over your life with great care. I fear that our home here will never be the same. God forbid that I have to say these words, but if I were you, I would find some excuse to depart, or you may never leave again."

*

Eadred's heart quickened as he approached the bishop's chamber. No one else was in sight. He unlatched the door and entered. Tears began to trickle down his cheeks. The stink from sweat, piss and shit in the freezing air made him gag. It was mixed with the lingering mousy odour of medicinal dwale, given to ease the bishop's pain. Eadred had turned to the wall and now returned his gaze to the shrivelled body that barely shaped the woollen blanket lying upon it. The bishop's head faced upwards, drawn, bone-coloured, motionless. Only the eyes, through desultory blinks, showed any sign of life remaining in the old man.

Eadred unfolded another blanket and laid it over Aethelbert. "My Father, it is Eadred." He bent across the bed so the bishop did not need to strain his eyes to see him. The old man emitted soft but agitated whimpers, like a wounded hound upon seeing its master. A faint smile broke through. "Our Heavenly Father awaits your glorious coming. I see him with his arms outstretched. Flesh and blood will soon end its toilsome march, and your spirit will leave for its heavenly journey." Eadred's smile faded, and he turned away to weep and wipe his face.

The whimpers grew more intense. Aethelbert's lips cracked opened and moved, as if he were trying to shape some words. The muscles in his face trembled; his breathing grew frenetic.

"Calm yourself, it is I, Eadred." The bishop struggled to nod and made it clear that he knew as much. He tried once more to shape a word. He wanted Eadred to come closer. Was that the meaning? Eadred moved his face closer to the bishop's and listened with intent. Aethelbert breathed deeply and coughed.

The rush of foul breath startled Eadred, and he lurched backwards. With reticence, his face returned to rest just above the bishop's sunken eyes. Another forced cough. The faint odour of dwale mixed with herbs. Eadred stared into the bishop's eyes and understood. In moderate measure, dwale would help a man sleep and heal some kinds of sickness, but too much, for too long, and it was deadly.

"Poison?" The bishop's agitated groan in response to Eadred's question was enough. He had spoken, and the meaning was made clear. "Who?" Aethelbert groaned in response. He struggled to move his lips, but no name was formed, just gasps for air.

A short-lived smile animated the bishop's face, then an expression of peace and resignation. He was ready to go, however it happened. Eadred pushed his hand beneath the blankets and found Aethelbert's cold and trembling hand. He squeezed it gently. The old man's lips flickered as he struggled again to form words. None came, and he groaned with frustration. The moans and facial contortions grew more intense. Eadred watched every movement, especially the eyes.

"Am I in danger?"

Aethelbert's whole face became animated. *"Go, go!"* The meaning of the bleats was clear.

"I will. God protect your precious soul. You have been my dear father in so many ways." Eadred wiped away tears, remembering some of Aethelbert's kindest words and actions towards him. "I swear before the Lord God, I will find who did this to you." The bishop's eyes were closed, his breathing shallow. Exhausted from his efforts to communicate with his favourite son in Christ, the bishop had drifted into sleep.

Careful that he was not seen, Eadred returned to his cell. Loneliness weighed upon him as he packed a joint of mutton in his woollen bag. He could not stop the tears from falling. All he desired was to be a simple priest. Now, even if he wanted to, he could not creep back into a cloistered life. Someone had polluted the bishop's final days and brought him to a premature, degrading death.

The evening service came, and Eadred participated, but his mind was far from the psalms he sang. He planned to leave the minster shortly before first light and make towards Deerstow, then the Cauldron. He had one true friend, and Tatwine was there.

Eadred looked up, and his eyes met those of Abbot Cuthred. His mouth was also inattentively reciting the holy words. The abbot stared at him. Eadred looked away but was drawn to glance again towards the abbot. Cuthred's eyes had not moved. When the service drew to a close, Eadred watched the abbot gesture to Brother Diuma and whisper to him. The brother nodded briefly and went to leave the church. Eadred watched carefully. Just before he disappeared into the darkness, for the briefest instant, Diuma's head rose, and he looked across to Eadred. He decided not to wait until morning; he would flee within the hour.

In his cell, Eadred secured the knife that Tatwine had given to him at Elmstow. The loud thumping on his door caused him to cry out and break into a shiver. He quickly hid his knife and bag under his bedclothes and asked who it was. Diuma grunted his response.

"Brother Diuma, please sit, if you will." Eadred moved a stool closer to the monk.

"This will not take long. You were seen making a visit to the bishop today, which our abbot did not authorise, and you left the bishop in a distressed state."

"I apologise to the abbot, but the bishop is like a father to me, and I needed to see him and pray for him before his end came. I—"

"This cannot be tolerated. The abbot has decided to relieve you of all your duties, and you will remain in your cell until he decides your punishment. You are to have no contact with the other inmates. Any further disobedience and you will be removed from the priesthood. Is this understood?"

Eadred slumped against the wall. Diuma repeated his question.

"Yes, it is understood," Eadred said with uncharacteristic irritation. "But how is it possible for this minster to serve God if it cannot deliver the sacraments? Other than the bishop and the abbot, I am the only ordained man left in the minster. Who is to perform the sacraments for the community outside of our walls?"

"I will perform your duties from now on, not that it is any business of yours. Some advice for you, do not ask so many questions!" Diuma grunted once more and left.

Eadred waited a short while until all was quiet in the corridor. He took his bag and knife, checked there was no one nearby and hastened to the minster gate. The air was clear and cold, and the light of the moon cast shadows from the bald branches across the path to the river. In his agitated condition, Eadred imagined these were the last sentinels of the minster that he had to pass. Soon, he had left Snailwell behind, and he pushed himself hard and breathless into the night.

There was a limit to how far he could progress without erring and taking a false track. Eadred began to slow his pace and search with greater caution for his route. When an abandoned hut appeared off the side of the path, he decided it was as good a roof as he could hope for and would keep the frost from his back. It would be well past midnight, and his absence would have been discovered. Would Diuma already be on his trail? Fearful that it was possible, Eadred moved away from the hut and chose a narrow clearing further into tree cover and also abstained from a fire.

The discomfort of the open air during the cold, dark hours seeped into Eadred, but he was not fighting misery. There was a purpose in him. Finally, he had made a crucial discovery, and he needed to share it with Tatwine and then the ealdorman. There was no doubt that Abbot Cuthred would unleash his dog, Diuma, to follow Eadred—if he were not already on the scent.

The night was strangely short. Eadred's body and his mind had kept him from rest, not troubled, but quickened from working through what he had been told and what he had seen over the past few weeks. Was his imagination leading him towards the truth, or was it playing tricks? If Tatwine had managed to uncover even a single man connected to the crimes against those living on the vast estates of Forthred and Cerdic, then Eadred might learn where the truth lay.

When the ducks and bitterns heralded the coming of light, he rose, exhausted, but with thoughts of the monstrous crimes that had been committed, and were still being perpetrated, driving him on. Eadred returned to the road and began to run. The future of the kingdom and of the Church of the East Angles rested on the information and ideas he carried in his head.

TWENTY-ONE

The Gates of Hell

It was Tatwine who had taught Eadred how to cover great distances without the aid of a horse. He had stared in disbelief and mocked the hermit monk when he picked a hill or a river bend at the limit of his vision and said they should be able to reach the landmark in half a day. Yet, by steady running, the objective was achieved.

For the year after first meeting Tatwine, Eadred had followed the monk's instruction to improve his strength and resilience so if he found himself again needing to fight for his life, he would be prepared to wield axe and shield. He also practised the monk's style of running to cover vast distances. It was strange for his brothers at Snailwell and for the folk from surrounding villages to see a priest bounding along the pathways, but they became used to this next eccentricity from him.

As darkness approached once more, he was nearing

Deerstow. He had no desire to explain himself to anyone, so when night fell, he crept through the vill and continued by moonlight a way further. The night was freezing, but Eadred's body cried out for rest, and it was close to daybreak when his eyes awoke. After the first hour, he had run off the stiffness in his legs, and he continued, his eyes focussed on discerning the path ahead to the Cauldron.

The deep orange light of the sun, filtered through the smoke of late-afternoon hearths, beamed low in the western sky. Eadred smiled with the knowledge that he recognised the huddle of houses before him. He stopped to regain his breath, watching a couple of children run inside, doubtless to alert parents of a stranger. A few moments later, several men appeared.

"Is it you, Father Eadred?"

"Alfred!" In the time it took for the priest to run to the houses, Elfwyn and Tatwine had joined the gathering of villagers. Everyone was smiling.

Eadred and Tatwine embraced each other, laughing. "You have the look of a man who has run a long way." The monk eyed Eadred's grubby face and boots. "Surely, my eyes are deceiving me?"

"No, my dear friend, I left Snailwell the night before last and am here without horse. These have carried me." Eadred pointed to his feet. The two men would have continued with their banter, but Alfred had a pressing question.

"The bishop has made you our priest?"

Eadred shook his head. "No, Alfred, the decision has not yet been made, but I will serve you for a while, and gladly."

"Then we must feast tonight to welcome you back."

Alfred smiled. "Let me leave you now to reunite your friendship, and I will prepare for this evening."

When they were alone, Tatwine looked at his friend with a sceptical eye. "So you are here once more but without a decision from the bishop?"

Eadred muttered, "It is complicated. I will tell you later."

"I will be glad to hear it," the hermit replied. "And I have a secret to share with you. The sisters, Eadgifu and Eadburga, came with me for their own protection. They left Brihtwold. To hide the truth of their escape from the folk here, I said they were seeking to become postulants at Elmstow. It was only a small sin. I pray that the sisters will not feel the wrath of Lord Forthred for their actions. I daresay that Brihtwold has condemned their escape to anyone who will listen and seeks to avenge himself. He is the most vile of creatures. Eadburga told me of the foul language he used when penances were imposed upon him, and he will assuredly be seeking revenge on her, for she stole a share of his coin. They will be safe here, but there will be a day when they must face justice."

"You made the right decision, my friend," Eadred replied. "They are defenceless. In all the misery that we are witnessing, protecting those women is an act of mercy. We will face Forthred's ire when we need to.

"Good Tatwine, horrific things have been committed at Snailwell. I fear the bishop is being poisoned. He is close to death and beyond any help I could provide. He was unable to speak, but in his own way he told of his terrible fate. And the Abbess of Elmstow was found hanged just beyond the walls of Snailwell! She was the hope of all of us who wanted a better, more caring Church."

Tatwine held his head and wailed. "How can such evil be possible? The two beacons of our Church struck down." He collapsed to his knees. Eadred also knelt.

"And there is more, if that is possible. I heard that at the translation of Saint Wulfmaer to Lord Leofric's new church at Thornham, the body of an executed man was found in his coffin. It was almost installed in the new church! What purpose is served by such an atrocity?"

Tatwine shook his head and groaned. "I have seen this before. If the body of one who has put himself beyond the mercy of our Lord is buried within consecrated ground, then the land is profaned. If the body is not discovered and removed, and the land purified by a solemn ritual, then it becomes a place for devil worship and the calling up of demons. This is devilry, Eadred, done by man but commanded by demons. All of this is far worse than I imagined. Let us keep these dreadful events to ourselves for now, for it is beyond me to understand who is our friend and who is our enemy. I must go and pray now, for we are all in need of protection, and I must walk in the spirit world."

The feast was sombre with the weight that Eadred and Tatwine were carrying. It caused them to empty more cups than their usual practice. Alfred was perplexed that the two friends seemed to find little joy in their reunion. He spoke of the capture of Boisil and how, despite rough treatment, he had refused to name any of his murderous accomplices. The captive had also claimed, even with blood pouring from his mouth, that no one had ordered his activities, that he and his companions were simple outlaws.

The hours passed, and Eadred felt his eyes and legs grow ever heavier. He wanted to share the thoughts that were troubling him about Abbot Cuthred with his soul companion, but there had been more than enough anguish for the day. Tiredness and the maudlin punch of the ale that rolled in the cup before his eyes were also taking their toll. He was not the only one whose speech was slurred, so he bid his hearth companions good night and shortly after fell onto his bed. Evil was at work around the kingdom and within the Church. Eadred hoped the bewildering idea that had come to him was the truth. Tomorrow, he would find out.

*

A tap on his door, probably one of several once Eadred realised it was not a dream, led him to moan aloud that he would meet Tatwine in the village hall as soon as he was ready. This was followed by a belated apology.

A short while later, after breaking his fast with a rapid intake of bread, cheese and ale, Eadred, in the company of Tatwine, Alfred and several other men, went to the hut where Boisil was secured. He sat, bound hand and foot, naked, back against the wall. He had been beaten around the face and doubtless elsewhere, and after a flickering glance to see who had entered the darkened room, his head dropped forward. He was hauled to his feet and his hands tied to overhanging ropes.

"Who is this priest?" The captive's question was met with a blow to the stomach.

"I am from the minster at Snailwell, and I am here to give you one last chance to save your eternal soul before you are maimed and executed."

Boisil looked at Eadred and smiled. "Do not trouble yourself over my soul, priest. It is not your concern."

Eadred stared into the captive's eyes. "You have murdered your own folk; you tried to kill this monk and the women who travelled with him; you led the boy called Coenwulf into a pit of crime, which led to his death; you sacrificed a priest; you have slaughtered your own people's livestock; and you may well have helped murder the daughter of your rightful lord and her husband. Your crimes will bring eternal damnation, with no relief from the pain or misery. Greater misery than men can understand. Yet by true repentance, you will gain a clean execution, and God may still grant you his grace."

Boisil shook his blooded head in mock horror and laughed. "Whatever you call a crime, I call a just sacrifice. Leave me, priest, and let these men do what they have to. I do not fear the end they have devised."

"I know you do not," Eadred replied.

Boisil looked with fleeting surprise at Eadred's certainty, then spoke. "Then that is that."

"Not quite, my friend," Eadred replied. "You have no fear for your soul, and I know why."

Boisil smiled. "Why?"

Eadred continued to stare into Boisil's eyes. "Why would some men, like you and others who have since been killed or executed, not fear a painful death or misery and starvation for their family, if they have any? Certainly not for gold, for it would have no purpose. Could it be for their country?" Eadred shook his head. "I think not, because their actions are harming their own land. Unless, perhaps, they owe allegiance to another kingdom—Mercia—and their hearts burst with the honour of knowing that they are harming us. But I have been told of your lineage and of others who have been caught and executed, and you and they are no more Mercian than am I and certainly have no honour. No, Boisil, you and others like you share one important mark." He stopped speaking and faced away from the captive.

"Pray, tell me. I am interested to know what your mind has contrived." Boisil maintained his smile.

Eadred returned his gaze towards him. "You are all stupid and easily led. I have seen this before. A man seeks out weak-headed criminals, dissatisfied with their lives, easily bought, easily led, who would do his bidding, then go to their deaths without fear and without revealing what they know. But what you were not told is that it is all a lie."

"What is the lie?" Boisil replied in his assured voice, but Eadred could see the disquiet seeping into Boisil's face.

"The man who leads you and your sort told you that the men and beasts you killed, and the priest you buried alive, were blood sacrifices. You do not fear eternal damnation because you do not fear the Lord God. You serve the dark one, and were told by his creature that your murderous actions and silence would gain you an everlasting time of plenty in whatever strange afterlife you imagine. The more blood, the better."

"The spirits I serve work greater magic than your weakling God," Boisil countered.

Eadred shook his head and smiled. "The men and beasts you slaughtered, and the priest you defiled, were never sacrifices. The killings were to destroy the wealth of the great families that stood in the way of a man's greed and lust for power. Tell me, did this servant of these dark spirits perform ceremonies before you and your companions, where animals were slaughtered, strange words spoken and solemn rituals performed? No, I thought not. Beasts left to the wolves are not sacrifices.

"I know you will not confess or give us the names of your accomplices or the man who fed you this lie, at least not now. But in the days to come, I will have his name, and he will be captured. And I tell you, Boisil, he will talk to save his pathetic life. He will give us names and seek to blame them as much as he can. He will leave you to perish in body and soul, and then you will plead for a clean execution with tears in your eyes. That day is not far away, my friend."

"I killed no priest of your God, and I had no hand in the death of Lord Cerdic's daughter. That is all I will say." The captive said no more nor looked at Eadred, but Eadred could see that Boisil was troubled.

*

Eadred, Tatwine and Alfred sat close to the hearth fire in the great hall. Each filled their bowls from a cauldron of thick stew. Two took a cup of ale, and Eadred of wine.

Tatwine spoke first. "Now, my brother in Christ, that was interesting. I am not sure whether to feel fear about this obscure man who persuaded Boisil and others to commit such atrocities or some flicker of relief that we are closer to his capture. Pray, what have you discovered?"

"I am not certain, myself," Eadred replied, "but I will tell you both all I know or believe, and you can tell me where you think I am right, and where I am wrong." Eadred could not help but smile at the memory of when Tatwine and he had sat around a fire and talked about a murder in this way. They were times of wonderful companionship and freedom for his mind. He glanced at the one-eyed monk, and Eadred knew he felt the same. The burden of misery that had oppressed Tatwine the night before seemed to have lifted somewhat, as it had for Eadred. The war within the world of men and in the spirit world was well underway, but Eadred believed that he could at least see the enemy emerging through the vapour.

"If a man does terrible evil but does not give up his secrets, even to save himself from an agonising death or to protect his family, and seems to have no fear of hell, then he does not fear the Lord God. Boisil confirmed his for me. Men such as him, Dudda and Cuthbert have been duped into the service of the devil. The mind who led them into this mire has a corrupted soul. It is my belief that his greed for temporal power has driven him to seek the help of demonic spirits and to engage weak-minded and vulnerable men to do his bidding. For the devil works through men's sinfulness to gain their souls. The greatest lords in our land after our beloved king are Aelfric, Forthred and Cerdic. This wave of crime seeks to destroy the wealth of Forthred and Cerdic and to bring the ealdorman to ruin. A thief would have stolen the herds of cattle, but this man has a different purpose, not senseless killing of beasts, but purposeful destruction of the rich and powerful and the impoverishment of their tenants."

"But you thought the killing of livestock could have been a secretive approach by the Mercians to harm us and to sow discord within our communities," the hermit questioned.

"I did until I discovered that despite the huge numbers of cattle owned by the Church, especially at Snailwell and

Elmstow, which are closer to the Mercian border and have less protection against thieves, these were not attacked. It is a monstrous crime birthed in our own kingdom. I suspect that whoever is behind this wave of death did not expect the two families, which had feuded since before memory, to accept the need for a marriage alliance. He did not know of the wedding, so there was the attempt to create mischief at the wedding feast. That also failed, through stupidity and the quick and courageous action of the Lady Hilda. Dudda, Cuthbert and, I believe, a third man were then ordered to murder Forthred's son, Edmund. That also failed in one sense because Censwith was never meant to die. Perhaps the plan was to kill Edmund when his bride was not with him, or the killers believed that she might even condone the murder. When the heavens opened and threatened the settlements, the killers were forced to act quickly and took their chance when other folk were not there. Censwith had to die because she witnessed her husband's death and may have even fought to save him."

Eadred emptied his cup and filled his mouth with stew. "Now, who is this man? Sadly, I do not yet know, but I think there are some paths that lead to him." He looked into the eager eyes of his two companions and breathed deeply. Up until now, Eadred had walked on fairly solid ground, which his mind had traced and taken many times, but he knew that what he was about to discharge was new, obscure and treacherous.

"There could be two men. One is the hand that gave Boisil and the like their orders, and the other is the mind." Eadred turned to the hermit. "Tatwine, who has the greatest knowledge of the darker beings of the spirit world, not to battle against them, but to petition their power to do evil?"

"Men of the Church who have fallen or who slink in the shadows," Tatwine responded. "Some men enter the Church and learn the rituals of faith and the deeper meaning of holy words and numbers and gain the power that these possess, but also call on other spirits. These men are false in their hearts and seek to control the spirit world for their own purposes. When the Church encourages those who are worldly and powerful to give their lands and gold, they invite such men into the fold."

Eadred nodded. "Yes, and there are too many of them. I know that the bishop has had to expel several junior monks for their involvement in dark magic. He told me that one monk from a remote monastery on the coast saw no difference between the magic of demons and the miracles of Christ and the saints! And remember, when Elmstow was cleansed, we discovered men and women who saw no issue in sitting at the table of the Lord God and of the Evil One and eating whatever they chose from either. There are two other reasons why I think churchmen are involved."

"Our herds have not been attacked?"

"Yes," Eadred replied to Tatwine. "The Church has rich herds, ripe for someone if their aim is to create misery across the kingdom. But while Forthred's and Cerdic's men and beasts have been slaughtered, ours rest peacefully. And there is another reason, and one that I have dreaded telling you." Eadred proceeded to talk openly of the murder of the Abbess of Elmstow and the bishop's belief that he was being poisoned. "I smelt dwale on his breath. It could have been given as medicine, but when I said the word 'poison', he became very agitated. It is clear to me that only a member of the Church at Snailwell could have administered the dwale."

Tatwine and Alfred crossed themselves. "We will avenge him," Alfred swore.

Eadred continued. "Who would poison our beloved Father? Certainly not those who have lived there with him for many years. There are only two who have joined our community recently: the abbot and Brother Diuma. My friends, I am suspicious of Diuma. There is a sense of malice about him. I am not certain whether he was lying or not, but he told me that Abbot Cuthred, who was Abbot of Wexning before coming to Snailwell, brought him from Wexning and wants him to deliver the sacraments to the people."

"Is he ordained?"

"Exactly, my hermit friend, I have asked others, and they do not believe he is. I have not met an ordained monk, and Cuthred, so I hear, was ordained only when he became an abbot. All of our Christian flock know that they see an ordained man to hear their confession and to officiate at Mass. If a grown man does not know this, then—"

"He is not of our faith!"

Eadred shrugged his shoulders. "I believe he may be one of those men who became a monk to learn more of the words and rituals. And I know that the abbot and Diuma visited Deerstow last summer. It was from this time that the attacks on cattle started. But this Diuma is not a clever man. He is not the mind behind these foul acts."

"Then who is?" Alfred asked.

Tatwine seemed hesitant but ventured his question. "Are you saying that the abbot is behind these atrocities?"

"My friend, I do not know, but someone at Snailwell Minster did order the poisoning of Bishop Aethelbert. The Abbess of Elmstow was also murdered close to Snailwell while she was staying there. Yet she also drew the ire of powerful secular men who had used Elmstow as their whoring nest before she turned them out. Her murder could have been ordered by one of them. And we should not forget that Father Ingeld, a priest from Snailwell, was buried alive at Deerstow. Did they all make some diabolical discovery? The man that is conjuring this evil is at Snailwell. My heart does not want to believe that it is the abbot, but my mind is suspicious of him. Remember how Lord Forthred said that knowledge of his son's wedding was kept close to avoid the risk that someone might contrive to stop it? The bishop knew of it and would have performed the ceremony himself but for his failing health. Aethelbert did not tell the abbot of the wedding and sent me. Did the bishop suspect Abbot Cuthred? The abbot was furious when he discovered that I had officiated. What if his anger came from his desire to stop the ceremony, but the bishop's secrecy removed the opportunity? Hence the need to act at the wedding feast."

"But he is a senior churchman! And why would he do all this?" Alfred asked.

Eadred replied, "We know that the devil often works through men's sinfulness—lust, greed, pride, anger, vengeance. A fear of demons might draw men together, but sin divides them. The powers of hell are working here, but their limbs are men." Eadred bent forward, clasping his hands behind his neck, and stretched against the tension in his head and shoulders. "What evil do we face? I see no other path than to go forth and seek out the truth. We need proof to make an accusation, especially if it is against a powerful man, and we have none."

Tatwine put his arm around his friend and hugged him. "Then let us do that. You are God's warrior, and I am with you in the battle, and I will not stop fighting beside you until we have won."

"Nor I," said Alfred. "There can be no peace until this stops, and I owe it to Father Ingeld and my own lord to find the murderers and see them executed."

"What of Elf? We two are unmarried churchmen, but you have a wife and have seen enough trouble," Eadred replied.

"She has grown used to this life of uncertainty and is as brave as I. Whatever I need to do to protect our people, Elf will support me."

"There are three of us," Tatwine smiled, "not one. How should we proceed?"

"You are good friends. I pray to God that we succeed and live. If I am right, the nest of this evil lies in Snailwell Minster, but it may also lie at Deerstow. The feud between Lords Forthred and Cerdic is deep and bloody. If it were only intended that Forthred's son be killed and not Cerdic's daughter, then could Lord Cerdic or his kin have had a hand in the murder of Edmund?"

Alfred became indignant. "No, I cannot believe that our lord is involved in all this misery. His livestock have also been slaughtered, and he has always been a good protector."

"You are right to praise him, but who is to say that there are not those who are kin to him who have long harboured thoughts of revenge?" Eadred replied. "One of us must search further in the estates of the two lords. Another should go to Snailwell Minster to watch the abbot and his so called monk. And it is there that we must look further into the death of the Abbess of Elmstow. It is to Elmstow where the third must go to see if there were deeds there that led to the abbess's murder. What say you?"

"It is a good plan, Eadred. If Snailwell is the seat of this misery, then you, who have a gift for discerning the truth, should return there."

"Ah, Tatwine, I have something more to say, and I am not sure how to say it." Eadred looked at his friend with blank eyes for a while, waiting for the words to form. "I have broken my vow of obedience. I was ordered by the abbot, who is now in charge of the minster, to remain in my cell, and he relieved me of my priestly duties. I chose to escape. If I am caught, my life will be very difficult." In reply to his friend's groan, Eadred continued. "With what I suspect, I had no choice. I also had warnings from the bishop and from a brother whom I respect that my life was in danger if I stayed. My friend, I have no idea where I belong or where this will end."

Tatwine shook his friend by the shoulder. "Dear Eadred, we will triumph over wickedness. It is said truly that the devil and his horde fight the hardest when goodness is closest to victory. The Lord God is with you. I will go to Snailwell. My name is known there, but not my face. I have but one eye, but so do many of our countrymen, through war or ill fortune. You cannot go to Elmstow. The abbot would have sent a rider to alert them of your flight. It would be as bad as returning to Snailwell."

Eadred understood the sense of Tatwine's words but argued that it was pointless for Alfred to worm his way into Elmstow. He had little experience to help him in the minster. Alfred was happy to agree with this. So, despite the risks of the venture, Tatwine was persuaded that Eadred would go to Elmstow and Alfred would search out what more he could from the estates of Forthred and Cerdic. Alfred said he would take Boisil, who had harmed Lord Cerdic's tenants, wealth and honour and deserved to be executed. But Eadred dissuaded him, saying they needed to keep Boisil alive, at least for now, and it was better to keep him bound in the Cauldron.

"My friend, there is something more I would ask of you," Eadred spoke to the hermit. "Do you know of the *Rule of the Master*? The abbot told me that I would gain instruction from reading it, but I have never heard of or seen such a book."

"I have heard of this but, as you, have never set my eyes upon a copy. It is a book containing rules of how a cloistered community should live. All I know of it is that it is more severe than the rules of any house these days. It would fit with the abbot's strict mind."

"Alfred," Eadred continued, "find out, if you will, whether Cerdic had daughters at Elmstow Minster, and if so, whether they were sent from its doors by the abbess."

*

The following morning, the three men met to break their fast, and, as agreed, two of them had altered their appearance. The changes caused some merriment and bewilderment. Tatwine had taken a blade to refresh his tonsured scalp and remove his beard, and he had dressed in a new habit that Elfwyn had miraculously found for him. Eadred laughed that if his friend had two eyes, he would have failed to recognise him. Eadred had also changed his appearance, shaving his head completely and dressing in the breeches and tunic of a peasant farmer. Tatwine spent some time counselling Eadred on how to sound less like a priest and more like his adopted function. Eadred confessed that it would be difficult for him to maintain this deception, for priestly interests and language were what he knew. He prayed that no one would question him closely.

The three men prayed together for God's favour on their work, then hugged each other. They were walking into danger, and their levity soon faded. With only Elfwyn and a few of the other women out of their beds and busy with their tasks to witness them, the trio went their separate ways.

TWENTY-TWO

Tatwine

Many years had passed since Tatwine had last journeyed to Snailwell Minster. It was not as grand as in his memory. He had since spent many years attached to Elmstow. He had taken to living in a cleft near the top of a chalk hill overlooking the minster. Within a short walk from his modest abode, he could come to a clearing through which cut the road from Elmstow to the border with the Kingdom of Mercia. There he would often sit and pray, gazing with wonder over the buildings below. Both minsters had been built within the sturdy bones of buildings contrived during the time when Roman warriors had marched through the island many generations earlier.

Elmstow had grown from a former home to the legions and was a wonder of stone-and-wooden buildings. It had seen repairs by King Athelstan because of its closeness to the Mercian border, and its walls had been strengthened by a great curtain ditch. Before the king had declared it a minster, it had served Romans and East Angles alike as a fortress. Snailwell was different. Although the seat of the bishop, it was less imposing. In ages past, it had perhaps been the home of a wealthy merchant. Its church and several other buildings were of stone, but most were of wood. Though more modest, Snailwell possessed rich lands, cattle, sheep and pigs, fish ponds and mills, the equal of Elmstow.

After a restless night under the stars, Tatwine entered the minster enclave in late morning under the name and mission he had assumed. "Good morning, Brother. I am Brother Paulinus from the monastery at Icanho. I am travelling to Elmstow Minster and humbly ask whether I might rest here for the night."

"Brother Paulinus, you are welcome, of course. I am afraid we are not as organised for guests as we should be. Our blessed Bishop Aethelbert left his earthly life five nights past, and, as dreadful as it is to say, he was poisoned by dwale! Forgive me, I am Felix, not yet a cloistered man, but hoping to become so. Let me take you to the guesthouse. There you can cleanse your limbs of the dirt of your journey, and I can get you some bread and cheese and a cup of ale."

Tatwine crossed himself. "Poisoned! Our poor, beloved bishop. Who would poison a man of God, and one who has already seen so many years? Is there a suspicion on anyone?"

Felix drew closer to Tatwine. "Our abbot has already spoken to us—it is truly alarming. One of our own brothers!"

Tatwine shook his head.

"And one who had achieved great things and had the ear of the ealdorman," Felix continued.

"Pray, no! What is his name?"

"A priest who was the favourite of the bishop, called Eadred. No one can understand it, but he has vanished. He left secretly on the night of the bishop's death. The abbot was reluctant to believe it himself but said there was no other explanation. Why would one of our own steal away in darkness, and break his vow of obedience, unless he had committed a great sin? And listen to this: Father Eadred went to see Bishop Aethelbert, alone, the day of his death. He had been told by Abbot Cuthred that under no circumstance should he visit the bishop unless he was granted permission, and he disobeyed."

"No, this cannot be." Tatwine's mind creased in agony. He knew his friend to be innocent, but Eadred was now blamed for the very crime he had himself unearthed! "The priest you named is of high repute. I have heard of what he did at Elmstow to wipe the place clean of the ungodly. He risked his own life. And the affection between our bishop and he is well-known. The murderer cannot be Father Eadred."

Felix's eyes flared open, he inhaled deeply, and his body gave a little shake from the confusion he confronted. "Those who know him are as surprised as you, but for Eadred's sudden disappearance the night our bishop died. A rider was sent to the king to declare Eadred as an outlaw, but, so we have heard, the king is hesitating, in remembrance of the great deeds Eadred performed for him last year at Elmstow. Thanks be to God! Apparently," Felix whispered, "King Athelstan wants Eadred captured and questioned and will hold anyone who seeks to harm him without a trial as blameworthy, to stand trial themselves for whatever harm comes to him. It is good to have great friends, is it not?

"Now, this is where you can sleep. Come with me to the kitchen, and I will get some food and ale, and I will see when Brother Diuma can see you. He assists the abbot and will want to meet you."

Tatwine nodded and followed the postulant, broaching the name Eadred had given to him and using the words the priest had suggested. "I have heard of a monk, known for his knowledge and wisdom, whom I believe is an inmate here—Brother Anselm. His reputation has reached Icanho. I would be grateful if it were possible to meet him."

"He has just returned from a visit to our abbot's cousin, Lord Leofric, so he may be tired. I believe he assists the thegn with his reading and writing. He goes most weeks. It is best to ask Brother Diuma whether it is possible to meet him. Now, here is some food and ale, and I will see you at our afternoon service."

Tatwine picked over his meal in despair. This had turned far worse than he could have imagined. He had parted from Eadred with his friend facing the likelihood of his removal from priestly orders. Now, Eadred had been accused as a murderer. The demons who had been adjured to harm Eadred were more powerful than Tatwine had imagined. He resolved to pray with more intensity, for this needed all of his faith.

Tears streamed down his face. Tatwine had never sung psalms or prayed with such passion. His dearest friend was in mortal danger. The service ended, and he wiped his face.

"I can see the love of our Saviour in your face, Brother Paulinus."

"Father Abbot, I am overwhelmed to be worshipping in Snailwell Minster."

"I hear that you are journeying to Elmstow Minster. May I know the purpose of your visit?"

"There is a hermit monk who lives nearby. He is known for his prophetic visions, and I have long wanted to spend some hours with him. I am told that, like myself, he has but one eye, and I have wondered whether our Lord God has granted him such a gift to compensate for the loss of his human eye. It is a question I wish to ask of him. My abbot gave me permission to travel and also to visit Snailwell. Although, I have been told of some very sad, very disturbing, events."

"You talk of the murder of our beloved bishop?"

"Yes, Father, and also of the Abbess of Elmstow. What is happening to our Church?"

Abbot Cuthred moaned. "It is sick, and I am afraid that it has been in decline for a while, but it will be remedied. We need a new bishop who is strong in purpose and faith."

"I hear your name mentioned, and, God willing, it will happen and there will be renewal."

The abbot bowed his head. "A word of warning before my duties call me away. I hear that the hermit monk of Elmstow does prophesy words of knowledge, to be sure, but he is also tainted by his friendship with the priest accused of murdering our father bishop, and who is now a fugitive. Do not risk falling under his sway. It would not surprise me if the murdering priest, Eadred, seeks out this monk, or indeed the cloistered sister of Elmstow with whom he fornicated. Be wary, Brother Paulinus.

"And with the evil murder of the abbess, it is my duty to visit Elmstow very soon to ensure that there is no backsliding in standards. I would ask of you to tell the senior sister to expect a visit from me soon. I have not been to Elmstow since last summer, and I will want to meet each of the inmates to satisfy myself of their piety."

"It would be my honour to be useful to you, Father," Tatwine replied. "And thank you for the warning. I too want our beloved Church to be healed and will do my utmost for you. With your leave, I will go now to see your assistant, Brother Diuma, whom I understand wishes to speak to me."

Abbot Cuthred waved an imperious hand. "That will not be necessary. I will tell Diuma that we have spoken and have an understanding. He is often blunt and unreliable in his words and actions and can turn a friend into an enemy. And he is not my assistant. He should not say that."

Tatwine gave an unctuous bow. "Then I am mistaken, Holy Father. I understood that you were training Brother Diuma for ordination."

"That is certainly not the case," Cuthred replied. "He is unsuited and has expressed no such wish, and I do not take kindly to men who try to rise above their station."

The abbot said he had important duties to attend to and suddenly hurried off, clearly not wishing to discuss Diuma any further. Tatwine regretted immediately that he had not taken the opportunity to talk about the death of the Abbess of Elmstow, but he felt as if his head was about to explode with all the information he had gathered in the past few hours. The worst of it was that his friend Eadred was an accused murderer. The priest would, by now, be well on his way to Elmstow, where the accusation against him was bound to be known—the abbot would have made sure of that. But Tatwine had confirmed that Diuma was, at the very least, an uneducated and uninformed monk. But was he also someone who used, and misused, spiritual rituals to call upon demonic forces?

He felt a desperation growing within to warn his friend. Yet he still had tasks ahead of him at Snailwell. Eadred had charged him with talking to Brother Anselm about the abbess's comings and goings and to talk to Brother Diuma. Tatwine had no desire to talk to Diuma and would have happily accepted the abbot's counsel that it was unnecessary, but Eadred felt that the strange monk might divulge important information by accident. Wishing to delay an encounter with Diuma for as long as possible, Tatwine enquired of Anselm's whereabouts and took the walk to the minster's fish ponds, where he had been told Anselm was likely to be found.

It was still a troubling task for Tatwine to introduce himself to Anselm. He may well have shown himself to be a friend to Eadred, but that did not make it any easier for Tatwine to expose himself. The concealment of his true identity was the only advantage he had in this pit of danger, and who was to say that the abbot or his dog, Diuma, had not already corrupted Anselm's mind with the false story that Eadred had murdered the bishop? He would tread with some care, but without the luxury of time, he could not be too cautious.

"Brother Anselm?"

The sprightly monk rose from his task of weeding around the pond edge. He bore an inquisitive smile.

"Indeed, I am. A new brother. Unexpected and how exciting!"

"I am Brother Paulinus, visiting from the monastery at Icanho. I have heard many good things about your wisdom and devotion to our Lord, so am overjoyed to finally meet you."

Anselm smiled and shook his head. "That is very pleasing, but I am sure I am a very ordinary monk. Perhaps there is another Brother Anselm. I am sure there must be, and you are mistaken."

"You are as modest as I have been told. But there can only be one of your name here at Snailwell, so I am sure what I have been told refers to you."

"Well, I am still sure that I do not warrant such praise. Who from Icanho has commended me thus?"

"Not one from Icanho, but one whom you helped and who journeyed on a mission to the Cauldron Folk, returned and then had to leave in haste. One who is distraught at the murder of his beloved bishop."

Anselm looked at the ground and murmured. He stayed thus for a while, his face agitated, then he looked directly at Tatwine. "If this priest were here now, what do you think he would say to me?"

"He would say that he searches still for the truth but is getting closer and that he hopes you will trust me, for I am his friend, and tell me what you know of the death of the Abbess of Elmstow."

Anselm continued to look into Tatwine's single eye. "If you follow the pathway behind the church and turn to the left, you will find three storage huts in a row. Meet me behind the third of them just before evening prayers. There will be torches lit by then. Now, you must go."

Tatwine was returning to the guestroom when he saw a monk on the other side of the courtyard who, from the distinctive harelip he bore, could only be Brother Diuma.

He was alone and heading in the direction of the abbot's reception room. Hopefully, the abbot had yet to speak to his self-styled assistant, so it was now or never. Tatwine's heart raced, not from fear, but from the elation he felt from the mission he was upon. He was used to the perils of spiritual combat, and he sometimes hungered after the hazards of physical battle, but the mental struggle with another man was a recent joy he had discovered through Eadred. Tatwine had, many years ago, embarked upon the life of a hermit, but once in a while he ached for human contact, and what better than with his soul friend when they fought evil? Yet this journey was different. It was the first occasion when he had ventured alone to search for pieces of the riddle. Tatwine shouted out and moved quickly to head Diuma off. He introduced himself.

"I would not want you to cast your eyes upon me and wonder who I was or my purpose here. I met the abbot earlier and explained my mission, and he gave me good advice. He has the bearing of a leader. Our Church is sorely in need of a strong and intelligent man who is pious but also walks easily with men of power."

Diuma remained silent, watching Tatwine's expression with intent. "What office do you hold at Icanho?"

It was not a question or a tone that Tatwine expected. "None, I am a simple monk."

"Are you really? I have heard that you ask many questions."

Tatwine flushed red. "This is my first journey to the bishop's seat. It has held a special place in my heart since I became a monk. I look and talk in wonder and reverence and forget myself. I must seem foolish."

"You do," Diuma replied. "Some advice on your mission to Elmstow. Make sure you remain a simple monk. Ask questions, if you will, about the Scriptures, but not about those who command the minster and conduct its activities. That is not your role. And be careful, the road to Elmstow is dangerous. I would not want anything unpleasant to happen to you. Is that clear?" Diuma spoke with a poisonous stare.

Tatwine had not been spoken to like this since before taking holy orders, and that had ended in a knuckle fight. He was being threatened. The furious anger that in his youth had led to his murdering his best friend, and had taken him into a solitary existence, fired within him, and he clenched his fists.

"Is it clear?" Diuma repeated, sneering and advancing on Tatwine until he stood so close that Tatwine felt the man's words scorch into his face. Tatwine nodded. "The Church is changing," Diuma continued. "It will be run by men of discipline, used to wielding power. Men who will make the Church rich, so its words are heard throughout the kingdom. It would do you well on your journey to Elmstow to consider how you can help achieve this worthy aim. For those who do not feel they are able to support this cleansing, life will become very hard. And I hear you are seeking to talk to Brother Anselm?"

Diuma's face turned dark, so Tatwine trod cautiously. "Only if he is not too tired. I hear that he has just returned from visiting the abbot's cousin, so I understand if he wishes to rest. Brother Anselm is widely known for his piety. I had hoped for the opportunity to pray and talk with him awhile, but if it is not possible, then it is God's will," Tatwine spoke softly, having mastered his anger.

"Indeed, he would be exhausted and may find it impossible to talk to you."

Tatwine continued. "To read and to write are wonderful skills, and teaching is a noble task."

"Lord Leofric seeks improvements for himself and his estate. But to teach is arduous, so I expect Anselm will not be able to meet you. Now, are you familiar with the spirits?"

If it had been anyone other than Diuma asking the question, Tatwine would have broken into a smile, but he controlled himself. "I walk daily in the spirit world with God's Spirit, the saints and all manner of others."

Diuma looked into the distance, seemingly reflecting on his response. "They can be called to help us in our purpose. If you are who you say you are, and ready to help rather than hinder our reforms, then see me on your return journey and we will talk. Remember, I have eyes and ears everywhere—here, in Elmstow, in the deep fens, in the spirit world, everywhere. They know your name. A false step and these days might be your last."

Tatwine had not felt such fear for many a season. He understood well enough the power of the spirit world, for good and for evil. There was a war, which the Lord God was sure to win, but it was to each man whether he partook in God's glory or succumbed to darkness. In Diuma, there could be a man who would exhort the powers of evil to wreak harm on rivals and enemies and to build wealth and power in the world of men. But was the abbot his master? Tatwine harboured some doubts, but he had a more immediate concern. Could he trust Brother Anselm, whom he was to meet within the hour? Someone had alerted Diuma to Tatwine's inquisitiveness: Anselm or Felix. Tatwine felt he had little choice. He had to discover more about the murder of the Abbess of Elmstow and of the poisoning of the bishop, and Eadred had borne witness for Anselm.

At the appointed time, Tatwine found the row of three storage huts, and with hand on knife, he edged from the light of the flaming torches into the shadows.

"I am pleased you decided to come. This is not a place where it is easy to trust anyone," Brother Anselm, who was leaning against the wall, whispered. "I know Eadred would not have murdered our bishop. That Aethelbert should have come to his age and die from poison within his own minster is beyond understanding or grief!"

Tatwine looked at a man arched with worry and decided to speak what was in his mind without inhibition. "Eadred is now an accused murderer, although he does not know of the charge. He is in such danger. I have to find who poisoned the bishop and bring him before a court. And Eadred has charged me with finding more about the terrible murder of the Abbess of Elmstow. He is my friend, and I pray that you may know something that could help me. He has faith in you, Brother Anselm."

Anselm exhaled. "That it has come to this! I will tell you what I know, for I cannot contemplate what might happen to Eadred. As to the bishop's death, the abbot tells us it was poison. I do not know whether to believe him or not for our dear bishop was well loved and had lived beyond his natural span by many years. So why would anyone take to killing him?"

"Eadred suspects Diuma of having a hand in this vile act, and perhaps even the abbot himself."

Anselm rested his hand on Tatwine's shoulder. "The

abbot is a cold and ruthless soul. If he deems a man, or a woman, to be his enemy, then the Lord God help them. I pleaded with Eadred to leave Snailwell when I saw him, for I feared what the abbot could do to him. But, God forgive me, I did not expect his departure to be so sudden or to be used against him in such a foul way. Now, Eadred is accused by Cuthred of murder! But Diuma is different from the abbot.

"I have seen both Cuthred and Diuma together and never with anything but contempt on the abbot's face. The abbot is from a great and noble family. He is well educated and has elegant tastes. He is, without doubt, ambitious and has the skill to achieve his aims. Diuma, I think, also has ambitions, but not the mind to achieve them. He is a brute, and some may fear him because his appearance scares them, but I doubt that he is a murderer. I have seen him terrify brothers by flaring his nostrils, baring his teeth and hurling abuse. I have watched him since his arrival here. He is jealous of rich and powerful men, jealous of their minds. He is only an animal. He came from the abbey at Wexning, on the eastern side of the deep fen. I believe that is the land where his family comes from. It would not surprise me if his violence has something to do with raising them up. His attempts to gain higher positions by calling himself the abbot's deputy, or some such word, are laughable. His intentions and his abilities are small, but those of Abbot Cuthred, I fear, are vast. It is not Diuma but the abbot you need to stalk and trap, then this evil may be stopped.

"As for the abbess," Anselm continued, "I did not see her leave Snailwell myself on the morning of her death. I know that she rode alone to spend time with the Lord God, as was her custom—and many knew of it. The only other help I can give is that I and many brothers heard raised words between her and the abbot, but I have no knowledge of what. That is all I know, my friend. Now, it would be wise for us to leave here before we are seen, and I must rest awhile. My mind and limbs grow heavy."

"Thank you, Brother Anselm, for the great risks you have taken for Eadred. I understand that you would be tired from your efforts to teach the abbot's cousin the blessings of reading and writing."

"Ah yes," Anselm smiled, "the thegn Leofric struggles but is an attentive and serious-minded pupil, and Cuthred has instructed me to do my best. It makes me useful to the abbot, which is a good thing these troubled days. Where you see a simple faith, a warrior heart and a contentment with life, as it is in Lord Leofric, you see arrogance, guile and ambition in his cousin. Now, give my blessings to Eadred. I pray that he is in a safe place, far from danger. Is he well hidden?"

Tatwine shook his head. "I wish he were so. He is on his way to Elmstow, but he is at least clothed as a peasant, and with his head shorn and face unshaven."

Anselm sighed. "Well then, may the Lord God protect him from his foolishness!"

*

Tatwine's night was unsettled. He attended each of the services, watching the abbot and Diuma closely. Neither even glanced at each other nor at him. Everything appeared as it should. There was no sleep, though, for him. Brother

Anselm's words were troubling but also strangely exciting. Tatwine had come to Snailwell believing, as did Eadred, that the abbot and Diuma were tied in a monstrous crime. It was true that the abbot had stopped at nothing thus far, in the world of men and in the spirit domain, to further his ambitions. But Brother Anselm had put a new thought in Tatwine's head about Diuma. He was a violent but stupid man, with a different and far more limited purpose than possessed the abbot. It had reinforced to Tatwine that Abbot Cuthred had to be stopped. He had the bishop's and the abbess's blood on his hands but was clever enough to keep himself at a distance from the crimes. Tatwine had persuaded the abbot that he was an ally, and this could bear fruit in the future. He was keen to tell Eadred of his discoveries, but had he found proof of the abbot's involvement? In truth, he did not know. It would be for Eadred's intricate mind to see if there was some key in what Tatwine had learnt that would unlock another door.

The following morning, after breaking his fast, Tatwine left Snailwell, armed with a stout staff and his knife, and set off for the Cauldron.

TWENTY-THREE

Elmstow

He could feel his heart thumping, not through exertion, as the pace was gentle and the goat he had bought was surprisingly compliant, not needing to be coaxed or pulled along. It was excitement. Not much further and Eadred would reach the summit of the low chalk hill and look down once more upon the minster at Elmstow. It was where his life had changed. And there it was.

He sat upon a fallen tree trunk, happy to take in the view and to collect his thoughts. He had travelled slowly, spending three nights sleeping in the woods to allow the hair upon his face to grow, as Tatwine had suggested. The goat, which he had bought two days earlier, browsed cheerfully nearby. The minster seemed even more majestic than when his eyes had first seen the collection of stone-and-wooden buildings just over a year earlier. The heart of the minster was its church. It had started its life as a temple to the deities of the Roman legions. Bishop Aethelbert, in the company of the king and queen, the nobles of the land and a throng of the clergy and cloistered men and women, cleansed the building of its demons and consecrated it to the service of the One True God. Now, through the smoked rays of the morning sun, its walls shone like gold. Another stone-walled and thatched building stood on the other side of the courtyard from the church. Once the barracks of the army of Rome, it now contained the dormitory and cells for the abbess and the inmates. The other buildings—for communal activities, for cooking, for the sick, for guests, for the few remaining slaves who had not been freed by the abbess, for storage and butchering of beasts—were largely of wood and cramped within the encircling walls. Beyond the ramparts, the burgeoning settlement, the farms, fertile meadows and fields, fish ponds, woods, the fast-flowing river and its mills told of a prosperous community.

The cloistered women who had proven themselves delinquent had long since departed the minster, pushed through the door by the new abbess. They were, almost all, the daughters of powerful men, unfamiliar and unamused by the actions of a forceful woman who wielded such authority. They would have all taken offence, but would any have gone so far as to murder the abbess?

This was one of the thoughts preoccupying Eadred as he descended the hill towards the minster. Another, and the most prominent, now the difficulty of his mission stood squarely before his eyes, was the adequacy of his disguise. The removal of close to half of the former female inmates and the death of the few priests during the Mercian attack had reduced the number of souls who might recognise his face, but there were still several handfuls of nuns who might remember, and one especially, although she would not betray him. But what Eadred hoped might weigh the scales in his favour was the increased sturdiness of his body, his broader shoulders and chest and muscled arms and thighs. These, at least, gave him the appearance of a hardworking farmer.

Eadred prayed silently as he passed through the minster gates with his soiled face lowered that his changed frame, attire and features would be enough to maintain his secrecy. The goat seemed happy with its role and wandered peacefully behind him. Only one person would be willing to help him, and he had to find her. It was almost the hour for the midday service, and, through habit, Eadred found his pace quickening towards the minster church, only to remember that he was now a farmer. A solid, high wooden wall also barred his way. Then he recalled something that Tatwine had said. The abbess, in her reforms, had built the barrier to keep guests and the minster's workers away from the cloistered women, as far as possible. The gate was locked. Eadred would need to find a way into the central enclosure. He noticed several carts standing not far away which could serve his purpose, and when darkness fell, he would make his attempt. For now, he would go into the minster's fields and see what information he could glean from those working there.

*

No light from the moon or stars could penetrate the lid of motionless clouds that pressed down upon the minster. A few torches had been lit earlier, and these stood in pottery containers within the minster walls. Eadred saw how these failed to reveal the full contour of the barrier and left sections of darkness and shadow. The midnight service would have begun within the church, and on Eadred's side of the barricade no one stirred. He had watched a shadowed length of the wall for some time, knowing that a cart rested there in the gloom. Earlier, Eadred had placed a barrel on the cart, and the time to take his chance was upon him.

In an instant, he was past the cone of light from a torch and onto the cart, then onto the barrel. The extra strength he had developed in his arms was sufficient to haul him up and over the top of the wall. The base on the other side was unlit. Whether it was a clear drop or onto something unpleasant or noisy was a mystery. Eadred hung by his fingers for a few seconds, but he had no option. He let go.

He landed with a thud and a subdued groan, but at least he had landed on a clear patch of earth. He took a few moments to settle his eyes. Slivers of light emerged to his left and right. He edged forward with his hand outstretched until it touched wood. He was behind a small building, probably a storehouse. He needed to find the church. So he felt for the wood and found his way around the hut and into a passageway. Eadred was quickly some distance from where he had landed after scaling the wall.

Eadred's memory began to do its work. He turned left then right and came to the edge of the central courtyard opposite the entrance to the minster church. He could hear the chanting within the building, so he had time to position himself. The usual practice at the end of the service was for the cloistered sisters to follow the abbess or senior nun in single file across the courtyard to the dormitory door, in order of seniority. The novitiates and postulants brought up the rear. Edith had been accepted as a novitiate during the preceding year, but if any postulants had sought entry to holy orders, then they would walk behind Edith. Eadred prayed that there were none.

Several torches lit the way from the church to the dormitory, and he positioned himself in the shadows just around the corner from the doorway through which the holy sisters would emerge. There was a single torch set in the church wall some distance behind him, and this was nearing the end of its life. Eadred had already checked to see that it cast no shadow that might alert the procession of his presence. The singing stopped, and, with his heart thumping in anticipation, Eadred waited for the door to open. It was not a long wait.

The door creaked, and soft candlelight bathed the back of the senior nun as she stepped into the courtyard. At a respectful distance, the line of cloistered sisters followed. Eadred had resolved to watch them, to see where in the line Edith walked and then to wait until the three o'clock morning service. Once the sisters repeated their journey to the dormitory, he would act, for once they were within the dormitory, the door would be locked and Edith would remain in the company of her fellow sisters in Christ, beyond contact until daylight was near.

Eadred counted sixteen figures passing through the church door, and he was certain that Edith was not one of them. From his position, he could see each face, although partly shadowed. He could never forget the profile of her face or her willowy form. Surely, there would not be many more in the congregation. God willing, she would be the last to leave the church. And there she was!

He stifled a gasp. How could any face be that delicate or any expression so full of grace? Eadred had imagined Edith every day since he had last seen her. He had remembered every minute they had spent together, and though it was a sin, he had relived those blissful moments when they had caressed each other's nakedness and brought each other to earthly rapture. But the reality of her presence, so close to him now, was more intoxicating than any memory. She was the last to walk out into the courtyard, and did her step falter momentarily? Could she have heard his breathing? Eadred had devised a plan to catch her attention, but something so slight in its movement that no one else would discern his presence. As he thought over his intention, he realised how unlikely it was to succeed. Yet he had no alternative. He watched Edith disappear, and, awash with fears about what would happen following the next service, he drew his cloak around his shoulders and prepared to wait out the cold hours of night. The scraping sound against the stone wall of the church behind him was the last thing Eadred expected. He spun around.

A figure had just emerged from around the back wall of the church and came running at Eadred. He saw the flash of a blade. He ripped away his cloak and threw it at his assailant. It did enough to mask Eadred's movements for an instant. Enough time to avoid the downward thrust of a knife and for Eadred to draw his own.

Eadred had not had to face a man intent on his death since the horrors of Elmstow, and the worst of those memories flashed in his mind's eye. The man facing him was taller, but as far as Eadred could see, he was of a slighter frame.

"You are Eadred the priest?"

"You seem to think that I am. Who asks?"

"It is you—cloaked as another to deceive those around you. Do not concern yourself with my name. You will die at my hand now."

"I will not be that easy to overcome. I have fought many men who have tried to separate me from my life—murderers and warriors—and they are the ones who lie dead. You will have to work hard tonight to earn your gold, but it will be beyond you." They were difficult words for Eadred to say. He had known men who blustered and swaggered, and he was as different from them as it was possible for a man to be. For some, it was who they were—proud of their name, strength and skill, eager for glory and arrogant. For others, it was an ephemeral mask, hiding their want of courage. And for others, it was a weapon, designed to instil fear. Eadred could not dwell on why he had said such words; it was enough that his friend Tatwine, who had more courage than anyone Eadred had ever known, had said that he should.

"You are a priest, Eadred, not a warrior," the hermit had said, "and if a man threatens your life, it is natural that you will feel fear. The Lord God will seek to keep you from harm if you are doing his work, but he expects you to use your own mind and body to protect yourself, for that is why they were given to you. When you are a priest, dress, speak and behave as one, for this is expected. But when you need to fight with a blade, then put aside your priestly bearing and become as a warrior. If a man seeks to take your life, then use words, not to bring him to a better Christian life, but to put fear and terror in his heart. Give him one chance to sheathe his blade. If he backs away from the fight, then no blood is lost."

The assailant was not to be dissuaded. "You are a follower of demons and a murderer. The fires of hell await you. Whatever happens to me now, I am destined to dwell with my Heavenly Father." And with that, he flew at Eadred.

The unexpected strike sent Eadred tumbling backwards, winded, his knife knocked from his grip. In panic, he thrashed around, trying to grab the hands of the man who pinned him to the ground. The point of the blade pierced Eadred's thigh. He groaned but clutched the man's wrist, struggling against the attempts to bring the knife higher on his body and then deeper into his flesh. Eadred sensed that he could hold the blade from inflicting further damage, but his other hand failed to find his own knife. Tatwine had taught him a move that needed no weapon, an attack that had already inflicted terrible damage on the one-eyed hermit. Eadred needed it now to save his life.

Eadred dug his finger into his attacker's eye socket with immediate effect. The man cried out with sudden pain, pulling his head back, but Eadred's determined hand followed, and his finger reached and dug deeper. He snatched the knife from his assailant's trembling hand and thrust the blade into his chest. Eadred's other hand covered the man's mouth until the risk of his crying out had ebbed. He prayed that no one had heard the sounds of struggle.

It had been a surprisingly quick encounter. The figure's breathing was slight and erratic, but the opportunity of discovering who the man was still presented itself. Then, in the dull light issued by the solitary torch in the church wall,

Eadred recoiled in confusion. The man's head was tonsured. He was in holy orders! Little wonder that he was slight of build and easily overcome. If it had not been for Tatwine's urging that Eadred strengthen his own frame, then he would have been of a similar build and the outcome of the struggle far less certain. The man was young, fresh-faced and close to death. His eyes flickered.

Eadred gently rubbed the monk's forehead. "While you can hear me, I swear to you that I am no demon-worshipper or murderer. I have enemies within the Church and beyond, and they are doubtless spreading rumours so men can kill me without penalty. Whom am I supposed to have murdered? Who said such a calumny?"

The dying monk gasped and whispered. "Our beloved bishop, by poison. The abbot told us. Tell me the truth. Are you innocent of the charge?"

Eadred's head dropped. "He is dead, and I am charged? He was like a father to me. The charge is contrived. If I lie, may God strike me down now! For taking your life, forgive me. I did not know who attacked me. If I had known you were a companion brother in Christ, I would have spoken differently to you, and I would have done anything to avoid a fight." Eadred's cheeks ran with his tears. "Please let me know your name so I may pray for you, and I beg that you forgive me."

"Then I have been misused and forgive you." The monk let out a wretched sob and gave up his soul.

Eadred would have howled if anywhere else, but he shook silently and wept. The kingdom would believe that he had just committed another murder. He was as good as dead, but he swore that somehow Abbot Cuthred would

241

face justice for the death of this young monk. For now, all he could do was drag the monk into the shadows, where he found a half-empty storehouse in which to hide the body. There, he prayed for the young monk's soul. His words were not stale or spoken quickly, but wrung from the heart. Eadred had killed men before, here in the battle at Elmstow a twelvemonth earlier. As with the young monk, they had attacked him and he had responded. Why then, Eadred asked himself, did he feel such remorse for killing the young monk? If Eadred had told his attacker at the outset that he was innocent, it would probably not have altered the outcome. It was simply a pointless death of one who had believed a lie told by his superior and had taken up his clumsy blade with zeal in the belief that he was serving God.

TWENTY-FOUR

Edith

The soft waves of chanting voices stopped, and there was silence. The short service, held at three in the morning, had ended. Eadred positioned himself, as before, just around the corner from the front of the church. The door creaked, and the cloistered sisters proceeded across the courtyard. There were some muted groans in the chilled air and yawns from those desperate for the warmth of their beds. Eadred was ready. He counted each of the figures as they stepped from the church. Edith should have been next—the last to leave. She did not appear. Eadred's tension almost caused him to sigh aloud. Then, after a few moments, she appeared and turned to close the church door. This was Eadred's opportunity.

He had clasped in his hand the small crucifix and chain that Edith had given him when they met last, a year earlier. Eadred cast it towards her feet. It hit her cloak and fell with the faintest ring. She looked down, stooped and took up the object in her hand.

"Hurry along, Edith," the sister in front of her called. Edith responded by breaking into a gentle run. Once the sisters were within the dormitory building, the door was closed, and Eadred remained outside and alone. His hope was that Edith would recognise the object and seek him out later that night. He crouched against the church wall and waited. His hands and feet, which had lost their warmth while he was praying for the nameless monk, began to throb, and his body ached. The wild exhilaration he had felt when seeing Elmstow that morning seemed now to have happened months ago, and gloom had spread within his mind. Eadred's life until a year ago had barely known anything but routine or gentle undulations, but now he seemed to swing chaotically from peaks of joy to shadowed voids. He wondered in his quiet moments who he was. Whether there were some deep roots within him that would not change or whether he was a block of clay to be moulded by circumstance. He had been made by his God, but did that mean he was like a statue, or did God have a journey and a destination for this obscure priest's life? Whatever was in God's mind, it was deeply troubling for Eadred, for it meant that his faith could not be a gentle voyage through known waters, but one set for storms and battles in far-off places.

The creak of the dormitory door set Eadred's heart racing. The torches had all but died, leaving, at most, some glowing cinders. He stared across the courtyard to a figure carrying a shrouded candle. His mind told him to be cautious, but his heart had already won the battle.

"Edith, is it you? It is Eadred."

"Where are you?" came the response.

Then she was standing before him, although all he could see was the outline of her face. He took her free hand and kissed it. The nun did likewise with his.

"Come, dear Eadred, we must find a safe place." She led Eadred through the darkness to a hut where farming equipment was stored. Inside, she lit another candle.

"I did not murder our bishop, Edith." The misery of his position and the joy of once more being with the woman he loved overcame him. He fell into the nun's embrace and wept. She also shook with her weeping. "And, my dearest—" Eadred's words disintegrated into meaningless sounds, and he groaned with the agony of what he had to tell Edith. "I have tonight killed an innocent brother in Christ who believed the lie he had been told and tried to kill me to avenge the bishop. He attacked me here, in the minster, and I defended myself against his blade. His body lies in a storehouse nearby. I am a wretched man."

Edith looked into his eyes. "The sin is not yours, Eadred. It belongs to whoever murdered Bishop Aethelbert and seeks to blame you. You told me when we were last together that your gift will bring you powerful enemies. Here is the truth of those words. There are men who will risk their own souls to gain their desires, who will commit unspeakable crimes. My dearest Eadred, I fear for you. Every day we have been apart, I have prayed that God will keep you safe. You have powerful enemies."

"I know who it is, dear Edith." Then Eadred looked into the deep beauty and care in the nun's face and managed a smile. It was returned. He wanted to forget the dangers that pressed on him and let the joy that was bursting within him live again. For months, he had struggled to suppress the image and the memories of the woman standing in front of him, but now, with his life falling apart, it seemed a pointless effort. If physical passion was birthed from affection, care and deep connection of minds and hearts, then to call it fornication was a crude, deceptive word and should not deter consummation of their love. Eadred hoped beyond hope that Edith felt the same.

"My dearest Eadred, I tell you the truth that I love you more than any man alive, and not a day goes by when I do not remember those sweet moments we shared in passion a year past. If I let my mind now take its natural course, it would be overwhelmed with the feelings I have for you, and my body would be yours. But this is not the time. I know that if we give way to our carnal feelings now, your enemies would profit. This has come to me in prayer, Eadred. I do not say that we will not melt together as one ever again, but let us wait, dear priest."

Eadred searched his beloved's eyes, but there was not one chink of weakness. He nodded with sadness and they sat side by side with their cloaks wrapped over them. "My enemies knew somehow that I would come to Elmstow. And when they find the poor monk's body!" He shook his head. "They will harm you to find me."

"They have been watching me anyway. I did not know of it until recently. The abbess has been protecting me. Several men have come this past year to misuse me—powerful men—but the abbess stopped them all, despite threats against her. Some of them had defiled me in the past, when I was a postulant here under the former abbess, when this place was a whoring nest."

"Did she give you names?"

"No, but only a week or so before our abbess was murdered, I saw two of them here in the minster. I dared not venture too close. One shouted the foulest words at our abbess and drew his sword, but she crossed herself and shook her stave and did not take one step backwards. The abbess said they demanded information about you, whether you had been allowed to see me. She said she gave no answer. The man who drew his sword had a misshapen face. He had a harelip."

"Ah, Diuma! Do you remember anything about the other?"

Edith continued. "He had a sense of arrogance about him, as would a thegn or warrior, and was finely dressed. He even pushed the abbess with his hand several times, but she brushed it away. The man with the harelip seemed to owe obedience to him. That is all I remember. My face was so drawn by the deformity of one man that I did not notice much of the other. But it was the one who was vane who wanted me. He offered gold in abundance, but the abbess refused.

"But wait, I do remember something more. He wore a striking medallion of gold upon a chain around his neck."

"Abbot Cuthred!" Eadred exclaimed. "He wears it proudly, usually alongside his pectoral cross. But he would not have come dressed in his religious garb, not if he were aiming to spend his visit whoring. Someone murdered the abbess, and it is becoming clear that it was because she had shut the door to the debauched and powerful men who had grown familiar with using God's house for their enjoyment.

"My dearest," Eadred continued, "now the abbess and

the bishop are dead, you are in the gravest danger. Come with me. I know of a place of safety, where the people have good hearts. It is deep in the fenland and called the Cauldron by the local folk."

Edith looked desolate. "Oh, Eadred, I cannot. There are other women here who are in as much danger. I cannot leave them." Eadred began to protest. Edith placed her finger on his lips. "I will be safe. Go now, my darling. Find the ealdorman." Eadred knew she was not going to change her mind.

"The crucifix you gave me when we parted last year, and which I threw to gain your attention, it has been with me ever since. It is a treasure and a reminder of our love. Could I have it? It is as powerful to me as a holy relic."

"I left it in my bed. I do not think I dare fetch it now. But here, take this." Edith felt for the pocket in her tunic. "It is my comb. See, it is beautiful, well crafted and with a design of vines woven into it. I thought I had lost it, but there was a miracle and I found it again."

"It is indeed a wonderful thing, but I do not want you to be without it," Eadred replied.

"I have another, which a beloved sister gave me and which I use to show my gratitude to her. This one I carry for its beauty. Here, take it with my love." Edith kissed the object, and Eadred took it.

A few minutes later, he stood with Edith over the body of the dead monk. She moved her candle across his face.

"He is not from Elmstow. We are still a community of nuns, with but two new priests. Now you must go!"

Eadred watched Edith use her feet to scuff the earth from where the nameless monk had met his end to where he had been dragged into the storehouse. After a final tearful embrace, Eadred watched her make her way back to the dormitory and prayed that no one would be woken by her movements. Then he found a path to the door in the inner wall, raised the latch and was soon beyond the outer gate. It would be a few hours yet before sunlight welcomed the new day.

*

Eadred's progress was slow until the way ahead began to emerge as darkness gave way to daylight. There was only one place in the kingdom where he would feel safe, and it was at the Cauldron, where he would also meet Tatwine and Alfred once more. For much of the day, Eadred managed to maintain a steady run, in the manner that Tatwine had taught him, broken by periods of rest, and he hoped that he would find the settlement of Deerstow by nightfall. It was not to be, and when it became too dark to continue safely, he diverted himself from the pathway and found a small patch of flat ground, where he covered himself in what dry sedge he could gather.

This was not the only hope that was dashed. Eadred lay, cold and shivering. The course of his life since his triumph a year earlier at Elmstow had proven not only to be empty, but a curse. He sighed at his simple-minded expectation that an apparent gift from the Lord God would bring him worldly affirmation and some measure of happiness. If it had brought these, they had been transient. He lay, disguised and lonely, hunted as the murderer of the head of the Church, a man he loved. Every man and woman in holy orders, other than Tatwine, Anselm and Edith, would be praying for his capture and death. God did not promise his followers an easy life, but he surely would not abandon them to the desolation of the devil. Even his reunion with Edith now seemed hollow. Eadred had hoped she would be eager to join him, but not so. He fingered the comb she had given him. It had an unexpected warmth about it on such a freezing night. He was holding it when sleep finally released him.

His whole body ached when he tried to rise the next morning. He had slept further into the day than he had expected, and a smear of light already was giving form to the trees around him. He had prayed much during the night that his faith would be restored, and though he could not comprehend what was happening to him, Eadred begged the Lord God to continue to protect and guide him.

Less than an hour later, Eadred recognised the road that led into Deerstow. The village was surrounded by waterlogged meadows and fen, making it impossible to skirt the settlement quickly and then reach the Cauldron by nightfall. He had no option but to take the path. Eadred had spoken to many of the inhabitants not long past, but his appearance and speech had changed, hopefully sufficiently. It was cheering to Eadred to practice Tatwine's advice that he try to adopt the identity of a farmer; it reminded him of his youth, before he had entertained thoughts of taking holy orders. It was a warm memory and provided Eadred with some lightness of heart. If he could move past the houses without much contact with their inhabitants, then he could push on at pace.

Eadred passed the church at the edge of the village and continued on close to Lord Forthred's great hall, the houses, huts and the pens for the pigs and chickens. The smith's hammer rang out as he fashioned or repaired a blade. The day had drawn others to their labours. Eadred heard voices coming from inside the houses, but apart from a few children playing or carrying eggs or wood for the fires, the scene was quiet, and thankfully he encountered few others.

Eadred neared a section of the road where the remains of a ruined building lay some way off to the left. He was familiar with the burnt wreckage and the small cross planted at its centre from his earlier visits. It signalled that he was nearing a bend in the path and then he would be free of Deerstow.

"The church caught fire last winter." The voice startled Eadred. An old man, bent and supported by a stave, sat on a fallen tree trunk on the other side of the road.

"Good morning to you," Eadred responded. "I had thought that this was where some poor soul died and was buried when their home caught afire, but this was your church?"

"It was, young man, and the ruin just over there was our lord's hall. It caught alight and embers set the church off. God be praised that we had no other damage."

"And the church at the other end of the village?" Eadred was perplexed.

"It is grand, is it not? Built last summer, as was the new great hall."

Eadred's brow creased, and he looked back to the ruin. He knew this was important, but he was not quite sure why.

The old man mumbled as he sifted through his memory. "Your voice is familiar. Have you been here before, not long back?"

"I have been this way once or twice over the past year. My home is in the Cauldron, and I return from a visit to Saint Wulfmaer's shrine. My lord granted me permission to travel." While the old peasant mumbled and nodded, seemingly accepting the explanation, Eadred's mind cleared. "It is a fine new home for God. I daresay that your lord granted his best land?"

"It is passable land if cared for," the old man replied. "It used to be farmed by an honest man and his wife. Sad to tell, he lost the use of his eyes, she lost her mind, and they both passed into God's hands. The son struggled with farming; he did not have the wits or the intent and soon failed to render Lord Forthred his customary share. So when land was needed for a new church, cemetery and hall, our lord took the land and gave the son some disagreeable plot. No one much liked the boy anyway, so we were all pleased the earth was granted to God's glory—that he might bring us good days."

Eadred gave a sage nod. "I remember seeing the son, I think—a face of warts, growths and lumps—and hearing that he was keen on other men's wives. What was his name?"

The old man groaned. "Brihtwold, a man of few friends, if any, and that is not the end of it. Now, his wife and her sister have disappeared. No one knows the reason. Our lord questioned him about their absence, but Brihtwold swore that when he awoke on a new day, they had gone. God forbid that there has been some violence; we have seen enough of that these past days. But if they left willingly, then they left without our lord's permission and will have to face his anger when caught."

Eadred wished the old man God's blessing before setting foot once more on the road.

"You remind me of someone I saw some time back. I feel as though I have spoken to you before."

Eadred dismissed the idea and hurried off, soon breaking into a gentle run. He knew the way now, and this awareness freed his mind to think over what he had just stumbled across. He dug from his memory deeds he had been told about, where and when they had occurred, who had told him and whom they involved. Some strands of the truth began to emerge, and Eadred understood their importance.

The church in which Eadred had married the murdered couple was not the church the bishop had built years earlier. How had he missed this until now? He remembered the bishop telling him that he had the church at Deerstow built and consecrated many years back, but Aethelbert had also said that Abbot Cuthred had recently consecrated the church. Eadred had let the apparent contradiction pass at the time, and all he could imagine now was that he had supposed the bishop had been confused. Yet Abbot Cuthred had also told Eadred that he had consecrated the church at Deerstow the last summer. Whatever the reason for Eadred's lapse, it was a mistake with serious consequences.

TWENTY-FIVE

A Troubled Reunion

Eadred stole a glance at Elf, whose blue eyes gazed at her husband with more love and admiration than he had ever seen in a woman's face, even more than from his own dear Edith. The priest had earlier witnessed Alfred embrace his wife with his eyes sparkling and with a shower of kisses that made her gasp. Eadred smiled at such open affection. God knew that he needed some solace. Eadred, Tatwine, Alfred and Elfwyn sat around a blazing fire. Their stomachs were full, an excess of ale and wine had taken the edge off some of their misery, but the gloom of Eadred's plight would not be easily assuaged.

Tatwine had already spoken of his time at Snailwell Minster. The death of Bishop Aethelbert and the accusation by the abbot that Eadred had poisoned him overshadowed everything. Eadred sat silently, head bowed. Alfred then told of his experience at Deerstow and its neighbouring vills.

Although the distance between the Cauldron and Deerstow was but a day's walk in fair weather, Alfred's face was unfamiliar to most of the folk who lived there. Fortunately, he had come upon a farmer he did know, who had bought some of the famed Cauldron cattle, and Alfred had been invited to stay with him for three nights. It proved to be a productive arrangement, as the evenings had been convivial and informative.

The murder of his only child by two of his own kindred, so the farmer told Alfred, seemed to have changed Forthred's nature, at least for now. The hot temper and rabid acquisitiveness for which he had been known were no longer evident, although Forthred was not often seen these days. There was a wasted look to his expression when he emerged from his house, as if he were a base slave freezing through winter's agony with no hope of better days. Alfred also happened to be in Deerstow on the last day of a peace mission sent from Lord Cerdic. As well as bestowing three oxen, the mission gifted a delicately illustrated psalter for use in the lord's church. The mission had been led by one of Cerdic's sons, had stayed several nights and the bond between the two former antagonists appeared to have been strengthened.

Yet the real pearl that Alfred had discovered involved Cerdic's wife. Alfred continued. "The Lady Hilda told her husband her secret, and he shared it with his closest hearth companions, beaming with admiration for his peace-weaving wife. When it seemed that the two families were about to fall into deadly conflict at her daughter's wedding feast, she took the courageous decision to appear to stumble into the fire. The sight of the great lady screaming in pain caused the conflicting warriors to withdraw. If she had not put herself in great danger, then the age-old feud would have broken out once more."

"It is true," Eadred said. "I had no hope of quenching the hatred. The lady deserves her great reputation."

Alfred lowered his voice. "I also discovered that one of Lord Cerdic's daughters was expelled from Elmstow Minster by the abbess, and it was none other than Lady Censwith! From what I could glean from those who would talk, Lord Cerdic and Lady Hilda were furious at their daughter, for she was a wayward girl, but they bore no animosity towards the abbess. Yet I did hear a whisper that Lord Cerdic ranted that the action was unjust, given the endowments he had made to enrich the minster. But I swear on the Holy Book, Lord Cerdic would not murder a man or woman who served the Lord God."

"You have done well to unearth so much," Eadred replied, "and to share your knowledge honestly. Lord Cerdic is no Forthred, but we cannot ignore any part of what you have learnt, no matter what pain it may cause us."

"Now, Eadred," Alfred returned his cup to the ground, "we have been patient and told you of our journeys, as you asked. Come, we are keen to hear what you discovered. I know that the false charge against you is a crime, but the king himself has refused to proclaim that you are an outlaw. He is the closest of our kingdom to the Lord God. Take heart from that, my friend. What I have learnt most in the short time I have known you is that your mind can see into the shadows of a crime. Is that not a great gift and a great purpose? Think of this torrent of crime that has almost broken our land. You may be the only person who can stop it." Alfred went to say more, but his wife placed her fingers across his lips. Then she moved around to Eadred and wrapped her arms around him. Startled, he looked up to see Elf's loving eyes embracing his misery.

"Forgive us if we seem to expect so much from you. We are wrong to do that, and you are also wrong to expect so much of yourself. You are a wonderful man and priest, Father Eadred. We will not put burdens upon you. Just know that you are loved by your Saviour and are amongst friends." Her smile spoke more than words, and Eadred returned it. He nodded, coughed several times and spoke.

"Forgive me, my dear friends. I did want to listen carefully to your words, to see if the stories they weaved, and my own, created a picture that will lead us closer to the truth. This was our hope when we departed on our separate searches. So let us fill our cups and let me meander awhile.

"I came upon two things that help our cause, although one of them especially troubles me. Firstly, I discovered that the land in which Father Ingeld had been buried alive was not a cemetery when he was murdered. It was farmland at the edge of Deerstow. The old church burned down last winter. The new one was built and its cemetery consecrated last summer. Blessed Father Ingeld's body had already been buried there. Thus his brutal murder took place away from prying eyes—on land farmed by Brihtwold of Deerstow. When I visited Brihtwold before I left Deerstow for the Cauldron on my first journey, he was not there, but the sisters Eadgifu and Eadburga were. My eyes fell upon a sizeable bag of silver pennies that was partly hidden from sight. At the time, I thought Brihtwold's cattle had earned those coins for him, but I now consider that they would have amounted to far more than an incompetent farmer could ever possess by his own honest toil."

"And Eadburga took some to ease the life of her and her sister," Tatwine added.

"Indeed, Eadburga discovered the bag, but it is hard to think of her action as theft, for I cannot conceive that Brihtwold came upon that wealth honourably. You will remember that Dudda and Cuthbert were also paid a bag of silver for murdering the married couple. There is little other way that Brihtwold could have gained such riches but by theft or payment for a great crime, and there has been no recent talk of such a theft. And surely, when Brihtwold found that the sisters had secretly left, and with some of his silver, he would have denounced the theft if the silver had been his by right—but he has said nothing. I had pondered that a third man was involved in the murders, but I never considered Brihtwold. I should have thought more clearly when I saw the silver in his house, but it was not until I discovered that Father Ingeld was buried alive on Brihtwold's land that my poor mind made the connection. Often, a single dim spark of information means little. It is only when it is connected with others that it shines a light on the truth. My friends, if I am right, we may well have found another murderer. Thank the Lord God that Eadgifu and Eadburga are safe here, in the Cauldron."

"So the pig murdered our brother in Christ because of the penances Ingeld imposed for his womanising?" Tatwine asked.

"It could be so," Eadred replied. "He certainly holds no affection for the clergy. But I think it is more likely that Father Ingeld, who was like a father to Coenwulf, discovered that Brihtwold was leading the boy into the evil that cost him his life. On his journey last spring to Snailwell, Ingeld could have confronted Brihtwold at Deerstow, threatening to expose him, and Brihtwold tortured and killed him. Though we know Brihtwold to be violent, I cannot yet prove he is Ingeld's killer or was involved in the murders of Edmund and Censwith. I must accuse him and bring him to court and see how he explains the riches he has accumulated."

Eadred finished his cup in a single draught and refilled it with his favourite ruby liquid. He stared for a while into the dancing flames before speaking. "Friends, the second matter has greatly unnerved me. Someone knew enough of my journey to Elmstow to send a young monk to follow me there with the intent to kill me. The monk was not from Elmstow. I checked with Sister Edith, who had never seen him before. I do not know if he was from Snailwell. I heard that several young monks entered at the same time as Diuma. He was a man of faith, that was certain, young and eager to serve, but misled. Tatwine, you see how I owe you my life, for you urged me to strengthen my frame so I could defend myself." Eadred proceeded to tell how he had easily overcome the nameless monk who had tried to kill him. Tears were soon etching stripes in his soiled face. "Friends, I fall sometimes into despair that someone wants me dead, and God help me that I killed a fellow member of our Christian family. I will never forget the loneliness and despair in his face as he passed from this life at my hands."

"It is as I have said before, dear Eadred," Tatwine replied, his hand on his friend's shoulder. "You have a God-given gift of discerning the truth about murders. It is known throughout the kingdom. The foul soul behind the many murders in recent times fears your gift and sent an innocent boy to his death, hoping he would take your life. Yet we will find him, make no mistake. Light always defeats darkness."

Eadred nodded with a fleeting smile and shook the hermit by the shoulder, then he looked his companions in the eye, one after the other. "Then let me ask, who could have soiled the young monk's mind with the lie that I conjured demons and poisoned the bishop? And who knew of my journey to Elmstow?"

They stared in silence, then the hermit spoke. "We knew of the plan, of course, for we helped devise it."

Alfred shook his head. "God strike me down if I lie, it was not I who shared it with the one who wished you harm!"

"Alfred, I believe you. If you wished me ill, you could have killed me when first we met and I was weak and defenceless. You are a man of honour. I know it was not you or my dear friend Tatwine, of course. But I ask you both to think very carefully if anything you may have said could have alerted others that I was journeying to Elmstow?"

Alfred pondered for a while and shook his head. Tatwine looked anxious and spoke. "I am searching through the memories of my time at Snailwell. It was only a few days past, but much happened. I told Brother Anselm that you were going to Elmstow, but, as you had asked me to contact and confide in him, it did not concern me to put myself in his trust." Eadred nodded his agreement. "I told the abbot and Diuma that I was on my way to Elmstow to see a one-eyed hermit monk! I was warned about myself." The monk allowed himself a brief smile. "Ah, I do remember, the abbot did say that it would not surprise him if you sought to journey to Elmstow, knowing that we were companions and

Edith was a sister at the minster. He could well have ordered the unknown monk to Elmstow to search for you."

"Yes, it is more than possible," Eadred replied. "Cuthred accused me falsely of the bishop's murder. It makes sense that he would then send someone to the place where I would want to hide, knowing that you, my dear friend Tatwine, lived nearby. And, of course, where Sister Edith lived." Eadred picked up a stone and threw it against the wall. "He knew that my affections would lead me there."

"And what of the murder of the Abbess of Elmstow? Are we any closer to her killer?" Alfred asked.

"The abbess had many enemies amongst the rich and powerful, but I have no idea which one had her killed," Eadred replied. "And the diabolical act of attempting to inter the body of an executed man in Thornham church, it is part of this wave of crime, I have no doubt. The mind behind all this misery communes with dark spirits; this we know. He sought to make Thornham a temple for the devilish brood. But the body of the executed man has now been burnt and his ashes scattered, and we know nothing of him."

Tatwine added, "His hand was missing—that is all we know."

Then Alfred spoke. "We have shared our knowledge, and there were grave risks in gathering it. Good folk lie dead, and doubtless more will perish, and the slaughter of our cattle continues. Now we have started on this journey, how are we to act to stop this misery?"

"You are right, Alfred," Tatwine replied. "We are the ones who know that Abbot Cuthred is the mind behind this evil. He keeps his hands clean while Diuma does his bidding. The kingdom believes he is a stern churchman, disciplined, intelligent and the obvious successor to Bishop Aethelbert. Without strong proof, there is no chance of bringing him before a court, yet Eadred is called a murderer. The abbot is a shrewd and ruthless enemy. And when last I heard, the ealdorman, who is our only hope, is at the southern border where it meets the sea." Tatwine tossed his empty cup into the fire and swore.

"I see one hope," Eadred replied. "Alfred told us that he came upon no hint of evil at Cerdic's or Forthred's halls, but a budding alliance to fight off their attackers. Alfred is a man of honour and known for it by his lord. I say Alfred seeks an audience with Lord Cerdic and takes Boisil. We will go with him. If God judges that our purpose is true, Cerdic will listen to what we know and help us convince Lord Forthred. Then we will journey to Snailwell, where I will accuse Diuma of murder and bring him to court. It is there that I will battle with him. It is a risk, but I feel sure that when Boisil sees Diuma before a court, he will confess that it was Diuma who recruited him. The case against Abbot Cuthred will, with God's help, follow. This is our only path to stopping the evil. We must tell Boisil before we leave for Lord Cerdic's hall that Diuma has been captured and his role in the wave of destruction has been identified. This will unnerve him and loosen his tongue. Now, what say you?"

The plan was discussed well into the night. Its risks were great, particularly for Eadred, but for the others too, as they had harboured a criminal. It was acknowledged that Eadred was the best man to present the case against Diuma and Boisil, but the priest could be arrested on the spot. It was a terrible dilemma. In the end, after many cups had been emptied, it was agreed that the three men would journey to

Lord Cerdic's hall. They would take Boisil and most of the fighting men of the Cauldron, for these folk owed allegiance to Cerdic, who was their temporal lord, and they would be needed if Cerdic decided to take the dangerous journey that would lead to an accusation against the abbot.

After a few hours' sleep, Eadred awoke. The night was deathly cold and silent. His head throbbed when he turned, and misery filled his heart. When the earth was touched once more by the radiance of heaven's candle, he and his companions would set off for Lord Cerdic's hall. Eadred had relived the half dozen times he had spoken at trials or to great men to convince them of the truth of his thoughts about the guilt or innocence of others. Tomorrow, he would all but put his own head in the hangman's noose with only his thoughts and words to keep him from execution.

He had entertained the thought of rising early and slipping away to the coast and the possibility of stealing a fishing boat and pleading to God that it might take him across the sea. It was a grim thought but tinged with hope— an unknown set of dangers for a boy who had never set eyes on the sea, compared to a risk that was staring him in the face. There was no bishop now to defend him. Eadred had seen executions, and he had witnessed brutal torture to extract the truth from accused men and to wreak vengeance on those who had offended the powerful. All in a Christian kingdom. God forbid that this would be his end. But as the night crawled on, Eadred knew ever more clearly that he could not run. For then, evil would win, and even if he still drew breath, his spirit would die.

TWENTY-SIX

Life and Death

E adred stood hidden in the shadows within Lord Cerdic's great hall, listening to every word that was spoken. As arranged, Alfred and Tatwine had sought and gained an audience with Cerdic and his wife, Hilda. Before leaving the Cauldron, Eadred had told Boisil that Diuma had been caught and was facing trial in Snailwell. Boisil had broken down. It was a lie, and Eadred asked God to forgive him.

Boisil swore before Cerdic and Hilda that his mind had been twisted by the evil monk Diuma's demonic spells. That he was a poor peasant who knew not what he was doing when influenced by the devil's creatures. Boisil's lord stared with unmoving eyes. When Boisil finished speaking, his lord replied.

"Wretch, you murdered my tenants, and with a coward's arrow in the back, and you slaughtered my cattle. By any law of this land, you deserve a traitor's death."

Boisil burst into tears, repeating his claim that he was under demonic influence and could do nothing to withstand Diuma's control over him. He turned to Hilda and begged for mercy. Her face did not soften.

Alfred spoke. "Lord Cerdic, Lady Hilda, it is true that this monster led a boy we cared for, who could have lived a good life, into the dark abyss of crime. The boy was hanged. Boisil deserves an end worse than that suffered by those who died because of him. And he has admitted taking Diuma's silver for his trouble. But, my lord, I beg that he be allowed to live for now, for his knowledge will help condemn others who committed these crimes.

"The monk Tatwine has written on this calfskin the names of the criminals Boisil knew of. Some are from your estates and some from Lord Forthred's. Many are already dead. But those who devised and controlled these attacks upon your own family and wealth remain free. There is a man nearby who knows more of their plans, and I ask that you would hear him."

The intriguing request was agreed to, Boisil was led away, and Eadred appeared into the light. Alfred had urged the priest to enter with his head bowed, to remain humble and to appeal to Cerdic's wife if the audience deteriorated badly. Eadred was more than happy to accept the advice.

"Ah, the murderer!" In response to their lord's words, two guards advanced upon Eadred. He fell to the floor and begged for mercy. Once more, Alfred showed the skill he carried modestly.

"Lord, I beg that you listen to Father Eadred. You and the Lady Hilda will remember how this priest used his gift to uncover the murderers of your daughter and her husband.

Those dogs refused to name their master, yet this priest has discovered his name. Father Eadred is no murderer, but his enemies want him dead. There is more to hear, if you will?"

Lady Hilda whispered in her husband's ear. "Very well," Cerdic replied. "Speak."

Eadred rose from the ground, wiping soil from his face. He had thought over his words and arguments dozens of times, and in the silent hall, with expectation and dread oppressing him, Eadred, the priest of God, began to present the evidence he had gathered. He stuttered and gasped at the outset but soon settled his nerves. As Alfred had counselled, he looked often to Hilda, for unlike her husband, who sat with a stone-hard countenance, some sign of her reaction would sometimes escape in her expression. He began by swearing upon the precious blood of Christ that he was innocent of the murder of Bishop Aethelbert and had been falsely charged, and he pleaded for Cerdic's support when the time came that he be given a proper trial to prove his innocence. Eadred also spoke of the importance of Boisil's knowledge in bringing others to face justice, for he alone could identify Diuma as the man who had recruited the gang who had wrought such death and destruction.

Eadred continued. "I have had time to think more about those awful acts. Though the brothers Dudda and Cuthbert were rightfully executed, they were not the mind behind those murders or the only ones present at the killings. Lord Forthred's son, Edmund, was the greatest warrior from these parts, known for his strength, ferocity, vigilance and fighting skill. Could a lame, weighty fool and a weakling dare to overpower him and his wife? It may be possible but carries great risk of failure and terrible retribution, not only from the families of the married couple, but also from the man who paid them to commit the murder. They had already failed once—at the feast—and could not afford to fail again."

Eadred's eyes quickly scanned across the expressions of Cerdic and Hilda. Both seemed absorbed in his account, as he had hoped, and with his confidence emboldened, he decided to present some other ideas that had come to him in the dark hours.

"And I have considered why it was that the bodies of your daughter and her husband were not thrown, in haste and without dignity, into holes in the nearby wood, but instead wrapped in winding sheets and buried in the time-honoured burial ground. Firstly, because they were murdered nearby. They could not have been killed in their home without others hearing the attack. On the second day following their wedding, Edmund went to view the condition of the earthen bank protecting the settlements. Lord Forthred told us thus. I believe his wife went with him. The men they took must have been Dudda, Cuthbert and another. All of whom were known to Edmund. With Edmund's mind on his task, two of the attackers thrust knives into his back. The other had engaged the attention of your daughter. She broke free and in the struggle was herself killed. Perhaps the killers did not wish to harm her, but they had to take their chance to kill Edmund when he was some distance from the vill, and they could not allow a witness to survive."

"Who, then, was this third man who helped in the murder of our daughter?" Cerdic asked.

"My lord, I think it is doubtful that he was one of Lord Forthred's kin, for he would have been discovered by now,"

Eadred replied. "I believe it to be a disgruntled tenant of Lord Forthred who was dispossessed of his land and income and enticed by Diuma's silver: a man called Brihtwold. I myself saw a bag of silver coin, well beyond his natural wealth, in his house. I also think he killed Father Ingeld. The body was found buried alive on Brihtwold's land. He is a vindictive and violent man.

"Let me return, with your assent, to the burial of husband and wife. The burial ground that has enclosed the bodies of Forthred's family and all of the nearby communities for generations was close by. Despite the horror of the crime, Dudda and Cuthbert, who I believe were not Christians but acknowledged the spirits of their ancestors, could not bring themselves to foul that earth and anger the ancestors by treating the bodies as common criminals.

"It was Diuma who recruited Dudda, Cuthbert and Brihtwold to murder Edmund, as he had recruited Boisil and others to slaughter your beasts and men. While the evidence against Diuma is growing, lord, it will be far harder to link these crimes to the man whom I believe is the mind behind all this evil—Cuthred, Abbot of Snailwell."

Both Cerdic and Hilda gasped. Eadred endured an awful and sceptical silence.

Lady Hilda then spoke. "Abbot Cuthred comes from a rich family, and with the death of the bishop he will assuredly become head of the Church in our land. What would he gain from such infamy?"

Eadred replied. "To raise his family and his name, my lady. He is rich, but not as you or Lord Forthred. His ambition is boundless. If he becomes the new bishop, he will be head of the Church with power over estates that will surpass your own, Lord Forthred's and all except the king. He sought to wreck the marriage alliance between Lord Forthred and yourself. The terrible slaughter of livestock owned by both your houses was also designed to weaken your power. The vast estates and herds owned by the minsters of Snailwell and Elmstow have been unharmed, while yours face ruin. Cuthred remains in the shadows and beyond accusation, while he has accused me falsely of the murder of the bishop. All this speaks of a cunning mind at work. A mind that happily calls on demons to aid his cause. Our only hope of bringing him to justice is through Diuma."

"It is a dangerous road you are asking me to take, priest."

"Lord, I ask only that you request Lord Forthred to listen to my thoughts, then, if you are both in agreement, to support the convening of a court where I can defend myself and lay a charge against the abbot and Diuma. I may fail, and I will bear the consequences. But if these men are allowed to continue, soon the abbot's family will be the most powerful in the kingdom after the king himself, and yours will lie in ruins."

*

Two days later, Eadred presented his case to Lord Forthred. Even more than Cerdic, the thegn had felt the slow bleeding of his wealth from the destruction of his livestock, but more than anything he wanted revenge on the man who had ordered the death of his son. Eadred outlined the evidence that supported his belief that Brihtwold was the third man involved in the murders of the young married couple and had also killed Father Ingeld.

"I have done no wrong, I swear it." Brihtwold was dragged from his house by two warriors. Others entered and pulled the flimsy shelter apart.

"There is no silver, my lord," a warrior spoke to Forthred.

"He would be a greater fool than we know he is to leave it here," the lord replied. "Read the charges."

"Brihtwold of Deerstow, you are charged with aiding in the murders of Edmund, son of Lord Forthred, and Censwith, daughter of Lord Cerdic. Also, you did murder the priest Father Ingeld. Your trial will take place at Snailwell Minster. You have a day to gather eleven men to swear that you are worthy of trust and your denial of the charges should be believed."

"How can I gather any oath-helpers?" the farmer screamed through his tears. "I have done wrong to many here, but never murder."

"At last, you will face justice," a villager shouted. The sentiment was echoed by others. Brihtwold was bound and led away.

Thus, on Eadred's plea, the two thegns agreed to ride to Snailwell with their warriors and to send word in advance that they brought with them the fugitive priest as well as others accused of murder and slaughter. They also sent a message to the ealdorman, petitioning him to assemble a court at Snailwell to judge the culprits. Eadred also convinced the thegns to have Eadburga brought from the Cauldron, for she had stolen much of Brihtwold's silver and needed to explain from where it had come. It would be an unjust twist if her theft was allowed to remove evidence against Brihtwold. Eadred also sought to have Sister Edith fetched, and Tatwine was despatched with a warrior to collect her from Elmstow. She had seen Diuma and an imperious noble threatening the abbess to gain access to Edith for carnal enjoyment. If Edith could identify the man as Abbot Cuthred, then it would build the case against him. Eadred had believed Edith to be finally safe after Elmstow was cleared of rats and the new abbess installed, but to discover that there were still men who would kill to have his beloved Edith in their beds brought him to tears and fury. He was again caught in a terrible dilemma: to keep Edith safe, he had to endanger her.

The wave of crime that had surged across the kingdom could be stopped in only one way. The black soul and his accomplices at the centre had to be uncovered, brought before a court and executed. So, three days later, Forthred, Cerdic and their sizeable force arrived at Snailwell. Aelfric, Ealdorman of the East Angles, also arrived. The enterprise had begun, and, God willing, truth would win in court and without unnecessary bloodshed. The weight of it all was crushing Eadred. Over and over in his mind, he continued to gather and weigh the evidence and arguments he had amassed. Sometimes, they appeared solid, like flesh, but more often they seemed weak and easy for a sharp mind to deny. He sat sobbing, locked in his cell. Tatwine was allowed a short visit, and Eadred rested against him while the hermit's arm was wrapped around his shoulders. While Tatwine recited constant prayers, Alfred could be heard outside sharpening his axe. Both would be needed in the days to come.

TWENTY-SEVEN

The Trial of Eadred the Priest

On the flat pasture surrounding the hill on which the minster rose, warriors encircled dozens of fires. On one side of the road to the minster gate, the hearth companions and many of the tenants of Lord Leofric were encamped. On the other side, the followers of the thegns Forthred and Cerdic were establishing their camp. And behind the minster were the fires of what remained of Ealdorman Aelfric's force that had been chasing down criminals across the kingdom. The three prisoners, Eadred, Boisil and Brihtwold, hands bound behind them, were led into the minster's courtyard by the ealdorman's men.

"I have been empowered by our king to convene the trials of the three accused men," Aelfric said.

"Naturally, you will have my complete cooperation," the abbot replied. "I have long held the view that Father

272

Eadred has done more ill than good, and his murder of our beloved bishop confirms this sad but true fact. I know nothing of the other two men, but I welcome the trials and swift and suitable sentences of the guilty."

"My experience of the priest differs from your view," the ealdorman said. "It is widely known that at Elmstow he discovered the murderers. And recently, as you know, he unearthed the killers of Lord Forthred's son and Lord Cerdic's daughter. There is little ill in any of this." Before the abbot had a chance to reply, Aelfric continued. "I was surprised to see your cousin's men arrayed in force beyond the minster. This was surely not necessary."

"Nor is the force brought here by the two fenland thegns," the abbot replied curtly.

"They brought the three prisoners through land known to be dangerous. Attempts to free the prisoners or to silence them were expected. I am grateful that the accused arrived here unharmed because of the protection provided by the fenland lords. My men are now guarding the prisoners at all times."

Cuthred bowed slightly. "Have you given thought to the order in which the accused men will be tried?"

"I have," Aelfric replied. "The man Boisil has admitted to involvement in the murder of many men and the slaughter of herds of cattle, which have blighted the kingdom. He has named some of his accomplices and will name more. His trial must come first."

"The Church thinks differently about the order of trials. I will give you our reasoning. While there has been much damage to Lord Forthred's and Lord Cerdic's property—men and beasts—the murderers of the two persons of rank have been caught, tried and the sentences carried out. Not so for the bishop. He was head of the Church and one of the leading men of our kingdom. It is right and proper that the man accused of his murder be tried first. If you wish to remind yourself of the customary methods and procedures of the courts, then I will summon men who can advise you."

Aelfric glared at the abbot. "I am grateful for your advice, but that will not be necessary." The arrogance of this overbearing and ascetic churchman, with his jutting jaw and disdainful expression, tested the ealdorman's temper. Over the past months, Aelfric had become used to gaining justice by use of his sword arm and leaving Hygelac to apply his blunt methods to extract the truth. It was not always the best approach, but Aelfric thought it honest.

"As you wish," the abbot replied. "You would know that the king will expect a faultless trial, given the magnitude of the charges. I am sure you understand that the next few days will be the most important in the kingdom for many a year. A people are granted peace and prosperity by God if they fear him and live good lives. The king should do no less. He must uphold justice, and those who act for him must do the same. I assure you that under the time-honoured customs of our people, the trial of Eadred the priest should take place before the others, and I, as the senior churchman in the kingdom, will bring the accusation against him. That is the king's law."

Aelfric stared at the abbot. "The trial will start the morning after tomorrow to give the priest time to gather his oath-helpers."

"I need assurance that he will be guarded closely while

he does so," the abbot added. "The priest is not trustworthy and could well attempt an escape."

Then, with some menace, Aelfric spoke in a slow voice. "He is my prisoner; do not presume to advise me further. As to the trial, I, and I alone, will officiate." Aelfric rose and left the abbot before he could utter another word.

*

Aelfric sat at a table in the courtyard in front of the church. Before him, seated or standing according to rank, were the thegns Leofric, Forthred and Cerdic, Abbot Cuthred, men from the king's own guard, the inmates of the minster and freemen from nearby settlements. The three prisoners stood guarded and with their hands bound. Daunting warriors surrounded the perimeter.

Aelfric rose and opened the proceedings, stating that the three men faced an array of accusations. The first to be tried would be Eadred, priest of Snailwell Minster, and the abbot would bring the charge. Abbot Cuthred, dressed in the finest vestments, then rose.

"Until a new bishop is chosen, I am the senior churchman in this kingdom. It gives me no pleasure to accuse Father Eadred of the murder by poison of our beloved Bishop Aethelbert. I personally ordered Father Eadred not to see the ailing bishop until I gave him permission. He disobeyed and then broke his vows again by running, like a criminal, from the minster that same night. Before the sun rose on the following day, our blessed bishop was dead. There is only one explanation: Father Eadred poisoned Bishop Aethelbert." The abbot returned to his seat, and as he descended, his head rose in admiration of his own comments.

"Father Eadred of Snailwell, how do you plead?"

Eadred responded in strict accordance with the customary legal procedures. "By the Lord, I am guiltless, both in deed and counsel, of the charge of which Abbot Cuthred accuses me."

Aelfric replied, "Then you are required to furnish eleven oath-helpers to swear that your word is true."

Abbot Cuthred leapt to his feet. "My Lord Aelfric, this priest is accused of murder, and his reputation and honour are certainly not without blemish. Against the vows he solemnly took, it is widely known that he engaged in fornication. Under our customs, he needs to supply three times the number of oath-helpers, and each has to be questioned as to whether they know the accused personally. How else can they vouch for his word? Surely, he knew this obligation before this trial began."

Aelfric issued a loud sigh. He knew it was impossible for Eadred to furnish the required number of men, even if all of the inmates of Snailwell vouched for his word. The abbot knew the procedures that needed to be followed, and he did not. Aelfric stared into the distance in anger and absolute futility.

"Lord Aelfric, I ask that you grant me leave to speak in my defence," Eadred suddenly shouted.

The abbot sprang to his feet.

"This cannot be allowed. The law is clear. The priest must furnish the required number of oath-helpers, or the case is proven against him."

"Are you nervous of what I might say, Reverend Father?" Eadred retorted.

The abbot flushed red and opened his eloquent mouth, but he was never given the opportunity.

"The priest's life is in the balance. Whether it is correct by the letter or not, I give him leave to speak." Aelfric made certain that the whole assembly heard him and understood. The abbot stood in shocked silence for a few seconds, then returned to his seat. Eadred proceeded.

"My lords, the abbot is right that I did once commit fornication, but I confessed my sin without compunction and accepted the penance. Many men of the Church have sinned, as have those in the laity. If a man confesses and accepts the penalty required by law and the Church's penance, then he is absolved. This is our law and custom. I never sought to hide the truth, and my word remains pure. But there is more I wish to say." The young priest ploughed on at speed.

"When I entered the bishop's cell, there was, sadly, the smell of one who is close to death, with his bedclothes damp and soiled. But there was another odour. It was dwale. It is, as many know, both a treatment and a poison. I do not know if it were given to help our beloved bishop or to kill him, but—"

"How can an accused man be allowed to speak thus?" the abbot shouted. "This is improper and insolent."

"I will hear the priest!" Aelfric thundered. The abbot remained standing and continued to stare at the ealdorman. "Continue!" Aelfric bellowed.

Eadred stuttered but found his voice. "Lord, if the bishop's death was murder from poisoning by dwale and with the intention of accusing me, the murderer made this serious mistake. The scent of dwale when mixed with herbs is difficult to detect by smell or taste and thus may go undetected by the bishop or other inmates. Whoever secreted the dwale in the bishop's drinks would hence go unnoticed. Yet dwale finds its way into sweat and the body's leavings. The bishop's clothes and bed were fouled from several days of these wastes, and the stench became unmistakeable. The abbot's charge against me may have seemed true but for the fortifying of the smell of dwale issuing from the bishop's body and collected on his bedclothes.

"While I was gathering my oath-helpers, I spoke to several brothers who had prayed with the bishop on the days before I did, and they all talked of the same odour. I know that it is sometimes difficult to know the difference between an amount that helps and an amount that kills unless you are skilled in such things. So it cannot be said that the bishop was wilfully murdered. However, it is impossible that I administered the dwale that killed him, for its odour was detected on the bishop before my time with him, and even before my return to Snailwell."

Aelfric glanced at the abbot, whose eyes bulged. His lips quivered, and his frame tensed, as if he were readying to jump to his feet. Aelfric shouted, "Are these brothers willing to swear that they smelt this odour?"

"Yes, my lord, and they did tell others of the smell. It is widely known."

Aelfric addressed himself to the abbot. "I cannot see that the charge against this priest of murdering the bishop by poison can be proven. If you wish to continue with the charge, then you risk accusation yourself." It seemed that Cuthred was listening with one ear; the other was occupied by the monk called Diuma. He had quietly brought himself from the outer edge of the assembly and was whispering to the abbot. He then furtively moved away.

Abbot Cuthred rose. "My lord, a young monk who recently joined this minster, Brother Asser, whom I sent to Elmstow on a mission, has recently been found dead at that minster. It is my strong belief that he was murdered by Father Eadred."

Sudden uproar broke out; some voices abusing Eadred, others demanding that the abbot explain himself, and others holding their heads in shock. Aelfric rose and did what was natural to him. He slammed his sword down upon the table.

"Explain yourself! There has been no talk of this before now."

"Forgive me, Lord Aelfric." The abbot gave a fawning bow. "I have little information on Brother Asser's death, but does Father Eadred deny the charge?"

Aelfric countered before Eadred had time to speak. "There has been no charge as yet. Do you wish to accuse the priest of this apparent murder?"

After a long pause, accentuated by the expectant silence of the assembly, Cuthred spoke. "I will gather more information before making a formal accusation."

"Very well," Aelfric continued, "I will return to the charge against Father Eadred of murdering the bishop." He turned to Eadred. "Do you have the necessary number of oath-helpers to swear that your word is pure?"

"I do, my lord."

"Then let them come forward."

A line of men approached a table, and, in turn, they placed their hands on the Bible and so swore.

Aelfric rose. "It is not possible to be certain whether the

dwale administered to Bishop Aethelbert was intended as medicine or poison, but what is clear is that Father Eadred did not murder the bishop."

He may have been less familiar with the intricacies of the law than the abbot, but Aelfric knew well enough that if Cuthred wished to pursue more charges against Eadred, he risked exposing himself to charges. He looked at Abbot Cuthred, sitting crimson-faced, staring into his lap. Once more, Diuma appeared, tapped Cuthred on the shoulder and whispered. This time, the abbot pushed the hand away, not looking at his so-called assistant. A second attempt by the monk was met by a stern, silent stare and a dismissive wave of the hand. It seemed that Cuthred was done for now. The risks were, for the moment, greater for the abbot. If a man brought an accusation against another and it was not accepted in court, it was often the case that the accuser faced a charge of bringing a malicious suit, and he suffered the consequences. The more serious the claim, the more onerous the punishment.

Aelfric had come to value Eadred's gift of detecting the perpetrators of great crimes since the two men had met in the pit of Elmstow. Abbot Cuthred had pursued the priest with the venom of one who feared what he would uncover. Cuthred needed to close Eadred's eyes and extinguish his mind for good. When triumph proved harder than he anticipated, the abbot had made the astonishing charge that Eadred had murdered Brother Asser. To make two unsuccessful accusations of murder against the same man courted disaster for the abbot. For the first time in many months, Aelfric felt there might be some breach appearing in the armour of those who directed the wave of killings. God knew that he needed a victory, and it seemed that this was a vital one. He allowed himself a brief smile before rising.

"I proclaim that Father Eadred's word has been found clean, and the accusation against him has been proven false. He is a free man. Unbind him. The trial of Boisil of the Cauldron Folk will take place in the afternoon."

*

Eadred fell to his knees, rubbing his wrists, weeping but elated. "Lord God, you have delivered me from my enemies. Bless you! Thank you!"

Many a monk came to congratulate him. It was a wonderful feeling not to be a fugitive. Yet when he tried to make sense of the abbot's actions, Eadred was troubled. The charge that he had poisoned the bishop was easily refuted. It seemed as if it were a quick and poorly thought through strategy, taken in the hope that the king would declare Eadred an outlaw so any man could legally kill him on the spot without the need for a trial and without penalty. The abbot's second accusation, so soon after the first, also seemed a mistake. If anything, Cuthred had unmasked himself. Eadred felt that he had bested the abbot for now, but he worried that Cuthred had more arrows to fire, and what would they be?

A hand fell heavily on his shoulder. He cried out in alarm and heard a familiar laugh. "God has delivered you from your enemies, as was his promise." Eadred turned his tear-stained face upwards to see Tatwine beaming down at him. "She is here and now guarded closely by the ealdorman's best warriors. Hygelac has been charged with protecting her."

"My wonderful friend, thank you for delivering Edith safely." Eadred fell into the hermit's arms, blubbering and convulsing with an explosion of feelings. "She is in hell's mouth here."

"She is far safer now, surrounded by Aelfric's hearth warriors, than she would be in Elmstow," the hermit replied. "If Hygelac were charged with keeping me alive, my soul would never leave my body! Now, hear this: Edith told me that when the young monk's body was found, a rider was sent to Snailwell. A few days later, two warriors arrived from the abbot to retrieve the body. They would not allow the boy to be buried at Elmstow. The warriors spoke to the senior sister, and loud and stern words were heard. They then came to see Edith and brought the senior sister with them. Edith expected the worst but said the men were courteous to her. The sister said that she must answer their questions honestly and made her swear on the Bible that she would. Edith is an honourable woman, and we would not expect anything less than truth-telling.

"They asked if you had visited her secretly, under the guise of a peasant. Sadly, she had to confirm this to be true. They then asked if you did murder the young monk, and she said that you were attacked by him and killed him when defending yourself. Edith also said that you were full of remorse for the deed but that he came at you convinced you had murdered the bishop. Our sister told me that the warriors then asked an exceedingly disrespectful question—whether you had fornicated with her, either under duress or by choice." Eadred held his head and groaned that she had been subjected to such prying and discourtesy. "She replied in anger that you had not. But this was not the end of it.

They asked if she could recognise any of the men who had visited Elmstow in recent weeks, and Edith replied only one: a man with a harelip. Though there was another with him, one who was proud and arrogant, she could not bring his face to memory."

"Cuthred and Diuma!" Eadred spat the names. "She told me so herself."

"Yes, it could be no other," Tatwine continued. "The warriors told Edith that she was in no danger and under their protection. But when they left, the holy sister who had assumed leadership of the minster until a new abbess is chosen told her that she should flee without haste. So it was that we met Edith close to the summit of the hill near Elmstow. She thought we were the warriors returning and hid, but, recognising me, she came out from hiding and journeyed with us."

"Sister Edith's courage and wisdom match her beauty," Eadred gasped. "The abbot has been beguiled by her. Her courage and wisdom will be needed to bring both him and Diuma to justice."

"Will you accuse them of this wave of murder and cattle slaughter?"

"I have little choice, my friend," Eadred replied. "It has shaken the kingdom to its core and will continue to weaken the rule of justice unless they are stopped. But I must wait until I can prove they are the culprits. I cannot accuse the abbot now; he would walk free. I will seek an audience with the ealdorman, for so much depends on Boisil's trial.

"Yet, I cannot help but feel there is something I am missing."

"What do you mean?" Tatwine replied. "Have we not

hunted these animals with care and resolve? If we continue thus, they will be snared."

Eadred shook his head. "Does it not seem too easy thus far? The brothers Dudda and Cuthbert, who killed the married couple, were unveiled and confessed without much effort. The abbot's charge that I poisoned the bishop was easily refuted in court. These give me a strange feeling that we are being led somewhere fruitless. And with what the abbot surely knew of my encounter with Brother Asser from the information Edith had given to his warriors, why did he seem so unprepared and make such a fumbled claim that was easily rejected?"

"The abbot is not the first leader to be let down by his followers," Tatwine replied. "Just because you had the better of the crude-bladed fool Diuma does not mean that you are being drawn into the wilderness by a shrewd mind."

"I hope you are right, my friend. We will know more at Boisil's trial. When he identifies Diuma, then I will accuse that malignant so-called monk, and we will be closer to the truth."

TWENTY-EIGHT

Confusion Redeemed

The guard of Aelfric's warriors surrounding Boisil, and their presence throughout the assembled court, had noticeably increased. Eadred's confidence rose to a similar degree, for it signalled the importance placed on Boisil's testimony by the ealdorman. Cuthred had also understood this, so he had argued and succeeded in having Eadred tried first. Unfortunately for Cuthred, he had not succeeded in having Eadred convicted, so now the priest could participate in Boisil's trial—if the ealdorman so agreed. Lord Cerdic rose and pointed to the miserable-looking captive.

"My lord, I accuse Boisil of the Cauldron Folk of murder and the wicked destruction of the herds owned by me, by Lord Forthred and by the men of our estates. The terror inflicted by this man and gangs of criminals has brought us to our knees. Those who were not killed by their cowardly arrows to their backs face starvation. This man knows the names of the others involved, and if he seeks to withhold any of their identities, leave it to me to extract them from him."

Aelfric demanded of Boisil if he were guilty of the charge of not. The prisoner replied that he had already admitted his guilt and fell to his knees, weeping. "My lord, I am a wretched man, foolish and easily led. I am destined for the pit of hell, for I have taken the lives of others and destroyed their wealth. Worse, I have turned my back on the Lord God and sought the help of the devil's brood. I beg you for a clean death, and if any can find it in their hearts, to pray for my soul that the Saviour of man may have mercy on me."

Aelfric sought the names of every one of Boisil's accomplices if his plea were to be considered. So, slowly and tearfully, he gave about twenty names and the vills where they came from. Cries of horror greeted some of the announcements, especially of two monks: Brother Oswine from Wexning and Brother Daniel from Snailwell. Eadred sighed on hearing Daniel's name. He was an indulgent and aggressive young man whom Eadred had always thought to be ill-placed in the cloister. Unsurprisingly, Brother Daniel was nowhere to be found. Over half of the individuals Boisil named had already been killed in fighting or by execution. Then came the moment Eadred had been waiting for. The ealdorman spoke.

"Answer this truthfully and you will be spared the worst excesses of a tortured execution. Who ordered you to commit these outrages?"

Boisil looked around the assembled men carefully, scanning from side to side several times. "Lord, I had expected him to be here as a prisoner."

Eadred remembered the tale he had spun to persuade Boisil to speak, but that seemed of no consequence now. The ealdorman snapped, "Tell me his name!"

"Lord, I never knew his name, but he had a harelip, and his head was tonsured as a monk. Solid of frame and fearful when angry."

Diuma's name echoed across the courtyard. The abbot rose, also shouting the monk's name. He turned and looked across the faces. "He is not here!" Eadred had been looking at Abbot Cuthred's expression from the moment Boisil described Diuma's face. What he saw alarmed him. The abbot seemed as astonished as anyone. Could he have known that his self-named assistant was going to be unmasked as the hand that had organised the murderers and prepared himself to exhibit the same shock as everyone else? Or was he genuinely astounded and horrified?

The ealdorman ordered his men to search the minster for Diuma, then he slammed his sword upon the table. He announced that Boisil had admitted his involvement in the reign of murders and cattle slaughtering and would face execution. One man remained to be tried, and that would take place the following morning. The court was adjourned.

Eadred rested his back against the church wall and sat preoccupied with his thoughts and the image of Abbot Cuthred. It troubled him to the core that his mind had written a story of the wave of lawlessness across the kingdom with the abbot and Diuma as the obvious culprits. He had no doubt that the monk's part in the story was largely correct. Diuma was the grubby hand that recruited the murderers and instilled fear within them. But Eadred was no longer as sure about the abbot. If not him, then who was the mind behind the terror? As Eadred pondered this question, he groaned. Suddenly, so many people could be the culprit.

"Eadred, my boy, thank the Lord God that you are safe and freed from the charge of murder. What a foolish accusation to make. Anyone who knows you would understand that it is not in your nature." Eadred smiled to see the warm countenance of Brother Anselm and rose to greet him.

"How good to see you, Brother Anselm. Unfortunately, it was someone who does not know me well who thought I was capable of such a crime. But I will never forget that I killed a fellow brother in spirit and will not rest until I find who sent him to kill me."

"When Diuma is found and questioned, I have no doubt he will confess."

"And name the abbot as his leader?" Eadred replied.

"I cannot see any other explanation," Anselm responded. "Then we will be free again, but the Lord forbid that I am wrong and there is another beast amongst us."

A voice called out Eadred's name. It was Tatwine, who hurried towards his friend. "At last, God willing, we have that wretched soul Diuma. He will not escape."

"Brother Paulinus!"

"Ah, good Brother Anselm," Tatwine smiled, "I humbly ask for your forgiveness. I came last to Snailwell in disguise to discover more about the deaths of the bishop and the abbess. I did not divulge my true identity at that time." Eadred then added his own apology to Anselm.

"It is of no matter," Anselm replied. "I understand the need for such secrecy, and Eadred, it speaks much of you to have such friends."

The conversation between the three men was interrupted when Eadred's name boomed across the courtyard. This time from a warrior—one of the ealdorman's men. Eadred yelled in return, and the warrior came running towards him. "I am to take you to Lord Aelfric now! You are to come alone."

*

"Two arrows in the back. He was found behind a hut on the far side of the minster." The ealdorman spoke with Eadred, Hygelac and several warriors in an empty, candlelit storehouse. Diuma's body lay supine upon a table. "He was taken unawares; there are no other wounds."

"His tongue was silenced not long after he was named in court. He is still warm," Hygelac added. "I was hoping to question him. His many secrets would have spilled out then."

Eadred slumped against the wall. The war between good and evil was playing out before his eyes. From the elation of his own deliverance that morning and the naming of Diuma in court, to the misery of Diuma's death before he could name the one who was behind all the destruction.

"I pray that we can come upon the threads of these crimes once more, for all seems blank and dark to me now. With your permission, lord, I will withdraw and pray." Aelfric nodded his assent, and Eadred went to seek out the one man who could help him.

As Eadred walked to Tatwine's cell, his heart almost burst from his chest. Emerging from a doorway onto the courtyard and protected by three warriors, Edith smiled. "I prayed for your deliverance, my dear priest, and God has freed you," she shouted. Her guards were doubtless certain of their fate at Hygelac's hands if anything happened to the nun and were wary when Eadred approached. "Let him come to me, please. He has been found innocent by the ealdorman." They accepted this reassurance but with their hands on their sword hilts.

"I cannot stay long, Edith, but it is a joy to see that you are safe. It was I who had you brought here and put your life at risk. I needed you to identify Diuma in court as the man who threatened the abbess, and now he is dead. But there is still a purpose. Do you see that tall and colourless man walking across the courtyard? Was he the man who was with Diuma when they came to Elmstow?"

Edith looked carefully at Abbot Cuthred. He raised his face, and his eyes fixed soberly on hers for a few moments. He seemed forlorn. "I think that is the medallion I saw, so I suppose it is him."

"Look closely," Eadred encouraged.

"He looks familiar, but I was so distracted by the harelip and the violence of the other man, I cannot be certain." Her guards made it clear to Eadred that they needed to take Edith away from the open courtyard and into the protection of one of the buildings. With a smile from both of them, they parted ways.

Edith's answer was not what Eadred had hoped for, and his mind was full of confusion. Once inside Tatwine's cell, Eadred was met with a squeeze around his shoulders by his friend's strong arm and by his genial spirit. Eadred could manage only a listless smile in response. "Come, my dear brother, I have seen you in this temper many times before, and each time you have recovered and more," the hermit chuckled. "How you fall about, as if you were ready to die! Even a beast of the woodlands struggles to regain its feet if it has been felled by a hunter. You are more than this. Remember the vision I was granted when the Lord God showed me the gifts he had granted you? You were blind to them then because your eyes had not been opened. Now they have, and you have seen things that other men could not. You have discovered deeds that cruel men would commit murder to keep hidden. It is an insult to God not to use your gifts, and he has sent me to remind you of this and to help you back on your feet. Now come with me. I have claimed a hut for the evening."

The glow and warmth of the fire raised Eadred's spirits, and he sat on one of the stools and smiled. Without a word, Tatwine took a candle and bolted through the door. A minute or so later, he reappeared with two enormous pitchers. "Ale for me and wine for you," the hermit grinned, then disappeared once more. When he returned, it was with three roasted chickens. "One of the joys of having great lords staying here is that there is plenty of food and drink! Now, let us fill our stomachs and free our heads and see if we can find our way through this marshland of sin and come to the other side. I promise you that before we see the bottom of these jugs, you will be smiling with some revelation. I know that the harder all this seems, the more your mind works, and the more your mind works, the clearer the truth becomes. I will begin. Do you now doubt that the abbot is the mind behind all this destruction and misery?"

Eadred took a sip of wine, then another, then he downed half the cup. "My dearest friend, how you persevere with me. I do not feel much cheer, but I cannot let you down, of all people. Let me wander awhile. I had never taken to the new abbot. Compared to Bishop Aethelbert, he seemed as a cold, grasping manager of an estate, not a loving father. The bishop was suspicious of Cuthred's motives and warned me of his intentions and behaviour. The abbot stood in my way when I wished to divert myself from my priestly duties to look closely at the murders. Then he accused me of poisoning the bishop, then of murdering Brother Asser. Diuma claimed to be his assistant, and we know that he mustered the criminals and sought to drag Edith into carnal activity to sate the abbot's lust. I do not doubt that Diuma also paid Dudda, Cuthbert and Brihtwold to murder Forthred's only son. So I came to see the abbot as the mind and Diuma as the hands behind all the misery the kingdom has endured. As the Abbess of Elmstow stood between the abbot's wicked desires and Edith, I also led myself to believe that Cuthred had ordered the abbess's death."

"My friend, these are all sound reasons as far as I can see, to think that the abbot is the mind behind all this evil," Tatwine replied.

"Yes, I suppose they are. But let me continue. Why, then, would the abbot do all this? I saw two reasons. Firstly, he comes from a wealthy family and is exceedingly ambitious, both within the Church and within the ranks of noblemen. He sought to weaken other great families by whatever means he thought best. If he were successful, then his family would become the second-most powerful in the kingdom, after the king, with temporal and spiritual power. Secondly, he wanted to destroy me. Brother Anselm told me that he felt the abbot was jealous of my eminence, that he thought I had been falsely raised above my station. The abbot told me that himself. He was also jealous of the affection that Edith and I share, for he lusted after her. Also, he believed that I might uncover his many secrets. So, my friend, for all these reasons, I came to believe that Abbot Cuthred was the mind behind the kingdom's woes. Then when I saw the abbot as astounded as everyone when Boisil named Diuma, I began to doubt this edifice I had built."

"But Cuthred named you as Brother Asser's murderer! How could he do so if he had not sent Asser to kill you?" Tatwine's expression carried significant doubt. Eadred returned a chicken leg to the platter and looked into his empty cup, then he shut his eyes. The two friends sat in silence for a while, while the fire crackled and hissed. Then Eadred spoke, still with eyes closed.

"Think on this, my friend. The abbot could have indeed instructed Brother Asser to go to Elmstow on a mission, but then Diuma secretly intervened and told the young monk that I was also journeying there and he could gain glory by defeating the bishop's killer. The abbot did not know that I was heading for Elmstow, but Diuma did because someone had told him so. A man who has recruited a band of murderers to inflict misery on Lord Forthred's and Lord Cerdic's tenants would have spies everywhere. It is well within the bounds of possibility that one of these recognised me on the road from the Cauldron to Elmstow. It was an opportunity that fell into Diuma's lap. I can see him filling the boy's head with righteous anger, and that venom led Asser to attack me without thought. I do not think it mattered to Diuma whether that poor monk defeated me or not. What concerned Diuma was that one of us died. He probably expected that I would overwhelm the lesser-framed boy, then when caught, I would be charged as a murderer and hanged. I would leave this life in despair and humiliation, throttled in front of my brothers in spirit." Eadred filled his cup, took a deep mouthful and sat once more in silent contemplation of what could have been his fate, then he continued.

"What if Abbot Cuthred genuinely thought that I had fled the minster that night because I murdered the bishop? My flight appeared to confirm my guilt. When it seemed in court as if I would escape the charge of poisoning the bishop, do you remember Diuma whispering to the abbot? He could have been giving Cuthred another opportunity to have me convicted for murder. So incensed was the abbot that I might escape a just sentence that he mouthed the accusation that Diuma had fed him."

Tatwine looked unconvinced. "But I thought Edith recognised the abbot when he visited Elmstow with Diuma to procure her for his lust?"

Eadred shook his head. "That was my mistake—one of many. Edith described him as a man who was arrogant and who wore a medallion. I then said he was the abbot because of her description and because Diuma accompanied him. I went to her not long past and contrived for her to look upon Cuthred at a distance no further than we are from the nearby hut. She could not be certain that he was or was not the man she had seen with Diuma. Edith said again what she had told me at Elmstow, but I was too stupid to realise its importance. She said that Diuma's face had absorbed so much of her attention that she scarcely looked upon the other man.

"Ah," Eadred groaned and slapped his thigh, "of course. What is it about Diuma that we all see? The split in his face.

Everyone recognises him and his violent nature. Whoever is behind all this anguish knew that Diuma would draw men's eyes. He would be the one who men would remember when they sought the black mind behind all this turmoil. The real culprit let Diuma be noticed, while he went about his foul work in secret. And when Diuma was named in court, the mind behind the murders had him killed."

"Well, if not the abbot, who is this monstrous murderer?" Tatwine stared in confusion.

"I wish I knew. Someone who is powerful and ambitious or someone who carries bitterness towards Forthred and Cerdic. And the man who seeks my death may be the same man or different." Eadred groaned and emptied his cup. "Oh, how I erred by thinking the abbot was the chief of this evil band, but now I see my mistake, I can think of no one else. It could be Lord Cerdic, his losses are far less than Forthred's, and it was only Forthred's son who was the murderers' target. There are years of animosity between those families, and Cerdic's daughter was sent from Elmstow as a delinquent by the abbess. Were we simple-minded to think that their children's deaths would bring them together? Then there is Lord Leofric, the abbot's cousin. He has influence, though not the equal of the others in power, whether land, livestock or the capacity of his mind."

"Leofric is trying to lift himself and, as far as I can see, by honest means. Brother Anselm told me he was teaching him to read and write."

"That is surely to be welcomed," Eadred replied. "To be able to read the Scriptures and to write are good for a man's faith and for estate management. I would rather a man learn those skills than spend his time murdering his countrymen! And I doubt that Lord Leofric would put his cousin in danger."

Eadred continued. "It is a difficult thing to ponder, but we may have to return to an unpleasant thought I discarded earlier. I had thought this to be an enemy from within, but could another kingdom be behind this misery? It has brought our land to its knees."

The obvious suspect was the Kingdom of Mercia, which bordered the Kingdom of the East Angles to the west, and the two kingdoms had been enemies for generations. Occasionally, one of the contenders had crossed the border with a great army and had eventually been opposed by an armed force of similar size. These were costly and dangerous ventures, and neither kingdom had struck a killing blow. In the years between these challenges, there had been endless raids by smaller forces. Mercia was not the power that it used to be, but the mutual antagonism had not disappeared.

Eadred continued. "The Mercians are not strong enough now to muster an army against us, but with gold they could be turning us against ourselves. What better ploy is there but to have your enemy eat itself?"

"So Diuma was a Mercian spy?" Tatwine mused.

"It is possible. We both know it has happened before," Eadred replied. "Both kingdoms would still have men and women taking their coin. It would explain why we have not found the man who has conceived these attacks. I was certain that the targets were our great families, but the target was the kingdom itself, and the feuding families were the weapons!"

"Eadred, all is not lost. Surely, there is one of them still here—the man who killed Diuma?"

"My dear friend, there are armies camped here. How can we find one man? He may have already fled."

The two men fell into silence. More wood was positioned in the fire, and soon it recovered from its slumber. The chickens had been reduced to bones, but there was a cup or two left. Eadred's gaunt face reflected his loss of optimism, but in his mind's eye he was still sifting through everything he had learnt about the crimes and what new meaning they might have.

"Come, we will get to our destination." Tatwine shook his friend's shoulder. "Now, what do you make of the murder of the bishop? Is it connected in some way to this great crime, or is it separate in its nature and purpose? I cannot, no matter how hard I rake over what we know, make sense of the poisoning—unless it was no murder at all, but a mistake by those who cared for Aethelbert. He had lived beyond the border of his natural span; what purpose would anyone have in ending his life a few weeks before God intended?"

Eadred raised his head and smiled feebly, yet still in silence. So the hermit continued.

"And the diabolical end to the abbess's life! That we should lose both wonderful children of the Lord God so close together."

Eadred bit at his thumb and looked intently and silently at his friend.

"What is it, Eadred?"

"No, no!" Eadred imagined that his own eyes were growing to twice their normal size with the enormity of the thoughts swimming in his head. "I must go. Forgive me, dear Tatwine. I believe I see the truth emerging through the mist! I think I know how the deaths of the bishop and abbess are connected and who killed them. It is the same mind behind the deaths of Edmund, Censwith and Ingeld and this wave of crime and destruction."

"Who is it? Where are you going?" Tatwine shouted.

"To the ealdorman. Swear you will tell no one of this. Heaven help us!"

TWENTY-NINE

The Risk

Eadred watched the pale sun beam through the smoke of morning fires, clothing the courtyard and its inhabitants in a deep orange cast. He was enjoying the possession of a lighter spirit after his exoneration. It had been fear rather than belief in the accusation that he had murdered the bishop which had stopped the inmates of Snailwell from openly questioning the abbot's charge against him. Now, Eadred had returned to the fold. He had also learnt something fascinating from Ealdorman Aelfric. A Mercian warrior had just been captured and was enduring Hygelac's torture to loosen his tongue. The outcome, Eadred hoped, would shed more light on the campaign of terror and murder across the kingdom.

As the taint of murder on Eadred had been removed, he was free to accuse Brihtwold in court. A rider had returned from the Cauldron saying that Eadburga had been laid low by the fen ague and it was not possible to bring her to Snailwell to explain that she had stolen Brihtwold's silver. It would have been advantageous for her to identify the silver as belonging to Brihtwold, but Eadred had seen it himself, so he felt that this would not lessen his accusation.

After Aelfric had opened the proceedings, Eadred spoke. He accused Brihtwold of being the third man involved in the killing of Edmund and Censwith. As with the other two murderers, silver had been seen in Brihtwold's house, and he bore a grudge against his lord for having removed him from the fertile land that his parents had farmed to some worthless waterlogged meadows. It was this grievance that also provided the fertile soil for his recruitment by Diuma. The accused bellowed out his innocence until he was knocked to the ground for his trouble by the flat of a guard's sword. Eadred continued.

"I saw with my own eyes a bag of silver in your house. It is not possible for a poor and deficient peasant to amass such wealth through his own honest toil."

"If you saw such coin in my house, it was not mine. I swear it," Brihtwold cried out.

Eadred continued. "I also accuse this man of murdering, in the most foul of ways, our beloved Father Ingeld. The father was buried alive in the very land that Brihtwold farmed. This man is a womaniser, despite being married. All of Deerstow knows this. Many times, Father Ingeld was obliged to hear his confession and to impose penances. I have also had to do the same and know from his own wife and her sister how Brihtwold ranted against the penances and against priests. He took to beating his frail and disfigured wife. He is a violent man. He has often failed to control his lust and temper, and took his revenge on our poor brother in Christ."

"I did rail against the penances, I confess this, but I never attacked the father. You must believe me."

The outcome was inevitable. No one vouched for Brihtwold's word, and he was declared guilty of both crimes. The ealdorman announced that he would be executed, and he was dragged away sobbing his innocence. And that was meant to be the end of the proceedings. The three accused had been tried—one found innocent, and two found guilty. The low hum of chatter had turned to loud discourse, awaiting Aelfric's announcement that the court was closed. His sword hammered on the table three times, as was Aelfric's practice, before the noise subsided.

"This court is not yet done. I give leave to Father Eadred to speak."

Over the past few weeks, Eadred's skill with mind and tongue had received some validation, and he could, with reason, have returned to the normal life of a priest with his name and honour intact, if not raised. Why, then, was he about to risk it all? To Eadred, the answer was simple. Whether the plot had been devised in Mercia or within the Kingdom of the East Angles, the source had yet to be discovered. If this were an act of the Mercian kingdom, then it could be a prelude to an open attack. If the mind that had created the wave of violence was an East Angle, then it was treason, and if the man remained free, he could continue his destruction. Whatever the case, Eadred felt an allegiance to the new ealdorman, Aelfric. He was a good man and had supported Eadred several times already in his short time at the king's right hand. The burdens were crushing the young ealdorman. If he fell, there was no obvious man of the same character, and the kingdom would be open to endless strife, even to its destruction.

Despite his own diffidence and bouts of self-doubt, Eadred also knew the truth of Tatwine's words—that he had been granted a special gift by his God. The wicked servant hid his talent through fear and was thrown from his master's company. The faithful servant used wisely what had been given to him and entered the master's presence. He may have wanted to leave the blessing lying fallow, but Eadred's faith would not accept such a response. And far less noble, but no less inspiring to him, he found that he enjoyed the task of discovering the crooked path that led from a murder to its perpetrator. It gave his mind a freedom from the burdens of his priestly duties. So, despite the dangers to his own life, Eadred took the action that his mind had determined was necessary. He breathed deeply and spoke the fateful words.

"I accuse Brother Anselm of Snailwell Minster of murdering Bishop Aethelbert by poison, of murdering the Abbess of Elmstow and of sending Brother Asser to murder me. I know—"

The groan that met Eadred's words was angry and almost unanimous amongst the assembled brothers in Christ. Abuse was thrown by many, and even Eadred's closest supporters shook their heads. There were shouts that he had overreached himself and was not just confused and wrong, but mad and arrogant. Several cloistered men crossed themselves, shouting that the devil had taken control of his tongue. A ring of warriors converged on him and drew their swords to protect him from the throng that pressed forward. Eadred looked to Aelfric, who looked dismayed, even though he had known what Eadred was going to say. Eadred mouthed a silent prayer that the ealdorman would continue to support him. The sword slammed down, over and over, until silence returned.

"I have given this priest leave to speak. He will be heard, as will Brother Anselm's response. Now, continue!"

Eadred's voice trembled, but he pushed the words from his mouth. "I know this charge seems baseless and abhorrent, but I have just reason to accuse Brother Anselm."

Anselm rose from his chair, his body shaking with fury. "I reject this malicious charge and have no understanding of why a brother whom I have always loved and supported should speak such a calumny. If I must, I will present more than enough oath-helpers to prove the truth of my word. I have never been so abused, even by pagans! Why? Why, Eadred, do you spout such a vile lie?" Again, Aelfric had to use his sword arm to stem the torrent of foul language aimed at Eadred, who then continued.

"If I am given the chance, I will explain my reasons in court. It was Brother Anselm who contrived to give me time with the bishop the day before he died of poison, thus I was accused of the crime. It was Brother Anselm alone who knew I was journeying to Elmstow dressed as a peasant, and Brother Asser was then sent to kill me. It was—"

"Enough," Anselm cried out. "It is not right that this priest can stand here and abuse my honour. I have a right to gather my oath-helpers, and I demand it now!" The monk's appeal was echoed by many voices.

The ealdorman rose and, seeming to tire of the need to use his sword, roared above the noise. "Will you have your oath-helpers ready by the morning?" Anselm replied that he would, without difficulty. "Tomorrow morning, Father Eadred's accusation will be heard in court, and Brother Anselm will reply."

As the assembled men were dispersing, Eadred yelled at Anselm, "I know who serves you and whom you serve. And I will shine the burning light of truth on all of you and your black deeds tomorrow."

*

Eadred knelt alongside Lord Cerdic's hearth group of warriors camped just beyond the wooden walls of the minster. Aelfric's and Forthred's men were nearby. It was close to morning, and in the previous evening, Eadred had persuaded the ealdorman and the two fenland lords to prepare for battle. It had been far from an easy task, but they had agreed when Eadred convinced them that there was no other way of bringing to an end the months of strife and misery. The whole community of Snailwell, other than Brother Anselm, had been secretly removed, including Sister Edith and Abbot Cuthred, although he had to be knocked senseless and gagged to be certain of his silence.

The single peal of metal striking metal caused Eadred to gasp. A hand moved quickly to cover his mouth. "Silence!" Tatwine took his hand away. Around them, in the loosening darkness, scores of warriors tightened their grip on their weapons. Eadred fingered the shaft of his axe. If he were correct in his accusation, there would have been an attempt that night to silence him forever.

Tatwine drew close to Eadred and whispered in his ear

with an unsettling voice. "Are you certain that Anselm did what you have accused him of?"

Eadred was defiant. "I am, and more. God willing, the strength of men we have here will persuade Anselm and Leofric to put down their arms, and I will present my case in court. There is much more to say and to learn." The rising commotion within the walls told that Eadred's escape and the evacuation of all of the inmates had been discovered. The gate opened, and, lit by flaming torches, armed men began to disgorge. Eadred's eyes were not the only ones to be stunned. On and on they came, spreading to both sides of the road.

"It is as you thought. They could not silence you in secret, and now all deception is abandoned."

"It seems so," Eadred replied to his companion. "There are certainly more torches than I imagined. When I spoke to Lord Aelfric, he told me they captured a Mercian warrior yesterday, almost dead from days lost in the meres. Under Hygelac's torture, he revealed that he and others were malcontents, fortune-hunters, men without inheritance, all paid by Diuma. Not a Mercian plot against us, but one of our own using Mercian mercenaries to swell their ranks."

Tatwine put his hand on his friend's shoulder. "You did well to flush them out. First Diuma, then Anselm and now Leofric. They could hide no longer."

Before the faint light of morning stained the eastern sky, the magnitude of the opposing force became clear. Torchlight shuddered in the breeze, shadowing a hundred men or more.

"In the end, it is the matching of blades that decides an issue," Cerdic spoke to Eadred and Tatwine.

Eadred replied, "Indeed, but I hope we survive to bring the guilty to trial. Let them look at their countrymen and explain why they did commit such evil, and then let them endure the noose."

Several minutes passed without movement, then a figure astride a horse appeared through the gate. "My lords, I wish you a good morning."

THIRTY

Blade-Sweat

The three most powerful lords of the East Angles after the king himself, Aelfric, Cerdic and Forthred, stood side by side. A shield wall protected them from whatever might come their way. Facing them was Lord Leofric. As he had hoped, Eadred saw the mark of Leofric and Cuthred's family—a rearing horse—depicted upon a chained medallion around the lord's neck.

"Lord Leofric, may we know the reason for your family's treason?"

"Ah, the young ealdorman. I am no traitor! I love the king with all my heart, but he is badly served. You were made ealdorman when your father died because the king chose quickly with war descending, and he hoped against hope that you would follow your noble father in boldness and strength. How he has been let down. Do not call me traitor for wanting our kingdom to rise again! And I loved your great father. Many a night, I shared his company around the hearth. Who do you think bore the wounds of defending this kingdom against its enemies and keeping it safe? His companions fell in the heat of battle. He wept for them but returned to the fight. Many a gold ring he gave me for my service in battle. You are not fit to walk in his steps or to possess his title. You are barely a man at all."

Eadred was praying as he had never done before that Aelfric had the strength to withstand yet more ridicule. Leofric had not finished.

"And my Lord Forthred, the days of your ascent are over. You had the best land in the kingdom, but still you coveted more. Two wives brought you more riches, and both died young. Such a misfortune for you. And you gained more wealth at the expense of Lord Cerdic. So I took to destroy your wealth and your line." Warriors raised their shields to catch the arrow that sped towards Leofric at Forthred's order. "You have spent your useless life acquiring what is not yours."

"Did you kill my daughter?" Cerdic shouted. There was no response. Cerdic cried out again.

"I would have preferred it otherwise," came the answer. "But she was with her husband at his life's ending, and we could afford no witness."

"The Lord God of the Ages will bring you to justice, godless traitor!" Eadred blurted out.

"Is this the petty priest I hear? I am not godless, you fool. I have kept faith with many gods and spirits, and they support me now. I have tried the God you embrace and found him weak and useless in life's battles, so I abandoned him. And while I have your ear, listen hard. If you still live when this is over and I am victorious, I will have you tortured and hanged. Your fall and your end have already been determined in the spirit world. I hear that you took Edith with you when you crept from this minster last night, but you do not possess her heart. That is mine, and once she has watched you die, she will also be mine in body."

Aelfric had remained behind the shield wall, close to the other lords, but Hygelac had used the concealment to remove himself. While Leofric continued his attempts to fracture the skin-thin alliance, the battle-hardened commander of the ealdorman's force was quietly readying his men at both wings of the line of warriors. He gave a shout.

The centre of the shield wall opened, and Aelfric, Cerdic and their men burst out towards Leofric. At either end of the line, Aelfric's men also charged. The ragged lines hit with splintering, bone-crushing force. Eadred and Tatwine fought side by side, each with axe and shield. Alfred was not far from them, leading the Cauldron Folk. Eadred knew what to expect from Tatwine, and he was prepared. The last time the two men had faced an enemy, it had been Eadred's first battle. He had wondered then if Tatwine were the same Christian man he had come to know. The monk had transformed into a raging beast, seemingly unconcerned for his own life. He had hacked the life from man after man. When Eadred had faltered, Tatwine had sworn and hit him hard. "When a man comes at you with his weapon ready to take your life in the ferocity of battle, you are no longer a priest, you are a warrior. Kill him to save yourself, and if you live through the day, pray for his soul when night falls." They were words that had saved Eadred's life that day, though he had seen the darker side of his friend. There was a shadow over Tatwine's soul, seen at its most clear in the violence of battle.

And here, before Snailwell Minster, the battle for the kingdom's riches and its soul exploded. When one of Leofric's men swung his axe down towards Eadred's head, all else disappeared other than the need to defend, then attack. He killed the warrior and sustained his first wound of the day, but Eadred had become a bear with slashing claws.

The fighting was close, bloody and evenly poised, then Forthred led his men forward. The hacking grew more desperate and fierce. Leofric's shield wall began to break as some of the mercenaries turned to flee back into the minster, and in a few moments his force was disordered. Eadred and Tatwine continued to push forward and supported each other more than they cared for their own safety, as had become the mark of their friendship. The Cauldron Folk proved their worth, eager to stand with their unyielding leader. While men hacked and thrust with their blades, others fired arrow points, and the difference between life and death became more a decision of fate than of skill. Alfred's fearsome roar was cut short when a point hit him in the chest, and he faltered.

"Protect Alfred," Eadred yelled to the Cauldron warriors. He saw Alfred fall and screamed his name before one of Leofric's men smashed into Alfred's unprotected head with an axe blade. Eadred slashed his way through to the place where Alfred had fallen, but it was too late. The advance pushed him forward, and mourning would have to wait.

The attackers cleaved into exposed backs and heads. Through the buildings and passageways, the pursuit continued. Battle turned into a rout, then a massacre. It was soon over with only a few of Leofric's men managing to escape. The rest lay dead or captured. The base lord himself was found hacked and mutilated; the opportunity of questioning him had passed. But there was still a chance to discover more about the extent of Leofric's iniquity. It was fortunate that Eadred recognised Brother Anselm, who was caught trying to leave the minster. He was bound and hauled away by Aelfric's men.

With their blood up and Leofric's force defeated, Forthred and Cerdic found themselves with their closest hearth warriors facing each other. The recent skin of cooperation that had grown facing a common enemy looked perilously thin compared with generations of antipathy, and the Lady Hilda was not present to weave the threads of peace. The warriors of the two lords struck out at each other. "Hold!" Forthred bellowed. "Enough blood has been lost." He stared at Cerdic and sheathed his blade. The lord of the deep fens nodded, did likewise and shouted, "It is time to heal."

Eadred sat with his back against the church wall, binding a wound to his thigh. His body shook with weeping. His one-eyed friend sat beside him, washing a wound to his forearm. His face also ran with tears. "What of Elf?" Eadred sobbed. "I saw the love they had for each other. She would be praying now that he is safe. God help her, and us, when we tell her."

"How I feel his loss," Tatwine struggled to speak. "I had hoped we three would be friends for all of our lives. Let us go first to the church and pray for Alfred's soul, and for all those who died with good in their hearts." The two friends wrapped the cloak of their arms around each other and went into the minster church. They were not alone. Inmates, warriors, folk from the settlement—men and women—wept and prayed.

Eadred and Tatwine prayed and cried until the gloom of night descended and they could bear no more misery. They struggled out into the cold air to find some bodily sustenance. "I saw you during the fighting." Tatwine smiled at his friend. "You have become a fearless warrior. I taught you well! And the day, in so many ways, belongs to you. I spoke to Hygelac; he weathered the day well. I think he will live to an old age, despite his hot temper and love of war. He told me that one of Leofric's senior men, who was suffering at his hands, betrayed that our arrival came when Leofric's force was still growing in number and skill. In a month or so, it would have become far stronger and ready to move openly against the other lords. You brought us here to confront the enemy when they were still quite weak. Your charge against Anselm unnerved them, they sought battle, and we prevailed."

Eadred managed a feeble smile, then looked around the solemn courtyard with its weight of the dead, burst bodies, separated limbs and heads, the ground moist with blood. "How can this happen in a Christian kingdom? I have learned to fight to preserve peace and my own life, but I tell you I will always be troubled by the taking of a man's life by another. Where is Christ in all of this?"

"He is in the hearts and heads of Forthred and Cerdic," Tatwine replied. "The fenland feud between them has, I pray, ended. It was not the day you wanted by choice, my dear friend, but it can be redeemed. The malignant presence of Leofric has been destroyed. His cousin, the abbot, says he knew nothing of Leofric's ambition or methods. I am not sure of the truth. And, so I am told, the ealdorman will convene Anselm's trial in a few days. I am sure that the last scraps of this foul plague will be discovered and dealt with, and you will be called upon to use your skills. May Anselm be punished for what he has done. Make sure that you extract all that he knows. I fear he has too many secrets.

"Come," Tatwine continued. "We have lost our dear friend, and many here will also feel his death and the death of other companions, but let us find food and renew our bodies, for we still have tasks to achieve."

THIRTY-ONE

Eadred's Battle

It was a trial that no one had expected and, up until a handful of days earlier, only one man had wanted. Eadred sat at the front of the assembly, absorbed in his own thoughts. The court assembled on the fourth day after the battle, once the courtyard had been cleansed and the dead from all sides had been buried in consecrated soil, other than Leofric, Diuma, Boisil and Brihtwold, whose bodies were burned and their ashes disposed of in a shithole. Much had changed over those days since the battle. Brother Anselm would have easily gathered his oath-helpers on the day Eadred had accused him, but now there was not one man willing to say that Anselm's word was true. Still, Eadred had no idea what the accused man would say.

Barely half of the number of men who had witnessed the earlier trials now congregated in the courtyard. But the desire to catch every word and watch every nuance on Eadred's and Anselm's faces told in the silence that greeted Aelfric's opening of the court proceedings. Eadred accused the brother of collaborating with Leofric in the thegn's murderous campaign against the fenland lords and of murdering Bishop Aethelbert and the Abbess of Elmstow. Aelfric ordered Anselm to respond to the charges.

"Lord, this accusation grieves me much." The monk shook his head in sadness and disbelief. "I am guiltless, both in deed and counsel, of the charges made against me by Father Eadred. But I am now defenceless, which is why I sought to leave this minster during the battle, and did no more than did Father Eadred when he left here in the dark of night some weeks back to protect his life. No man will support my oath because of Leofric's treacherous behaviour and his actions of a few days past that cost so many innocent lives. But what has that to do with me? I ask any man who knows me, has there been any taint upon me these many years that I have been a brother here in Snailwell? Is there any link between Leofric's crimes and me? Father Eadred is a good and faithful priest and friend. Have I not always supported him? My heart is broken by his actions against me. Surely, if I am to be hanged by the neck, there must be a reason. I am no thief or murderer with a heritage of lies and crimes against my name." The monk looked to Aelfric. "Lord, you are a just man. Though I have no oath-helpers and it is irregular, I plead with this court: let Eadred show why he believes his accusation to be true."

The hum of voices testified that Brother Anselm's defence of himself and his plea seemed reasonable. Eadred's face also betrayed the disquiet within him at the action he had embarked upon. He tried to quell the tremor in his hands, but he could not contain the sweat that broke upon his back and forehead. He turned away from the faces looking towards him. There was Tatwine, with no fear in his expression, only the firm certainty that his friend knew what he was doing. He gave an almost imperceptible nod and smile. Eadred breathed deeply for as long as he could until the ealdorman instructed him to explain his charge against Anselm.

"Brother Asser was sent from this minster to kill me because he had been told that I had poisoned the bishop. He knew that I was journeying to our sister minster at Elmstow, and he followed me there. Who told him to kill me, and who here knew where I was going? Brother Tatwine, who had ventured here, told only one person of my plan, and that was Brother Anselm, whom I trusted at that time. Brother Tatwine will swear this is true."

"If I may speak," Anselm responded. "It is true that Brother Tatwine, who came here under the guise of another brother, told me of Father Eadred's plan to journey to Elmstow. To my eternal shame, I did tell someone, but only because I was scared for my life. Diuma or one of his spies saw Brother Tatwine talking to me. The foul man questioned why I was meeting Brother Tatwine in such a secluded spot, and he threatened me with a beating or worse. In panic, I think I may have exposed Father Eadred's intention. We were all terrified of Diuma, and I am sorry that I thought no further than my own safety, but I am not strong."

For several reasons, it was not what Eadred wanted to hear, but he pressed on. It was strange for anyone to question an accused man in court and almost unheard of to muse upon the possible elements of a crime and motives of the accused. Yet that was what was happening. Perhaps it was the enormity of the crimes that allowed such peculiar behaviour to be accepted. Whatever the reason, the assembly seemed to fall under the spell as the two men talked. Eadred continued.

"I have thought much about the deaths of the bishop and the Abbess of Elmstow. Why did they die not many days or much distance apart? If anyone had wanted the abbess dead because of her cleansing of the filth from Elmstow, then they could have killed her on many other occasions over the past twelve months. She had a daily habit of a short solitary ride from her minster, followed by prayer, so there was no need to wait until she was here in Snailwell. The abbess was killed because of something she discovered here or something she and the bishop spoke of that would expose the man behind the wave of crimes. Though Bishop Aethelbert was old and within the last weeks of his life, he also had to die, so that whatever he and the abbess had discovered died in Snailwell before it was divulged to someone he trusted. He was already bed-bound and thus was given dwale. I know the consequences of this concoction. It is a medicine in small doses, but given a little more over time, it destroys a man's strength, his speech and his breathing, and eventually he dies. Our beloved bishop was given enough to remove his ability to form words and eventually to kill him. The taste and odour were too slight to detect in a single cup, but over several days the stench of dwale came to fill the bishop's cell from the waste of his body. It was either fortunate for the killer or it could have been planned that I returned to Snailwell when I did and was then blamed for the bishop's death.

"I do not know what the abbess discovered or what she and the bishop spoke of that meant they both had to die. But now Diuma is dead, only you know that, Brother Anselm."

The monk shook his head. "You are clever with your use of words, Eadred, but it was not I who killed these wonderful leaders of our Church. It was Diuma and Leofric. Surely, that must be clear?"

"It was what I also believed for a while. At other times, I thought the abbot was the mind behind all the destruction. I now know that the abbot, although not a warm-hearted father of his flock, is heedful of his duty. Brother Anselm, you knew that the bishop was close to death, and you gave me the opportunity to pray with him by granting me the time that was allotted to you. When I fled the minster in fear of my life that night, you succeeded in making me the obvious murderer."

"But that was an act of kindness, my boy." The monk smiled, looking at the faces around him.

"I thought so too, then I remembered that the abbot gave instructions that the inmates were to visit the bishop in pairs. If I were to ask the monk who was to attend the bishop with you why he did not come with me, I wonder what he would say?"

Anselm shook his head. "He would answer truthfully that I asked if you could attend the bishop alone because you always shared a special friendship. There is no dark purpose, Eadred, only care, as there has always been."

Though Anselm looked with a soft and affectionate face towards him, Eadred did not reciprocate. He had learnt from Tatwine that a contest between two armed men, especially if it was not one-sided, was often a bloody game where each man tested the other to see their strengths and weaknesses and favoured moves. Though the result was seldom certain, the better warrior would begin to position his enemy so he could not use his strengths and makes mistakes, until a final blow ended the matter. Eadred's guts twisted and ached because the outcome of this battle was unclear, but he knew with certainty that he could not allow his mind to believe that Anselm would win. He had to take more risks; there seemed little point in doing otherwise.

"You have made several mistakes, Brother Anselm. Perhaps each one alone might be defended, but together they show that no one else could have committed these crimes other than you." In response, the monk smiled. Eadred continued. "You erred in not killing the abbot when you had the opportunity. I made certain that he left with us for safety on the night following my accusation against you. You told Brother Tatwine that you visited Leofric to teach him to read the Scriptures, at the abbot's request, and that he was a good pupil. But the abbot told me that he never gave this instruction and will swear so before this court."

"I thought the abbot might not agree, so I used to visit the thegn for that purpose without the abbot's knowledge. I thought this was a small sin."

"Indeed," Eadred replied. "It is doubtful that the abbot would have chosen you as a teacher, for you can neither read nor write. Your instructions to me on how to find the Cauldron were given as a song that you made and learnt by heart. So why were you visiting the thegn every week?"

Anselm's face tightened, and he gripped his hands together. "I had not the time or energy to explain to Brother Tatwine the purpose of my visits to Lord Leofric. The man could not read, so I was teaching the thegn the Scriptures in the same manner that I taught you the way to reach the Cauldron."

Eadred retaliated. "It is hard to see why such a noble mission should be kept from the abbot or that it was too tangled to explain to Brother Tatwine! And if Leofric wanted lessons in such a form, surely he could have asked his cousin, the abbot, if you could provide them. Neither you nor Leofric uttered one word to the abbot about these meetings.

"Now, let us return to Diuma's threat against you to reveal what Brother Tatwine told you. Surely, with one who professes so much care for me, even if you were compelled to tell Diuma of my destination, you did not have to tell him that I was disguised as a peasant. Brother Asser and I had never met. I did not recognise him, but he knew me. He discovered me amongst all the other men at Elmstow, and it did not take him long to do so. You wanted that young monk to find me." Eadred stared at Anselm, who had reddened and was beginning to breathe heavily. Eadred continued. "You described me in as much detail as you could. The only other person who could have accomplished that and passed the information to Diuma in time for me to be followed was Brother Tatwine. It could only have been you who set Brother Asser on the road to kill me."

Anselm stared in silence. Eadred knew he had struck a telling blow and continued. "At the end of Brihtwold's trial, I accused you of murdering the bishop and the abbess and said that I knew who served you and whom you served. It was a trap, of course, and you fell into it. I pondered that night whether you would suffer the same fate as Diuma.

He was killed to silence his tongue and because he was no longer useful. But this was not to be your fate. You not only survived, but Leofric rode out that very night to protect you, even though his force was nowhere near being at its full strength. This was surely not an action taken to save a simple monk who taught him the Scriptures. Indeed, it was very strange; a high risk for the thegn. If you had poisoned the bishop or killed the abbess on the thegn's order, and there was a danger that you would tell the truth at your trial, you would surely have arrows in your back by now.

"Why did Leofric confront us with his force, and at that time? No one had accused him of any crime. He was not on trial. There is only one explanation for all of these happenings. You did not serve the thegn, he served you. Leofric and Diuma may have been the brute force behind this time of murder and misery, but you were the mind that devised it all. You were the dark and evil force that worked in the worlds of men and of the spirit to wreak devastation.

"Your words encouraged me to believe that the abbot incited the torrent of crime and that Leofric was an honest thegn. Yet when Abbot Cuthred accused me of murdering poor Brother Asser, I could see in his eyes that he really did not understand what he was saying. Diuma gave him the words, and his dislike of me made him say them. Did the warriors who fetched Brother Asser's body and who questioned Sister Edith come from the abbot, as they said they did? No, they did not. For if they did, the abbot would have known what had happened that night at Elmstow. The warriors did not serve the abbot, did they? He had no idea what had happened. They were sent by you.

"I believed your condemnation of the abbot for a long

while. Thus, when Sister Edith told me that Diuma and an arrogant nobleman, who wore a rich medallion about his neck, had come to Elmstow to gain access to her body for carnal pleasure, I imagined that it was the abbot. But it was Leofric. I should have realised then that the abbess and the abbot would have behaved very differently towards each other. It was clever of you to have a creature such as Diuma to do your bidding. He recruited the witless men who murdered and slaughtered. He gave silver to the two brothers and to Brihtwold to kill Lord Forthred's son. He scared people, he filled their heads with demonic thoughts, and he also drew their eyes. He was the one they remembered as evil.

"Brother Anselm, you have been the clever mind in the shadows that let others take the consequences for your dreadful campaign, and you almost succeeded. But it could only have been you who sought my death at the hands of poor Brother Asser. You were the only one who knew of my disguise that led him to attack me. Leofric has openly admitted—indeed, has glorified—his crimes against the fenland lords. You met that traitor often, and behind the abbot's back, for some dark and perfidious purpose, which you sought to hide by a complete and stupid lie. My threat to unmask your actions, the actions of a monk who seemed innocent and harmless, led Leofric to unleash all of his forces against us. He would not do that for a simple monk. He and Diuma were your dogs.

"Your word is worth nothing. You have no oath-helpers to support you. You are exposed as a murderer, a traitor and as a practitioner of devilry. All are punishable by death. Leofric declared before us all that he called upon demonic spirits. If your creature called upon demons, then he was following your directions. It was he that cut the right hand from the body of an executed man and then secreted the remainder of the body within Saint Wulfmaer's coffin."

"It was the left hand! I saw it myself. There is no power in the right hand, you fool!"

The assembly gasped at Anselm's words, and cloistered men crossed themselves.

Eadred knew the time had come. He turned to face Aelfric. "My lord, Brother Anselm's words have condemned him. He has led a foul, treasonous and diabolical war against this kingdom, in the world of men and in the dark spirit realm. He has caused many deaths. He has had slaughtered countless cattle owned by the fenland lords and by common folk. I ask that he be found guilty of these many crimes." Cries of support greeted Eadred's words.

Aelfric rose. "Brother Anselm of Snailwell, I find you guilty of murder, treachery, devilry and destruction of other men's property. You are the most loathsome creature. You are sentenced to be mutilated, hanged, your body burned and your ashes thrown to the winds."

Despite Anselm's fate, Eadred saw a faint smile upon his face as he listened in silence to the abuse being hurled towards him by the assembled court. The monk's reaction reinforced the importance of a final question from Eadred before Aelfric closed the proceedings.

When the angry voices began to abate, Eadred shouted, "Lord Aelfric, may I ask one final question?" The ealdorman nodded, albeit with apparent exasperation, and he smashed his sword on the table.

"Pray, why did you unleash this wave of misery upon your fellow men?"

323

Anselm gave a reflective smile. "I thought that the thegn's desire for Edith might be the end of you, Eadred. He lost his soul for a spell that would turn her heart from you to him and would see your life end in misery. I taught Leofric every action and every word until he knew them by heart. When the abbot ordered your return to Snailwell and I could contrive a plan to see you blamed for the bishop's death, I believed the spell was working. But it seems it was not! You are better protected in the world of the spirit than I believed."

Anselm turned to the ealdorman with a sneer upon his face. "We were successful in keeping you from protecting the wedding, but the idiots Diuma chose to destroy the marriage alliance instead drew those lords together. I was beyond anger. But is it not a gentle thought to send you to sleep at night, my lord, that if you had not failed to attend the union of the fenland lords, then their two offspring might still be alive?"

Anselm looked to Eadred. "I was one of the old ealdorman's eyes and ears. Aethelbert knew there was one of us in Snailwell but I think he only came to suspect me recently, when he began to question me about my absences from the minster. He also seemed to become suspicious of Leofric, and could well have understood some of our intentions. Cuthred's appointment as abbot made life difficult for us, so Leofric played upon Cuthred's ambitions and ties of kinship to distract him from our purpose. Fortunately, I think Aethelbert believed Cuthred was one of us, and he never seemed to trust him. So when the abbess arrived for her meeting with Aethelbert, we feared that he would entrust her to tell the ealdorman of his discoveries, for he was beyond travel. We could not let the bishop or abbess live.

"As you probably came to suspect, we are not simple-minded believers in God. We used to call on God once in a while, but he did not take kindly to being entreated to help us in what he considered to be evil. The idea to have a church built at Thornham came to me from the demon I called upon to help Leofric in his carnal quest for Edith. The abbot was all too helpful. It was never intended to be used as the abbot hoped, but to mock God. I could have reversed the abbot's purification of the Roman bricks with ease, and then I could call upon the powerful gods of the legions. The demon's price for helping Leofric was to install, by procession, the body of the executed man whose hand we had used in the spell. This would have desecrated the church, without others' knowledge, and we could have used it for our rituals. It almost worked when Cuthred agreed to translate the saint to Thornham. We put the body in the saint's coffin and saw it carried to the church, but did not anticipate that Cuthred would want to transfer the saint to a new coffin.

"Most of my life I have harboured secrets. It was no difficulty for me to wear the mask of a brother but without the beliefs that most men consider should accompany a tonsured man. I mouthed the words and played the rituals. It was easy.

"Leofric, Diuma and I found a common purpose. The thegn was jealous of the power and wealth of the fenland lords and lusted after that woman. I helped him. Diuma was also obsessed with worldly ambitions, but they were quite narrow, in keeping with his mind, but he was useful.

It was Diuma who told me of the present shape of the road to the Cauldron after journeying to those parts when he was recruiting our band of willing hands. For even if I had recalled the path from a single journey a dozen years past, the shifting meres would have changed its shape and rendered my memory useless."

Anselm looked again at the ealdorman. "As for me, my purpose was greater. You would barely understand. I could see that the kingdom would be a lesser place without your great father. He had the heart of a great warrior and straddled the seen and unseen worlds. Some like-minded men proposed that I take his place and keep faith with the spirits. So I did what I could. I called on all manner of spirits—that was my strength—and almost destroyed the powerful lords of the kingdom.

"What of our ancestral gods and spirits, who had lived alongside us for generations? They lived in this land, in its forests and meres. Then the forces of the so-called One God came in strength and sought to push them from our hearts. I dared to show the limits of his power, even within his own house, for a short time. Do you really believe that men like Cuthred, who have barely a spiritual thought in their heads, are a fitting bridge between the people and the unseen world? Is that the future you want? I did not seek to destroy the kingdom, but to save it. I pity you all. I should have won if not for a petty priest."

THIRTY-TWO

Return to the Cauldron

"Anselm can trouble us no longer." The priest and the monk rose from their brief rest and continued their journey towards the deep fens and the Cauldron.

"I am sure you are right," Eadred replied to Tatwine. "As for his black soul, it has gone to hell, I have no doubt of that. It is beyond any man to call him back or to engage his spirit in any crime. So it was Leofric who called upon the powers of darkness to harm me, and Anselm willingly helped him. The affection between Sister Edith and myself was widely known after I saved her from the pit of Elmstow, and I paid my penance. Her heart could never belong to another, and it galled Leofric to the point of losing his soul. It is true that there were times when I thought the Lord God had abandoned me, but I am safe, and it is Leofric and his brood who are dead.

"Yet in the world of flesh, many will continue to suffer

because of the damage Anselm and his nest inflicted. How many deaths already? And how many more will perish from starvation with their herds slaughtered? And how many more grieve? How are we to tell Elfwyn? When I saw Elf for the first time, she reminded me of my dear sister," Eadred sighed. "I daresay I have already told you of this, but it preys upon my mind."

Tatwine's smile spoke for him. He wrapped his arm around Eadred. "The days can be hard, there is no doubt of that. There are not many that are free from pain, but we must not let this weigh on us for too long, or we become dark in spirit and cannot see the light, which is everywhere. There are men, like Anselm and Leofric, so dripping in sin that their greed and lust consumes the lives of others. But we are different. If Christ is within us, we must shine, so others see him within us. When I am alone, as I am for most of my days, I can drift into melancholy. Yet I can always find something that brings a smile or remember some happiness if I put my mind to it. My memories of our days together always lift my spirit. I smile and often laugh when I think of those times. And I reflect on those truly wonderful hours when we ponder over the footsteps of a secret criminal to see if we can catch him. For now, let us give thanks that we have conquered the evil that risked the ruin of our kingdom, and much of this success rests with you. How you trapped Anselm with your words; it was wonderful to see." Eadred blushed, and a diffident smile crept over his face.

"Let me tell you, my gut ached with fear for most of the time I was talking," Eadred admitted. "It is a hard lesson for me that an evil mind, who is also clever, can block my blows, one after the other, and almost win the contest. It was only after I had struck out at him many times that I began to feel I had his measure. Sadly, it is seldom won by a single overwhelming blow but by many strikes and wounds."

"And that is what you did, my friend," Tatwine smiled. "Remember also that Sister Edith is, at last, safe. She is returning to Elmstow with warriors to protect her on her journey. That is indeed a joyful thought."

Eadred reached for the chain around his neck. "And see, I again have this crucifix that she gave to me at Elmstow last year."

"It has a simple beauty, Eadred. And even Abbot Cuthred now sings your praises! Surely, this is a miracle and a cause for happiness and mirth. The ealdorman too is strengthened in his position because of you." Tatwine started to sing a psalm, Eadred joined in, and the hours passed happily.

*

In late morning, Eadred and Tatwine were not far from the Cauldron. They had seen a few of the local folk on the road, and these had rushed back to alert the community. So when the two friends turned the final corner, they saw a knot of close to a dozen souls, talking anxiously amongst themselves. When they saw the two figures, there was silence. No one came to greet them. When Eadred and Tatwine approached, Elfwyn, with Eadgifu and Eadburga by her side, stepped forward. Eadred looked into Elf's moistened eyes as they searched for hope. He opened his mouth, but Elf stood ashen-faced, staring past him, and his words were lost in her cries. Eadburga looked at Tatwine, and he shook his head. The two women held on to Elf, and all there began to sob.

"How?"

The hermit replied to those who asked, and soon his tears fell. "There was a battle at Snailwell Minster. The thegn Leofric was one of the evil souls behind the misery that has been inflicted on the fens. Alfred fought bravely, as he did always, and as did the other men of the Cauldron. He carried the cause of your people, and he helped win a great victory to protect all of the kingdom. Evil has been defeated, in flesh and in spirit. He has been buried with the kingdom's heroes in sacred soil." Tatwine continued to sob as he turned to Elfwyn. "Alfred is now in the Lord God's gentle hands. There, in triumph, he awaits you when your time comes. Our time as flesh is brief and often harsh. Our time in the Lord's house is forever, for those who have chosen him as their god. There, you will both rejoice and love."

"And the others?" another woman spoke with much apprehension.

"All the men who left with Alfred will return. They carry many wounds, but none that are deep, so I am told. You will see them in a few days." The hermit's words tapered away. Many who heard him made the sign of the cross and sighed with relief, but none openly rejoiced. All that could be heard were sobs and the whistling of the wind and creaking of branches.

In silence, those present came to Elfwyn and embraced her, then they began to slip away. Eadred understood their dilemma. He had seen it before in his duties. For some, there was the embarrassment of feeling joy while a wife was enduring the worst hour in her life. For others, it was the bleak unknown of how they would move forward without the man who had bonded them together and seen to their safety for a decade or more. As if to reinforce Alfred's loss, it was left to Elfwyn to shout to those returning to their homes that when the men returned, there would be a feast. One woman spoke to Eadred, saying that the house where they had stayed before was ready for them and food would be brought later.

*

The two companions slept all night and until the light of the following day had started its solemn departure to the treetops, and their fire had long since died. They emerged cold, confused and with empty stomachs. The communal hall was blissfully warm with the comforting smell of a rich stew steaming in the cauldron. The door creaked behind them.

"Eadgifu, what a joy to see you once more, and indeed you do look well." Eadred squeezed her shoulders. Tatwine wrapped her in his arms and kissed her cheek. "I have something to tell you that I hope will cheer you," Eadred continued. "The beast, your husband, Brihtwold, has been executed. He can no longer cause you harm. And listen, the ealdorman has ensured that you will inherit your husband's land, and any charges against you and your sister from leaving your lord's land without permission have been withdrawn. You are both free and have land!"

Eadgifu fell to her knees and wept. "We are free to return to Deerstow?" Eadred confirmed that they were.

"Father Eadred accused Brihtwold of killing Father Ingeld and aiding in the deaths of Edmund and Censwith. It was upheld," Tatwine added joyfully.

331

Eadgifu rose and went to leave. "I must tell my sister, and we will share a cup or two tonight." She turned at the door. "Oh, I almost forgot why I had come. Please take what food you need. The two jugs of ale on the shelf are for you."

"And I also forgot," Eadred added, "I pray your sister is well again after her illness. The ague can be most terrible."

"She is well," Eadgifu replied. "I cannot think why you thought she was not. Now, please see to your stomachs."

Eadred took platters of thick bread and stew, and Tatwine carried the ale back to their house. They had already transported some of the burning logs from the hall, and their own fire now crackled happily, issuing shadows that flickered and leapt against the wall.

"Is it not a wonderful thing to see happiness in another and know that you have helped in its birth?" Eadred belched. Two cups later, the priest stared at the pulsing golden heart before him, his tears hissing on the embers.

"My dearest friend, may I tell you what I believe is the greatest difference between us?" Tatwine asked, and Eadred waved his hand by way of permission. The hermit's words were already slurred, and he looked at his cup with apparent surprise at the impact of what he had drunk. "I am sad in the moment. The worse the circumstance, the sadder I am. But I know I return to happiness because that is my nature, for I know I am loved by the Lord. In my youth, I succumbed to evil many times, and you know I killed my best friend in anger. But God forgave me, and as the years passed, I came to forgive myself. The Lord God told me to live alone, not just as penance, but until I felt that I was in control of my darker emotions. That day has not yet come. You also know you are loved by the Lord, and he has given you great gifts. Yet, while I and my past wrongs have come to an understanding, you are tortured by your past mistakes and even those happenings that cannot in all conscience be your responsibility. You did not make Alfred come with us to Snailwell. He came through duty to his lord and to protect his people and his country. And look at the good you have done. You have freed Eadgifu and her sister from that monster Brihtwold."

Eadred could not bear to look his friend in the eyes. "I am tormented by much of life, that is true. And it is the nature of the tasks I have taken upon myself that I will venture along a path for some distance sometimes before I understand that it is a mistake. I have come to terms with this, I think. But when I am responsible for the death of someone, how can I forgive myself? Someone who should have lived is dead because of my mistake."

The hermit replied with some mild annoyance. "Though it is sad beyond measure, you are not the one responsible for Brother Asser's death."

"It is not Brother Asser. Lord God, help me, I have just understood that I persuaded the court to execute the wrong man!"

THIRTY-THREE

Redemption

"Good morning, Eadgifu, you are well after last night?" Eadred smiled at the woman who opened the door.

"My head hurts a little, Father, and I do not doubt that yours and Brother Tatwine's do as well." She chuckled and smiled at the monk. "Come in. We owe you both much; you are welcome here."

"It is your sister we wish to talk to. Is she within?"

"Father, she is not, but by the mere's edge gathering withies. She will be awhile. Is there something I can do?"

"No, I think not. We will go and meet her there." Eadred gave Eadgifu a quick blessing, then he and Tatwine left her.

It was usually a joy for Eadred to be close to the mere. Soft underfoot, the fragrance of peat in the sharp, mist-flushed air, the wind singing through sedge and reed, the melancholy cries of the birds and the dark, mystical face of the water reflecting the clouds puffed in the vast sky. But it was not a cause for happiness today. He walked in sombre silence, and Tatwine left him to his thoughts.

Eadburga turned to the sound of the footfall. She cut the blade of her knife into the osier trunk and made a pleasant greeting. Eadred had honed and repeated his words over and over, but he was praying hard that God would help him through the next minutes. He had no appetite for an agreeable welcome.

"Eadburga, I cannot blunt the purpose of my words. Brihtwold was a loathsome creature. His mistreatment of your sister was known by all. Father Ingeld married them and became the first priest to condemn Brihtwold's behaviour, imposing penances many times. I also gave him penances and know how he decried them to anyone who would listen. You know that the cornerstone of our laws is that an honourable man is considered most likely to be innocent of a crime, and a man of bad character is most likely to be guilty. Brihtwold was undeniably a dishonourable man and took silver, did he not, with Dudda and Cuthbert, to kill Edmund and Censwith? I came to think that he also killed Father Ingeld."

Eadburga was sitting on a fallen tree trunk with a mildly bemused expression. "He was capable of all manner of evil, Father. I daresay you would have said so yourself in court. I am occupied with my work now, so I will return to it if there is nothing you want from me. There is much to do."

"Sadly, Eadburga, I was mistaken in believing he killed Father Ingeld. Last year, the father arrived in Deerstow from the Cauldron, as usual, when the days were beginning to lengthen. He stayed for a few days only this time. Many people saw him and presumed he had left early for Snailwell.

If I had not been so preoccupied with my own concerns about officiating at the wedding, I would have remembered that Brihtwold told me that he was not in Deerstow at the time of Father Ingeld's final visit, but in the upland, together with other men from Deerstow. This has been affirmed by others." Eadburga shrugged her shoulders at his words.

"It was only last night that I realised Brihtwold could not have murdered Ingeld. I then lay awake during the black hours thinking about who else could have done such a terrible thing as to bury a priest alive."

"Did your thoughts lead you anywhere?" Eadburga questioned.

"They did. Before I accused Brihtwold, I had initially thought that Father Ingeld was murdered by Boisil after the priest confronted him for leading the boy Coenwulf into crime and execution. But although he faced his own execution, Boisil denied this murder. In my experience, if a man already condemned denies another murder, then it is likely to be true. So I looked elsewhere. The mistake I then made was believing that Ingeld was killed because he imposed such heavy penances on Brihtwold. But when I knew that Brihtwold could not have been the murderer, then my mind considered the opposite—that he was murdered because the penances were too light and did not change Brihtwold's foul behaviour. Someone, or perhaps two people, whose lives were made miserable by Brihtwold's conduct, confronted Father Ingeld, and when he said he could do no more, their fury overtook them. Perhaps Ingeld's horrific and silent death reminded them of their own lives, and they wanted him to feel as they felt—powerless in their suffering."

"Father, I know you have a reputation for solving

crimes, but answer me this. If Ingeld deserved to die for his weakness when punishing Brihtwold, then surely this killer would have also killed Brihtwold? It makes no sense to let the cause of the misery live."

Eadred nodded. "He did not live, did he? Ingeld's murderer also killed Brihtwold, but not by their own hand. If Brihtwold had been murdered, not executed, then suspicion would fall on those Brihtwold had harmed. It is true that some husbands might be suspected but also his own wife, whose life he had made a misery. Ingeld's body was found buried on Brihtwold's land, but it was not only Brihtwold who lived there. Is this not true?"

"If you are saying that my sister and I killed Father Ingeld, then you are not as clever as men say. That is absurd!"

"I will question Eadgifu later and see what she says," Eadred replied.

"She will be at a loss to understand, for she knows nothing, and you have no proof of anything, you stupid man." Eadburga pulled her knife free from the wood. In a heartbeat, Tatwine had unsheathed his blade. It was the action from Eadburga that Eadred had waited for.

"I have also wondered about the murders of Edmund and Censwith. Dudda was bulky and slow, and Cuthbert was weak, but Edmund was the greatest warrior in these parts—strong, nimble and watchful. In a struggle, Censwith would also have fought and screamed. The killers could not afford to fail, as they had already at the wedding feast, or suffer heavy wounds or have the sounds of conflict heard. Thus, I believed that there were three killers. I had always assumed three men, but a woman's presence would have calmed the mood. Perhaps a woman to occupy Censwith in conversation while Dudda and Cuthbert plunged their knives into Edmund's back? A powerful woman could subdue Censwith and keep her from crying out.

"I saw the silver coin in Brihtwold's house. I believed it was his and was payment for his part in the murders, but it was yours all along. It was clever of you to tell Tatwine that you had stolen it from Brihtwold. I only realised my mistake—my fatal mistake—when I understood that you did not return to Snailwell for Brihtwold's trial because you had the ague, but because you would have been named as a witness to the silver in his house. In his desperation for life, Brihtwold would have cried out that you also lived there. The risks of your deception falling apart were too great. And I was so easily deluded by my disgust of Brihtwold and your deceit. You needed to be free of that man, and you needed money to care for your sister, but you have damned your soul."

Eadburga stared at the priest. "My sister had no protection from her husband, none from her lord and none from the Church. Eadgifu had no involvement, and you have no proof. You accused someone of these murders, and they have been hanged. Would you now accuse another? Now, I will gather my withies and return home."

Eadburga disappeared along the path back to the settlement.

"Can we do nothing? She killed Father Ingeld and Edmund and Censwith!" Tatwine looked at Eadred.

"I fear not; not within the law. An accusation would fail. I have no evidence, and she has a good name, here and in Deerstow, but I will not stop trying. I had hoped and prayed that Eadburga would prove me wrong, that she was innocent and I did accuse the right man. But I now know that she was the murderer. My friend, I made terrible mistakes. I was so consumed with preparing for my battle with Anselm that I wanted Brihtwold's trial out of my way. I was the witness in court to the bag of silver that took him to the rope. If anyone is to blame, it is I. I pursued a man to his death. I killed him and let the real killer go free. What have I done?" Tatwine sheathed his knife and put his arm around his weeping friend. "We are human; we make mistakes. He was not a good man."

Eadred could not shake the monstrous feeling of his failure. It was made worse the following day when Eadburga disappeared without warning. She took her knife, cloak and a few pennies.

"Why would she leave, Father?" Eadgifu wept. "Did she say anything to you?"

"I think she is oppressed by something in her life. But I know how much she cares for you."

It was one of the few times that Eadred did not take the fullest advantage of the food and wine put before him. He smiled, as best he could, at the farewell feast for Tatwine and himself, but his joy was plain when Elfwyn was acclaimed by all as the new headman. As her first task, she raised the names of Eadred and Tatwine, then offered for Eadgifu to live with her until she decided whether she wanted to return to Deerstow. It was an offer Eadgifu happily accepted.

*

Eadred knelt in silent prayer beside the grave markers for Edmund and Censwith in Deerstow as the noise continued not far away. A voice startled him. It was Tatwine.

"Come, good priest, see what they have found!" The hermit's excitement caused Eadred to rise and hurry to catch his friend. Four slaves, watched over by two of the ealdorman's warriors and a local man, had finished digging close to a dozen holes, and from the last cut they were extracting a body. Eadred cried out his anticipation. "At last! See if Lord Aelfric can come." The body had been thrown into a pit without preparation. The skin had turned brown from its time in the waterlogged, peaty soil and seemed remarkably without corruption. Eadred poked his finger into a rip in the back of the tunic and then into the gash in the flesh beneath it. The slaves turned the body over. "See, another strike to the chest. Now, look carefully," Eadred instructed the local man.

"I know him." He nodded. "His name was Wilfred. He went missing a while back." Eadred asked when. "Last year, I think, when we had seen the back of winter." Aelfric arrived.

"Lord, if I am right, this is the man who brought news to the bishop that Father Ingeld was ill and could not make his usual visit. He was enticed to say this, and having done so, Ingeld's killer made certain that he took his secret to this crude grave. If you agree, I would like some of the monks from Snailwell to see if they recognise the body."

Eadred continued to cast his eyes over the corpse. He tried to open one of the fists but failed. A slave also failed, so a warrior cut away the fingers. Eadred pulled out a sizeable clump of hair, which dislodged a small object from the hand, and it toppled into the grave. He untangled the hair and held out the long strands. Then he reached down, retrieved the object, rubbed it and held it up, then gave it to the local man. "Have you seen this before?" The man spat on it, rubbed it hard and held it close to his eyes.

"She had some fine jewels! It is hers, the Eadburga woman, and no mistake. A pendant like no other that I have seen a peasant woman wear. It used to bounce well against her tits. Ask any man from Deerstow and they would remember and swear upon it. Then one day it was gone. She said it was lost in the mere." The man fell silent for a few moments while he ruminated on his memory. "But, as I remember now, she stopped wearing it at the same time Wilfred disappeared. I do remember also that Wilfred and Eadburga used to fornicate. Ask others and I feel sure they will remember." He returned it to Eadred, who addressed the ealdorman.

"Imagine a struggle during the dark hours. She stabbed him, but he tore her hair and pulled the pendant from her neck as he fell. Then Eadburga thrust her knife into his back. Time was against her, and she buried him quickly. If our brothers at Snailwell remember this man as the one who brought the message, and I am certain that they will, then it could be no other than Eadburga who killed both Father Ingeld and Wilfred."

THIRTY-FOUR

The Final Act

"I did not believe she would ever be caught," Eadred said to Tatwine. "A woman with her looks and guile is never friendless. But drawing her blade and slashing at the ealdorman's men who stopped her boarding a ship to Francia was a mistake." The young priest and the hermit stood in a port where a great river met the southernmost part of the kingdom's coast. The leaves had begun to bloom into their earthy colours, signalling the return of the cooler months.

"We owe that to the ealdorman," the hermit replied.

Eadred nodded. "He is building his eyes and ears quickly. He is a good man, and I never stop praying for him. And tomorrow, I am to accuse Eadburga in court. I will not let her escape this time. My mind is clear. I have brought sworn witnesses to verify the pendant I found in Wilfred's hand, and monks from Snailwell who remember his visit. And her sister is safe, now she has chosen to enter the cloister at Elmstow."

"Eadburga deserves her death."

Eadred returned his friend's words with a feeble smile and politely denied his offer of company into the evening.

The following morning, the court was convened in the open air to accommodate the level of interest, together with the many witnesses Eadred had called. Seabirds swooped and screeched, and some encroached disinterestedly upon the assembly. The ealdorman opened the proceedings and called upon Eadred.

He breathed deeply and stared into the distance. "I, Eadred, priest of Snailwell, accuse Eadburga of Deerstow of the murder of Father Ingeld of Snailwell and of the man known as Wilfred of Deerstow. This Wilfred was identified by monks of Snailwell as the man who brought the false message that Father Ingeld was ill in the spring of last year. Wilfred was killed to keep this lie hidden. And finally, I accuse Eadburga of aiding the criminals Dudda and Cuthbert in murdering Edmund, son of Lord Forthred, and Censwith, daughter of Lord Cerdic."

Aelfric turned to Eadburga. "Do you accept the charges?"

"Lord, although I have no oath-helpers, it is certain that I must deny these charges. Surely, Brihtwold of Deerstow has already been hanged for three of these crimes, by the word of Father Eadred himself, and I cannot remember this Wilfred. I ask that this priest give some reason for his strange accusations. Lord, pray, let me also say this. I am protective of my body, for many men have desired it in the past, and I drew my blade when men accosted me when I was lawfully about to board a vessel. I was unaware they were your men and ask for your forgiveness."

Eadred sighed when Aelfric bid that he speak once

more. "I will regret for all of my life that I caused the death of Brihtwold and that I believed the lies told by this woman, but no more. Lady, this cannot be denied." In his upstretched hand, Eadred held the pendant and the strands of hair. "Many men from Deerstow have sworn on their honour that this was your pendant. It is different in design and quality from anything else they have seen on a village woman. It and this hair were found locked in Wilfred's dead hand."

Eadburga shouted her denial. "He was angry when I refused his attentions, and he stole it from me weeks before he went missing. That is why he had it, and I know nothing more of it after that."

"No, lady, did you not just tell us that you could not remember the man? I have brought witnesses who will swear that you were never seen to wear this pendant from the day Wilfred went missing and that you told all who would listen that you lost it in the mere." Eadburga stared at the row of men from Deerstow, whom Eadred had brought as witnesses. He continued. "The day after I confronted you with your crimes when we were at the Cauldron, you disappeared, leaving the sister you professed to love and whom you had always protected. There is no escape this time. Wilfred had to die to protect the lie that Father Ingeld was still alive. You had already persecuted and murdered the father. Why commit such a monstrous sin?"

Eadburga suddenly appeared exhausted. "You are right that I finally left my sister, but I knew she was safe, protected by those who had come to love her, and I left her most of the coin. Who protected my sister from her loathsome husband all those years? Everyone had more important duties. She was dutiful in her churchgoing and her prayers. She prayed that the rebukes from the priest and the penances would alter Brihtwold's behaviour, but they did nothing but anger him and set him further against her. I confronted Ingeld late one day, pleading that he do more to fill Brihtwold with the fear of God. He said he could do no more than talk to the brute, impose the accepted penance and—listen to this—absolve him of his sins! Ingeld said he was tired and needed his bed. What care is that of a poor woman who suffered daily abuse but paid her tithes? He turned to go, and in fury, I picked up a length of wood and hit him on the back of the head. There is a dark side to me that I have long known, and I wanted that priest to understand how it felt to plead for help but to be left unheard. So I bound him, hand and foot, forced a ball of cloth into his mouth to keep him from crying out and fetched a length of more cloth from our house. I wrapped him as a corpse and dug his grave. When his eyes flickered open, I told him of his fate. He tried to shout, but he discovered what it is like to be in such pain and terror, and screaming for help, but no one listens. Then I bound his eyes, pushed him into the hole and filled it. No one saw me or heard me.

"Killing the priest came from an anger that took hold of me suddenly. It flared, but once I had finished with the burial, I had feelings of regret. But even more, I worried that I might be discovered and taken, then my sister would be at the mercy of her vile husband. I knew that the priest was expected in Snailwell, and if he did not arrive, the monks would come looking and soon discover that he had visited Deerstow. His wagon still rested in our vill. Wilfred would do almost anything for a chance to lie between my thighs

345

and had no time for the priest, so I spun him a tale. I went to him that night and gave him what he desired, then said that Ingeld had taken ill and wanted a man to tell the bishop of his illness and to take his tithes. I told the idiot that if he undertook the task, starting by moonlight, I would give him more of what he wanted on his return. He agreed, of course. As an afterthought, I told Wilfred to tell the bishop that Ingeld was still at the Cauldron, for neither he nor I wanted more monks and priests coming to Deerstow to see to the priest's health. Wilfred agreed.

"Days later, Wilfred returned and was bewildered to hear of Ingeld's sudden disappearance. My lies were already stumbling over themselves. There was only one path forward, and I continued to take it. I told Wilfred that Brihtwold had secretly returned from the upland, and I suspected him of murdering the priest and burying him on his own land. I said if he came that night, we could try to find the body and then accuse Brihtwold. It was arranged, and when Wilfred was digging, I stabbed him to death and buried him."

Eadred stood in silence. He was surrounded by others, also shocked into mute horror.

The accused continued with the same detached voice. "The man called Cuthbert of Deerstow told me one day after we had fornicated that he would pay me well to help him with a task. He would not tell me what it was to be, but gave me ten silver pennies to promise myself to the undertaking, saying that I would have four times as much again once I had fulfilled the task. I agreed, of course, for such a sum. It would give my sister and me freedom from her foul husband. Some months before, I had caught sight of Cuthbert talking secretly with the monk who had a cloven

346

lip and came to suspect later that he was also involved, for neither Cuthbert nor Dudda had the brains or courage to commit such crimes without another man's ambition. And when I asked Cuthbert why he had whispered with the monk, he said it was talk of the weather, or some such nonsense, but he turned as white as a spirit.

"It was a surprise to most of us when the marriage of Lord Edmund and Lady Censwith was announced. Then the day following the wedding, Cuthbert met me and said he would call upon me soon to meet my part of the agreement. He showed me a bag of coins that would then be mine.

"The following day, when the rains were falling hard, he fetched me from my work. There was fear in his eyes. I followed him to the earthen wall around Holm, where Lord Edmund and Dudda were talking. I was told that if Lady Censwith did arrive, I should engage her in talk and stop her from shouting out. And as we neared the wall, she did call out to her husband and came running to him. So I went to meet her, saying she should return home, for the rain was growing stronger. I heard groans behind me. The lady began to scream at what she saw, and I struggled to stop her. It was only then that I saw Lord Edmund struggling with Dudda and Cuthbert with blood pouring from the lord's back. Cuthbert yelled for me to draw my blade and to silence Censwith. The lady and I clashed, and I killed her. It was not what I wanted. We all had tears at what we had done when we looked upon the bodies, but we were fearful of being discovered. Dudda and Cuthbert then had great unease about the wrath of their ancestors and spoke special words to the spirits while we quickly wrapped the bodies in good linen cloth the men had brought and buried them

347

together. They were no different to Christian men who murder then ask for God's forgiveness.

"I was later paid and told that there may be more work for me to do and more silver for it. It was never to happen. I did harbour a great concern that during Dudda and Cuthbert's trial and torture they might tell of my involvement in the murders. But they did not. I can only suspect it was because they feared I might talk of that monk with the harelip."

An eerie silence followed Eadburga's admissions. It was finally broken by Aelfric. "Eadburga of Deerstow, you are found guilty of these terrible crimes and for allowing your sister's husband to be executed for them. This has gone on for long enough. You will be executed before sunset, and your soul will face the torment it deserves."

Despite bringing Eadburga to her life's end, Eadred felt anguish when she rejected his offer to pray with her. He still prayed for her silently as she stood, hands bound, with the rope around her neck, waiting for the moment when her life would end. She had done some evil things, blinded by her love of her sister, and they could not be excused. But had she not also pleaded with those who should have done more to stop the mistreatment of Eadgifu? They, including himself, had all failed her. If anyone who possessed authority had listened and granted her justice rather than leaving Eadburga to fight and kill for it, would she, Ingeld, Brihtwold and Wilfred still live? It was a black thought. He closed his eyes, hearing her sobs.

"Tell Eadgifu that I died with her name upon my lips. All I ever wanted was to protect her," Eadburga wept.

Eadred cried out, "She is safe and has joined the minster at Elmstow. Sister Edith will see that she is always

348

protected." The stool was pushed away. He could not watch the final twitches as Eadburga's throat was crushed.

*

Eadred and Tatwine stood on the shore. "I have never seen or smelt the great sea before. It is a gift after all the misery and torment." Eadred's eyes moistened.

Tatwine responded, "It is only the second time I have seen this glorious vision, my friend. Does it not cleanse the head and fill you with wonder?" Tatwine punched his friend's arm playfully. "I am also filled with awe at how you have resolved all this evil. You uncovered the head and the hands behind the wave of crime that almost brought the kingdom to its knees and saw them cleaved from this life. Your name is raised by the great lords of our people, even by the king, and you have avenged all of the murdered dead. The Lord God bless you, Eadred." Tatwine shook his friend so hard that the two men almost fell to the ground.

Eadred composed himself as best he could but was left crimson-faced by the praise. "I am really a simple priest, my friend, who perhaps has found how he can best serve his Maker in the world of men. And your spirit, good Tatwine, has always inspired me. There is a joy you find in life that often struggles to find a home in me."

That night, they camped on the shore. The friends spoke little but listened to the bewildering and entrancing sounds, the pounding waves that filled their thoughts and imaginations. Sometime that night, Eadred awoke. His mind, as it often did in his times of solitude, fell into a restless inquiry of how he had fought evil and come to beat it, despite his many mistakes, and how close death had come to claiming him. As hard as he tried, he could not shake the misery pressing on his soul from the life he had unjustly taken and how his mistake had come to pass. He had allowed his mind to become distracted, beguiled and blinded. He also pondered the oppressive weight that Aelfric must bear each day, knowing that each decision he took could cost the lives of others. Then he saw his hermit companion, at a distance, kneeling on the pebbles, deep in prayer. Tatwine also had a burden, a heavy torment, but still he seemed to find happiness all around him. Eadred fell into sleep.

The morning was fresh and clear. The two friends left the sound of the waves behind them and found the road they had to take. "See," said Tatwine, "how the trees are laden with jewels! Let us enjoy this time and take a slow road back to our homes."